CHOSEN

THE STOLEN SERIES
BOOK THREE

MARLENA FRANK

For Patrick and Amelia,
May you find hope in even the darkest of times.

PREFACE

It's been nine years since I dreamed up the world of Stolen. That's honestly hard to believe right now. At the time I never expected to be an author, let alone capable of completing a series. And finding a publisher was daunting.

I tried finding an agent at first for Stolen, but I felt defeated after too many rejections. I worried that the story wasn't good enough, that it would never be read by anyone after I had poured years into creating this world and crafting these characters. It's like I lived in a fandom of one. I was about to put this series aside, to work on something else and forget about it, but *Stolen* felt different.

Unlike other novels I wrote and discarded, left aside to collect dust on my computer, I felt that this series had potential. The story felt like an incomplete tapestry, and I desperately wanted to find someone who believed in me enough to give it a chance. Fortunately for me, The

Parliament House Press gave me a chance. Since then, it's been a whirlwind.

Since then, the Stolen series has been an incredible ride. I've been blown away by the love and support I've received. Sometimes I want to pinch myself when someone mentions that they know who Mawr is. I want to cry happy tears when people tell me how much they love Shaleigh or Teagan or Talek. People message me, telling me how much they have enjoyed these books, telling me what the story has meant to them. It gives me purpose. It puts fuel behind all the typing, all the editing, and all the stress of being an author.

Chosen was written during a time when the entire world was changing. The pandemic struck, and all the truths we had taken for granted were torn away. It was a time of finding justice and demanding truth. The Black Lives Matter movement began and, just a short drive from my house, I watched in horror as people were corralled by armed military.

Books aren't written in a vacuum. All of it got poured into words. It was poured into writing *Chosen* and will probably be reflected in more of my books.

Change isn't easy, but it's necessary for things to improve. Sometimes it requires listening, learning, and believing in hope even when the future seems dim and dire.

I hope the Stolen series has brought you hope regardless of where you are.

Marlena Frank
January 5, 2020

CONTENTS

PART I
STRONGER TOGETHER

TO BE LOVED

*I*t was difficult to breathe. The sky was filled with smoke and the waves of heat made Shaleigh sweat through her clothes.

She didn't belong on top of an active volcano near rivers of lava. She shouldn't have come to the Peak of Gwern with her friends. She shouldn't have pretended to be a warrior when she knew very well that she wasn't.

And she certainly had no business trying to talk to a fire dragon.

She could have gone home when Queen Mab offered it back in the City of the Faeries, but she thought she could help. She should have accepted it and gone back to her schoolwork, to her best friend Kaeja, and to her father. Had they forgotten her completely by now? Would she live long enough to see them again?

Shaleigh licked at her parched lips as her eyes began to water from the heat. At least back home there were problems she could fix; there was no fixing a dragon.

The ground shook and she took a step back, dipping

her foot into a thick mound of volcanic ash that covered her ankles. She knew what that meant: Tanwen was emerging.

Instinctively she reached for Mawr, placing a hand on his flank even as he flattened himself to the ground and covered his eyes. She stroked his mane in a feeble attempt to calm him, despite her own heart thudding in her chest. A hand clasped hers, clad in fur, and she turned to see Colin staring at her with absolute terror. She squeezed his hand, staring into his eyes. Beads of sweat dripped off the black fur of his cheeks.

"I wish you had left!" she cried to him, tears streaking down her cheeks. "You both could have been long gone by now."

He shook his head. "I couldn't leave you any more than Mawr could. We're both going to stand with you, whether you like it or not—it's too late to leave now." The ground quaked beneath them again and Colin moved closer to her side; they put an arm around each other to stay steady. "I'm so sorry for all this," he said.

"Me too."

A loud crack tore through the air and all three of them jumped. The ground close to where Talek stood tore apart, creating a great chasm, and ash fell into the gap that highlighted red from an inner light. He wasn't far from where they huddled to the ground. Talek put one arm up to shield his face while his other hand gripped Teagan's, backing away from the heat toward Shaleigh.

Teagan stared with unblinking eyes at the chasm, his skin horribly pale against the smoky sky. He had been stabbed through the heart with a ball of hot lava, thrown by a magician who was controlled by Keriam. Talek had used his magic to close his wound, but he couldn't bring Teagan's life back: Despite Talek's Madness and despite the powers he had been given from his pact with Keriam, even he couldn't overcome death.

Flames licked upward from within the giant crack, growing higher. Two wisps of flame crept forward along the ground, white in color like kindling caught ablaze. But there was nothing there to burn besides ash. There was nothing alive up here except for them.

At the base of the white flames, Shaleigh realized that it wasn't just flame, it was a glob of volcanic rock that she knew hadn't been there before. It was crusted black, as though cooled in places, but it was also veined with white molten lava within. The pair of rocks seemed to shift left and right, though it was hard to tell if they were really moving or if it was from the heat waves coming off of them. That's when she realized that they weren't merely rock—they were claws.

"Mawr..." Shaleigh crouched down beside the stone lion, moving her hand from his flank to his cheek. He didn't say anything, but she could feel him trembling under her palm, his stone body almost painfully hot to the touch. Colin took her lead and crouched down beside her. Only Talek remained standing, still holding Teagan at his side. They were close enough she could make out their faces now.

"Please," Talek said, tears marking streaks down his soot covered face. "I merely want council with you. That's all!"

The molten claws dug into the earth, and the ground

shook again. Shaleigh heard another crack and wondered if they were all going to be sent tumbling down into a fiery abyss.

She looked up and watched as the dragon pulled herself up out of the chasm.

First came her head, surrounded with long, floating tendrils of flame, and then came her serpentine neck and body. She was black like a cooling lava flow from head to toe, and occasionally bits of her body crumbled and fell to the ground, adding to the mounds of ash all around them. The cracks exposed her true, molten essence. Much of her body was still on fire, lit from the pit from which she emerged. She snorted steam into the air and took a deep breath. As her chest expanded, Shaleigh could see the cracks of her body expand and begin to cool as well. It was as if she wasn't used to breathing air from aboveground.

Slowly Mawr got to his feet, much to the shock of Shaleigh and Colin.

"What are you doing?" Colin asked, as though staying on the ground would somehow avoid getting her attention.

"It's her," Mawr whispered, clearly in awe despite still trembling. "It's really her. I never thought I would actually get to see her. I've read about her for so many years, studied so many of the books. She's beautiful. They never said she was beautiful."

Despite the heat that was building and her own heart thundering away in her chest, Shaleigh had to agree with him. Tanwen was beautiful in the way encountering a big cat in the wild would be beautiful, but then it would also lead to death. Every fiber of her being wanted to run away as fast as she could down the mountain, but Shaleigh couldn't look away.

Tanwen was graceful but terrible, a presence so raw and powerful that she seared onto the mind. Shaleigh knew that nothing she could photograph would ever live up to her.

The dragon craned her neck back and surveyed her guests, settling her white hot gaze on each of them, her eyes burning with an unending flame. Shaleigh heard Talek cry out as Tanwen's gaze fell upon him. It sounded like he was physically in pain and it made her want to bury her head down against Mawr's side, but she couldn't do it.

Then Tanwen turned to Mawr and the poor lion just yelped and began shaking again. Shaleigh patted his side, trying to calm him, but she couldn't bring herself to speak. She couldn't even think of any words to say.

When Tanwen's gaze fell on her next, the weight of it made her stomach drop. A bizarre chill went through her even though she was still sweating like crazy from the heat. Shaleigh couldn't turn her head or glance aside, all she could do was stare even though it hurt. It was as though the dragon saw everything within her, knew everything she had done, and lifted up every flaw from within to examine and explore.

A sob escaped her lips. Her own thoughts dimmed and suddenly she knew with certainty that she was a trespasser. She was an intruder, a disease, a parasite that had no inkling of where it landed. Shaleigh wanted to apologize, to say something to explain, to help the dragon understand why she was here and why she wanted to help her friends, but words didn't come.

A high-pitched hissing sound assaulted her ears, like the whistling of a teapot about to explode with steam. Absently Shaleigh put her hands up to her ears to block out the noise, but it didn't even muffle it. The sound came full force still and it took a moment for her to recognize that there were words in the sound.

"Yes, this must be your language. You have something that belongs to me, Shaleigh Mallett." The ground shook and Shaleigh fell forward, but Colin caught her before she hit the ground.

"What was that?!" Colin screamed; his breath warm against her neck as he pulled her upright. "Was that her?"

"She speaks in a fury of scream and flame!" Mawr cried, clearly quoting some kind of book he had read. He was crouching down again. "All who hear her will regret their ears!"

Shaleigh blinked and shook her head, finally free of whatever the dragon had done to her.

Tanwen looked out over the chasm, staring directly at her, patient and threatening without making a move. Shaleigh wracked her mind. What did they have that belonged to a dragon? They barely had anything with them as it was.

She glanced to her friends, surely, Tanwen didn't mean them. Even if Talek was near to losing himself to the Madness and taking them all with him, she would still never let a dragon take him—take any of them.

"I don't know what I have," she confessed. "If we have anything of yours, we don't know it."

Tanwen dipped her head and gave a slow nod, the wisps of flame behind her rippled as though from wind. Then the jar that Shaleigh still had tucked under her arm, the one she had forgotten about and had almost left at the edge of the Dark Lands, felt very cold. She reached for it, surprised that she even still had it. The sweat from her fingers left marks on the glass. Inside looked empty except for maybe a cobweb or two, but she knew for certain that it hadn't felt that cold before.

When they had left the Dark Lands, Shaleigh had nearly tripped on it. She wasn't sure where it came from, but she was certain they didn't just happen to come across it. Now here Tanwen asked for it, as though she had left it there and had them fetch it for her. Shaleigh held the jar up for the dragon to see; Tanwen nodded again, her flaming white eyes never leaving Shaleigh.

She must have seen Shaleigh's confusion. "It's only empty if you look through your eyes," Tanwen said simply, the steam whistle shriek of her voice made Shaleigh's head pound. "Give it here."

Shaleigh froze, not sure how to even do that. She couldn't just hand it over; she was barely able to keep from backing away as it was. She thought of just lobbing it at her, but that would probably end with it breaking, and with Shaleigh in an even worse situation. Even if she could get the jar close, wouldn't it just shatter from the heat, especially with how cold it felt?

Tanwen rose up, the length of her lava cracked, blackened body coming out farther from the ground. Two black shapes tore loose from her body, throwing ash into the air, and unfurled. Her wings were enormous, like bat wings, and ribbed with shifting lava beneath the skin. The heat they gave off was unbearable.

"Give it here!" Tanwen shrieked again, opening her jaws and revealing rows of sharp teeth and a white light inside her mouth and throat. It was blinding, and Shaleigh winced as she held up a hand to shield her eyes.

"Do as she asks!" Talek called to her, acknowledging that she existed for the first time since they landed on the Peak of Gwern. "She'll kill us all if you refuse!" He was walking toward her with Teagan following at his side.

"How?" Shaleigh swallowed down the dryness of her throat. "I can't get close to her, and I'm afraid it'll shatter!"

Mawr stood up suddenly and wrapped his teeth around the jar as gently as he had when he helped her onto the sled by the lake in Aife. He picked it up then nuzzled her with his stone whiskers.

"Mawr, what are you doing?"

He muttered something unintelligible.

"Be careful!" Colin cried in understanding. "Don't get too close! She can melt you too, you know."

Mawr nodded and then inched forward a little, then inched a little more. His tail was tucked so far between his legs that Shaleigh was afraid it might trip him. He only got a foot or so in before he laid the jar gingerly onto the ground and hurried away again.

"I can't believe you did that!" Shaleigh wrapped her arms around him. He was shaking, but his face wasn't charred or worn from the heat. She rubbed behind his ears.

In the distance above the crack, Tanwen settled back down, her fury now focused on the jar that was clearly still out of her reach. She cocked her head to the side and a small blue flame licked up out of the ground at the jar, cracking it into a dozen pieces.

Shaleigh gasped.

At first it looked like the jar was empty, but then she caught the strong smell of dust and the undeniable stench of decay that she recognized from the Masked King. A thick fog emerged from the shards and floated up to form a humanoid shape.

"Mighty Tanwen, I beseech you."

Shaleigh's jaw dropped as the voice of the Masked King hovered in the air from the haze before them. The fog shifted until it made a vague replica of the Masked King, himself. It reminded her of something her imagination might have dreamed up staring at her through a window at home on a foggy morning. Only it wasn't that; it was him. Somehow, he had found a way to join them, and Shaleigh didn't know what kind of message he had to deliver.

"You have guided me for decades, dear Mother. When I had no understanding of what I was, you showed me. When I couldn't grasp what had happened to me, you guided me. I beseech you to help this pathetic group on my behalf."

Shaleigh's eyes went wide. He was helping them? She had expected him to try to sabotage them somehow, not to help. That high-pitched steam whistle sounded again and Shaleigh looked to Tanwen. The dragon was laughing.

"The Madness is present here, you see," the Masked King continued. "It has nearly taken the white-haired

Faerie and it has already led to the death of the other. I understand if you, Mother, wish to kill them all, it is entirely in your right."

"Can you believe this guy?" Colin asked. "I can't tell if he's trying to help or turn us into barbeque."

"However, I hope you will show mercy," the mist replica said. "Not for them, but for me. I wish not for another Dark Land to form upon our land. If he must be destroyed, let him destroy the Human World, but not here. I do not wish for another such as myself, Mother. I would not wish that upon anyone. Act in the wisdom that you know so well, Mother, but please, forget me not in your decision." As his voice faded, so did the misty visage of him. It dissipated along with the heat waves and soon they were back to facing Tanwen alone.

"I never would have thought that guy was friendly, but apparently he was," Colin admitted quietly with a lopsided smile.

"Talek scared him," Shaleigh said with a glance to the two Faeries who stood nearby. "He got to see what it would be like to have two Masked Kings and he didn't like it. He helped us, but only to help himself."

Tanwen didn't look at any of them. Instead she stared at the broken jar that lay in a bed of ash. "Perhaps Fineen is right," her voice shrieked and Shaleigh winced involuntarily. "I ought to at least listen to what you have to say before I devour you."

Her claws dug deeper into the earth, causing the ground to quake as she pulled the full length of her body up out of the chasm. It was like watching a coil of rope get pulled out of the sea—more and more of her just kept appearing. Finally, her back claws emerged and landed on the earth as well. The ground shook so hard that Shaleigh fell into Mawr's side.

"It's too hot!" Mawr cried. "You all will get hurt! We need to pull back."

He was right, the heat was starting to singe her skin. Together the three of them backed away, but it was difficult because Tanwen was drawing closer, her body impossibly long and her heat enormous.

Then her features began to change. Her eyes became smaller as she shut them tight and the length of her body shrank inward. It was crazy to see the full length of her body shrink down, looping in on itself, until she looked more like a lizard with wings than a dragon. She stretched out her wings, peeling them off her body again, and the bat-like membrane shrank inward into long, spindly arms. Her bulky back legs pulled forward. As she transformed, the heat seemed to dissipate until finally Shaleigh could look at her without backing away.

A woman stood before her; her skin as black as the volcanic ash at their feet. Her body was still cracked in places and Shaleigh could see the lava that flowed in those cracks, bright and hot and dangerous. Tanwen shook herself and tensed, knitting the cracks closed. When she opened her eyes, they were human looking, except for the pupils which still shone that white fire within. She tensed again and bright hair in shades of crimson, amber, and ocher emerged from her head and toppled down her shoulders to the middle of her back like water.

She squared her shoulders and walked toward them.

"Is that easier for your frail bodies?" Tanwen smiled, revealing pointed teeth.

Shaleigh just stared at her. She was still a dragon, she had to be, but for several long moments Shaleigh's mind was too frozen in shock to respond. She was trying to wrap her brain around the ridiculous concept of that enormous fiery dragon fitting into the body of the woman before her.

"You're... human..." she finally forced out. Full sentences were not an option right now. Her brain could barely come up with single words let alone a fully formed sentence.

Tanwen laughed, and Shaleigh could see the fiery white flame at the back of her throat. It made sense somehow that she should be made of fire. She had always read that dragons were hungry, perhaps they were just as hungry as fire.

Shaleigh took a deep breath, trying to ignore that her skin still hurt in places, mostly her hand from touching Mawr's back. She tried to ignore that Colin had hold of her other hand again and was half-heartedly trying to pull her backward, away from the dragon. She glanced to Talek, who stood in awe and confusion, both of his eyes swirling with the violet of Madness. She only hoped the shock of all this didn't cause an explosion like Queen Mab said happened before with the Masked King.

"You bring me a corpse that's been forced to walk, a Faerie on the brim of destruction, a statue that's been taught to speak, a ferret as big as a man," the amusement was bubbling through her words, "and a shrimp of a girl from the Human World." She laughed and the wind picked up slightly with her humor.

Pieces of ash and dirt flew into their faces and Shaleigh had to squint to be able to see through it.

"I've eaten entire armies, crumpled villages in minutes, and devoured more Mad Faeries than I can count. My dear friend the Masked King may want me to spare you for his own devices, but I don't see why I should. This is the biggest disappointment I've had since Flidais came to build a castle on my home." She laughed again, and this time the wind was so strong that Shaleigh fell to the ground.

"You have to help me," Talek urged as her laughter finally died. "Teagan, he should not be dead! I need him at my side, and you're the only one who can—"

"Another Faerie heartbroken, why am I not surprised? Your kind's affection leads to more Madness than any other magical being in my land." She swished her hair to the side, and Shaleigh saw a flame emerge between the strands for a brief moment before being snuffed out.

She could kill them with a glance.

She was humoring them.

Shaleigh thought of how the Masked King was excited to have visitors who actually wanted to speak with him. She thought of Queen Mab and how so many Faeries chose to leave her city even though she worked so hard to keep it protected. Finally, she thought of Madam Cloom forcing the bloodshed at the Games in the hot air balloons in the Garden.

Boredom, she realized, was probably the only reason Tanwen hadn't already destroyed them.

Although Shaleigh's memory of the Memorial Chamber in the High Castle of the Garden felt like a lifetime ago, she remembered passing many statues in that room. One was a woman sitting in a chair with her head thrown back laughing. It was an odd pose, very different from all the other statues in that room, and that was what made her remember the name she had seen there: Flidais. She must have been a friend of Master Cathal, and if that was the last visitor Tanwen had gotten, then that had been centuries ago. Despite living in a volcano, she doubted even a dragon was immune to boredom. If she could prove they shouldn't be dismissed, maybe they had a chance.

"Please hear us out!" Shaleigh urged and she couldn't help but wince as the dragon aimed her gaze at her. She might be in a human form, but there was still a weight with that gaze that made her body quake. "Talek was forced into a pact with a cruel magician known as Keriam. The magician was the one that killed Teagan and turned the magicians in the Sanctuary against us. We're Teagan's friends." She glanced to Talek, his eyes were wide as he watched her, clearly shocked that she was speaking up for them. "We're Talek's friends, too."

"Shaleigh..." Talek whispered.

She turned back to Tanwen, "Please, we've come very far. I could have gone home, but I chose to help my friends instead. I chose to...speak with you rather than leave."

Tanwen smiled and Shaleigh squeezed Colin's hand. "Do you regret that decision?"

Shaleigh studied her, trying to decide what was the right answer, trying to figure out what she wanted to hear, but there was no telling. She took a deep breath and nodded. "Yes."

"So, you do value your life then?" Tanwen approached her, bare feet leaving deep impressions in the volcanic ash on the ground.

"Yes," Shaleigh choked. "I value all our lives, even Teagan though we lost him."

"Ah yes," the dragon said, stopping only a foot in front of her. "The dead one."

Shaleigh nodded again. She could feel the heat emanating off of the dragon, and there was steam rising from her freshly cooled skin.

There was a pressing feeling, and suddenly a hot spark in her head that made Shaleigh cry out and fling her hands to her skull. Distantly she heard her friends call out to her, but Shaleigh couldn't hear the words. Her brain was on fire. Her mind went blank, because all she could feel was the pain shooting around her head as though she put her finger into an outlet.

Then the pain was gone, and she realized she was on the ground, staring into the ash. Mawr was beside her, nuzzling her with his sharp whiskers and Colin was keeping her from falling face forward. She sniffed and wiped at her nose to find wetness and pulled her hand away to see blood. A funny thought ran through her head that if she hadn't had the sickness from overexposure to magic before in the City of the Fae, she would be dead.

She swallowed down the taste of copper in her throat and stared up at Tanwen to find that Talek was on his knees in front of her, begging.

"She's an innocent in all of this. You and I both know she doesn't belong in this world." Fresh tears streaked down his cheeks as his voice cracked. "All I want is to have Teagan back! All I want is for him to be happy. Whatever you wish, I will grant if it is within my power. Please spare them. Take me instead if you wish!" He reached out to her as though to take Tanwen's hand, but she slapped it away and Talek cried out. His hand was bright red where she had touched him, leaving a nasty burn.

"Don't insult me. I've eaten far too many Faeries infected with Madness. I will not be your executioner. I'm fed up with your addled minds being sent to me to incinerate." She turned to Shaleigh and that familiar adrenaline rush made her dizzy for a moment. "This Keriam. I saw that he was immortal in your mind, but he is a magician. How is that possible?"

"I don't know," Shaleigh admitted, her throat felt dry and her tongue too thick and slow.

"Stand aside," Tanwen commanded at her friends. Colin glanced down to Shaleigh once with apology before scurrying away, but Mawr stood fast.

"No," he squeaked. "I won't let you hurt her."

Tanwen stopped and stared at him. "You are excellent at your work, Mawr the Guardian, but I need you to stand aside for me."

Mawr began shaking. "I won't let you," he muttered.

Shaleigh reached to stroke his mane. "It's okay, Mawr. Don't get yourself killed, okay?"

He looked back to her, his glasses rattling on the bridge of his nose. "I don't want to lose you!"

She leaned forward and hugged him tight. "I know, it's okay," she said but she doubted it really would be. She couldn't let him be harmed though. He was made of stone and Tanwen lava.

"I won't leave you," he whispered.

"This is very touching, but I do need you to move aside, Guardian of Aife," Tanwen growled.

"If you're going to stay with me," Shaleigh whispered to him. "Stay close but stay out of her way, okay?"

He nodded and his glasses fell askew. Shaleigh straightened them, then used him to climb to her feet. Mawr moved out of the way, but still stayed with her as she faced Tanwen once more.

"Tell me about this Keriam. Tell me about what he's been doing to the Shadow Wolves."

Shaleigh stared at her in confusion for a moment. "The Shadow Wolves? The ones from the Slumbering Forest?"

Tanwen nodded and glanced back to Talek who crawled to his feet to take Teagan's hand again.

"They may not belong to me like the others do, but I must know what he does with them." She waved a hand, adding, "The others are all mine: the Faeries, the minotaurs, the magic of the magicians, they are all mine. Even the magic that was used to create your friend here," she gestured to Mawr. "The magic they borrow is mine, and I give it freely. However, they must return it to me upon death. Which is why I must ask again," she leveled another heart-pounding gaze at Shaleigh, "tell me more about the immortality of Keriam the magician."

"I'm not sure," Shaleigh fumbled. "All I know is that the Masked King somehow made an arrangement with him."

Her eyes blazed. "The Masked King, you say? Making such arrangements without my knowledge, oh no, we can't have that. Who is this Keriam?"

She shook her head, "I don't know him very well. I only know that he is in a Faerie pact with Talek."

At mention of his name, Talek held a palm out to her. "I have left my master. He abandoned me and killed the only one dear to me in the world, great Tanwen."

She swooped toward him. "But you know of the magician who dares defy death in my land, the one who defies the ultimate payment?"

"Yes," he admitted, his voice wavering.

"Don't hurt him!" Shaleigh called, rushing forward. Her legs didn't want to work quite right, and she nearly tumbled over her own two feet, but she fell toward Talek and he caught her.

"Shaleigh," he whispered, staring down at her. His white hair was peppered with ash and his eyes swirled with the iridescent violet of the Madness. She reached forward and hugged him, and he gasped. "What are you—"

"Stop trying to get yourself killed. You're a good person! I don't want any of you to die!"

He pushed her away gently, his hands still shaking. He glanced to Tanwen then back to Shaleigh. "You can't save everyone."

"Don't tell me that! I don't care what you've done, I don't want you to get killed like Teagan. I can't stand to see someone else I care about die!"

"Calm down, little Human," Tanwen cooed. "I merely

want information. And since none of you seem willing to talk easily, I must reap it myself."

As soon as Talek met the dragon's eyes, his body went rigid.

~

THE BLOOD DRAINED from Talek's face. His mouth went slack; his eyes widened. Shaleigh fancied she could see the violet of his eyes pulse, but it was hard to tell. Then he whimpered.

"It's okay, Talek, I'm here. You're not alone." She tried to ground him somehow like she had Teagan in the Dark Lands. She was afraid for him. He was the one who had dragged them up here, but he was also the most vulnerable.

He gave out a short scream that was quickly cut short and Shaleigh jumped. "What are you doing to him?"

Tanwen didn't even glance to her. Whatever Talek was experiencing made his entire body tremble. His eyes were wide, as though being forced to watch something horrible. It was draining him, and the violet of his eyes grew brighter.

"No," she muttered. Was this it? Was this what he looked like just before destroying and killing all of them? She couldn't stand aside and watch, she couldn't just sit and passively take in what was happening. That had never been Shaleigh's way, and so she jumped at him with a snarl and knocked him to the ground, breaking Tanwen's control over him.

They hit the ground hard, billowing ash up into the air like black snow.

"Don't you think you're clever?" Tanwen hissed from behind them.

Shaleigh ignored her and got onto her hands and knees to stare into Talek's distant gaze. "Talek? Can you hear me?"

He gave a weak cry, but his eyes were moving again, and soon he pursed his lips together. Finally, he seemed to recognize her. "Shaleigh..."

"It's okay, I—" The words caught in her throat as hot pain licked around her ankle. She jerked her left leg and screamed, scrambling away from Talek. He reached for her, saying something, but the pain bit deep into her skin and erased everything else in her mind. Something bright and thin flipped away from her like a whip. The pain was excruciating.

She panted, staring at her leg that looked like it belonged to someone else. The ringlet around her left ankle was dark red and she could see the smoke rising up from the heat. It would turn into a terrible blister, if it healed at all.

Tanwen's whip returned to a claw that was attached to a partially transformed fiery wing, then it pulled in completely to reform into a humanoid hand and arm. Shaleigh stared, her mind empty as she reeled from the pain, trying to make sense of what happened.

"Do that again, and I'll take your head," Tanwen said simply and stalked toward Talek again. He was still lying on his back but trying to push himself up into a seated position; he was weak. She knew why, too, she had seen how it drained him. Whatever the dragon did to him, whatever it made him experience, it had to have been terrible.

"Don't do it," Shaleigh breathed and rolled onto her stomach to push herself up. Bits of black ash stuck to her dress and arm. It smelled like sulfur and she winced as she pushed her face away from it. If the dragon continued to torture him, continued to push him, Shaleigh wasn't sure if he would last. If the Madness took Talek completely, it meant they all died, including Mawr and Colin. She couldn't let that happen.

"Talek, hold on!" she called as she tried to stand despite her injury. Every flex of her foot sent pain up and down her leg. Then an arm wrapped around her waist, and another folded in her knees with great care to avoid her hurt ankle: It was Colin, picking her up like he had when he kidnapped her in the Tree House. She winced at the pain that throbbed through her leg.

"What are you doing?" she cried. "We have to help him!"

"Keeping you from getting yourself killed," Colin grunted as he carried her over to Mawr, who was prancing his paws in the ash.

"I don't need your help, Talek does!" she argued after he placed her down on one leg.

Talek cried out again and Shaleigh's chest tightened as she looked to where he lay at the dragon's feet.

"I sorry, Shaleigh, I know you don't like it, but I don't think we have a choice," Colin said.

The dragon loomed over Talek, her hair falling down around her shoulders as she stared into his eyes. Tiny little flames sprouted up within her hair before snuffing out again—Shaleigh worried that the flames would drop down onto Talek's face, but they didn't.

"Please, his mind can't take it. The Madness has eaten it away," she cried to Tanwen and tried to step forward but the pain on her left leg seared as she tried to put pressure on it. Mawr pushed up next to her when she stumbled, and she gratefully leaned against him.

"Thank you," she whispered.

"She could have killed you," Mawr whispered back. "You can't go over there!"

Colin put a clawed hand on her shoulder. "Mawr's right. I won't let you kill yourself trying to help him. He got himself into this mess. You can't save him now, only he can. And you've already angered Tanwen once. I believe her when she threatened to take your head next. I won't..." He paused, taking a deep breath. "I can't let that happen to you." There were tears in his eyes and he clutched at her shoulder with desperation.

"I'm sorry." She put a hand on his arm, gently urging him to relax and release his hold. Then she reached out a hand to Mawr, petting him reassuringly. "I can't sit by, waiting and hoping. I have to try to help." She shook her head, feeling her heart ache. "I can't bear to watch anyone else get killed."

Colin's voice was small and pleading. "If you try again, she's going to kill you." His voice broke. "And I can't watch you die either. *Please*."

Talek screamed again and Shaleigh winced.

"Maybe we could go together?" They both turned to Mawr, who trembled from his nose to his tail. "She won't listen to you, Shaleigh, but maybe she would if we all tried to help."

Shaleigh nodded and turned to lock eyes with Colin. "Do you think there's a chance she'll listen?"

He glanced to the dragon, to Teagan's body, to a distant lava flow and sighed. "She didn't kill you the first time, did she? Maybe Mawr's got a point."

Shaleigh let out a slow breath. She knew it was the right thing to do, but she was still terrified to do it. "Together then." Her voice was hoarse.

Colin gave a weak nod as fresh tears fell down his cheeks. "That's the only way, isn't it?"

"It's always best to work together," Mawr agreed, his deep baritone making Shaleigh's hand vibrate on his flank. He was watching Tanwen and Talek in the distance with his ears flattened back, looking like he wanted to flatten himself to the ground again.

"Mawr," she whispered, wishing she could get closer to his face, but unable to use her injured leg. "Do you really think this is a good idea?"

He shuffled his paws in the ash. "I'm scared too, but I don't think I can stand here either. If it was up to me, I'd be on the ground with my eyes closed, but maybe together, maybe then I'd be strong enough to try."

She reached over and rubbed above his shoulder.

"Promise you won't run in again?" Colin's voice was high-pitched like he might break down bawling at any minute. "Promise you won't try to be a hero without us?"

"I promise," she said, and took his hand in hers, giving it a squeeze. He was trembling—they all were. Her left leg throbbed, and the pain made it hard to think.

Around her tears, Shaleigh looked back to Talek. The dragon was still boring into his mind, but Teagan was also there. He was crouched down beside Talek, holding his hand and stroking it.

It was as if he was alive, but he wasn't.

He couldn't be.

"What—?" She gasped, trying to find the right words.

Staring at the two of them, with Colin's warm hand in hers and Mawr's stone fur in the other, her mind felt empty, numb. All she could do was stare as Teagan stroked Talek's hand. She sniffled and blinked, trying to see around her tears. Teagan's gaze was still flat, still just as empty as the day he died, but there was care between them that she'd only seen in the drawings she had found strewn about their home in the City of the Faeries. This was different though. Teagan was doing it out of his own volition.

Shaleigh turned to Tanwen, watching her white eyes burn. "Stop," she called. "Leave him alone. He doesn't deserve to be destroyed. He deserves to live."

Tanwen looked up and Shaleigh felt her stomach drop. For a brief moment she wondered if she was going to tumble to the ground, but Mawr and Colin held her steady.

"I have seen what he has done. I have seen the fires that drive him. You suffered at his hands. He betrayed you." Tanwen took a deep breath and stepped around Talek to approach them. Her bare feet seemed to rock the earth as she strode closer.

"Shaleigh," Mawr whispered. She didn't have to look to know that he was fighting his own terror to stay by her side. Yet, even with all he had read, even with all the warnings, he still stayed with her. He still supported her. She smiled, feeling a flicker of confidence.

"I have seen some of what he's done. I know he's hurt people." Shaleigh thought of the piles of minotaur corpses in the woods and the magicians from the Sanctuary. "I know he's probably killed people, too, but that doesn't mean he deserves to die."

Tanwen glanced to Colin and Mawr, who despite flinching, stayed on either side of her. They stayed because they believed in Shaleigh. They stayed because they trusted her. A fiery resolve formed within her, not for herself, but to protect those she loved. She glanced to Talek— his eyes were closed, and he was far too pale. And Teagan was still beside him, stroking his hand as though a dragon hadn't just passed beside him.

"You wear your fears on your skin," Tanwen said as though it was an insult. "He is not dead, but his mind...that was quite enlightening." Her tone was different from before. The hot rage and fierce warning that had led to Shaleigh's leg being injured was gone. Now it was replaced with a more somber, more subdued tone. "You don't want him dead. You don't want your captor who forced you up this mountain to be killed." She pointed to Colin next. "And I assume you don't even want your kidnapper dead either."

Colin gasped and Shaleigh pulled him closer to reassure him. "It's okay," she said and turned to him, "calm down."

"She knows," Colin whimpered, biting his lip. "She knows what I am."

"I know all, Colin Cawley, Human child of The Garden, once beggar, once soldier, and now..." Tanwen smiled. "Professional lacky, it seems."

Colin's voice trembled. "No! I—I mean, I try to help people. That's all I do is try to help."

"That's not true at all!" Mawr pleaded. "He's my friend, and he saved my life! If he's a lacky, then so am I."

Colin glanced to him. "Mawr..."

Mawr was no longer hunkered down but standing up straight. He was still trembling, but Shaleigh hadn't seen so much confidence in him since they reached the Peak of Gwern. "If being friends and caring about each other makes us lackies, then I guess that's what we all are."

Tanwen laughed and the ground shook beneath them. Shaleigh and Colin both had to lean on Mawr to keep from falling, and the stone lion had to drop his belly to the ground to stay stable.

"What did I say?" Mawr asked. "Did I say something wrong?"

"No," Shaleigh reassured, stroking his mane. "I think you said exactly what you should have."

Finally, Tanwen's laughter ended and she crossed her arms. "I don't plan to kill you all at the moment—you are more entertaining than I anticipated."

She stared up at the dark skies and dragged her hands through her hair, dropping ash and flames to the ground as she paced. She looked sad, Shaleigh realized. She looked like she was trying to solve something, and Shaleigh stood up again on her good leg, one hand against Mawr's flank.

"Thank you," Shaleigh stated awkwardly. "For not

wanting to kill us." It seemed like the right thing to say when a dragon showed mercy.

"There was so much pain," Tanwen muttered as though speaking to herself. "I've seen true misery, true misfortune, and this is probably one of the more heart-wrenching tragedies I've encountered in many millennia." She turned to them, and the white hot flame in her eyes had burned down to red embers. "As you know, Shaleigh of the Human World, Queen Mab has brought many unfortunate Faeries here. Their minds fractured, much as your friend's is. Their magic overwhelmed by their emotions."

Tanwen sat down on a stone and stretched out her long legs. "I'm tired of seeing it. I'm tired of devouring their grief and their sorrow. They should sort out their own problems instead of throwing them into my volcano, my home. I see their lives in my dreams, their despair, their hatred. Sometimes it takes centuries for that chaos to dissipate, yet I must live with it for all that time." She looked up and met Shaleigh's gaze with a pleading expression. Shaleigh felt her pain, her guilt, and her disgust.

Shaleigh thought back to the burned ruins they had passed on their way up the mountain. She thought of all the Faeries that must have come up here to be consumed by the dragon, at Queen Mab's insistence. She had always considered what the Faeries felt, not what it did to the dragon. The Madness itself was clearly volatile. What did it do to someone to consume that much negativity all the time? Her heart pounded in her chest as she considered this as Tanwen continued.

"Perhaps it's time I take away the magic I gave to this world. Perhaps they would be better off without it."

"Take away the magic?" Mawr asked, his voice barely a whisper. "All of it?"

Tanwen nodded.

"But that would mean... me..." Mawr trailed off, and Shaleigh glanced to him with terror.

"No," she whispered. "You can't do that! Mawr's better than anyone I've ever met! He's too good to be killed like that. Besides, you said you wouldn't kill us!"

"It wouldn't be killing; it would be removal. An unmaking."

"I won't let you!" Shaleigh wrapped her arms around Mawr's neck. In her fear, she fell to the ground on her hurt leg and cried out, shifting her weight quickly to her good leg and trying to get the pain under control. She glanced down to see bits of ash were now stuck to the wound.

"Shaleigh, be careful. Don't hurt yourself." Mawr licked at her arm to gain her attention.

Tanwen shook her head, completely oblivious to Shaleigh's pain. "He is but a statue, nothing more."

"He's my *friend*!" Shaleigh shouted. "He's my *stars*! I won't let you take him away from me."

Shaleigh's whole body was shaking as she hung onto Mawr. She waited, watching the dragon sit on her stone that was like a makeshift throne, surrounded with the ash of destruction and the rivers of lava and death.

"How can you possibly understand the emotions you see?" Shaleigh asked in the silence. "You don't love or hate anything. You just sit here in your mountain and live through others. You're annoyed by the lives you devour but those lives were all they knew!" Hot tears rolled down her cheeks, but Shaleigh couldn't stop. The words were flowing freely now, as though she had known what to say all along. "You don't understand what it's like to lose someone you care about. You don't care about anyone."

"I care," Tanwen replied, but there was no truth in her words. It was an empty phrase, and even as she said it, she blinked, as if she too realized the hollowness of her words.

"I know you don't see me as anything other than the beggar I once was," Colin said, his voice thick. "I've loved, I've lost, and I don't want to lose my only friends. I've been alone before, and I know what that feels like. It hurts. I'd rather be dead than be alone again."

Shaleigh reached over to put a hand on his arm as Mawr nuzzled him. Colin stared at the dragon in defiance.

"Stop that," Tanwen hissed. "I don't care what you think about loneliness. I don't care who your friends are or what you've experienced."

"Of course, you do," Mawr added. "All you've ever known are the lives of others. You do care, and that's why it bothers you so much."

Tanwen was on her feet in a flash of heat and fire that made Shaleigh wince. Before them stood the fire dragon once again and Shaleigh knew they were dead. She knew it in her bones as Colin rushed over to wrap his arm around her waist and put an arm around Mawr.

"I'm so very sorry, you two," she whispered.

"It's okay, Shaleigh, at least we're together," Colin added.

"I love you both," Mawr squeaked.

"Love," Tanwen hissed. "You all have so much love for each other. You care so much for one another. I wish..."

"What?" Shaleigh looked up at the dragon hovering above them. Her head was still covered in black stone, but it was cracking and chipping away, releasing more heat. Her tail snaked around behind her, dipping into the mouth of a lava river in the distance. "Everyone brings their problems here. Everyone makes demands of you, but what do you wish for, Tanwen?"

"To be loved," the dragon hissed, and the light of her body grew too bright and Shaleigh had to close her eyes against it. The heat hit her in waves. "I wish to be loved."

THE LIGHT DIMINISHED SLOWLY. Shaleigh gasped as the heat dwindled along with it. She opened her eyes, feeling how raw the skin felt around her eyelids. Though her skin didn't sting, she felt like she had fallen asleep in front of a space heater for too many hours.

Turning, she found Tanwen sitting on her stone once more in her human form. She was hunched forward, her hands clasped before her and her eyes downcast. "I'm sorry," she whispered. "I lost control for a moment."

Shaleigh looked at Mawr and Colin, asking, "Are you both okay?"

Mawr nodded with wide, fearful eyes, and Colin rubbed at the fur on his arms.

"I think so," Colin whispered. "Just slightly singed." He whispered to her, "That was a close call."

She gave him a nod. It was closer than she liked, but they were still alive and that had to count for something.

She looked across at Talek to see that Teagan had thrown his body over him, possibly to shield him from harm. There was no way that Teagan wasn't somewhere in that body, hidden deep down. She wondered if he'd been there the whole time and she just hadn't noticed.

Shaleigh focused on calming her rampaging heartbeat as she turned back to Tanwen. That was the second time the dragon had refrained from killing them, even though she clearly wanted to. Shaleigh couldn't risk losing this connection, even if it was tenuous. She only hoped Tanwen wouldn't lose control...again.

"You've never known love, have you?" she asked once she had her voice under control.

"No," Tanwen stated simply, as though she hadn't come close to boiling them alive a moment ago. "I've been reviled, ignored, or used, but never loved. Certainly, never appreciated."

It was odd for a dragon not to feel appreciated, and Shaleigh had to stare at her for a long moment, trying to figure out what she meant. She thought of the books that Mawr had read, but her friend was too frightened to say anything. The display of power had taken away the brief bout of courage he had. Surely having books written about her was appreciation. Surely having everyone terrified of her was appreciation in a strange way.

Tanwen had said that she could take the magic out of the world, but did that mean she could put magic into it again? She needed to learn more, but this time she needed to be careful how she asked questions.

"You're linked to the magic here, aren't you? How?" Shaleigh asked.

"I gave myself to this land, buried myself deep in the soil, and allowed the earth to soak up the magic I emit. I allowed it freely, wanting others to experience the joy it gives, the power." Tanwen took a deep breath, and Shaleigh could see the cracks in her dark skin from the lava beneath. She wasn't as put together as before. She wasn't as in control.

Shaleigh swallowed down the lump in her throat, determined to take cautious steps.

"They don't see the magic I give as a gift, from a mother to a child, they see it as a birthright, as a tool. They use it for such hateful, disgusting acts. I'm tired of giving so much of myself and seeing so little good done with it."

"Sometimes doing good is hard," Shaleigh said. "It's tempting to take the easier path instead of doing the hard work it takes to be good. I've tried doing what I thought was right before, but I hurt so many." A hollowness filled her chest and she thought inexplicably of Madam Cloom, but she pushed through it. "I made mistakes in trying to do right. I didn't know any better, but I also didn't really want to know better. I assumed I was right even though I wasn't."

"You're saying I'm being too hard on them," the dragon said with a snarl.

"No, I'm saying that they're trying their best, but it's difficult. You've had centuries to see what's right or wrong, but we don't get that luxury. We don't live that long." Shaleigh tried to hop forward on one leg. She wanted to get closer to Tanwen, she felt like she needed to, but Tanwen's outburst had made her leg flare up, and it was throbbing like crazy. There was no way she could chance putting weight onto it, and it was difficult trying to concentrate through the pain.

Then Mawr leaned against her hand.

"It's okay, you can lean on me." He smiled, and his voice was warm. "I'm here to help."

An arm looped around her and Colin drew up beside her. "We do this together, remember?" he whispered with a half-hearted smile, his eyes red. "One way or another."

She smiled at them both. "Thank you. I couldn't do anything without you two."

"I think you could," Mawr added. "I believe in you."

A warmth filled her, and a stability that she hadn't expected. Step by slow step, with both her friends' help, they approached Tanwen. The dragon was watching them with unshielded curiosity this time. She was studying their friendship, their affection, their love. Shaleigh realized in that moment that she was being fully honest with them when she said that no one loved her, and in that moment Shaleigh pitied her.

"I'm sorry that so many have disappointed you. I do think they try their hardest, and I can tell you for a fact that if the Faeries and the magicians I've met knew that they have you to thank for the magic they use for all aspects of life, they would love you."

Tanwen scoffed, but the briefest pang of sorrow was clear across her face.

"If they knew what you gave them, that you were the mother of all the magic they know, they would love you and visit you. You wouldn't have to be lonely anymore."

"You speak of impossibilities. There is no love for a rampaging fire dragon."

Shaleigh shook her head slowly, choosing her words carefully. "Perhaps you have to learn to control your temper more." At the glare she received, she quickly added, "If you push them away, why should they risk their lives to understand you?"

"I've read many books about you," Mawr said in a small voice, and Shaleigh felt her chest swell with pride for her friend's bravery. "I've read many who would have loved to speak with you in their lifetimes. I think, if you gave them a chance, many would love to meet you and understand all the knowledge you have to give."

Tanwen shook her head. "You give them too much credit. I've seen their ways. They try to build villages on my land just to spite me. They try to build castles on my home. They throw their unwanted into my flames, and they share stories of my ferocity. None truly know me. None want to know me. You say they would have loved to converse with me, Mawr, Guardian of Aife, but where are they?" She gestured to Talek and Teagan then. "Even you have come asking for favors."

Colin shuffled with concern. "I mean, we have, it's true. You're not wrong there. They're both good people though. They both love each other very much."

The dragon scoffed again. "And you have proof, Colin Cawley? You've only seen their despair and their hatred for each other. I saw that in your mind. I saw Teagan mocking him in the jail cells beneath the High Castle of the lost Garden. I saw Talek crying over his bedsheets. You assume they love each other, but you have no proof. It's merely speculation. They hated each other and that hatred once sewn can never be cured."

Colin pulled away from Shaleigh, letting her lean against Mawr.

"Are you okay?" Shaleigh asked, unable to keep the fear from tainting her voice.

He nodded and reached into one of his pockets. "I have proof. Teagan let me take it." He pulled out a drawing, one that Shaleigh had actually seen before.

"You went there?" Shaleigh asked, and Colin nodded.

"Talek was a total wreck, too. Here, if you don't believe me, maybe this will help." He stepped up to Tanwen and placed a piece of paper on the ground. Tanwen flicked her hand and it flew up to her fingertips.

It was a small sketch of Teagan laughing, one of Talek's more endearing drawings, and one where the artist's love was clear and heart-wrenching knowing their history. Tanwen took it and stared at the ink scrawled across paper, her fingers singeing a corner. She gave a small smile, and a longing came to her gaze.

"Talek made this," she said as though she could feel it through the paper. "It's filled with his love."

Colin nodded. "Yes, ma'am. There were a bunch more, but I really liked that one. I liked seeing Master Teagan—er, *Teagan*—happy. I never saw him that happy when he was working as the High Faerie at the Garden. I liked it."

Tanwen studied the drawing again then looked over to Talek still lying on the ground, eyes closed, with Teagan holding his hand. She took a deep breath, and this time Shaleigh could see that her skin was fully formed without cracks of lava beneath. Perhaps she had taken Shaleigh's words to heart and was trying to control her anger. If that was the case, then already they had made some small victory.

"Your determination and affection for each other, their love for each other, all of it is so very different from what I'm used to experiencing. You didn't come here with swords or try to make waterfalls to extinguish my flames. You didn't come here as a last mercy to put someone out of their misery. You came here against your will, of course, but I think you could have left your captor if you truly wished it. I think you came here for your friends as well." She leveled Colin with her heavy gaze, "Am I right?"

Colin stepped back to wrap his arm around Shaleigh's arm again as though looking for something to distract himself for a moment longer to keep from answering. "Yeah, I could have probably gotten us away. I knew Shaleigh wanted to help them though, so I didn't. I didn't kidnap her again, though I was tempted to."

Shaleigh laughed. "I know you were, and honestly I don't blame you. If Tanwen has to work on her anger, you really have to work on this kidnapping problem."

He gave a sheepish smile.

"I will help you," Tanwen said suddenly and Shaleigh felt the tension release from her shoulders.

"Thank you," Shaleigh said, not knowing what else to say. "Any help you can give us, we would appreciate."

She honestly never expected the dragon to be willing to help them, and even her throbbing leg might be worth it if they had somehow achieved that.

Tanwen got to her feet and stepped over to where Talek lay. Teagan was at his side, but when the dragon waved her hand to the side, Teagan dropped Talek's hand and stepped back several paces. She then gestured toward them. "Come closer, Shaleigh."

Shaleigh looked between Mawr and Colin. "Can we all come?"

"Just you."

"Damn," Colin grumbled, removing his arm from around her. "Maybe you could ride on Mawr's back?"

Shaleigh shook her head. "I don't think she wants that. She wouldn't have told me to come by myself if she did."

She let out a huff of frustration as she stepped away

from Mawr and hopped on one leg, aiming for the rock that Tanwen had been sitting on. If the ground was flat, it wouldn't be so hard, but with the ash covering everything, it was difficult to keep her balance. Every hop also sent a jolt of pain through her bad leg and the last few hops made her grimace as the pain got worse. Finally, she reached the stone and leaned heavily against it, gasping in the hot, thick, sulfuric air. Sweat dripped down her brows as she stared at her hands splayed out on the stone. It was warm to the touch, but everything here felt warm.

She looked ahead and saw that there was still a good twenty feet of space between her and Talek, and worse yet, there were no rocks for aid. She would have to pace herself. She could do that. Shaleigh took a deep breath and hopped—one, two, three. She was feeling good about herself and didn't have much farther to go, but then on the next hop she lost her balance, falling hard to the ground. Pain reverberated up and down her leg and she couldn't hold back the grimace or the cry.

"Shaleigh!" She heard Colin cry behind her.

Mawr's voice was unmistakable when he said, "I should go help her."

"No, you can't. She only wanted Shaleigh. And you know I can't carry you."

Shaleigh held a hand up, palm out to her friends, and their conversation went silent. She didn't want either of them risking themselves for her. Like Talek, she had gotten herself injured, and now she was dealing with the consequences. Tanwen, who was crouched over Talek, glanced over her shoulder, flicking her hair to the side. "What's wrong with you?"

Shaleigh closed her eyes. She had to admit it, she didn't have a choice. She wasn't at all sure how the dragon would react either. "My leg. It's badly burned. I can't walk on it."

Tanwen got to her feet with annoyance and stalked over, looking down to her leg as though seeing it for the first time. "Ah, yes, it is."

Shaleigh glanced down at the wound; the middle of the burn was bright red, looking almost straight through to her tendons beneath the skin. All around it was unnaturally pale on her dark skin, almost white, and the pain was terrible. She wasn't even sure if she could hop again because the pain was so bad. The natural heat that Tanwen gave off only made it worse.

She tried to ignore that the leg existed, tried to ignore the throbbing pain, but it was impossible. When Tanwen crouched down beside her, Shaleigh whimpered and closed her eyes. It felt like her leg was on fire again.

"Child, look at me."

Shaleigh opened her eyes; Tanwen's white, smoldering gaze met hers. "This will hurt. Brace yourself."

Shaleigh took a deep breath. She had no idea what was coming. She just hoped that she still had a leg by the end of it.

Tanwen put out a clawed hand, hovering over the wound, and Shaleigh felt the heat flare up. She cried out again as her skin burned. Then the heat seemed to be pulled outward from her body, and the pain slowly diminished. It reminded her of when Talek had pulled the smoke from her lungs on the stairwell in the Sanctuary. After a minute, Tanwen placed her hand on the wound, wrapping her whole hand around her calf and covering the length of the injury—Shaleigh screamed.

It felt like a knife was being dug into the wound. It felt like fresh claws were scraping under her skin. Shaleigh beat onto the ground, tossing ash into the air as she tried to squirm away out of instinct, but Tanwen's grip was powerful, and the pain intensified.

"Stop, please!" she begged, pain tore up and down her left leg. She wondered if her entire body was about to burst into flames. She wondered if this was what burning alive felt like. Then she felt cold fingers slip into her hand and looked up to see Teagan's lifeless eyes staring down at her. His skin was chilly against hers; he began stroking the back of her hand.

"Teagan," she gasped, wondering if she would black out, wondering if she would survive, wondering if Teagan heard her, and wondering if some part of him knew what was happening. She squeezed his lifeless hand tight as the pain finally began to dissipate.

"There you are," Tanwen said with a wide smile, looking quite pleased with her work. "You'll have a mark, but it is now fully healed."

Shaleigh leaned back, panting and coughing from the ash that got in her mouth. She was covered in sweat, but her leg no longer hurt. In fact, she felt no throbbing or even heat.

"Shaleigh, are you alright?" Mawr called.

"I'm okay, I'm alright!" she gasped, giving them a thumbs up without even knowing if they understood what that meant.

She pushed herself up to a sitting position and examined her ankle. A scaly, black crust covered the burn, as though it had turned into a giant scab. She looked closer and could see that it wasn't a single giant scab, but many small scabs all lined up perfectly together. "They're scales," she said aloud in awe.

"I gave you the only skin that can withstand fire: dragon scales." Tanwen smiled and rolled her shoulders. "It's a small place, I doubt anyone will notice."

Shaleigh's eyes went wide. Of course, people would notice black scales on her leg. Kaeja noticed the mark on the small of her back with ease. If a little discoloration freaked her out, Shaleigh wondered how she would respond to actual scales.

"Is there a problem?" she asked.

"No, not at all," Shaleigh added quickly, "Thank you for healing it."

"Come. I need your assistance." Tanwen had gone back to Talek's side and crouched down with him.

Shaleigh started climbing to her feet, but Teagan put a hand out to her. She let him pull her up and stopped to stare up into his eyes. She wished she could see life there. She missed the confidence and intelligence she used to see in his eyes. Instead she saw nothing, no recognition, no witty remark, no questioning—just emptiness.

"Come on, Teagan. Talek needs both of us." There was a flicker of something in his eyes when she mentioned Talek's name, some flash that could have been a reflection from the distant lava flows. Some part within her hoped that he was in there still somewhere.

She kept ahold of Teagan's cold hand and led him over to Talek, who was still laying on his back with his eyes closed. Hearing the crunch of earth, she turned to see Mawr and Colin approaching.

In a panic, she whispered to Tanwen, "My friends, can they help?"

The dragon ignored her as she crouched down onto her knees, small cracks of deep red forming on her skin where her kneecaps were. She didn't respond, and Shaleigh had to ask again before her powerful gaze turned to her.

"As long as they don't interfere."

She nodded to Colin and Mawr who drew up behind her.

"What does she mean by that?" Colin asked. "We won't interfere as long as she doesn't hurt anyone again."

"Hush, she can hear you," Mawr whispered, his glasses rattling.

Shaleigh waved at them to be quiet. She turned to Teagan and patted his hand, "You need to back away now, okay? I don't want you to get hurt." He took several steps back. Maybe he was simply taking orders now? It was impossible to tell.

Shaleigh got down on her knees opposite Tanwen. Talek lay between them, either unconscious or asleep, she couldn't tell. She didn't want the dragon to change her mind, but she was grateful to have her friends close. She felt safer when they were near.

"What can I do to help?" she asked, holding back a cough from the black ash that came up into the air.

Tanwen smiled and pushed some hair out of Talek's face. "I need you to believe and trust that his mind isn't broken and lost forever."

"Maybe if she hadn't raided his head a few moments ago, it wouldn't be," Colin muttered behind her. Shaleigh turned to give him a glare and Mawr bit at his tunic and dragged him farther back so he would be out of earshot.

She nodded in appreciation then turned back to see Tanwen holding out a hand, her fingertips sharp points. Taking a deep breath to steady herself, Shaleigh took it. She expected it to burn her skin, but it didn't. It was warm and slightly crumbling against her palm.

"I believe," Shaleigh whispered. "And I trust."

TANWEN SMILED, and regardless of whether the dragon was trying to kill her or not, that smile sent a shiver down Shaleigh's spine. She felt her palms break out into a sweat and worried briefly that Tanwen noticed. She didn't want to let her know how terrified she felt, and although she wanted to believe and trust, she wasn't exactly sure she did. The wound on her leg had been made by Tanwen, and although she had healed it, she got the impression that the scales were permanent. While Colin had been rude when he said that Talek's mental situation was partly the dragon's doing, he was absolutely right, and his words dug into her mind like a parasite.

The dragon looked up at her with a frown. "You're not helping. If you can't trust me to help him and you don't believe it can be done, then the magic won't work. If you can't control your callous mind, then I might as well devour him here and be done with this charade."

"No, wait!" Shaleigh urged, gripping Tanwen's hand

before she could pull away. "I can do it, please let me try. You have to understand that it takes me a moment to..." she faltered.

Tanwen snorted through her nose, smoke emerging from her nostrils. "Try then. Prove to me that you can, or else he dies."

The finality of her words made Shaleigh's heart ache. She glanced to Teagan, hovering over her shoulder and looking down at Talek, swaying side to side as though ready to tip over. She thought of Teagan, cutting flowers in the Gazebo of the High Castle, preparing bushels of them for Madam Cloom. She thought of him nearly being tempted by the Masked King in the Dark Lands, and him carrying her through the treetops to escape the minotaurs. Her heart raced in her chest.

She had already lost Teagan, she couldn't lose Talek, too.

Taking a deep breath, she focused on Talek's face, and she let herself believe. She let herself trust that Tanwen, in all her years and all her power, could find a way to help him. Looking at his lax face, at the rise and fall of his chest, she wondered at how vibrant and violet his eyes would be when he awoke.

No, not violet. They would be normal. Could she even remember what his eyes looked like before the Madness had taken him? It was so long ago, and things had happened so fast at the Games. He had been wearing a helmet at the time. No, wait, there was the alleyway by the dress shop, when he offered her lizard tails to eat. She couldn't help but smile at the memory.

His eyes were warm and friendly that day, brown.

They were brown.

In almost an unspoken answer, Talek opened his eyes, gasping as though coming up above water. His eyes were still violet, but they had dimmed. They didn't gleam like they had before.

"There you are," Shaleigh said, "you had us worried."

Talek looked at her, completely bewildered, then turned to Tanwen and the blood drained from his face. "You..." he whispered, drawing away from her.

"Yes," Tanwen said with a smile that seemed more predator than human. "The magic within you is quelled, but I cannot cleanse you of the Madness until you deal with the source of it."

"The source?" he asked meekly, still clearly confused.

"We must deal with Teagan," she said, turning to his swaying form at Shaleigh's side.

His fear turned to anger far too quickly and the violet in his eyes flashed in warning. "No, I won't let you destroy him. I came here to save him, not to see him slain!" He was dragging himself away and trying to sit up. Shaleigh reached out, trying to take hold of his arm, to steady him.

"Talek, wait, let us help!" Shaleigh urged, "Tanwen has already healed my leg and brought you back from the brink. I'm sure she can do something for Teagan."

Talek sat up and wiped a streak of black ash across his face as he tried to wipe at his cheek. "Can you?" He sounded so childlike in that moment, so small and unlike the Faerie who had forced them up a mountainside to confront a fire dragon.

Tanwen turned and stared at Teagan, her face an unreadable mask. It was like she was trying to read his mind, but if he was dead, there would be no mind to read. Shaleigh watched and waited, but Talek had no patience any longer.

"You must tell me," he urged. "Everything I've done, all that I've destroyed, I did for him." He held up his wrist, the one tied with a black ribbon. "I only wanted him happy, but then he," his voice hitched, "...he killed him."

"He... you mean Keriam," Tanwen confirmed.

Talek nodded.

She gave a little snarl with a sneer of her lip. "The immortal magician who refuses to abide by the laws of my magic."

Shaleigh helped Talek to his feet, and he leaned heavily against her. His legs were shaky, but he seemed to be more aware than she had seen him since the Madness took over. But it was clearly still there, evident in the pulsing, glow in his eyes.

"There isn't much left of him," Tanwen said, laying a hand on Teagan's shoulder. "Much of him is gone, but not all of him. There is still some flicker of him here. Possibly tied to one of you." She gave a wicked smile. "I'm not sure how he managed it. Death should take all."

Talek whimpered and gripped a hand into his hair. "But he's there still! You can bring him back, right?"

The dragon didn't respond and Shaleigh steadied him. "Calm down, let me talk to her, okay? Please try to calm down."

Talek looked at her, his eyes wild and desperate. "Why are you helping me? I thought you hated me?"

"Because I care about you. You're my friend."

He barked a laugh but his eyes shone. "Really? After

everything I've done to you? I don't understand why you haven't left my side by now."

"I don't abandon my friends," she said, before clarifying, "Not intentionally, at least." She squeezed his arm. "Let me try, okay? Can you trust me? I trusted you, remember?"

He nodded, looking like he was about to burst into tears. "I remember," he said putting a hand on hers. "Thank you."

Considering that Tanwen had been in his mind for such a long time, she was amazed he was able to even speak. His mind seemed more fragile than before, though perhaps this was how he had been the night that she had helped him from the jail cell in the High Castle of the Garden when she promised to break Teagan's bond. Perhaps his confidence then was all an act, like the one he had shown for Madam Cloom at the Games. Perhaps this was his true mind, his true self, the one he usually kept hidden.

An idea came to Shaleigh then, one she knew was risky, but one she knew she had to take. She turned to Tanwen.

"If Keriam is immortal like the Masked King said, then how are we supposed to defeat him?"

The dragon shrugged in a strange way that looked more like how she must have normally stretched her wings. "If he is disobeying the laws of nature, then he didn't do that with my magic. It must have come from some other place."

She narrowed her eyes, "Like where?"

"From a land different from this one," she said plainly.

"With different magical rules? Different laws of nature?" Shaleigh pushed.

"A land with a different dragon sleeping in its belly . . . I see what you're getting at Shaleigh of the Human World, but I would not advise approaching another dragon. I'm far kinder than they are," she said with a glint in her eye.

Colin gave a nervous laugh, but Mawr quieted him.

"I don't mean approaching a different dragon, but perhaps," she glanced to Teagan, "you could give him something to help in fighting an immortal? It might give us a chance to defeat Keriam and I don't want to lose him again."

Tanwen smiled, and that familiar chill went down her spine like a cold fingertip. "You want me bring him back to life, but also grant him more magic? Faeries are magical beings already, imbued with my magic. Isn't that good enough? I know he's your friend, but you're asking me to break my own rules."

Shaleigh pursed her lips, treading cautiously but pushing all the same. Keriam still had the power to kill them easily if they went back without help, and she didn't want to work this hard to save her friends only to have them killed later. "I mean yes, but you just admitted that other dragons do it, so I assume you can too. That's probably what Keriam did to get his immortality."

Tanwen snarled at that and Shaleigh knew she was on the right track. "You tell us not to go to other dragons, but what choice do we have? If you can't help us, we surely can find a dragon that will."

Tanwen turned around and paced, the ground trembling beneath every footstep she took. Talek looked like he wanted to help her, but he kept his word and didn't say anything. He watched Tanwen with plain desperation.

Shaleigh glanced back to see that Mawr was ducked down to the ground again with Colin crouched next to him. Colin looked like he was searching for escape routes. Shaleigh gave them what she hoped was an encouraging nod and Colin rolled his eyes dramatically.

Tanwen approached again, seeming less angry than before. "I can't have you pestering my siblings with your ridiculous questions and begging for magic that doesn't belong to you. Especially after you regale them with stories of what I've done here." She turned to Teagan. "However, it's true that you may need some help against the immortal magician. I'll consider it." She put a hand under Teagan's chin, and Talek gasped. Shaleigh had to put a hand on his arm to keep him from intervening.

"First we must see how much of Teagan is left. I can't guarantee he can return, but let's try, shall we?" She turned to Shaleigh with a devious smile, "Would you like your friend back?"

Shaleigh stared at her, trying to figure out if what she meant was good or bad. Despite what Tanwen had done to help Talek, he still wasn't cured of the Madness, and she wasn't sure if she could really help Teagan, or if she was trying to take advantage of them all. Still, they weren't dead yet, and she even sounded like she might help them defeat Keriam on her behalf.

She felt a hand grip hers and looked to Talek. "What do you think we should do?" he whispered. His eyes were puffy and fresh tears had washed lines through the ash on his cheeks. He was trembling and terrified, but for the first time ever, he was coming to her for help, for advice. Shaleigh gaped at him, not sure what to even say. "Whatever she does has to be better than where he is now, right?" he added with a hopeful smile.

"I say do it," Colin called. "Anything is better than where he is now."

"She's crafty though," Mawr whispered, shuffling closer to them and piling up the ash on his front paws. "I don't know how, but she's surely going to do something we don't like. I want him back too, but I don't know if we can trust her."

Shaleigh looked to Talek, "What do you think he would want? You knew him probably better than any of us."

"I think I knew him pretty well!" Colin huffed. "And I think if it meant being alive again, he would be all for it. He was always trying new ways of using magic anyway, this would just be one more experiment to him."

"Well that's one vote," Shaleigh said, giving Colin a smile. "And you're right, sorry, Colin."

He smiled.

"Mawr's against it . . . Talek, what about you?"

He stared at her hard, likely sorting through all the possibilities, all the dangers, just like she was. "I want him back, and I don't care how. I know that's selfish of me, and I know he would say something about how careless I was to say that, but I don't care. I need him back."

Shaleigh let out a heavy sigh. "I know, and I understand."

"What about you, Shaleigh?" Mawr asked. "Do you want him back?"

Even though she knew the question was coming, it still felt like a blow to the chest. "Of course, I do! He saved my life so many times. I feel like I let him down." She pursed her lips, realizing what she had been about to say next: that he was like a second father to her. That wasn't fair though, that wasn't right. That felt like a betrayal to her real father who still needed her at home, who was still waiting for her, and was probably suffering. A cold guilt crept into her heart in that moment that she hadn't expected.

"So, the answer is yes, then?" Tanwen asked, a snake-like hiss in her voice.

"Yes," Shaleigh said, her voice breaking. She cleared her throat and tried again, "Yes, we vote yes."

"I didn't really disagree," Mawr whispered. "I just don't trust her."

"Hey, it's okay," Colin said and rubbed his mane. "We know, it's okay."

"Let's begin then," Tanwen said, turning Teagan's face to the left and to the right, like a model toy instead of her friend. A cold panic filled Shaleigh in that moment, and she almost said something to stop her. Almost.

SHINY, black scales began to protrude out along the back of Teagan's fingernails, covering each of his fingers, and then moving up his hands.

"Wait, what?" Talek asked, leaning in closer. "What are those?"

The black scales went up Teagan's arms, up to his

throat, up to his cheeks and ears. Teagan closed his eyes and shuddered.

"What's happening to him?" Shaleigh asked, as scales moved up and spread along his face and up to his hairline. "What's going on?"

The dragon Tanwen did not respond. She was clearly focused only on Teagan as more scales emerged, now around his ankles. The thin clusters of scales seemed to run like a roadway up and down his whole body. Talek had a hand to his mouth, whimpering as the scales clustered to cover the backs of Teagan's hands and the tops of his feet.

Then Teagan opened his mouth and screamed —Shaleigh and Talek both jumped. It took all of her control to keep from rushing in to help him.

The black scales seemed to sprout up like mushrooms from his skin, but there were no wounds and she didn't see any bleeding. They simply emerged like they had been there beneath his skin from the beginning.

Then Teagan opened his eyes, and they were no longer glassy, but alert. He looked at the dragon in front of him, at the flickers of fire that hid behind her long strands of hair, at the expression of pure delight on her face, and the cracked body that hid the fire of the dragon beneath, and he screamed again. He tried to pull away from her grip, but Shaleigh knew how powerful she was.

"There you are, High Faerie," Tanwen smiled and blew smoke at him. He winced as though it was too hot, and when she released him, he fell like he had never used his legs before. Colin darted forward in an instant, catching him just before he hit the ground.

"Welcome back to the living," Tanwen cooed.

"Master Teagan, are you alright?" Colin asked as he sat him gently on the ground.

"Colin?" he asked, coughing and trying to clear his throat. He blinked as he looked around, trying to take in everything at once, and shaking from head to toe.

At the sound of his voice, Talek lurched to Teagan's side and collapsed onto his knees, falling to wrap his arms around him. "You're alive, my love, you're really alive!" He pulled back and kissed him and then returned to hugging him again.

Teagan gave a small smile and put both arms around him, hugging him tight. "I'm so sorry for everything. I never should have treated you so poorly. I was terrible—"

"No, it's my fault!" Talek cried, interrupting him. "I'm the one who became a Faerie servant just to get you back. I should have known better; I shouldn't have done it. I just couldn't see past you. You're my *everything*. You always have been..." Talek broke off into sobs.

Teagan closed his eyes. "Shh, it's alright. I know."

Colin moved away, tearing up. He wiped at his nose with the back of his hand and grinned at Shaleigh. "I can't believe it. He's really back." He sniffed again. Shaleigh wanted to join them, she wanted to revel in Teagan's return, but she didn't want to interrupt his reunion with Talek. When she saw the black scales spanning his entire body, she thought of her own leg and turned to Tanwen.

"How did you do it?" Shaleigh asked.

"I brought him back. It wasn't as hard as I anticipated. As I said, there was a small piece of him still there, still lingering. Not in the body, of course, but present all the same. I didn't have to reach as far as I thought."

"He has dragon scales now," Mawr whispered, nuzzling up behind Shaleigh. "He has scales like you do." She felt his nose against her calf where the scales were, and it felt so bizarre to have something rub against them that her leg jumped.

"Oh wow, that feels weird!"

"Sorry!" Mawr said.

"Two of you are now marked as mine," Tanwen explained and Shaleigh looked up at her with a pit forming in her stomach.

"Marked?"

"Oh dear," Mawr whispered.

"The cost of my help, Shaleigh of the Human World. And I'm not finished yet." She shrugged and Shaleigh could see the imprint of her wings shifting beneath her skin. The dragon had to be very uncomfortable being confined to such a cramped space even for a little while.

"Mawr, what does she mean by 'marked'? What happens if a dragon marks you?" Shaleigh asked.

Mawr kneaded his paws into the ash and looked at Tanwen who was still stretching within her human form. He whispered, "It means that you are forever connected to her."

Shaleigh's eyes went wide. "Like a Faerie pact?"

He shook his head and his glasses slid down his nose. "No, I don't think so, but you can feel her presence. At least, that's how it was described in one of the books that I read when I was back in Aife . . . There was only one case of it ever recorded."

Shaleigh glanced down to her calf, taking time to notice the scales since they emerged on her own skin. The heat of the mountain was still palpable everywhere except there on her leg. It was a patch of cool and she wondered if the scales were imbued with magic, like the kind that gave her sickness when she visited the City of the Fae. She wondered too if getting the scales could have killed her before. Perhaps the dragon's mere touch would have killed her.

She spun on Tanwen, shouting, "You didn't tell us we would be marked when you offered to help."

The dragon threw her head back and laughed, it echoed across the barren landscape around them. "I wasn't intending to mark you, child, but you threw yourself in my way. You're fortunate. The burn alone could have taken your leg or your life. Instead I chose to mark you rather than let you perish." She flicked a hand through her hair, her smile fading as the flames burned and died within. "You were right, what you said earlier. All I see are the those who come here to throw their bodies into my home, who wish to be eaten by me. Those are the only lives I see, the only false love I experience. Perhaps what I ought to follow is true friendship, true love, what you all have for each other."

Shaleigh stared at her in shock.

"I want to dream other lives. I want to wander your worlds, to peek in on your experiences. It isn't the same as living the way you do, but it's a vicarious existence. Is that a worthy trade of my gift to you? Will you take a drop of my power in exchange for life, child of the Human World?"

"Drop of power," Shaleigh muttered, looking to Teagan, who had a roadmap of scales that ran over his skin. "That's how you brought him back. You gave him your power."

"It doesn't take much for Faeries, they're already imbued with my essence. And Humans are barely a breath of wind for me." She strode over to the two Faeries——Talek was trying to help Teagan to his feet but his legs kept slipping.

"What are you doing?" Shaleigh asked, starting toward her.

"Finishing this. You asked for my help, and I've given it. Now I have one more task to complete." She glanced back to smile at Shaleigh and it sent a shiver down her spine. "I'm collecting the rest of my payment."

Talek turned in shock as Tanwen planted a hand over his eyes. He cried out. His instinct was to reach up to force the hand off of his face, but he had no chance of moving her. Teagan fell to the ground with a grunt, trying desperately to help but unable to even stand on his own.

"Let go of him!" Shaleigh screamed. "Stop it, please!"

"Silence!" Tanwen roared as Talek's cries dwindled. She pulled her hand away, revealing the seared and scarred flesh around his eyes and nose. A red welt in the shape of her clawed hand marred his pale skin, until slowly black scales began to emerge. They cloistered out in little circles around his eyes and along the bridge of his nose, along his temple and outward, climbing up his forehead.

Talek whimpered, raising a hand as if to touch his face, but not daring to for the pain. His eyes were closed but his eyelids were swollen and raw. Colin was helping Teagan to his feet, and he was hugging him, trying hard not to fall apart into a crying mess.

Shaleigh grabbed his hand. "It's okay, we're with you still." She was trying to help but her voice trembled. "It's okay, just give it a moment." She remembered the searing pain in her leg when Tanwen's flame had wrapped around it and couldn't imagine what that must have felt like on the face, let alone her eyelids. The thought of it made her eyes well up with tears. She squeezed his hand, trying to give him some kind of comfort.

The black scales spread along the eyelids, and the swelling diminished until they returned to their normal size. "Why did you...do that to me?" Talek asked in a thick voice as though he was in shock.

"I needed to burn the Madness out of you. Once it latches on, there is no full cure, except through my flames. It is caused by your own instability, your own fear, mixed with magic used for the wrong reasons. My fires are cleansing and pure. The pain, however, is unfortunate."

"Unfortunate?" Teagan whispered. He finally managed to pull himself up to his feet and began stroking Talek's hair, petting him while knocking ash from his head. "You could have warned him, said something! He did not deserve that. He has been through more than enough already!"

Tanwen snorted. "Much of that was your doing, from what I saw."

Teagan fell silent and turned away.

Slowly Talek opened his eyes. The violet that Shaleigh had grown accustomed to was gone, and instead was replaced with the white flame that she had first seen in the dragon's gaze when she took a human form. It was brief before it settled into his normal dark brown.

"I can see," Talek whispered in awe. "They were on fire, the heat was so terrible, and I couldn't see. Now I can though. I can see...so much..."

"The Madness enabled you to see into realms other than ours. It enabled you to exist in many places at once, but with the magic of mere Faeries in you, your body couldn't withstand it. Your kind weren't built to exist in more than one place, but I was. I give you my sight, willingly." Tanwen gave a dignified nod, and Shaleigh realized the enormity of her actions. Had Tanwen ever granted anyone these gifts?

Talek gaped at her, then turned to look at the rest of them as though he had never seen them before. "Mawr, I can see magic flowing throughout you. It looks like music. It's beautiful."

"Thank you," Mawr said, dipping his head for a moment. "I didn't cast it, but I'm very flattered."

"Yes, but I can see it! I've never seen magic before or felt it so keenly."

Tanwen turned to Teagan then. "Teagan, former High Faerie of the High Castle in what used to be called the Garden." Teagan winced at her words. "I've given you my strength. You will find little that can harm you, which is how I was able to pull you back from death's door."

"Thank you," Teagan said and gave a half bow, but Tanwen held up a hand and continued.

"Before you give me thanks, be aware that there is a downfall to your gift. The only way your physical body can be destroyed is to return to me. Know that I will be watching your actions closely because you have already shown you are not to be trusted when granted power."

Teagan gaped but then closed his eyes and nodded. "Yes, I have to agree with you. I should not be trusted with too much power, though I still appreciate the gift you have given me. I will be forever in your debt, Tanwen."

She gave a wicked smile. "Oh, I haven't gotten to the other side of this bargain yet, but I will." Before Teagan could say more, she turned to Mawr.

Instinctively Shaleigh went to Mawr's side. She put a hand on his mane and felt him trembling. He was looking down to the ground, unable to look up at Tanwen as she approached.

"Please don't hurt him," Shaleigh pleaded.

Tanwen ignored her, watching Mawr with a smile. "Now what to do with you? You are gifted with a pure heart, a gift I've never encountered here. In fact, I rarely feel a pure heart anywhere in my lands. So, I feel that my gift should be special for you. What would you like, Mawr the Guardian of Aife?"

Mawr kneaded his paws on the ground, digging up piles of ash. Finally he looked up at Tanwen with fearful eyes. "I want my friends to be happy."

"I respect that, but what about you, Mawr? What would make you happy?" Tanwen gave a slow nod but Shaleigh couldn't decide if it was truly respect or if she was humoring him.

He looked to Shaleigh and his chest swelled as though a thought struck him; he hung his head. "I don't know if even you could make that happen."

Shaleigh stroked his mane in sympathy.

"I cannot grant what I do not know," Tanwen urged.

"But you were in my head already, you know everything about me!" There was no accusation in Mawr's voice, only hesitant admiration, as though he had spent years and years reading about dragons climbing into heads and wanted to someday have it happen to him.

Tanwen smiled and shook her head, answering then, "The Lady Sphinx."

Mawr gave a tentative nod.

"I'm afraid she has been gone for too long, though I suspect you knew that already."

"I did," Mawr said, hanging his head again. "I just didn't want to believe it."

Shaleigh put an arm around him and gave him a hug. He was still trembling, but seemed to calm as she squeezed.

Tanwen approached him and Mawr shuffled several steps backward, but the dragon neared then crouched down in front of him. "Hold still, please."

Mawr did as he was asked despite not knowing what exactly he was holding still for. Tanwen lifted a hand and held it in front of him. For a moment, nothing seemed to happen, but then Mawr's eyes went wide.

"Mawr, I give you the heart that you already possess, the strength to help your friends, and the courage to protect them from harm." She lowered her hand and Mawr blinked. "I give you a slight sliver of my heart, Mawr. Let it guide you when fear rises, let it protect you when danger looms, and let it enhance the love that you already possess. Perhaps you can do more with that sliver than I've ever done with mine."

"I feel all warm inside," Mawr said in a whisper. "It's wonderful. I like it so much more than being cold all the time."

She smiled at him. "Dragon fire is always lit." She turned to look down at Colin, who was partially hidden behind Mawr. "Did you think I would forget you? Or did you want me to?"

He shuffled to the side, his tail flipping back and forth. "To be honest, I was kind of was hoping you would."

"You are an enigma. You seem content in the skin Teagan gave you, but I think you wish to have more than that. You are also a messenger and a keeper, are you not?"

"Seeker, I find things," Colin corrected. "I was trained to, uh, kidnap kids from the Human World, unfortunately. But that job kind of ended when Keriam decided to show up, so I don't do that anymore."

She leveled him with a bemused expression, "I didn't ask what you used to do, I said you were a messenger and a keeper. You carry a message on you, do you not?"

"No, I—wait, I do!" He reached into one of his many pockets and pulled out the letter that he had received from Madam Cloom when she and Captain Briar revived him and gave him crutches. "I completely forgot about it."

Tanwen held out a clawed hand and Colin approached very slowly, holding the letter out. He dropped it into her hand as quickly as he could. It fell awkwardly, missed her hand, and landed silently in the ash. "You're not a very good messenger, are you?"

"No, I guess not." Colin gave a stilted laugh.

She leaned down and picked it up in a fluid motion. The back of the envelope was sealed with the emblem of the Garden; something Shaleigh hadn't seen in ages. She had gotten so used to seeing it on all the documents in the High Castle when she had lived there briefly, but now it felt like several lifetimes ago.

Tanwen ripped open the envelope and pulled out the simple letter, written by hand. She read it aloud so that everyone could hear, which seemed very impolite to Shaleigh, but at the same time, she was a dragon and could do what she wished. What use did she have for manners?

"Colin—I know you never liked me and that you never enjoyed working for me, but I have one last request:

"If you ever had respect for the Garden and all that it stood for, you will work to restore it regardless of your prejudices. And, despite my distaste of you, I have to admit that you did find the girl who would change the Garden—perhaps that was what the prophecy meant all along. I applaud your skill as a Seeker for that.

"Given what that damn Faerie did to me, I'm likely not long for this world, but I do not want to die knowing that the Garden dies with me. I worked too hard on building this place for it to crumble in such an embarrassing manner.

"You are a skilled soldier, so you know that the heartbeat of the Garden is more than its buildings and statues, it lies with its people. You and I both know that more than most. We both climbed our way up from the gutter and we'll likely die there, too.

"Don't let our beautiful home ever be forgotten.

"Signed, Geneva Cloom, Steward and Caretaker of the Garden, regardless of what that damn magician has to say about it."

Colin had a hand on his chest and his eyes were glassy. He looked like he was about to cry. "She said that *I* was a skilled Seeker? Madam Cloom *said* that?"

Mawr nuzzled his shoulder. "Just because you don't believe it doesn't mean it's not true."

"Yeah but she hated me. Master Teagan knows that, right?"

Teagan nodded, clearly upset by the letter. He wiped at his eyes. "She was a brilliant woman. Cruel, but brilliant. If she is truly gone, then I..." He pursed his lips and shook his head. "I wish I had been there."

"Enough of this prattle," Tanwen interrupted with a sneer. "You aren't a very good messenger, Colin, but perhaps I can make you better."

Colin stared at her. "How would you do that?"

She opened her mouth and the light in the back of her throat grew so bright that Shaleigh winced. Fire shot out of her throat onto Colin's feet and he leaped several feet into the air with a scream. Tanwen closed her mouth and smiled as Colin landed on the ground, his feet covered in white hot fire.

"Why?!" he cried, gesturing to his feet as the fire diminished. "Why would you do that to me?!"

She crouched before him in an instant and grabbed onto the tops of both his feet. Since Colin's feet were more stoat than human, he couldn't wear shoes. His clawed toes stuck into the ash as scales sprung up all over his feet, the fur singed off completely.

"I grant you speed," Tanwen said in a breathy voice as though the fire was still settling in the back of her throat. "Speed beyond anything you've known before, stoatling. Do you understand me?"

Colin was panting but he stared at her with his full attention. "Aye, aye, Captain."

Tanwen got to her feet and backed away from him. Shaleigh and Mawr rushed over to Colin's side.

"Are you okay?" Mawr asked, almost knocking him to the ground with his anxious nuzzling.

"Yeah," Colin squeaked. "Just a little toasty, I guess."

Shaleigh steadied him and he reached out for her arm. His grip was almost painful as he whispered, "I don't know what she did to me!"

Mawr was licking his opposite hand, turning his fur into a cowlick. Colin didn't seem to mind, or even really notice.

Shaleigh met Colin's desperate gaze. "At least we're alive, right?"

He gave her an expression as if to say this was hardly better. She looked down at the scales that covered his feet then at Teagan and Talek who stood close to each other, but distant from them. They studied Tanwen warily. Was this better than facing the dragon's wrath? Her generosity was dangerous.

"Now we reach the difficult case."

Shaleigh turned at Tanwen's voice and met her gaze. The weight of it shook her to the core. She took a deep breath and tried to ground herself. "Why is my case so difficult?"

"You already bare my mark, but I need more from you.

Your friends contain pieces of me, parts of my magic, and I'm afraid you are the key to it all."

Shaleigh narrowed her eyes. "What?"

"You brought them together. Every one of them are here because of you, so I must make you the key for the magic to work. Without it, you have no chance of stopping Keriam, his mind controlled followers, or the Pello Pines which have awoken in the Slumbering Forest."

Her heart sank at the dragon's words, especially as she recalled the Pello Pine that she encountered in the Faerie City. The memory of the barbs getting stuck in the palm of her hand made her flinch. "So, they have woken up."

Tanwen nodded. "And soon they will want to enact vengeance on the Garden and its remaining people. And you know whom Keriam will use as his army."

"Lieutenant Varg," Shaleigh answered, "and all of the troops—Graddic, the other minotaurs. Everyone."

"If they refuse him, he has the power to take choice away."

"With the scáil plant," Teagan gasped as he and Talek approached them.

"He sure has done it before," Colin muttered, leaning heavily on Mawr.

"Surely not the kind librarians!" Mawr shuddered. "They won't be able to stand against the Pello Pines. I've seen their wrath before. I've seen what they can do."

Colin put a hand on his mane. "Calm down, it's okay." He met Shaleigh's gaze. "We can't let that happen."

Shaleigh nodded and gave a shaky sigh. If Colin could be brave after having his feet caught on fire, she could too. "What do you need me to do?"

"You must wield my hands." She put out her palms but Shaleigh curled inward.

"You mean," she glanced over to Talek's face, remembering the red and raw scar from where the dragon placed a hand over his eyes, "on my palms?"

"Possibly. Or your arms, your wrists perhaps."

Shaleigh started shaking. The memory of the pain in her leg was still fresh in her mind. She wished the dragon had just grabbed hold of her like she had with Talek, but Shaleigh had been outraged at that, hadn't she? This was what it felt like to have a choice. This was why Tanwen must have surprised Talek with it because having to choose to have it done was a pain all on its own.

"I can't have it on my hands," Shaleigh said. "There would be no way I could hide it."

"Why would you want to hide it?" Tanwen scoffed. "My marks are to be honored not hidden away. My gifts are powerful, and I don't give them away to anyone." She drew closer, her eyes burning hot white. Shaleigh felt the heat rising in her and took a step back. "You should be grateful for my gifts. I give them so you can destroy an affront to my magic. I ask again: Why do you wish to hide it?"

There was no curiosity in her tone, only outrage. Shaleigh had to choose carefully what she said. If she misspoke, Tanwen could kill them all in an instant. All because of her own hubris.

Shaleigh's mouth went dry, but she took a deep breath, squinting at the heat emanating off the dragon. "I'm from the Human World," she said. "I have to be able to… blend in there again."

Tanwen snarled, that white hot fire appearing in the back of her throat as she spoke, "So you use that as an excuse to refuse my gift?"

Shaleigh felt her lip quiver and her hands shake.

"Please," Teagan begged. "Shaleigh won't live here forever. She isn't from these lands as she said. Let her be able to return home again to see her family and her friends. She does not belong here. She deserves to see her loved ones again."

Tanwen shook her head, veined lava flows glistening just beneath her skin as she glowered at Shaleigh. "And what makes you think you will ever go home again? This is your home now. You've already survived the magic of this world, been healed by it, and transformed by it. Do you truly think you would be accepted back home with such a mark?"

"My family would accept me, so would my friends." Shaleigh's tongue felt thick and uncooperative in her mouth. She pursed her lips and swallowed down the fear. "If you want Keriam dead so badly, why don't you go and kill him yourself? We passed the villages you destroyed down below at the base of the mountain. Why do you need us to do this?"

The dragon's smile faded, and her pale eyes flickered. "I cannot leave my homeland for long." Her voice became soft and almost pained. "I will dwindle if I depart from it. I can't take that risk."

"The mountains are your range," Shaleigh whispered as she understood what Tanwen meant. "You live in the volcano; you can't be away from it. All that heat... You need the volcano to survive."

Tanwen hung her head. "If I were to depart completely, the land would suffer. The creatures and beings who depend on me, the minotaurs, the Faeries, even the magicians would lose their magic. Many would perish."

Shaleigh gaped at her. "Everything depends on you."

"Yes," she said. "And now I depend on you."

SHALEIGH LOOKED DOWN at her hands, remembering again the seared skin on Talek's face. Her palms were covered in small nicks and scars, wounds from fleeing the minotaurs at the Sanctuary and from small twigs and branches over their trek up the mountain to the Peak of Gwern. They were covered in ash, the burned remains that had been bellowed out of the mouth of the volcano.

She looked to Teagan, whose body was a roadway of scales, to Talek, whose face was forever marred. She glanced back to Teagan, who was only now able to stand fully on his two feet. Even though she hoped that her dad and Kaeja would still accept her with scales on her body, she remembered the concern in her best friend's voice at the pale patch of skin on her back, the patch that had started all of this.

Could she be so vain that she didn't permit the scales on her hands and potentially lead her friends to death once again?

She curled her fingers into fists and pushed the fear away like she had when she faced the Masked King, like she had under the glare of Madam Cloom. She looked up at Tanwen, the terrifying and beautiful woman with a body of black lava rock and eyes of white fire. Then she held her hands out to her, palms up.

"Do what you have to do," she said, her voice low.

"Shaleigh, are you sure?" Teagan asked. She didn't turn to look at him, only stared at the dragon's eyes, allowing her into her mind and allowing her to check the truth in her words.

"I've already caused enough loss, enough death. I don't want to cause more. If your gift is more powerful on my hands, then so be it. If it will help the people I care about, the people I love, then go ahead."

"You don't have to do that for us," Mawr whispered. He was behind her, his voice deep and concerned. She felt his stone muzzle press against the back of her upper arm, warm and comforting.

"I know," Shaleigh whispered, closing her eyes. If she looked at Teagan or Mawr, she knew she would lose her nerve.

"You are brave, Shaleigh Mallett. Your friends will be revered for my mark, but you face scorn for the rest of your life in your beloved Human World." Shaleigh opened her eyes to see Tanwen's expression was soft. "You would do that for those you love?"

Shaleigh nodded.

"Your love for your friends is unlike any I have encountered." Tanwen shook her head in bemusement. "I was right to choose you to be the key," she said with a wide smile.

"I hope your faith isn't misplaced." Shaleigh gave a nervous laugh as a tear slid down her cheek. "I hope I don't let anyone down again."

"Believe in yourself," Tanwen said, taking Shaleigh's hands in hers—white hot pain seared through her palms. She tried to pull away on instinct, but couldn't, and instead fell to one knee. The dragon didn't say a word, only held her hands tight as the pain intensified, the heat was excruciating. Shaleigh screamed. She couldn't help it, the pain was far worse than it had been on her leg. It felt like holding hot embers.

When Tanwen finally released her, Shaleigh pulled her hands closer to her body. It wasn't even a conscious act, it was animalistic, protective. Her vision was blurry and she whimpered, not wanting to look at them. She didn't even want them to be part of her any longer.

"I choose you, Shaleigh, to be the key to my gifts, the one to unlock my boons."

Slowly the world came back into focus. She felt Mawr beside her, warm and steady. Shaleigh squeezed her eyes shut and opened them again, squinting down at the raw flesh of her hands, at the skin of her palms that barely looked recognizable. More tears came as she wept for the loss of the hands that she had always taken for granted.

"I believe in you," Tanwen whispered, "you just need to believe in yourself."

She waited for the black scales to crop up like they had on her leg, like they had on Teagan, Tanwen, and Colin. Where were they? Why was the pain lingering? Why did her hands throb still? Why wasn't it going away?

More tears came and she shook her arms, not really understanding why or believing it would do any good, but she wanted the scales to form to stop the pain. "What's wrong with them?" she cried. "Why isn't it working?"

"Shaleigh."

She looked up and met Tanwen's intense gaze. She felt the weight of the dragon in her mind, and the pain disappeared. Her breathing calmed; the world felt more correct than it ever had before.

"Believe in yourself."

"I'm afraid to," she admitted. "Every time I do, I make mistakes."

"That means you have learned and grown."

For the first time in a long time, Shaleigh felt a small spark ignite deep down, of confidence and clarity that she hadn't truly felt since before the Garden's fall. She had done so much since then, negotiated with queens and tyrants. She had even helped to bring a friend back from the dead. She wasn't naive anymore; she had learned her lesson. She wouldn't allow herself to be misled again.

The spark of confidence grew.

Tanwen looked down at Shaleigh's hands, and Shaleigh followed her gaze. The palms of her hands looked normal, slightly scarred, slightly damaged, but they looked better than she imagined they would. She brought them closer and saw that the scales were so very small, so minuscule, that she only saw them when she held them up to her nose. She dragged her fingertips over them. They were slightly hard, almost like calluses, but they didn't feel like scales at all. They certainly didn't look like them.

"Thank you," Shaleigh whispered.

"You did this." Tanwen explained. "You believed in yourself and you willed your hands to remain. If your friends wish it, you could help them to do the same."

Shaleigh stared at her in awe. "I did this?"

She nodded. "Alone, you are weak, but together you are powerful. As the key, you direct that power, but your strength is in your friends. Without their support, you have nothing."

Behind them Colin gave a tentative chuckle. "Keriam doesn't know what's coming for him."

"The magician is indeed quite clever as his self-imposed title suggests." Tanwen glanced to Talek. "I saw how suspicious he can be and how determined. He will stop at nothing to obtain what he wants, and if he learns of your power, he will do anything he can to dismantle it."

"But we have your gifts!" Talek smiled for the first time in ages. "And he no longer holds sway over me. He'll stand no chance against us now."

"Ah, but you still bear his mark. You would be wise to consider all that it implies."

Talek held up his arm and looked to the black ribbon tied to his wrist. Teagan's expression grew dark at the sight of it.

"You should destroy it," Teagan whispered. "We can find scissors that could do it. You should cut off his power immediately."

Talek clasped the loose ribbon between two fingers. "You're right, it wouldn't be difficult, especially not now. But I shouldn't."

"Why not?" Teagan asked. "Don't tell me you still feel loyalty to him."

Talek turned to look into his eyes and gave a bitter-sweet smile. "Look at us, the roles have reversed.

Remember me begging you in that jail cell to cut your bond with her?"

Teagan's mouth dropped open and he glanced away. "I do, and I regret my words that day. I was frightened for you and I treated you terribly. I should have ended my pact with Madam Cloom long ago."

Talek reached up and stroked Teagan's cheek before turning back to the ribbon. "No, I don't want to keep it out of loyalty, you misunderstood me. I want to be able to know what he's up to. I want to feel his panic as he realizes he's going to lose everything he's controlled for so long."

"He doesn't sound that different from Madam Cloom, to be frank." Teagan smirked.

Tanwen sighed and moved past Shaleigh, back to the crack in the ground in the distance. As she passed, Shaleigh could feel the heat lingering behind her, swaying the rocky landscape. Shaleigh took a step back and held an arm up to shield her eyes.

"You have your gifts now, and you have my trust that you will remove this usurper from my lands."

Shaleigh watched as her body began to crack revealing a river of yellow fire moving along the surface, breaking into tributaries and reservoirs.

"If you fail to do so, I fear for the future of my lands. If I should dwindle, so will any gifts I have given you." She turned to stare at Teagan with eyes ablaze, adding, "Including your physical form, Teagan."

He visibly trembled at her words and Talek wrapped an arm around his waist. "I understand. Thank you for...everything."

She turned to Shaleigh as her face broke apart and fell to the ground; she stretched out the long snout of her true face. *"Be the key,"* she said into Shaleigh's mind. *"You may not be Madam Cloom's chosen, but you are mine. Do not disappoint me."*

Raw dread and adrenaline surged through her and Shaleigh fell to one knee at the weight of it. Hearing the words and feeling the dragon's slight presence in her mind was one thing, but when she unleashed it in its full fury, Shaleigh found it hard to breathe. It was like her entire body shook with the weight of responsibility, the expectation, and the deadly unspoken threat if she did fail.

Tanwen suddenly broke out of her small caged human form and flapped her wings slowly as she stretched. Colin and Mawr had to back away from her, stopping to stand behind Shaleigh while Teagan and Talek watched her in awe farther away, squinting through the heat.

"Be grateful I have found a use for you, children. Continue on your journey, and I grant you permission to return if you wish—only if you bring those you fully trust."

"Thank you," Mawr said and bowed his head.

She gave a cry then that seemed to scatter like hot cinders across the stone. Finally, she jumped into the air, her great wings flapping so hard that the heat waves made Shaleigh's eyes go dry in an instant. She hovered briefly above the chasm from which she emerged before plunging down into the hot depths of the volcano.

Behind her the ground sealed closed, shaking the earth beneath their feet, until nothing of her presence remained.

AN UNCERTAIN FUTURE

Shaleigh wiped at her eyes, blinking through the tears that never seemed enough to sate the dry heat. Her mind rang with the dragon's words to her, "*You may not be Madam Cloom's chosen, but you are mine.*" The words made her skin tingle and put her nerves on edge. How had that even happened? When did that shift occur? One minute the dragon was threatening to kill them all, and the next she was tearing into their minds, until finally deciding to help them. Shaleigh's heart beat so fast in her chest she was afraid she might pass out, so she sat down in the ash and tried to take deep, calming breaths.

"Are you okay?" Mawr's voice pulled her out of her head and she absently reached up to pet his muzzle.

"I don't know," she admitted. "That all happened so fast. I don't know if we did the right thing or not. I feel like every second I was being judged and fighting for my life."

Mawr hunkered down next to her and she leaned her

head against his side as he rumbled the ground with his purrs. They were so soothing, and she was so shaken.

"I know it doesn't feel like it, but I think we were very lucky. Do you know I've never read a book about anyone meeting and talking with Tanwen before? Not surviving it, at least. There was the one case of the dragon's mark, but nobody thought it was real. It could have been much worse."

"I don't feel very lucky, Mawr."

"I agree, we could all be dragon barbeque right now!" Colin walked over, stepping cautiously on his scaly feet. "But I guess we could have died, and we didn't. So that's something!"

Talek helped Teagan walk over to them. He seemed to still be struggling with walking, but at least he was on his feet; Talek had an arm around his waist to keep him from falling over. She matched Teagan's smile. She was so happy to see him smile again.

"I'm afraid I don't have the energy to fly us back down now," Talek whispered, clearly uncomfortable about what had happened. "I'm sorry . . . I shouldn't have dragged any of you up here."

"If you hadn't, I'd still be dead," Teagan drawled, and Talek gave him a pitiful look. "Calm down, love, it was a joke."

"A bad one," Talek grumbled, shaking his head.

"I guess we're walking then?" Colin asked, looking around. "Does anyone remember what direction we came from?"

While Colin and Talek were trying to figure out which path through the ash and lava was the safest, Shaleigh looked down to her hands. She dragged a finger across the miniscule scales of her left palm then used a fingernail so that she could feel every tiny point. They reminded her of the tiny barbs of a cat's tongue, only much smaller. She swallowed down the lump in her throat. As unsettling as they were, she would have to get used to them. They were a part of her now.

"Do you have any idea how we should get out of here, Shaleigh?"

She looked up into Mawr's fearful gaze, his golden rimmed glasses askew once again on his nose and gave a big sigh.

They needed someone to lead. They needed someone to point them in a direction, regardless of whether or not it was right, and get them moving. They needed to get back to the Garden, and the longer they delayed, the more time was lost.

She knew she should stand up and take charge, that she could do it, that she was expected to do it, but she felt drained. She was so tired of having to make the decisions, of taking initiative, of putting herself out there. It was exhausting after a while, and she felt like she had done just that ever since she and Teagan had been dropped on the outskirts of the City of the Fae.

"I have no idea," she admitted. "I had my eyes closed when we were flying over, and I barely paid attention to where we were when we took off. I'm not very good at being a leader, Mawr."

She felt the buildup of tears behind her eyes as she finished speaking and took a deep breath. She wanted to cry again, but she was tired of that too. She just wanted to curl into a ball and let someone else take the reins for a while, even though she knew there was no one else who could. She wondered if Queen Mab ever felt that way, especially knowing how many Faeries she had escorted up here to Tanwen's home. Did she want someone else to take over for a while too? Was there anyone else who could?

"You don't have to be a leader, Shaleigh. You don't have to do anything. You're my friend, and I will always be here for you. If you want to sit here for a while, I'll sit with you. If you want to go somewhere, I'll follow. I don't mind one bit."

"Oh, Mawr," she whispered, wrapping her arms around him and hugging his muzzle tight. He felt so warm in her grasp.

After several minutes, she pulled away and wiped at her cheeks.

"Feel better?" he asked with a smile.

"You always make me feel better." She reached over and straightened his spectacles then got to her feet as Colin and Talek both turned to her. They had been in a heated discussion but paused when she stood up--they wanted her to lead, she could tell. Instead of curling up into a ball like she wanted, instead of allowing the bitterness from the weight of leading take hold of her, she indulged herself.

She walked over to Teagan and hugged him.

He pulled away from Talek so he could hug her back. "Shaleigh."

"I've missed you," she said. "So much."

He squeezed her harder. "I don't know how you got

me up the side of a mountain to see a dragon," he said, the smile evident in his voice, "but I am quite impressed."

She laughed as she pulled away. "That was all your boyfriend's doing. How are you feeling?"

He sighed. "A little foggy like I've been asleep for far too long, and my limbs feel heavy. They were tingling a lot at first, but they're getting better as I move."

"I'm glad. I wish we could get you checked out by a doctor or something just to make sure you're okay."

"I don't think we're going to find a doctor out here," Colin muttered.

"He'll be alright," Talek said. "He just needs some time." He stared at her for a long moment before adding, "I'm surprised you don't hate me. I put you through so much."

"You did, but you saved us too. You saved my life back at the Sanctuary and you tried to save Teagan's life."

He blinked before squinting, "I barely remember that."

"The Madness had taken hold of your mind," Mawr chimed in. "You weren't in complete control of yourself."

"I'm glad to see you too," Teagan added, turning to his lover, and Talek blushed around the edges of the scales on his cheekbones. She wasn't the only one who had changes that were going to be difficult to get used to.

This mountain had changed all of them.

Shaleigh glanced down to her hands again and rubbed her thumbs against her palms.

"What's bothering you?" Teagan asked her, pulling her attention back to him. He and Tanwen were both staring at her with concern clear across their faces. She needed to focus and not get lost in her head, even if she was drained.

They needed her.

Tanwen needed her.

"I'm the key," Shaleigh muttered. "That's what Tanwen told me. I may not be Madam Cloom's chosen, but I was hers."

"She said you made your scales smaller by willing it," Colin remarked. "Maybe you can do other things too?"

Talek began counting out on a free hand as he spoke, "Let's see, we have Teagan's skin, my sight, Colin's speed, Mawr's heart... Shaleigh you give us purpose. Perhaps with Colin's speed we could move quickly through this deadly landscape?"

"With my skin, we should be able to resist the lava," Teagan said with growing excitement.

Shaleigh glanced all around them, at the lava flows in the distance and the black ash everywhere. Tanwen had said that Shaleigh's strength was in her friends, did she mean that literally? If they all worked together, what would happen? She looked up to Talek. "Can you see a path?"

He blinked. "No, that's what we were just discussing. This place hides all sorts of unknown dangers."

"No, not with regular sight. With the sight that Tanwen gave you––look with a dragon's sight."

"Dragon's sight? That's a bit melodramatic," he said, smirking. When he looked around, at first, he looked just confused, but then his eyes turned a pure white and he shuddered. "Yes, I see a path down the mountain. It is treacherous. There are many lava flows here."

"Okay," Shaleigh said with a deep sigh. "We can deal with that. If we can deal with a dragon, we can do this, right? Everyone take hands." She put a hand onto Mawr's mane and held a few strands of stone tight.

"Do you think this will work?" Mawr asked.

"If we work together, I think we can do anything," she said. The strange thing was, just by saying it she almost felt it was true.

Colin took her other hand, then came Teagan and Talek.

"You know, I missed you too, boss," Colin said with a smile as he took Teagan's hand.

"You know I'm no longer your boss and I likely will never be again. You need not refer to me with obscure titles."

"Will do, boss. Anything else, boss?"

Teagan gave a bemused sigh and shook his head.

Shaleigh laughed, and it felt so good to laugh again. She missed their banter together. "You two!"

Teagan smiled and gave a shrug.

Colin grinned. "Sorry."

"We need to work together, okay?" Shaleigh asked, still grinning. "Talek, I need you to visualize the base of the mountain. Teagan, I need you to imagine moving through lava. Colin, imagine running really fast."

"Oh wow, um, do I need to close my eyes or something?" Colin asked.

"Do whatever works," she added. "Closed or open, I don't care."

"*Really fast...*" Colin whispered to himself. "*Be really fast!*"

"Silently, please," Teagan muttered with a smile.

Colin went silent.

Shaleigh closed her eyes and concentrated, imagining them rushing over lava runs and down to a safe little grassy spot at the base of the mountain. She imagined lava bouncing off their skin. Then she opened her eyes and looked around.

They hadn't moved, and she huffed in frustration.

"Why isn't it working?" Colin asked.

"Maybe we're missing something," Talek said. "Magic like this is very particular. It's very easy to miss a step."

"Maybe we need to sing something?" Mawr asked.

Shaleigh put her hands out. "Okay, everybody calm down. We just have to think through this carefully. We're just missing something, that's all. I just wish she had given us some instructions on using these things."

Mawr licked at her hand, his tongue rough and warm. "Just believe in yourself, that's all. She said that's what worked before."

"I am, but nothing is working!" she said in resignation. "I'm trying. Maybe it doesn't work unless she's here."

"Don't get upset, please don't do that." He kneaded his paws into the ash and Shaleigh instantly felt bad.

She stroked his mane. "I'm sorry, I'm not upset, I'm just..." She stopped and looked at him. "Wait, you have the dragon's heart."

"Well she gave me a sliver of her heart, but I don't think it's a full heart exactly. I like it though, it's nice and warm."

"It's still her heart, which means you're powerful too."

Mawr smiled and hunched his shoulders. "I don't know about that; I don't even have hands to hold."

"Listen, you're my stars, remember?" He looked up at

her with a sweet smile. "I can't go anywhere without my stars."

"I love you too, Shaleigh."

She hugged him with one arm before pulling away. Turning to the others, she said, "Okay, let's try this again. Do exactly what you did last time. Mawr, I want you to think about everyone here and how much we care about each other. I want you to think of how happy you are that we're all together, finally."

Colin squeezed her hand at that last word.

All of them closed their eyes and concentrated, and Shaleigh did the same. She focused on the clearing at the base of the mountain, the lava flows, of speeding through the grass, and Mawr's warm purrs. The acrid smell of ash dissipated from her nostrils to be replaced with the scent of dirt and grass. Instead of the distant sound of hissing gas and crunching rock, she heard beautiful birdsong. A cool breeze swept over her, and she caught the smell of leaves.

Then they came to a stop.

Taking a deep breath, she dared to squint her eyes open and gazed up at the tall trees looming over them. She gaped then gave a soft laugh in relief, hardly believing it had worked, afraid to believe it could.

"Shaleigh?" Colin asked, his voice still anxious.

She looked to see the others were all holding hands still, concentrating with their eyes closed. They were doing exactly as she asked them to.

"It worked," she whispered and slowly each of them opened their eyes and looked around.

"Oh my..." Mawr trailed off, tears in his eyes.

Teagan put a hand to his mouth and choked back a sob. He stared up at the sky, his gaze moving between the trees.

Talek muttered, "I never knew how much life there was hidden away beyond reach."

"Are you okay, boss?" Colin asked, approaching Teagan who held up a hand.

"I just—" He cleared his throat. "I thought I had seen my last blue sky," he whispered. Talek, who kept ahold of his hand, pulled him into a hug and held him close.

Colin wandered over to Shaleigh. "I didn't think it would really work; you know?"

The air smelled sweet compared to the charred ash from the Peak of Gwern. Shaleigh took a deep breath, letting it fill her lungs before replying, "To be honest, Colin, I thought she was going to kill us."

Colin glanced at her with surprise.

"I didn't think any of us were going to get off that mountain." Saying the words were difficult, but somehow as she spoke it felt like a great weight was being taken off her chest. "I didn't think she would let us. Even when she started to help us, I thought there had to be a catch. I didn't think hope was possible."

He came closer, his tail twitching back and forth behind him, betraying his nerves. "I—never thought I would hear you say that. I thought you knew what you were doing the whole time."

Shaleigh leaned her head back and laughed. "Really? You thought I got my leg injured intentionally?"

"Well... maybe not the whole time," he said and gave a

small grin. "I guess you had me fooled." He shrugged. "You seemed like you had a plan."

Shaleigh thought then of Dean Hammond's speeches at the university parties back home. She remembered the applause that the faculty always gave him. She thought next of Queen Mab speaking to her people in the City of the Faeries--"Maybe I did, or maybe I figured it out as I went."

He nodded. "You had no idea, did you?"

"I mean, I knew it was the right thing to do even though I was terrified."

He gave a heavy sigh at that. "I wish I knew what the right thing was to do. Sometimes I think I know what the right thing is, but then I'm wrong."

"That's okay, Colin, you're allowed to make mistakes."

"I said I was going to kidnap you. That was terrible, I never should have said it. I was just scared and wanted out of there. But you were right, we stayed, and we were better for it."

"That's what you were trained to do. It's going to take a while to unlearn that, and that's okay. Just give yourself some time." She thought of the dragon's words, adding, "It's okay to make mistakes as long as you learn from them. That's how you grow."

The ground shook beneath their feet; Colin reached out to steady her as his tail whipped around to keep him balanced. Mawr was bounding towards them, and the ground shook with every leap. As he approached, his eyes went wide as he realized that everyone was staring at him.

"Oh dear, I'm so sorry! I didn't mean to frighten

anyone! I just wanted to let you know that there's a river over there. I thought maybe we could all relax a bit."

Colin hurried over to him with a wide smile. "Wait a minute, you went off to find a river?"

"Yes," Mawr answered, clearly confused.

"By yourself?"

Mawr nodded at him.

"Mawr, that's wonderful! Look at how brave you've gotten!"

"Wait, I am?"

Shaleigh laughed. "Of course you are! You stood up to a dragon, and we all used Tanwen's magic to get here. I think that definitely makes you brave."

Mawr moved one of his paws across the ground. "I don't know about that, I wasn't there alone or anything, it was easier with you all beside me."

Colin dragged a hand through his fur. "Really? You were our resident expert on dragons and you still don't think you're brave?"

He shook his head. "Oh no, I cowered almost the entire time. That's certainly not being brave."

"But you didn't cower the *entire* time, did you?" Colin smirked, patting Mawr's mane. "Come show me where this river is. I feel like I'm carrying an extra couple of pounds of ash in my fur."

Shaleigh made to follow but stopped as Teagan and Talek drew close. "Are you two okay?"

"I'm still shaky," Teagan admitted. "I guess coming back to life takes a toll on the body. If I still had my Healers, I'd have them do research on the phenomenon."

"But you don't have them anymore," she reminded him.

He sighed. "Yes, I know. But still, it's fascinating."

"I think he'll be okay," Talek said, his voice soft. Half his face was covered in the black scales, like a mask. He smiled at her lingering stare. "It doesn't hurt anymore, if you're wondering."

"What about the Madness? I noticed you're seeing things now that you couldn't before."

He hung his head and his white hair, now a dingy, dark gray from being covered in ash, fell forward. "My memories from the Madness are mixed and jumbled. It was hard to think then. I couldn't distinguish what was really happening and what wasn't."

"It sounds like the Dark Lands," Teagan mused.

"Yes, I met the Masked King there." Talek glanced to Shaleigh, "Or at least I think I did."

"You did, and you nearly killed him too, I think."

Teagan's eyes went wide and Talek winced. "I was kind of hoping I'd imagined that. I really hope we don't need to visit him again."

"But you are seeing things," she pressed again.

"I am, but it's different. Before I think I was seeing other realms, other places. I would see creatures that I knew didn't exist, like shapes in a fog, or things drawing me toward them. Now I see what I think is Tanwen's magic everywhere. It's in the trees, the birds, and it blooms up into the sky. I've been practicing to see if I can will it on or off when I wish, and I think I can. It's just going to be difficult traveling anywhere looking like this."

Shaleigh thought of her palms and of how the scales were so tiny. "I think we may have a way to fix that, but it might take some time."

"And time is something we don't have much of," Teagan whispered. "Come along, let's catch up with the others. I feel absolutely filthy. Did none of you even dunk me in a lake or anything to clean me off? I feel like my skin has at least ten layers of grime."

Shaleigh and Talek glanced at each other and smiled. It was so good to have Teagan back.

~

SHALEIGH SMELLED the running water before she heard its ripple. When they stepped into the small clearing, carpeted with fine clover and yellow flowers, she thought for a brief moment that she had somehow gone home. There was something familiar about the space, something that made her think of Kaeja's laughter and of the feeling of her arm around her shoulders.

Most of the photography explorations they used to do were in urban areas: abandoned factories, old subway tunnels, disintegrating houses. They rarely got the chance to be in nature. Their trip to the Treehouse was one of the few times they got to, and somehow this clearing in the woods at the base of a fire dragon's mountain made her think of Kaeja.

A feeling of homesickness came over her then, and part of her wanted to sit down on the clover and moss and bawl her eyes out. It was overwhelming for an instant, and she leaned a hand out to steady herself on a nearby tree. Maybe it was the magic sickness again, the same that Queen Mab and Teagan had warned her about.

It was the second time she had ever been transported with magic after all.

She took deep breaths to steady herself: A cool breeze swept over her from the river and she breathed in the scent. It smelled fresh and alive, so very different from the heat and flames from the volcano.

Mawr was crouched down shoulder deep in the river, his stone body blocking the middle of the stream and forcing the water to part around him. He wore an expression of pure relaxation and she couldn't help but smile. It was rare to see Mawr forget his worries and relax.

Near him, Colin stood waist deep and held his tail with one hand while he scrubbed at his fur with the other. It was a rather bizarre image, watching him scrub himself like a person trapped in an animal's body instead of an animal who had grown up with his own skin: It was a strange reminder that Colin wasn't born a stoatling, he was made one.

She looked down at the dark scales on her calf catching the sunlight bouncing off the stream. She wasn't fully human anymore either, not now. She wasn't really sure what she was—who she was. She had taken on so many names throughout her journey: from being the Chosen in the Garden to Tanwen's Chosen. And much like the scales she had grown, she was different, and could never become what she was before. That was difficult to accept, but she had to. That was the only way to move forward, to feel comfortable in her own skin, to learn how to scrub her own scales like Colin scrubbed at his fur.

Shaleigh took a deep breath and let go of the tree, finally feeling like she could stand on her own again.

Regardless of what the strange feeling was, it had passed far quicker than it had in the City of the Fae. She turned to find Teagan lowering himself carefully down in the center of the clearing while Talek collected firewood. Teagan had said he wanted to bathe, but he probably still needed help doing that——she decided to help Talek.

Searching through the underbrush for kindling, she heard splashes from the river and saw Colin and Mawr splashing in the water. She smiled, watching them play back and forth through the trees. They would never have met if Mawr hadn't found her by the lake near the ruins of Aife.

Her smile faded as she made a startling realization: she had helped them all get to this point. Every last one of them was here because of her, just like Tanwen had said. It was strange to fully realize that and not just see it as words——she felt a surge of pride in herself. She was no longer the urban explorer lost in abandoned places while searching for a purpose, nor a girl kidnapped and brought to a strange land; she was their friend and somewhat of a leader. They depended on her and they valued her input, even after she made such terrible mistakes.

She had brought them together, and here they were still at her side. They hadn't left, they hadn't feared her like Madam Cloom or Keriam, or put her on a pedestal like Queen Mab. They came back to her and wanted to stay by her side. She was proud of herself, of her friends, and of how far they had all come. She never imagined they would still be working together, let alone working so well together.

What would she do if she could go home?

What would happen to them?

She stopped in a patch of dappled sunlight and stared up at the tree branches far overhead. The spiraled leaves of one tree bounced in the wind as birds chirped to one another in the light of the setting sun. Tears spilled out over her cheeks as she asked herself the dangerous questions she hadn't wanted to really ask aloud.

What if she couldn't bring herself to go home?

Going home had been such a powerful drive since she had come here, that even considering an alternative felt like betrayal to her dad and to Kaeja. Her friends here relied on her now, she was Tanwen's Chosen, if she left to go home, what would happen to their gifts? Would their physical injuries be for nothing? Would everything they went through be forgotten, simply because she had classwork to finish?

"Shaleigh?"

She turned to see Talek standing a few feet behind her. She wiped at her eyes, feeling the grime of ash on her face scrub across her cheeks.

"Are you alright?" He stepped closer, holding a hand out, uncertain.

"Yeah," she said, the lump in her throat betraying her emotions. "I'm fine." The tears wouldn't stop though, and she cursed under her breath. She was running out of ways to wipe them away.

He watched her closely for a moment. "I'm sorry, I didn't mean to interrupt, I just wanted to make sure you were—"

"No, seriously, I'm fine," she urged, interrupting him. "I'm just scared, I guess. I don't know what's going to happen, even if we win and everything goes back to normal, what happens to all of us? Do we forget about each other? Do we move on? Do I never see you all again?" Her voice hitched on the last words and she choked back a sob, turning away.

"It's alright, we'll cross that bridge when we get to it," he reassured as he came over and put a hand on her shoulder. It was supposed to steady her, but she leaned into it, keeping him there.

"How do you deal with the guilt?" she asked suddenly, her words more hostile than she intended. She felt his hand twitch as he flinched.

"You mean from all that I've done?" He sounded so confident, like he had everything together, but she was unraveling at the seams. She balled her tear-soaked hands into fists.

"How do you do that? How are you so put together?" She turned to face him but wasn't prepared for the sorrow in his eyes. It was like a punch to the gut and she instantly regretted her words.

"I'm not." He gave her a half smile. "I feel pulled in a hundred different directions: of guilt, of regret, of doubt, but I can't let that pull me down. Teagan needs me."

She stared at him, "He's not the only one who needs you. You're a part of our group just as much as he is."

He nodded to her. "And you are too."

"I know." She wrung her hands, her voice shaky and uncertain. She could feel herself coming apart. "I realize that, I just don't know what's going to happen in the end. It's all so much, it's terrifying. I don't want anyone to get hurt, I don't want to mess up again. You're all putting your faith in me and I just can't—"

Talek pulled her into a hug and Shaleigh stiffened in surprise.

"It's okay to fall apart," he said, holding her.

It was the last push she needed. She slung her arms around his shoulders and cried: The anger, the frustration, the fear, the pain, everything poured out of her. For several moments it was just her, Talek, and the woods around them until she pulled away and sniffled, her tears spent.

"I'm sorry about that," she said. "This has just all been so much."

"You're allowed to feel, Shaleigh," he said with a smile. "Many consider it a weakness, but the secret is that it's a strength. Allow yourself to feel, allow those feelings to exist. You shouldn't have to hide them away. Trust me when I say that will only hurt you in the end."

She glanced back behind Talek toward the clearing where she knew Teagan sat waiting, "Is that what happened to you and Teagan?"

He nodded and took a deep breath. "We ignored the warnings, we ignored the frustrations, we refused to talk about anything other than superficial things, and then when he acted, I was thrown for a loop. When I lost him, I had no purpose in my life. I had no reason to be, and I couldn't imagine my life without him. Yes, he betrayed me, but I shouldn't have gone after him. I should have formed a new life, and we could have met again much later, perhaps. I should have let him be happy, even if it was without me."

Shaleigh reached out and took his hand. He looked down at her touch as though surprised. "But you didn't, and that's okay too. I guess you allowed yourself to feel those things too much."

He swallowed then sighed. "I suppose you're right. We've both been at opposite sides of the spectrum, and I don't know which is the right side."

"I think it's probably the healthy middle, like Mawr and Colin have taken."

He shook his head. "No, we all have our mistakes, our regrets. It's what shapes us, what teaches us to do what's right."

"And that's precisely what we'll do, right? Stop Keriam, save the Garden, and prevent the Slumbering Forest from slaughtering people."

"Mmm." He cocked his head to the side. "I think it's the right thing. We'll find out once we're there. Regardless we need you. We depend on you for more than just Tanwen's gift. You are a moral compass that was desperately needed even before this all began."

"And when it's all over? What am I then?"

"Why, you are Shaleigh Mallett of the Human World. You decide your future, you decide your path, just as we all do."

"For better or worse, I suppose."

He smiled. "Precisely."

As they walked back to the clearing together, Shaleigh was surprised to realize that having a good cry helped. Talek didn't judge or chastise her for it. He acted like it was perfectly normal, and that was so refreshing. She half expected him to get mad at her like she did at her dad when he started crying, but he didn't. He just let her cry and get it out, and it felt good.

For the first time in weeks, she finally felt like she had a tiny, shaky handle on her future, on the safety of her friends, and on trying to right the wrong she had made. She had begun to redeem herself, but she still had a long way to go. Like Talek said, she decided her path.

But, regardless of the hope that she and Talek shared, they both knew they had a long way to go and were running out of time. Between the fire at the Sanctuary, negotiating with the Masked King, and debating with Tanwen the dragon, Keriam had plenty of time to increase his followers, whether with or without their consent if he was still using the Scáil plant to make his mind controlling toxin.

With Tanwen's gifts, they had a chance though, a tiny glimmer of a chance. If they could continue to work together, if they could move past their own mistakes and regrets, and face Keriam's forces, they might just have a shot at taking on Keriam and the now awakened Slumbering Forest.

They just needed more time.

And if she was struggling with the weight of everything, she knew her friends had to be too. Despite the limited time, they needed to recover. It didn't matter what gifts Tanwen gave them, they couldn't head into a battle exhausted.

She entered the clearing and watched as Teagan and Talek set up a fire pit; Talek blowing on the embers to get the fire to catch.

"Is it difficult knowing you all could have done this

with a snap of your fingers when you were in a Faerie pact?" Shaleigh asked.

"Sometimes," Talek admitted with a mischievous smile. "But with the Madness, who knows what the drawback would have been. The limbs might have grown legs to walk over to the fire and thrown themselves in."

Shaleigh grimaced. "It wasn't your fault, you know, none of it was. As you said, we all decide our future. You do too. You're more than Keriam's puppet."

He frowned and sat down beside Teagan, absently putting a hand on Teagan's knee. "Sometimes I'm not sure if I'll ever be able to make up for all that I've done. I've caused so many deaths."

"If it led to you saving my life in the end, I suppose it was all worth it then," Teagan said with a smile.

"Teagan!" Shaleigh cried unable to keep from smiling as Talek's outrage melted into laughter.

"I'm only half joking. It's my life, I'm allowed to be a little selfish with it, aren't I?"

Talek wrapped an arm around his waist, leaning into him. "I missed you so much, you know that?"

Teagan kissed him and Shaleigh turned away and looked out at the stream to where Mawr and Colin were still having a splashing fight--Mawr was easily winning.

"We have an excellent fire," Teagan said, changing the subject, "but I'm afraid we have no food to eat."

"Maybe Colin can help with that," Talek said, getting to his feet and heading to the stream.

After Talek moved out of earshot, Shaleigh sat down by Teagan. "I'm surprised you haven't cleaned up already."

He sighed, "I realized it was probably best to wait until

Talek cleaned up. Besides those two are making quite a mess over there."

Shaleigh laughed, knowing how Teagan was with his pride. If he couldn't bathe himself properly, then she was glad they were taking time to rest.

She changed the subject, "So, you two are good now?"

Teagan pursed his lips. "We're talking, which is more than we've admittedly done in centuries. I don't know if we're *good* exactly, but we're much better. I'm no longer tethered to Madam Cloom and he's no longer Keriam's puppet as you so aptly stated." He paused and reached over to pat her hand. "We're working on it, Shaleigh. Rifts like ours don't repair themselves overnight."

"I know, I just worry. We all have to work as a team to fight Keriam, and I don't know how he's going to react. It's not fair to you either if you have to pretend."

Teagan shook his head. "No, I still love him. I always did, but I was afraid of indulging him, or at least that's how I thought of it. I was rather childish, to be frank."

"He's still wearing Keriam's ribbon on his wrist. I wish he would just cut it off. What if we get all the way down there and Keriam takes control of him?"

Teagan sighed and leaned back to dig his hands into the moss and clover around them. "I don't know if he can. The Madness severed a true pact between the two of them. And the very fact that he's here and not at Keriam's side tells me that their bond isn't as strong as mine was with Madam Cloom. If she asked me to come to her throne room, I could not disobey, even if I wanted to." He waved a hand in the air. "Oh, I could voice my displeasure about it, insult her perhaps, but I still had to go there. I was compelled to, there was no way around it."

Shaleigh stared into the fire, watching as a beetle tried to escape from one of the logs, its back on fire as it tried to flee from the flames, but it slowed as it got farther away before going completely still. She winced. "So, if Keriam doesn't have him in a full Faerie pact, what control does he have over him?"

Teagan shrugged. "I have no idea. As you can guess, there hasn't been much research done on Faerie pacts, at least not that I've read. When Master Cathal asked me to enter into a pact with him, I did it with the understanding I was going into a pact with him and not with the Garden." Teagan glanced down to his feet. "He changed it on me at the last moment, and I was too shocked to say no. It was a foolish move on my part, but I was so excited to have that power that I didn't consider the consequences."

"I guess we'll both find out," Shaleigh said. She noticed that Talek, Colin, and Mawr were coming back from the stream, and assumed their conversation was closed for now.

The sun was starting to dip over the horizon, casting long shadows all around them.

Mawr was stained dark from the water all the way up to his neck, and he had somehow not lost or damaged his glasses in the splash fight. Colin held something over his shoulder, and when he got closer, he flung it to the ground. He had caught four large fish, all about half a meter in length, and sporting rainbow colors as well as a long curling fin on their heads.

"I got us some dinner!" Colin exclaimed. "Hope everybody is hungry!"

"Famished," Teagan said.

"Same," Shaleigh muttered.

~

SHALEIGH WENT DOWN to the stream and washed. She preferred to do it when the others were busy, not really out of a need for privacy, but just because it was nice to be alone for a few moments.

The sound of crickets danced in the air as she breathed in deeply before splashing water onto her face. Using the dwindling light, she decided to wash her hair a little: it was mostly to get rid of the smell of ash, she couldn't stand it any longer, but it was also to get rid of all the grime. Her hair hadn't felt so clean in ages, even though the twists that had been put in so long ago were lost. Her wet hair made her cold; she got to her feet and hurried over to the fire pit just as darkness fully fell. The group was talking quietly, the jovial sounds from earlier now reduced to quiet murmurs.

As night fell, the sooner tomorrow came.

Talek had setup two tall wooden branches and dug them into the soft dirt to work as spokes. Colin passed her, grinning with the fish, heading for the stream. Shaleigh sat down by Mawr, turning so that the fire would help dry her hair. When a metallic tang reached her, she grimaced. Colin was likely gutting the fish—it was gross, but she was also really hungry. As long as it meant food, she didn't care how gross it was.

"I kind of wish they could just bring us food from the Garden like last time," she admitted aloud.

"There isn't much for you to eat out here, Shaleigh," Mawr said as he sprawled out beside her, digging his claws into the earth. His gold rimmed glasses flashed as they caught the fire light. "Only birds and fish, most animals don't come so close to Tanwen's mountain. Many suspect they can sense that this is her realm."

She glanced over to Teagan and Talek who were talking quietly to each other at the other end of the fire. She spotted the black ribbon hanging from Talek's wrist and pursed her lips.

"Mawr, you know a lot of history, what do you know about incomplete Faerie pacts? Teagan and I were talking about how the bond with Talek and Keriam isn't as strong as the one he had with Madam Cloom. Do you know why that might be?"

He cocked his head to the side, and she could hear the *thump* of his tail on the ground behind him as he thought. "Faeries who get the Madness don't usually live afterwards," he admitted. "And those in a Faerie pact don't usually get the Madness. I'm afraid this situation is unlike any I've read about, Shaleigh. Though there might have been more books written on it in the Library of the Garden, but..." His face fell, and his shoulders slumped. "There's no telling what happened to those books now. You didn't get to see the library, but all those books were on the ground and forgotten, the bookshelves were toppled, it was so sad."

She reached over to stroke his mane. "I'm sorry, I

didn't mean to bring up something painful, I just thought you might know something that could help."

"No, I'm sorry, Shaleigh. I'm afraid most of the books I read were outdated, and I normally liked to read about Tanwen anyway."

She leaned in close with a smile. "Maybe once this is all over, you could write a book about meeting her yourself!"

His eyes went wide as he turned to her. "That would be amazing! Would you help me write it? If we wrote it together, we would make sure we got it right."

The pain from her talks with Talek in the woods came back to her. Would she be able to help him write it? Assuming they were able to defeat Keriam, stop the Slumbering Forest, and take back the Garden? Could she make a promise to one of her best friends knowing that she might not be able to keep it?

"We'll see," she eventually rattled out. "I sure would like to!" That was the truth.

"Thank you! I've never thought of writing a book before, but with you by my side, I could do it." To hide her distress at his words, she gave him a big hug.

Colin returned then and skewered two of the fish over the fire; he turned them occasionally as he stood close by. "We're all going to have shish kabobs tonight!"

"Shish—what?" Talek asked, chuckling.

"That's a fancy way of saying food on a stick," Colin said. "They talk about it in the Human World, Talek, you wouldn't know about it."

"At this rate," Teagan drolled, "Colin is going to be more of an expert on the Human World than Shaleigh is."

Shaleigh grinned. She wondered if Colin would ever get to visit the Human World again. Was that magic lost too? Would Tanwen's magic even work in the Human World?

When the fish were done, he snapped the stick in half and gave one to Shaleigh and one to Teagan. The fish was probably the length of Shaleigh's forearm: she stared at it, not sure where to even start. She had the tail end at least, no head, but she could see pieces of the skin in places still attached. It was a little charred on one side. And while it smelled delicious, it was a little unnerving.

Teagan leaned over to her, pitching his voice low so the others wouldn't hear. "Wait for it to cool, then start at the bottom and work your way up. I recommend eating it sideways so it's less likely to slide off."

Shaleigh nodded but didn't start until she watched Teagan take a few bites. Then she dug in. It was flaky, light, and had a surprisingly natural spicy flavor.

They ate, taking turns on complementing Colin's cooking and quick thinking, while watching the moon rise into the sky.

Mawr was purring at her side, looking at the stars, a smile on his face. She reached out absently and stroked his mane and he purred harder, digging his claws deep into the soil.

"Talek," Teagan said, the seriousness in his voice pulling everyone's attention to him, "you were with Keriam the longest, what do you think his next move will be?"

An uncomfortable hush fell over them, only disturbed by the crackling of the fire pit and the crickets sounding a chorus in the woods. Talek was silent a moment, eying the skewered and partially eaten fish in his hands. His expression was grim when he answered--"I think he's bolstered his numbers, that much is certain."

"The people from the Garden," Colin said, his eyes on the fires between them.

"Not necessarily." Talek propped his fish to the side and got to his feet. "Keriam is not limited to the people of the Garden. Those are probably the least of your worries. He still has the army of the Garden under his control without the need for the Scáil plant."

"I don't think Lieutenant Varg wants to follow him though," Colin added. "I think he's only doing it because he's expected to."

"Captain Briar went missing," Mawr muttered, digging his front claws into the dirt. "At least that's what the soldiers were told. He had to take her place. The Captain is smart though, I'm sure she's planning something."

"If she's working with Madam Cloom, there's no doubt. If she's still alive," Teagan whispered, his voice trailing off.

Talek continued, "That's just the start. He also has the Shadow Wolves under his control, some of which I believe he does have under Scáil, but some he does not. There are ones who lead, ones who follow him regardless of where he goes."

"I thought they were from the Dark Lands," Colin said, the fear in his eyes evident in the firelight.

Talek shook his head. "No, the dogs of the Dark Lands are...damaged."

"Yes, I saw that too." Teagan nodded. "They were dead once, I think. Or they died within the Dark Lands.

Regardless, they are chained to the Masked King. They are his pets."

Shaleigh remembered the dogs with the red eyes, emerging from the mists of the Dark Lands. Some were so wasted away that they looked like they had been dead a long time. Whatever magic kept them alive was very different from the magic Talek had used to resurrect Teagan. The thought of Teagan looking like those dogs made her shudder.

Talek put a hand on Teagan's leg, studying his face as though afraid of losing him again in the coming danger. Then he shook himself. "Yes, you're right. His Black Dogs are very different. Shadow Wolves think, they speak."

"They also walk on their hind legs," Shaleigh said, speaking up for the first time and trying not to quake as all eyes turned to her. "They spoke to us, they knew Mawr's name, the dogs in the Dark Lands were threatening, but they were very different."

"My point is," Talek stated, "we are greatly outnumbered. We are a very small band compared to them."

"You're forgetting the Pello Pines," Mawr whispered, lowering his gaze to the ground. Shaleigh felt him tremble at her side and she reached out to calm him. "They're all awake now, and if anyone is left alive in the Garden, they'll go after them. They'll be hungry."

Teagan put a hand to his forehead and shook his head. "The Pello Pines. How could I forget them?"

Talek put an arm around his waist and pulled him close. "I think you're excused a small memory lapse here or there, dear. You were dead."

Teagan reached out to grip Talek's hand as though looking for a way to ground himself.

They fell into silence.

Shaleigh finished her fish and got to her feet so she could drop her stick into the fire. Embers flew into the sky as the flame caught the oil and wood. She looked around at all of their frightened faces, and she saw her own fear reflected in their eyes. They were all realizing the daunting task ahead, the nearly impossible task that awaited them, and she understood exactly how they felt: She had felt intimidated by having their gazes fixed on her earlier, but now, looking around, she felt connected to them.

They all wanted to fix what had happened. They all wanted to take down Keriam and prevent the inevitable slaughter the Pello Pines would bring. They were all guilty of making mistakes to some extent. She felt camaraderie with them, she understood them, but she also knew what they were all forgetting.

"I've been kidnapped, forced to play in Madam Cloom's games, and used as a pawn to bring down the Garden." She could see the hurt her words caused on several faces, but she continued regardless. "I've faced Queen Mab and survived being a Human in the City of the Faeries. I've traveled through the Dark Lands and faced angry minotaurs. I've negotiated with the High Council of the Sanctuary and survived one brush with Keriam's mind controlled masses. And we've all survived a dragon's wrath."

They were all staring at her now, Talek had tears in his eyes and Mawr looked concerned. She pushed forward.

"Mawr, you and Colin were able to work at Keriam's side regardless of his ruthlessness. You were also able to slip away from him."

Colin gave a strained laugh. "He thought we were going to die in that fire, I'm sure."

"But you didn't," Shaleigh stressed, turning to Talek. "Talek, you survived the Madness and have somehow avoided being Keriam's servant even though you're both still in a pact together."

He gave a weak chuckle. "I think that was mostly Tanwen's kindness more than anything else. She pitied me."

"She wouldn't have helped you if she didn't think you were worth helping."

He lowered his gaze.

"Teagan, you came back from death because Tanwen believed in you."

He met her eyes, his hair bright red in the gleaming firelight. "And you are her Chosen," he said, his words feeling like a bell ringing in her soul.

She clutched her elbows. "Right, well, she saw potential in all of us. She thought we could do something, that we could stop Keriam. She gave us the power to stop him, but we can't let ourselves fall into fear even though we have a lot of terrifying steps ahead of us. We have to remind ourselves that we can do this that we are able to do this." She held her palms out to them. "She put the scales on my hands the same as she did for my leg, but I was able to will them to be small. I didn't even realize I was doing it. I willed this to happen, I molded her magic and the gift that she gave me."

Suddenly all of them were talking at once.

"But what if it was just you?" Teagan asked, his brows scrunched up with worry. "Only you have this ability; if something happened to you, where would we be?"

"You've done all these things, but we've done so little compared to you," Mawr lamented, hanging his face so low that his glasses slipped again.

"I actually helped the fiend we're going up against." Talek gave a sad laugh. "For all we know, I might still help him. We have no idea what control he has over me."

Colin rubbed his palms together, staring into the fire. He waited until all of them had said their piece, before speaking up. "I think you're right, Shaleigh," he said as he got to his feet. "We're all sitting around and feeling sorry for ourselves, but we can't be like that. The magic that Tanwen gave us depends on what we feel inside." He put a hand on his chest. "If we doubt ourselves, if we doubt Shaleigh, then nothing will work. We'll all get slaughtered. But if we support each other, if we believe in each other, and we believe in ourselves, then we're all so much more powerful."

She smiled at him. "Thank you, Colin. We need to believe in ourselves."

Colin crossed his arms, looking proud of himself.

Teagan raked a hand through his hair. "How are we supposed to believe in ourselves when we've done nothing but make mistake after mistake?"

"You made me into a stoatling, boss. That was the best moment of my life."

Teagan gave him a meek smile.

"I have you back in my arms," Talek said with a smile.

"All the hundreds of mistakes before that were worth it to have you back with me again."

Teagan turned to stare at him with wide eyes. "Do you honestly mean that? I don't understand how you can love me so much after everything I've done, after everyone I've hurt."

Talek smirked. "I think we're both guilty of that." He brushed some hair out of Teagan's face. "If it has finally reconnected us again, then it was all worth it." He pulled Teagan closer and they kissed.

Shaleigh shook her head and turned to Mawr, who still hung his head. She walked over and crouched down in front of him, rubbing at the fur beneath his whiskers until he looked up at her.

"I know you don't believe it," she said, "but you've grown so much since I've known you. You're braver now than you ever have been before."

He smiled, and tears gleamed in his eyes. "Do you really believe that?"

"I do," she said and fixed his glasses. "You were our expert in dealing with Tanwen. All your years of reading about dragons saved our lives."

He shuffled a paw against the scratched up dirt. He had piled up a mound of moss from his nervousness. "Tanwen asked me to be the heart of the group, but I don't know how I'm supposed to do that. Everyone is so scared, and I'm scared, and I don't know what's going to happen."

"That's okay," she reassured then scratched under his chin again and he closed his eyes with a smile. She moved to scratching his cheeks. "We need you, Mawr. I need you.

You're my stars, remember? I can't go anywhere without my stars."

He reached up and licked her cheek, warm stone raked against her skin and she laughed. "If you need me, Shaleigh, I'll be with you. I'll always be with you when you need me."

That familiar pang of worry came at his words, that uncertainty about what happened after everything, if they were still alive. She pushed it away and pulled him into a hug. "Thank you," she whispered.

He leaned his large head against hers. "I love you, Shaleigh. You're my best friend in the world."

Hot tears seeped from her eyes and her throat tightened. "I love you, too, Mawr."

ALONE

*M*orning came crisp and early; Shaleigh shivered. She was still curled up against Mawr, who served as her heater overnight. He was so much warmer since Tanwen's gift and she was grateful to have him with her.

She was grateful to have all of them with her.

Sleep helped her more than she thought it would, and it dawned on her that she couldn't recall when she had last gotten decent sleep. She yawned and stretched her stiff limbs, her back and shoulders popping as she got to her feet.

"Good morning," Mawr whispered, moving his head to the side to see her, digging his claws into the ground happily.

"Morning," she said as she stretched her legs out and yawned. She pitched her voice lower, seeing that Colin was asleep on Mawr's back. "Sorry I slept so hard."

"You're always welcome to sleep by me." He watched

her a moment before adding, "You seemed so upset last night, I was worried about you. Did sleep help?"

She smiled at him. It was amazing sometimes how he understood her so well. He could tell she was troubled even when she barely said a word.

"I think it helped a lot actually," she said before walking around so he didn't have to tilt his head to look at her. Colin snored as she took a moment to straighten Mawr's glasses. It was colder than it had been last night, especially after leaving Mawr's side. She shivered and crossed her arms to retain some heat. "To be honest, I'm dreading where we have to go next, but I know we have to do it."

He paused for a moment as though having trouble finding the right words. "Shaleigh, where do you think we should go first? Back to the Garden?"

She sighed and wrapped her arms around herself, trying to stay warm against the bright morning. "I was thinking about that—I don't think that's a good idea, not yet at least. If we show up in the middle of the Garden, we'll be trapped in those jail cells like Talek was before. We have to see how to approach it first."

Mawr shuddered and Colin gave a sleepy groan on his back. "I've been in those cells before and they're terrifying. I'm sure they've only gotten worse with Keriam in charge of the city. Yes, I think you're right, that would be a very bad idea."

"Exactly, so I'm thinking we need to head to the Slumbering Forest first."

Mawr's eyes went wide, and his voice came out in a high pitched whisper, "But the Pello Pines!"

Shaleigh nodded and sacrificed a bit of warmth to reach out and put a reassuring hand on his cheek, rubbing just beneath his whiskers. "I know it's scary. I saw one of the Pello Pines while I was in the City of the Fae. They're terrifying, and I don't really want us to have to go, but—"

Mawr shook his head forcing Shaleigh to stop petting him. Colin groaned again from Mawr's back. "We can't go back there, not without an army. Last time it took a powerful magician and a powerful Faerie to put them to sleep, but this time they won't be easily fooled."

"Mawr—"

He stared at her with wide, terrified eyes. "Shaleigh, they're going to be so angry. They're worse than an army of Shadow Wolves. They don't just prick you; they'll fling you around like... like..." He had tears in his eyes, and she wrapped her arms around his muzzle and pulled him close.

"Shh, it's okay," she whispered into his ear. "You're not going to be alone this time. We'll all be with you. You'll have friends to help." She rubbed the top of his nose as he took a deep breath.

"I wasn't alone last time," Mawr said, his voice shaky. "I had many friends with me before, and I had to watch all of them die. They were some of the wisest scholars and some of the most powerful magicians. All of Aife tried to fight them before, and they lost. If an entire city couldn't stop them, Shaleigh, how can we?"

She frowned and found herself at a loss for words, recalling the memory of the hulking tree behind bars with its long brambles and piercing stings. She glanced down to the back of her hand and could still see the pattern of dots from where it had stuck its barbs into her skin, looking for blood to leech out of her. Were they attempting too much? Sure, they had gifts given to them from Tanwen, who claimed to be the heart of all magic in the land, but what if even that didn't help?

Strategically she saw no other option but to handle the Slumbering Forest first, but perhaps she was wrong. Maybe that was why Teagan had shown her the Pello Pine before, because he wanted her to know what they were up against, or how dangerous the fight would be.

She heard footsteps from behind and turned to see Teagan and Talek returning from the stream. They must have woken up early and gone to clean up before leaving.

"Mawr," Teagan said, concern in his voice, "are you alright?"

"I've upset him," Shaleigh admitted. "I told him we needed to go to the Slumbering Forest first before we went to the Garden, but he said it's too dangerous. Is he right? Do you think we stand a chance out there?"

Mawr was trembling all over. "I watched the Pello Pines kill so many of my friends, even the children." He said as fresh tears stained his stone fur. "I don't want to see you all die, too."

Talek stepped forward and got down on one knee before Mawr. "I traveled those dark woods for many weeks in my attempts to find a way into the Garden. I saw the Daegonrúsc that engulfed the Pello Pines and kept them asleep for centuries. Even in their hulking cocoons, it's obvious how dangerous they are. And some still fed from the occasional Shadow Wolf if they got too close to it."

Shaleigh felt her stomach drop at his words.

Talek asked then, "Do you know what we have that your friends in Aife did not?"

Mawr sniffled. "Luck?"

Teagan smirked at Shaleigh's side. "Yes, hopefully..."

"We have dragon magic. And we have a secret weapon, one they wouldn't in a thousand years suspect. We have someone with us who was able to put them to sleep before." He gestured to Teagan who gave a heavy sigh. Talek glanced up to him with a wide smile. "If anyone knows how to handle a forest full of bloodthirsty trees, it's Teagan, right?"

Teagan shook his head and clasped his hands behind his back as he had done when he was High Faerie for the Garden. "I think Talek has put a bit too much faith in my abilities seeing as I am not in a Faerie pact."

"I'm only partly joking," Talek continued. "If we want to save the people of the Garden, then we have to stop the Pello Pines first. Keriam has no plans to help whatever survivors are in the city. When the Pello Pines come to take their revenge and drain the city dry, Keriam will leave with the army at his side. I imagine many of the soldiers will be oblivious to what is actually going on in the Garden when they're given urgent orders to leave the city."

Shaleigh thought of the locket that Lieutenant Varg had looked at when she was brought in to fight in the Games at the Garden, of the picture of his wife and two boys. She wondered if his family was still alive and safe. She could only imagine what it would feel like if the army was brought back into the city and Lieutenant Varg found his family once the Pello Pines were done with them.

She didn't realize how hard she was clutching her elbows until the scales of her palm cut her forearm and she jerked them apart. "We can't let that happen."

Talek turned to her with a sad expression. "I didn't want to say anything last night, everyone needed rest. I needed rest before I broke the bad news, but I generally know Keriam's plans. He shared everything with me, and I doubt he's likely to change his mind."

"But all those children!" Mawr cried. "They're not involved in any wars or kingdoms; they just want to play and be happy. Why must he risk their lives?"

Teagan stepped forward. "Perhaps I can shed some light onto that. Keriam simply does not possess the ability to keep the forest in check. When I worked for Madam Cloom, I was tethered to the Garden. I had the power to maintain the magic to keep that forest asleep in permanent darkness. It was as easy as a quick thought every few days. Talek does not possess that ability."

Shaleigh's gaze automatically shifted to the ribbon on Talek's wrist.

"Although I am bound to him, I'm afraid I don't have the power to keep the place in check like Teagan did. To be fair, it took a powerful magician bonded to a powerful Faerie to change that land before. Once that magic was broken, there was really no way to put it back. The Daegonrúsc will grow weaker with each passing day, and the Pello Pines will emerge from their cocoons of darkness and grow more powerful, and likely be ravenous."

Shaleigh shook her head. "Regardless of how much

power your Faerie pact has, we have to take care of the forest first. We don't have a choice. We could defeat Keriam only to have the entire forest against us. I think it's smarter for us to tackle it first before losing our advantage over Keriam."

She heard Colin slide off Mawr's back and land on the ground. He yawned as he walked over to join them, his fur rumpled. "Wow is everybody awake already? Why didn't any of you wake me up?"

"You sounded so comfortable, I didn't want to rouse you," Mawr whispered.

Colin froze and studied Mawr's face, realizing that he had tears streaking down his cheeks and onto his whiskers. He hopped over to his friend in two bounds —"What's wrong? Are you okay? What happened?"

Mawr tried to respond but hung his head as he couldn't get the words out. If post-traumatic stress disorder was a phrase they had in this land, Shaleigh would have suggested it as what Mawr was struggling with.

She shared the information with Colin so Mawr didn't have to, kindly implying the details of murder that Mawr had seen before without going into too much detail. When she was finished, Colin wrapped his arms around the stone lion's head and hugged him tight.

"I am so sorry you—we have to go through this. If I could find a way for you to stay here where it was safe, I would."

"I can't though," Mawr sniffed. "I have a gift from Tanwen, too, and you all need me."

Colin sighed and pulled away. "I'd offer to let you ride

on my back, but I don't think that's possible." He turned to the others, his tail twitching behind him. "Maybe Talek could put you in a bubble like before! He could just float you around and you'll be safer that way, right?"

Teagan reached down to take Talek's hand and gripped it hard; Talek hung his head, his white hair hanging in his face. "I'm afraid when Tanwen took away my powers, I lost my ability to do such things. She has given me the gift of dragon's sight, which means I may be able to help see the paths to take. I can see Tanwen's influence now, and all that she breathes magic into. But I can't merely fly Mawr above our heads if that's what you're asking. I have no way to protect any of us like I did before."

Colin looked between all of them, then glanced back at Mawr. "Look, he shouldn't even be here. They should have let him stay in the Garden picking up books in the library there. He shouldn't have to deal with these things again, he barely survived them last time."

"We don't have a choice," Shaleigh said, stepping forward to put a hand on his arm. "All of us need to be present to use the power that Tanwen gave us. And if we want to help the people of the Garden, then we have to deal with the Pello Pines."

"It's okay," Mawr whispered, licking at the fur on the back of Colin's hand. "Thank you for trying to help, but you all need me. I just need to be braver."

"Yeah, but you've already had to be brave," Colin countered. "You've already done enough. You've done more than enough. We shouldn't ask for more of you."

"It's okay," Mawr said again and nuzzled the back of Colin's head, nearly knocking him off his feet. "We'll be together. I think as long as I have friends with me, I can do this. Just don't leave me, okay?"

"I promise," Colin sighed, rubbing Mawr's nose. "I hate that we have to do this. I hate that Keriam has forced you to have to go back to that place. I'm a soldier, I've trained for this, but you're…" He paused and shook his head. "You're too good for this kind of work, big guy."

"I think you're too good to be a soldier. You're more than that. You're a good person," Mawr whispered.

"Mawr!" Colin whimpered and threw his arms around him. "If they hurt a single stone hair on your head, they're going to pay!"

Shaleigh had to agree.

~

THEY LEFT the safety of the clearing they had found: they left the sound of the water and the remains of their fire pit that Colin kicked and scattered. Together, they went back to the path down the mountain that they had taken before. The birds were chirping happily in the cool morning air and Shaleigh took in the sweet smell of budding green leaves and dew covered grasses.

She didn't want to forget the smells, the sounds, or the comfort she felt with having a group of friends around her. She understood how fleeting these small moments were and she didn't want to forget them. She wasn't sure if she would ever experience them again. She wished she had her camera so she could take pictures of the birds in the tall trees, or the dappled sunlight on the ground, or the babbling stream. She wished she could bring the moment with her, and capture all of her friends' smiling faces just in case.

In case of what? She didn't answer, didn't want to think about it. She only wanted to focus on one step after the other. Mawr needed her to be brave, and so did Colin;Teagan and Talek needed her to be strong, they had both been through so much.

All five of them knew what they were going up against, and the risks involved. Yet none of them were brave enough to voice their fears except Mawr.

They walked out to the road then formed a circle without even planning to. Mawr came to her side and sat down. She put a hand on his shoulder, feeling his heavy, anxious breaths.

"Are you okay?" she asked him, preparing herself for how he might respond once they were near the Pello Pines again.

He nodded but didn't meet her gaze. He wasn't pawing at the ground, but his tail twitched behind him, left and right, betraying his nerves.

"At least you'll have glasses this time," she said with a smile and that made him laugh a little. She was glad because she hadn't seen him this tense before, even when they traveled through the Slumbering Forest with Shadow Wolves lurking behind every tree. The Pello Pines weren't awake then, she reminded herself, every-thing was safer, and the only real threat were the Shadow Wolves. Now that the trees were awake, things were different.

Colin walked to Mawr's other side and put a hand on his shoulder. "Let's see, we've faced down minotaurs,

Keriam the cruel, a mad Faerie—sorry Talek, but it's true — and a fire dragon! I think we can tackle a few blood-thirsty trees, don't you, Mawr?"

He nodded. "I hope so, I'll do my best at least. I don't want to let any of you down."

Shaleigh reached over and gave him a hug, "You couldn't let us down if you tried, okay? We're all with you and we all care about you."

His eyes got wet at her words, but he gave an eager nod. "Thank you, Shaleigh."

She pulled away and put a hand back on his shoulder, petting him reassuringly. Then she felt her other hand be taken and looked over to see Talek at her side. "Who could have possibly guessed we would be back in that damned forest again?"

Shaleigh smiled slightly before thinking about how much time he must have spent there, moving through the husks of Daegonrúsc encased Pello Pines. "How did you handle it before? Didn't you spend weeks there?"

Talek nodded. "Yes, looking for some way into the Garden, then when your camera fell from the sky . . . I doubt I'll have such good luck this time."

"Alright everyone," Teagan said, staring off into the distance as he prepared himself mentally. Shaleigh took a deep breath. "I need all of you to focus. We need to work together to do this, which means no chatter when we're preparing."

Talek scoffed and whispered to Shaleigh, "You would think he fancied himself still a High Faerie with that attitude."

Shaleigh grinned and Teagan cleared his throat. She

pursed her lips to try to get rid of her smile, but it didn't work.

"Let's refrain from pointless chatter, shall we?" Teagan glared at the two of them, then sighed when they laughed.

"Sorry, Teagan," Shaleigh whispered, finally getting herself under control.

He took a deep breath. "Alright everyone, concentrate—Talek, you know those woods, find us a path there."

"It's very far away," Talek muttered.

"Do you think we should take stops in between?" Shaleigh asked. "Just to make sure we don't get lost along the way?"

Teagan shook his head. "Talek knows the lands, he should be able to lead us. Every time we stop, we risk an attack, and I'd rather not deal with those minotaurs again."

"Or with Keriam's forces," Colin added. "We have no idea where they are right now and Keriam may not have all the troops with him. They could be at outposts assigned as look-outs for us."

"Yeah, we're not ready for that. We need to keep the surprise if we can," Shaleigh said, squeezing Talek's hand. "Can you do that?"

"I can try."

Shaleigh dug her fingers into Mawr's stony fur. "Okay, everyone, let's concentrate. Talek, envision the path we need to take. Teagan, keep us protected against any dangers as we pass. Colin, make sure we're fast."

"*Be really fast...*" Colin muttered then saw Teagan's look. "Oh, sorry."

"Mawr, think about how much we all care about each

other," Shaleigh said. "And I'll see if we can move as a group."

She closed her eyes, imagining them moving down the rest of the mountain, past the foggy boundary of the Dark Lands, and through the trees where the minotaurs roamed free. She imagined she could see the remnants of their bonfires, now cleared and scattered through the empty clearings–the only sign they were ever there were the dark blotches that marred the soil.

She saw the river that wound its way around the borders of the Garden, and knew they were close to the dark dangers of the Slumbering Forest. It was a very long way, Talek was right, and a pounding pain began to throb in her temples. Despite the pain, she couldn't help but be in awe as they all worked and moved together. She could feel all their energies, moving and acting as one: All five of them joined together to move with one purpose across the landscape with the speed, stealth, and power of Tanwen, the dragon. It was exhilarating.

She felt hot and cold breezes flow past, caught the occasional scent of a campfire, and grasped words in conversations before the people who spoke them were gone. They passed strangers who never knew they had been there as they moved through forests without leaving a single footprint. They floated across creeks and rivers as though they were on solid ground.

Shaleigh smiled, feeling her heart pounding in her chest. She felt like she was steering a ship, sailing along unseen waters at inconceivable speeds. The energy built up inside, and it took all her effort to keep from laughing. She felt like she was on the downhill of a roller coaster that just kept plummeting. The thrill of it was exciting. It made her feel alive. She had forgotten how good it felt.

As they drew closer to the forest, something changed.

They started slowing down. She could tell something was off. It no longer looked like the Slumbering Forest. It was too bright, filled with light, and the trees were moving past not in a blur like before, but with the speed of a landing aircraft. She felt a panic form in her belly that filled her chest and made it hard to breathe. Why though? She was loving it one minute—why would she suddenly feel so different?

She started to tremble and it took her a minute to realize that the emotions she felt didn't belong to her, they were from someone else in their group. Someone else in their circle was panicking so badly that it was seeping into her, and possibly into the others.

Their travel had been smooth and fast before, but now it was rocky, barely avoiding looming trees that were approaching too quickly. She knew who it was in an instant: Mawr. He was so distraught earlier, so upset, and now she could feel his fear too. She knew how he felt in that moment and wondered how in the world he could possibly be so brave if he felt so terrified. Did he feel like this often? Did it rattle his body like that every time he cowered?

She was afraid to act on it. If she tried to do something or say something that broke their concentration, there was no telling what would happen. But Mawr was struggling and the energy that had connected them and made their travel so impressive and quick was starting to break down.

A black hand reached out to them, somehow sensing their passing, looming toward Shaleigh. She tried to steer them to the side, but the hand reached out farther, aiming for her. When it got closer, she realized it wasn't a hand, but a tree branch with claw like limbs curled at the end. She felt the prick of it scrape against her upper arm and gasped.

The prick of pain pulled her back into her body.

Suddenly it was like the roller coaster ride was brought to an instantaneous stop. The lurch of it flung her hard and Talek's hand slipped from her fingers. She tried to cry out, but only managed another gasp; her eyes flew open. She looked just in time to see Talek's face staring back at her in terror as he disappeared amid the cloud of trees that whizzed by. She held onto Mawr's fur only briefly before losing that too.

Then she slammed hard into the ground: she skidded across wet soil, her left shoulder taking most of the damage–the skin was dragged raw.

She wasn't sure how far she flew across the ground, probably only a few inches but it felt like several feet. When she finally came to a stop, she laid there with her eyes closed, gasping for air and trembling from head to toe. Her head spun, the headache that had emerged earlier returning. Breathing in the scent of the wet earth, she opened her eyes to stare at the crumpled leaves in front of her.

As Shaleigh slowly made sense of what happened, the pit of terror in her stomach dwindled away; her connection to Mawr was gone. She couldn't feel any of them any longer, and the emptiness was painful. It was clear that

Tanwen's gifts were powerful, but also destructive. She wondered if it was wise for a mere girl from the Human World to even try to wield them like Tanwen did.

Slowly she got her breath back. The air was humid and chilly, and as she pushed herself up with shaking arms she had to pull leaves off of her skin. Many of them were embedded and left impressions in her skin or drew blood when she removed them--she winced.

Looking up, Shaleigh realized that the sky was clear and overcast. There was no canopy over her head, meaning that there were no trees. Somehow that was more terrifying than losing Talek and Mawr. She glanced around at the great heaps of overturned earth, the soil black and rich from a very old forest. A few dying shrubs could be seen along the edges, black leaves curled up and browning. It took her a moment to recognize the shriveled shapes of the Daegonrúsc--they were barely recognizable. The daylight that flooded the land had almost killed them.

The Pello Pines were certainly awake, and it looked like they could even uproot themselves and move. The thought of those giant trees pulling their enormous roots from the ground and moving on their own was surreal and terrifying. In all the stories that Mawr had mentioned, that Teagan had mentioned, or even Talek, she couldn't recall anyone telling her they could uproot themselves and move. That would have been a really useful piece of information to know.

She finally understood the pit of terror that Mawr had felt as they approached the Slumbering Forest. It was the daylight that probably upset him. He knew better than most what the Pello Pines were capable of, and she should have listened to his warnings more. She should have asked to know more from him, but she hadn't.

Slowly she got to her feet. It took longer than she wanted because every muscle in her body hurt and her head was still pounding. She wanted nothing more than to sleep, and she wondered if that was due to traveling so far with Tanwen's powers. Her brain felt numb like she had taken a full day of exams.

The upturned earth surrounded her for at least a mile--there were so many of them that were awake, so many that would be traveling and *feeding*. She turned around and gasped. The tree line for the rest of the forest was only about sixty yards away. She crouched down behind a mound of dirt, remembering all too well the Pello Pine that she had encountered in the City of the Fae. Her hand itched just at the memory.

She scanned the darkness within the forest, the dappled sunlight, and the clear paths that the Pello Pines had taken into the woods. Perhaps not all of them were awake. Perhaps the ones who had woken first were trying to wake the others. Perhaps they had already started their assault on the Garden . . . Either way, Shaleigh had not planned to face so many of them.

Or to be alone.

PART II
DIVIDED WE FALL

LOST

Shaleigh

Behind a mound of uprooted soil, Shaleigh scanned the woods. She and Kaeja hadn't explored many woods before, but they had delved into enough for her to know that large gaping paths through the trees weren't supposed to be there. There were also no weeds or vines on the edge of the tree line like there should be. Whatever vegetation that used to live in the Slumbering Forest had died long ago when daylight was snuffed out.

Deep amid the trees, she saw dark shapes moving. Her heart leapt into her throat. Even from her distance she could tell they were huge. Swallowing down the panic, Shaleigh started looking around for her friends. *Should have been doing that to begin with*, she chided herself. She should have looked for them immediately, then worried about herself. That's what they would have done.

The mounds of earth were making it hard to see around though. If any of them were lying in any of the ditches, she couldn't see them easily–even Mawr could have been hidden in them.

If the Pello Pines could sense her, if they could tell she was bleeding, perhaps they had sensed the others. Perhaps they were bleeding even worse than she was.

She got to her feet, careful to stay crouched down to keep from being seen. Could they see her? She wasn't sure, but it just felt like a smart thing to do.

As she stepped away, her foot tangled in something and she nearly fell face-first into the dirt. Normally it wouldn't have been so dire, but her whole body ached, and her reflexes were slow.

She reached down to untangle herself and realized it was one of the dying Daegonrúsc plants. She unraveled her foot then squatted down to examine it. The shriveled plants were scattered all through the loose soil like seaweed washed onto shore. They had been torn out of the ground and discarded to wither in the daylight.

The plants had been black bulbous beasts when Shaleigh had first seen them, riding on the sled pulled by Mawr. They were so small now in the sunlight, barely more than a weed.

Shaleigh wondered what would happen when it got dark. Would the Shadow Wolves come out? Would the Pello Pines haunt the landscape looking for food? Fortunately, it was only morning and she hoped she had time.

She had to find the others, but there was no telling where they had gone when she was flung away.

She crept from ditch to ditch, scrambling as quickly as she could through the mud and over the heaps of unearthed soil. After an hour of searching, the sandals she was wearing were full of mud, her dress wet and stained. She was cold at first, but the more she searched, the warmer she felt as the sun climbed high into the sky behind the blanket of clouds.

Shaleigh paused to catch her breath.

Each ditch brought her a little closer to the tree line-- she checked each time she had to dart to another ditch. Now that she was closer, she could see that the tree line was entirely made of Pello Pines, but unlike the ones that had churned the earth around her, these were still mostly covered in the Daegonrúsc. She could see the bulbous black vine covering large sections of the trees. Yet, each day their bindings grew weaker.

She could spot a tendril or two on the closer ones, gliding through the air like serpents more than limbs, but they were far too high up to reach her. She knew those limbs well, those had barbs on them. Unlike the Pello Pine she had seen in the conservatory before, these were wild and way bigger.

They were also not caged.

She paused, scanning the woods again for any movement before trying to get closer. She was aiming for a ditch that was only ten yards or so from the tree line and her senses were honed, looking for anything. The forest was eerily silent, even from this distance. There were no birds, no insects, nothing except for the sound of the wind moving through the branches and the creak of wood.

She was about to make her next move when a large shadow moved behind one of the encapsulated trees. It was tall, thin, and the barbed tendrils, ones that she had thought were more like the branches of a willow tree, were lifted like the feelers of an insect, hovering forward and twitching. Shaleigh watched it, barely wanting to breathe. She knew she should duck down, just in case the trees could see her, but she couldn't move.

Of all the terrifying creatures she had seen in the land since being kidnapped, the Pello Pines were by far the most disturbing. Teagan had told her that they had a tendency to put their prey into a trance, much like the one she encountered had done even from behind bars.

It moved like a monstrous Lovecraftian creature through the still, silent forest, its roots tunneling through the soil with hardly any effort.

It was like something out of a nightmare.

The Pello Pine stopped, and the feelers lifted into the air. Shaleigh's instincts kicked in and she ducked down into the ditch. Her body was shaking; her heart thundering in her chest. She felt sweat break out all over her body. She closed her eyes and willed herself to calm down. Then she heard the sound of dirt moving behind her.

The ground beneath her rumbled, then stopped. Above her head she saw the feeler limbs reach out, each one tipped with a triangular shaped leaf. From below she could see the layer of barbs on each one, reaching out and curling inward--searching. It was looking for her, but how did it know she was here? Was it able to see her or scent her? It was a plant; how would it know?

It had moved through the dirt to reach her, and she was fighting the urge to run. If it moved forward again, she would likely be crushed, but if she moved, she could draw its attention. If it had seen her, she imagined it would have reached down already, but it hadn't. Its limbs still hovered above.

Reach, grip, release...reach, grip release.

It made her think of an alien from those old science fiction movies she used to watch.

Uncertain of what to do, she stayed frozen and watched, trying to keep from trembling. More and more feelers emerged, six total.

Reach, grip, release.

It was looking for her, but she wasn't sure what had tipped it off. The minutes passed too slowly. Then came the rumbling again, the shaking of the ground, and she heard its roots churning through the earth. The feelers above her head drifted away. Shaleigh didn't move, but she listened as it disappeared into the distance. Only when she could no longer hear it did she allow herself to relax.

She took a deep breath, then another, trying to calm her adrenaline even as tears sprung to her eyes. What was she even doing here? How could she consider herself a leader when she almost had a panic attack at the first Pello Pine she had to deal with? Mawr had seen an army of them attack, Aife and Teagan had fought alongside Master Cathal against an entire forest of them. To think that they had all truly thought she was the reincarnation of such a powerful warrior was so funny that she grinned and had to refrain from laughing. The adrenaline was getting to her.

She needed to get away from the forest. That was just too close. She wouldn't be so lucky next time and she didn't even know enough about the Pello Pines to avoid them. She cracked her neck and felt some of the tension in her back ease. She had waited a long time, but these Pello Pines could be smart. It could be waiting just like she was. She decided to make a run for it.

She wiped her eyes with her palm and felt the subtle scratches of the tiny scales that Tanwen had gifted her with. Tanwen told her that she could control the power herself, but she was still waiting to see that happen. And though Talek could use his sight on his own, maybe that had something to do with his Madness from before.

Shaleigh closed her eyes and steadied herself, taking another deep breath and shaking out her arms. She had to get far enough away so the Pello Pines wouldn't attack her or notice her. That meant scrambling over as many hills and ditches as she could.

Once she finally got her body to stop shaking, she psyched herself up, then darted forward. She clambered to the top of the first mound then leapt off and hit the ground hard. That was when she heard the sound of a Pello Pine. The ground rumbled and the sound of shifting earth made her run even faster--up to the top of another hill, jump, land.

The Pello Pine didn't have any obstacles. It blasted easily through a pile of dirt behind her, and she felt the debris hit her back.

Climbing up the next ditch, she felt something try to trip up her foot, but she leaped down before it could, giving out a whimper as she landed sideways and had to put an arm out to steady herself. Something tugged at the skirt of her dress, there was a ripping sound, but she ignored it and kept going.

As she was climbing the fourth hill, she felt a shock of pain in her arm. It was in the same spot the other Pello Pine had cut her when they were traveling, and the barbs went deep into her skin. She cried out and tumbled backward, feeling another barb dig into the wrist of her other arm. Panicking she tried to pull them off of her, falling into a primal instinct to remove the parasites and forgetting what Teagan had done before in that dark, murky conservatory.

The enormous tree towered above her. It had no face, no eyes or mouth, but its bark was a dark red, almost black. The other feelers were coming towards her. The roots beneath looked like large tubers sticking out of the ground, churning the loose soil as it shoved closer toward her.

A third set of barbs was trying to dig into her calf, but the scales that Tanwen had given her were preventing it from getting through. She had to act. The pain was unbearable, but it would be worse if she didn't do something--fast.

She couldn't concentrate or focus.

Grabbing the feeler on her wrist, Shaleigh yanked on it, wincing at the renewed pain. She stopped, panting, remembering then how Teagan had removed it before, and pulled backward--the barbs pulled free with ease.

She flung it aside and grabbed the one on her shoulder, grunting and wincing as she pulled that one out too.

She ran again, climbing up the next pile of dirt and jumping off.

Only something grabbed her just as she hit the ground.

She felt something wrap around her stomach, soft, slimy, and cold against her skin through her dress. The pressure tightened around her and pain erupted from her sides as she was lifted to the air. She suddenly remembered Mawr's words, long ago when he had told her about his Lady Sphinx: She had survived the battles, but when they came for the Library of Aife and tried to protect it, the Pello Pines had ripped her out of the sky.

Shaleigh had thought the barbs were all she had to worry about, but now she knew that it was far worse. She looked down at the tendril wrapped around her. All it had to do was fling her onto the ground one good time, and she would break something.

She was easy prey.

It lifted her higher into the air and she kicked her legs beneath her, pulling at the tendril wrapped around her stomach. She had the fierceness of a rag doll.

In a flash of terror and alarm, Shaleigh realized that she would die here. It wasn't conceptual like it had been in the Masked King's realm, or for thrills like it had been in the basement of Ferris Factory. No, it was suddenly blaringly real that she would die here.

Nobody was going to save her.

Nobody would even know.

The finality of it tore her apart.

The Pello Pine lifted her higher in the air. She looked

out over all the mounds of dirt around them. It stretched for miles in an endless wasteland. Would her friends find her body here? Would there be anything left?

She thought of Mawr crying that he hadn't been there for her like he hadn't be there for his Lady Sphinx. She thought of Teagan and how he would blame himself entirely for her death. She thought of Talek, possibly triggered into a new Madness despite all the work they had done to save him from the brink. Then there was Colin, her kidnapper turned friend who would blame himself for ever bringing her to this place.

Without her, they would fall apart. It wasn't that she was holding them together, but her death could lead to them never being able to save the Garden. All of the gifts that Tanwen gave them would be squandered and the Garden would be overrun by Keriam.

She remembered her first meeting with Madam Cloom in her giant throne room, a place that didn't even exist anymore. She remembered Madam Cloom's mocking tone as she told her that she was no warrior and no leader. Shaleigh had bluffed her way through, but she couldn't do that here.

There was no one to care--she couldn't pretend her way through any longer. She had to act, and she had to act now if she hoped to survive.

Too many people depended on her.

Too many people had died because of her.

The ground looked so far away now, and she felt the tendril start to loosen around her. Hot tears streamed down her cheeks.

How could she ever right the wrongs she had made if

she died here, killed by a giant tree, and smashed into pieces against the earth in this strange land. What about her father? She had to see him again. She had to hug him and tell him she was safe. And Kaeja? Her heart hurt at the thought: Her best friend, the only person who understood her the way no one else could.

She refused to die here, not like this. She refused to be a victim to weigh down her friends and family. She refused to be another lost soul in the Slumbering Forest.

She had to *act*.

With a snarl, Shaleigh grabbed hold of the tendrilled limb around her stomach with both hands just as it fully unraveled from her waist. The bark was more slippery than she expected, and she nearly fell, but the scales on her hands helped her grip hold. The scales dug into the slippery bark, and the tree shrieked.

It was a high-pitched noise that made her ears hurt and she ducked her head down against the noise. The vine she was holding swung around and Shaleigh held on as long as she dared before it finally flung her. She hit the ground hard but rolled as best she could, feeling the wound on her left shoulder scrape against the dirt again.

She got to her feet quickly and looked up at the tree. The vine she had grabbed onto with her hands was covered in crimson. Had she bled on it? When had that happened? Then she realized that it wasn't her blood, it belonged to the Pello Pine—they bled red. It wasn't blood exactly, it looked more like runny sap than human blood, but she clenched her jaw as she watched it flail, its tendril wrapping close around its body.

It was a small wound, much smaller than the gashes

she had in her arms from the barbs, but those were made with dragon scales. She had no idea what that meant for a Pello Pine. Would it ever heal? Was it poisoned? If Tanwen made the earth itself pregnant with her magic, and it flowed through every magical being and plant, including the Pello Pine, what did that mean to be harmed by her magic? Was it more deadly than a blade or even fire? Shaleigh didn't know.

She watched though as the Pello Pine retreated back to the woods, much faster than before, upheaving soil as it moved with its large roots, almost like an octopus's tentacles--looking more like a creature of the ocean than something that ought to live on land, but then again, this was a strange place.

Shaleigh studied it for a long time, waiting to see if it would get brave and try to return, or if it would gather more trees to try to kill her again. She sat down and wrapped her arms around her muddy legs, waiting to see if she would need to fight again.

At least now she knew that she could handle herself... a little. She couldn't survive exactly, and her growling stomach reminded her of that as she got to her feet, but she could search.

She needed to reach her friends.

Separate they were strong but together they were unstoppable.

TRAVELING the muddy wastelands without knowing what awaited her used to terrify her, but since Shaleigh had faced down a Pello Pine by herself and survived it, she had more confidence as she searched for her friends. She didn't really want to have to enter the dark forest on her own, but she had all but ruled out the muddy pits as places where her friends had fallen. If they were still alive, they would have heard her fight with the Pello Pine, but none of them had come.

So with the sun far past its peak in the sky, she stepped past the tree line and into the much darker and much deadlier forest: Here the Daegonrúsc still grew and covered many of the Pello Pines that were still trapped in slumber. On the edges of the forest, where sunlight likely hits the hardest, she could see how much the Daegonrúsc had died back on those Pello Pines compared to those on the inside of the forest. The edge was clearly one of the more dangerous places to be, but it was the only way in.

Shaleigh stepped into the colder shadows of the forest, listening to the wind whistle through the gaping holes left by the Daegonrúsc. It almost made her think of a canyon––there was no sound other than the wind, and strangely enough she almost found herself wishing the Shadow Wolves were present. At least then there would be some other living creature here besides the blood-sucking trees that could emerge at any moment.

She passed by one Pello Pine that had its black leaves exposed at the top near the sky, but half of its trunk down to its roots was still covered in Daegonrúsc. As she moved beneath it, a couple of tendrils at the top curved down toward her, reaching for her even though it had no hope of coming close to the ground.

Still it reached for food.

She moved further into the woods. It was clear where Pello Pines had passed through: The ground was eaten up in large divots that looked like a giant gardening hoe had dug up the earth. Their paths crisscrossed the ground and Shaleigh had to jump down into the trenches to pass through them.

The farther she went, the more she feared that she was completely lost. The sun would be touching the horizon soon and the darkness coming across the forest felt like walls closing in. It reminded her of exploring the many underground levels of Ferris Factory with Kaeja . . . Only here there was no exhilaration and excitement from exploring places that had been forgotten for so long. Here there was only fear and the unknown of what the night would bring.

Would the Shadow Wolves roam looking for food? Would the Pello Pines return to this section of the woods? Were there other things lurking here that felt safer hunting at night?

She gripped her arms in front of her as the cold deepened. She was still wearing the flimsy dress she had gotten in the City of the Faerie. It was torn at the skirt from the Pello Pine attack earlier and her dirt in her sandals grew colder against her feet as the sun sank. It was supposed to be for far warmer weather, not for traveling within a forest at night. If she didn't find a way to stay warm throughout the evening, it would be easy to die from exposure.

Shaleigh started breathing harder as she climbed a hill. The wind was stronger up here and her skirt blew around her legs as she walked. The shadows of the trees were long now and soon it would be difficult to spot a Pello Pine moving through the forest, even if it was close. Fortunately, she at least knew the rumbling they made as they plowed through the soil, but that meant she would need to stay awake too.

"Shaleigh?"

She froze, turning around in circles, peering out at the deepening shadows all around her. She strained her ears and squinted against the cold wind. She knew that voice.

"Mawr?" she whispered, afraid to make too much noise.

Far up the hill she saw him, a pale speck against the dark shadows of the Daegonrúsc and husks of Pello Pines. His voice must have traveled downwind because there was no way she should have been able to hear him. She sprinted toward him and he bounded down toward her.

She was laughing as she ran, tears already springing up in her eyes. She wanted to scream out to him, to call his name out at the top of her lungs, but she knew better than that.

He was running, bounding with all his weight against the ground as he got closer. If there were any Pello Pines in the vicinity they would feel that in their massive roots too--she picked up the pace and leaped over discarded limbs and piled up leaves, scraping her ankle against an old branch and nearly falling at one point from the uneven ground.

Mawr had risked his life for her; had risked it so she would hear him, so she would see him.

When she reached him, she pulled him into a hug, and they were both in tears.

"Shaleigh," he whispered. "I was so scared, and then I was lost, and then I had to run, and then—"

"Shh," she urged, rubbing at his nose. "Let me crawl up and then we're going to keep moving. I need you to walk though, don't run okay?"

"Okay," he muttered, his voice betraying his panic. "Did I do something wrong?"

"No," she said as he crouched down, and she climbed up on his back. His stone was so warm against her skin that it was almost too hot at first until her body acclimated to it. It took her a moment to stop shivering.

"I heard your footsteps in the distance. Then as you got closer, I saw you. Your dress is so bright against the trees, that even without my glasses I could see you," he whispered up to her. "I lost them somewhere in the fall. I didn't mean to, but they just fell off! I tried to find them but couldn't—"

She rubbed his head, scanning the trees around them. "Shh, it's okay. Just stay calm and do as I say, okay? Just like last time. Make sure you walk quietly."

"Okay." He nodded, his tail twitching side to side. "Where should I go?"

Despite the cold and her worry, Shaleigh had noticed the patterns. Most of the Pello Pines were headed downhill not uphill. That didn't mean that there weren't more up ahead moving in this direction though; moving toward the vibrations Mawr had made with his running.

She tugged gently on his fur toward the side, leading him along the hill and away from the straight path she had made before. He followed her guidance as she prevented him from tumbling into ditches or slamming into a Daegonrúsc covered Pello Pine.

Then she heard them, tearing up the ground and churning through the soil. Shaleigh turned to look and saw not one but three Pello Pines in the place that she and Mawr had left behind.

"Are they back there?" Mawr whimpered, his voice quivering in fear.

"Yeah," Shaleigh said. "But don't panic, okay? That means no kneading those paws into the ground and no running. You have to walk carefully and quietly, okay?"

"Okay," he said. "I'm scared, Shaleigh."

"I am, too," she said, reaching to rub at the fur beneath his ear. "And I'm also so proud of you. You've got this, okay? You can do this. Just believe in yourself."

"I didn't mean to lead them to us," he whispered, and she could hear the sadness in his voice. "I didn't mean to put you in even more danger. I was just so excited to see you and to know that I wasn't alone. I just wanted to be with you again."

"Shh, you're getting yourself worked up. Just stay calm and focus. We have to get away from them, so they won't feel us through the soil."

"Is that how they found us?"

"I think so," she said. She wanted to expand further on what she had experienced before with the one she had fended off but didn't think this was the right time to share it. Mawr was terrified enough as it was. He didn't need anything else to make it worse.

The light was dwindling far too quickly on the horizon, which made it difficult to see if the trees ahead were active Pello Pines or not. She turned around again, seeing that the ones behind them were still in the same spot, their feelers raised as though looking to see if their prey was still standing there.

She continued to give Mawr instructions, avoiding trees, and now having to rely on spotting the large bulbous Daegonrúsc plants at the base of the Pello Pines to determine if they were active or not, and the darkness was making that more difficult. She wished they had a torch or at the very least a phone light. Instead they had to slow down even further, treading through the forest without knowing fully what was around them or where they were even going.

Shaleigh understood then what it had to have been like for Mawr when they traveled through the Slumbering Forest before when he couldn't see.

This was terrifying.

THE CLOUDS PARTED and a waxing moon rose into the sky. Shaleigh was so grateful that it wasn't a new moon because even though the crescent moon didn't give too much light, a moonless night would have been pitch dark.

Though they were moving slowly, Mawr occasionally tripped over a stone or a tree root, and each time she had to sooth and comfort him. Sometimes he would start shaking and it took several minutes of petting his mane before he was brave enough to start walking again, knowing that Pello Pines were all around them.

She could only imagine how terrifying it was for him.

He couldn't see without his glasses, and he relied on her, knowing she couldn't see that well either in the darkness. She tried to keep him calm, but it was difficult when she knew and understood why he was so terrified. She also had fears of her own.

The memory of how quickly the Pello Pines descended last time was etched into her mind. She and Mawr had only been a few dozen yards away when they tumbled through the soil. They were unsettling to watch, with their vine-like tendrils that hovered in the air. At every trip or stumble that Mawr took, she feared a whole crowd of Pello Pines would descend again, like predators rushing in for the kill.

But they hadn't, not yet at least.

She clung to his warm stone back as she whispered directions in his ear, avoiding trees and brambles and warning of ditches. The cold night air was filled only with the sounds of Mawr's soft footfalls and her hushed voice. No insects buzzed in tides of white noise and no night-time birds echoed over the dark forest. It was as though they were the only two beings in existence even though she knew that was not at all true.

Shaleigh wondered if they had taken a bad path, but she knew nothing about the place; she didn't know the forest and had never seen any maps. She felt panic creep up her throat as her chest tightened. How long would they be able to wander? What would happen when she had to sleep? She couldn't leave Mawr alone all night on his own, or even during the day.

Her fear threatened to overwhelm her, but she couldn't let Mawr know. One of them had to be strong.

She had to help him even though she had the rising concern that they might never find escape.

Then she caught a powerful floral scent. It was so strong she could almost taste it in the back of her throat; she held back a cough.

"Mawr, do you smell that?"

"I can't smell anything," he reminded her with a squeak. "What is it?"

She breathed in the air, letting her sinuses adjust to it. It was familiar, but she had no idea why. Where had she smelled it before? It was definitely a flower. Was it a rose? No, that wasn't right.

Mawr waited for a moment before asking, "Is it lavender?"

"Yes, that's it!" Shaleigh said. "It's lavender!" Suddenly she remembered the white statues standing solemnly in the center of walkways, fountains overgrown with ivy, and a tall stone platform engraved with Mawr's name. That's where she smelled it before. "Do you think we're close to Aife?"

Mawr looked around, and she wished once again that he had his glasses. "Maybe," he whispered. "I don't recognize any of this anymore, though I didn't leave Aife for a very long time." He turned into the breeze, asking, "Should we follow the wind?"

"That's a good idea," she whispered. "It's likely blowing the flowers this way so that's why the smell is so strong."

She helped get him turned around and on the right path. The wind blew hard across her ears and she shivered, hunkering closer to Mawr's back.

"I'm sorry you're so cold," he said. "I wish you had something warmer to wear."

"Me too," she said through clenched teeth.

"I wish I was more comfortable for you too," he added.

She reached up and rubbed the little divot between his ears that he loved to have scratched. "That's not your fault. If you weren't here with me, I don't know where I would be." She would be frozen to death in a ditch somewhere, that's where she would be. But she didn't want to upset Mawr with her talk—she pointed out a thick root just in time for him to side-step it.

Something dark shifted up ahead and she tugged on Mawr's stone fur. He came to a stop. The dark mass shifted again, but this time she knew what it was: water. It was a lake in the distance, catching the light of the crescent moon up above. It looked familiar.

"Mawr, it's your lake!"

"My lake?" He whispered, swishing his tail with excitement.

"No, hold on, don't run," she reminded him. "I can't tell if there are Pello Pines around here, I don't want to risk it."

"Me neither," he crouched down to the ground again and she felt bad. He was so excited in that brief moment and she hated having to pull him back, but she knew it was the right move. They had to be smart if they wanted to avoid any more Pello Pines. They were terrifying enough to face during the day, she really didn't want to fight them at night.

They picked their way forward, past several more tall trees. As they got closer, the scent of lavender grew stronger and the sound of water emerged. Shaleigh felt a wave of relief at hearing the buzzing insects.

She looked up to see the trees from when she first landed in this strange land. She recognized the springy, spiraled leaves of one tree bouncing in the strong wind and smiled. She spotted then a large, overgrown bush on the edge of the lake and realized that was where she had swum to shore.

As they drew closer, Mawr picked himself up off the ground and his ears perked up. "I know this place," he said with a longing that made Shaleigh's heart ache. "This is my home!"

Shaleigh looked up the path where Mawr had dragged her from beside the lake on top of a worn sled. "There's grass sprouting here," she said. "I thought it used to be dirt."

"I used to pace a lot," he admitted. "I haven't been back in a while. I forgot how quiet it was, but I was so lonely."

"I'm sorry," she said.

"I'm not lonely now." He tilted his head into her hand, and she gave him a good scratch. "It should be safe for you to sleep here tonight, I can find you berries, we can get you warm." He started to paw the ground again.

"Don't do that, remember? This place was safe when the Pello Pines were fast asleep, but they aren't anymore. They might still be able to feel the vibrations."

It took clear effort on Mawr's part to stop himself, but he gave a slow nod. "Okay, sorry."

The wind picked up and Shaleigh had to hunker down close to Mawr again. Being near the lake meant the wind was much stronger, yet the lavender scent was also powerful.

"I need to get you inside," Mawr whispered as he walked without Shaleigh having to give him direction. He didn't need them. He had walked this land for years, centuries even. Even with his poor eyesight, he didn't need her help now.

Mawr made his way up the path and toward the tall hedges that hid the city of Aife from view. He was so much stronger than people gave him credit for. He had survived so much, more than just the war, but also the endless days and nights afterward. And, even after all that time, he still cared about everyone, and understood why the simple pleasure of reading a book was to be cherished. He was more resilient than she was; able to survive in the Slumbering Forest on his own without his glasses, and together they had passed through unharmed.

Mawr had faced his worst fears.

Now here at his home that he thought he would never see again, he showed restraint because he knew it was important. If this was her home, Shaleigh knew she would never be able to have that much control.

Just as they were about to enter the gap in the hedges that was a little bit more overgrown than it was before, Shaleigh reached down and gave him a hug. She was so proud of him.

"What was that for?" he asked, a smile on his lips.

"You're such an incredible friend," she said, her voice cracking. "Thank you so much for being here with me. I know that was terrifying for you, but I'm so grateful to have you beside me. I couldn't have done any of this without you."

He turned his head to the side and licked at her outstretched hand: Rough stone rubbed against her palm and kind of tickled against the scales. "If it weren't for you, I would still be living here, without anyone to call my friend or even anyone to talk to. You helped me to not be lonely anymore."

She hugged him tighter as the wind picked up again. "Thank you," she whispered.

Mawr headed in through the hedges. "I need to get you to a warm place. Maybe we can start a fire inside."

The branches of the hedges were longer than Shaleigh remembered, though maybe it was different being high up on Mawr's back instead of being dragged on a sled. She had to keep several of them from scraping her arms as they entered. Mawr tried to lower himself to the ground to help, but it was such a narrow space.

As they passed through, the wind died down greatly—though the night was still cold.

"It's so much warmer in here!" Shaleigh smiled.

"It is, the hedges weren't quite this big when people lived in Aife, but they were meant to help with the wind. With the lake, it can get breezy."

She shook her head. It was clear that even after his time away, Mawr still loved Aife and there was no question as to why: Despite being abandoned, the beauty of the city still struck a chord in her heart as the dim moonlight encased the city.

Though springtime had ended in the Garden, the lavender of Aife hadn't noticed. The plants didn't care

about cruel magicians or mad Faeries or even fire dragons, they just kept growing and flowering regardless. The
lavender blossoms were covering several buildings and a
few statues; she smiled at the sight.

This place was unchanged and frozen in place. After
all of the tumultuous changes that had happened since her
arrival here, it was oddly comforting to find that the
Ruins of Aife were immune. It still felt just as magical as
before, and she rubbed the back of Mawr's mane.

"We did it!" she whispered. "We made it through!"

"I didn't think we had a chance." Mawr admitted,
turning to look up at her again. "But you and I make a
great team. I think I can do all kinds of great things when
you're with me."

Shaleigh was only partially listening. At the far end of
the path, near the derelict library, she watched a large
black shadow slink around the side of one of the buildings. Its red eyes glinted in the moonlight and she gripped
hold of Mawr's mane.

"Mawr..."

He caught sight of her gaze and turned forward again,
ducking close to the ground out of habit. His tail thumped
behind them. He looked right and left, and it took
Shaleigh a moment to remember that without his glasses,
he couldn't see it.

"What is it? I can't see!" he cried in a panic, inching
backwards and toward the gap in the hedges.

Another shadow slipped out from behind another
door, closer than the other, and this time Shaleigh recognized what it was.

"They're Shadow Wolves," she answered absently. Her

mind whirled with confusion. Why were they here at Aife? Weren't they still working with Keriam at the Garden? Had Keriam suspected they would come here?

"What do we do?" Mawr whimpered as he backed away again, not realizing he was backing into a corner instead of toward the exit of the hedge wall.

Shaleigh considered telling him to run. Maybe they would have a better chance out in the woods with the Pello Pines than they did trapped in the ruins of Aife with a pack of Shadow Wolves. She glanced to the opening in the hedges, feeling some of the cold wind entering in through the gap—did they really stand a better chance?

If they left Aife, they were lost and neither Shaleigh nor Mawr knew their way around the forest. On top of that, despite Mawr being an excellent heating source, she was in danger of freezing to death out there. And if she fell asleep, which was very possible, Mawr would be helpless. The thought of waking up to see Mawr getting flung by one of those Pello Pines like it had tried to do to her... No. She couldn't let that happen.

With a deep breath, she sat up straighter and looked at the Shadow Wolves. There were four of them now, coming out from around the buildings. They approached slowly, but they didn't growl or show their teeth. They seemed more curious than dangerous, but she knew how fast that could change: If they wanted to eat them, they would have lunged for them by now. She knew they could talk . . . Maybe they too were looking for safety from the Pello Pines.

She slid down off of Mawr's back and he turned to

look at her with wide eyes. "Shaleigh, what are you doing?"

"I'm going to talk with them," she said, trying to keep her heart from racing.

"But they'll kill you!"

"I don't think so," she said, rubbing his side. "I know the Pello Pines will though—they'll kill both of us before the night is over. I can't possibly reason with them."

"You can't reason with Shadow Wolves either!" He hunkered down to the ground, pressing his belly and his nose into the dirt. "I don't like this, not at all. This is too dangerous!"

Shaleigh took a deep breath of cold air, letting it fill her lungs. It was dangerous, probably too dangerous, but she had dealt with worse. She had faced down Tanwen the dragon and survived, surely, she could find out why these Shadow Wolves were here instead of near the Garden waiting for their master. She had to find out what had happened to them.

Four pairs of red eyes were watching her, waiting.

SHALEIGH STEPPED AWAY from Mawr as the Shadow Wolves moved towards her. She knew that her friend was trembling behind her, terrified of what she was about to do, but she knew this was the only real option. It was either this or perish in the forest.

The scent of lavender wafted by again. It was so surreal to see Shadow Wolves in the ruins of Aife, a place that she had considered to be Mawr's home. The city was so beautiful with its hand-carved fountains and gorgeous statues with ivy running over everything. The Shadow Wolves seemed like a blight here with their hulking dark shapes and glowing red eyes.

"I recognize you," one growled, taking a moment to form the words. It was the first wolf that had appeared. "Master Keriam wanted you dead." He gave a wheezing laugh that sent chills down Shaleigh's spine.

"I'm not surprised," she countered. "He wants a lot of people dead these days."

There was more laughter from the others. They sat down, but the one that spoke stepped forward—he had to be the leader. "You're Shaleigh," he started, tilting his head to the side, "the one who brought down the Garden."

Shaleigh shifted uncomfortably, wondering if she had made the right move.

He let out a low snarl. "You're the only one Keriam fears."

That made her pause.

"Shaleigh . . ." Mawr muttered, crawling up to be beside her. "This is a bad idea!"

"It's okay," she whispered to him, trying to give him an encouraging smile before turning back to the wolves. "The one he fears? How do you know that? Why are you all here in Aife instead of heeling at his side? I thought you all were all close buddies."

Three wolves hunched their heads and turned to their leader.

"Keriam... He made us believe things we didn't want to believe. We did things we didn't want to do." He shook his head. "We never intended to go to the Garden. That isn't our home and there's nothing there for us. Ever since he made us attack the gates, he turned us into a prime target for every soldier there." He turned away and huffed. "They slice through our hides with their swords and gut us like cattle. Only a few of us with our minds could escape."

Shaleigh narrowed her eyes. "It sounds like you don't get along with him anymore."

The leader licked his lips and took a moment to answer. "He brought us here from another land, our homeland. He promised us food, safety, respect... He promised we wouldn't be hunted like we were back home. He promised..." he trailed off.

One wolf flung its head back and whimpered. Another wolf gave a huff and flopped down on the ground, turning their head away.

"So, he tricked you to come here and then used you," Shaleigh said. "But there are so few of you left. I remember dozens when the High Castle fell. Surely you all weren't—"

"As I said," the leader snarled, "gutted like cattle. The mixture he gave us to eat, that he demanded we eat, he made himself. That's what made us lose our minds and lose our ability to think. That's what turned my brothers and sisters into his puppets."

"The Scáil plant... I bet that's what it was. He used that to control almost every magician in the Sanctuary and had them all turn on us."

Mawr dug his claws into the dirt and Shaleigh leaned to put a hand on his side.

Each Shadow Wolf was watching her now, their red eyes gleaming in the moonlight. There was curiosity in their faces, but also a clear wariness. "You know this plant?" The one lying down asked.

"Yes," she admitted. "It... nearly got my friend killed." She paused. "Wait, so when Mawr and I were chased in the Slumbering Forest, was that you?"

She felt Mawr tremble under her hand at her words.

"It was likely our pack, if that's what you're asking." The leader gave a snort. "I don't recall chasing a girl and a statue." He laughed, a dry, raspy sound. The noise put Shaleigh's nerves on edge.

"They knew my name, they chanted it. It was so scary!"

Shaleigh reached over to put a hand around him to help calm him; Mawr nuzzled his head against her.

"I remember that chase," the one on the ground snarled. "A Faerie shined a small sun in my eyes. It was so bright; I couldn't see for days."

The camera, that's what they were talking about—it took her a moment to figure out what kind of small sun they even had that day.

She turned to the leader. "So was Keriam controlling you all then, too? I know he had someone in the forest here at the time, a Faerie." She shook her head. "Sorry, I'm getting off track. What I don't get is why you're here? If Keriam had you mind controlled, why aren't you still? How did you break free of it?"

"He got sloppy," the leader said, his voice dropping low. "After the Garden fell, he didn't mix in his little plant into our food like he used to. Some meals were less powerful than others: Those of us who could, fled. Then the damn trees started attacking us. I swear, is there anything in this land that doesn't kill?"

Shaleigh had to smile at that. "I had the same question when I was brought here. You see, I'm not from this land either." That seemed to get all their ears to perk up.

"Right. From the Human World." The leader scoffed. "You mean to tell me a girl from the Human World is going to take down Keriam the Cruel?" He couldn't even finish his words without breaking out into laughter, causing the three other wolves to start as well.

Shaleigh sighed.

"Why not?" Mawr asked, trembling but standing up again. Once again he showed how brave he was. "She took down Madam Cloom, survived the Masked King, and even won the respect of Tanwen the dragon."

They seemed to believe him until he got to the part about the dragon, then a whole new set of laughter tore through them. The one on the ground covered its face with its paws and laughed into the dirt.

Shaleigh just planned to wait it out, but Mawr was offended—"I mean it! She's Tanwen's Chosen."

"Sure," the leader chuckled. "And I'm Keriam's big toe."

Another round of laughter came; Shaleigh drummed her fingers on her arm. "If you all plan to laugh about all of this, I suppose you four must be getting along fine out here in Aife." Their amusement seemed to fade. "I mean, I know the Slumbering Forest had plenty of animals for you to feed on, and I'm sure the Pello Pines have left plenty for you, right?"

The humor was gone and in its place was a low burning anger. "Yes, girl of the Human World, we have not eaten properly for days. But that might change now that you're here. Your friend might not be edible, but you certainly are."

She expected Mawr to back away or to cower and knead his paws, but instead he took a step forward as if planning to defend her.

"Oh, I figured you were hungry. You must be since you're living here. I didn't hear a single bird out there today, so I know you all aren't eating much. And the fish in the lake won't last, will they?"

The red eyes were turned to her again, and she heard Mawr's tail thwacking back and forth. The air was filled with tension and she wasn't quite sure how the Shadow Wolves would react, but she had to play her hand. So, with a deep breath, she finally went for it—

"Look, if you eat me, sure, you'll have food for one night. That's great for you! But I'm pretty sure I'm going to be the only meal on two legs to be through here for years, so unless you all enjoy the idea of starving here in Aife, you could help me out instead.

"You all know the layout of this forest, even with the Pello Pines uprooting everywhere, so you could help us get to the Garden. Together, we can try to help the rest of your pack to escape Keriam's control and prevent them from being decimated by the army that he leads."

The silence that fell over the courtyard was palpable. Shaleigh felt her heartbeat thundering in her chest and saw Mawr breathing hard as they waited.

"So, you help us save our pack if we help you, then what? Where are we supposed to live? We were brought over by Keriam and told to live in the Slumbering Forest. That forest doesn't exist anymore and the eternal night we were promised doesn't either." The other three wolves shifted at their leader's words.

"You're right, we haven't eaten much. There isn't enough fish in that lake out there that we can catch and none of us are keen on living inside of these buildings for the rest of our lives, hiding from the sun. But there are no places for us here, no dark caves or caverns to hide and dwell. Yes, we would have the pack back, but we would all die out eventually. That's hardly a reason to risk our lives."

Shaleigh pursed her lips. She had thought this would be easier, that her argument was logical and sound, and that they would be eager to get food again. But she hadn't thought about a long-term home for them, especially not in the Land of the Fae.

"Where you come from, I assume there is eternal night? I guess there must be if you all live there."

The leader came forward, and Mawr stepped in to intervene.

"It's okay, Mawr," she said, not entirely sure if it was, but not wanting to start trouble. Mawr backed away to her side again, clearly uncomfortable but trying to be protective all the same. She wanted to hug him.

The leader eyed them both warily before stepping closer. Shaleigh could see a white scar across his muzzle. "Yes, we live in the land of Ciar, a beautiful place of blissful darkness and colors that your Human mind could never fathom." Shaleigh resisted the urge to take a step backward because she couldn't tell if the leader was making a threat or not. He came within a few feet then paused, looking down to the ground. "I miss it," he admitted suddenly. "I miss my home."

Shaleigh gave a tentative nod. "I miss my home, too. That's where I want to go once everything gets resolved here." She saw Mawr glance her way, a sad expression on his face. "I want to see my father again and my best friend, but I can't do that yet. I have to help my new friends." She put a hand on Mawr's mane and felt him trembling but didn't mention it. "I would like to help you all get home, too."

The wolf huffed and shook his head. "You don't even know where Ciar is, you silly Human. You can't make promises like that when you don't even know how to get there. Besides, it seems you have already made promises that you intend to break."

Shaleigh furrowed her brows. She was about to lash out, her anger rising quickly at his words, but Mawr spoke before she could.

"It's true, I'm sad that Shaleigh has to eventually leave me and go back to the Human World. She's the best friend I've ever had, and she has taught me how to be brave when I thought I was the too scared to even leave Aife— the only home I ever knew. I know that if she chooses to go back to her home to see her father, that she'll be happy, and that makes me happy. She hasn't broken any promises with me. In fact, she knows that I will always be here for her."

He turned to smile at her and Shaleigh felt tears in her eyes. She had never known that Mawr knew her fears or that he was more prepared to deal with her eventual return home than she was.

"I also know what it's like to be lonely. I lived here for too long by myself, hiding in these buildings and thinking that I was helping. I wasn't really, my books were all moldy and my library was falling apart, but it was easier to hide than it was to deal with my fear and loneliness." Mawr turned to look around at all the empty buildings and abandoned statues. "I know it's scary trying to trust again when you all had to deal with such a terrible situation, but don't you think it's worth it to see your home again? Don't you think your pack would want you to try to help them, even if it was dangerous? I think being controlled by someone has to be the worst feeling in the world."

The leader stared at Mawr for a long moment, clearly struck by his words and probably trying to figure out how a giant stone lion was able to understand the complexities of the world and frame them so simply. Shaleigh felt bad for him. She understood how easily Mawr could crawl under her skin—she loved it about him.

Finally, the leader hung his head and shuffled his feet, looking uncomfortable and uncertain for the first time since Shaleigh had approached him. He turned to look at the other Shadow Wolves behind him, all of whom were looking to him for answers. He forced himself to stand taller and meet Shaleigh's eyes. He very studiously didn't look at Mawr.

"Perhaps you speak some truth, Human girl. We'll have to consider it. I don't want to make a decision for all of us, but we have been uncomfortable staying here. This place is barely hospitable. Still your offer may not be the best option."

Then he bowed his head low and Shaleigh watched him in astonishment. It was the first time that a Shadow

Wolf had ever bowed to her in her life, and certainly the first time one hadn't tried to bite her face off first.

When the leader lifted his head, the other Shadow Wolves got to their feet. She wasn't sure if that meant they were going to make a decision or if they were going to take her by surprise and attack. She really had no clue how Shadow Wolves acted when they weren't under Keriam's slimy control.

"We will take the night to discuss our decision. By tomorrow evening, you will have our answer. Regardless, you can sleep here and take shelter: As long as neither of you tries to attack us, I see no problem in sharing our den with you."

"Thank you," Shaleigh said with an awkward curtsy. She really needed to practice doing that more, she'd had to use it far more often than she ever expected. "We really appreciate it. I think Mawr and I are just happy to be in a place that's relatively safe."

"We have made some changes," the leader added, glancing toward Mawr for the first time since being shaken by his words.

"All those moldy books!" One Shadow Wolf exclaimed. "They were disgusting, we threw them out so we could actually sleep in there. The library is the only partially weatherproof building left!"

Mawr's eyes went wide. "You threw the books...away?"

Shaleigh stepped closer and scratched at his cheeks, ignoring how raw her fingers felt from petting him so much to keep him calm. "They were all moldy, remember? You couldn't have saved them even if you wanted to."

"Oh," Mawr said, lowering his gaze. "Oh yes, I forgot about that. I guess that does make sense."

Shaleigh gave him a hug. "Look, at least you know they're not just sitting on shelves getting even more moldy."

He didn't look up at her words, and she tried again —"Yes, it's no longer technically a library anymore, but it'll be safe and warm for us tonight, doesn't that help? The building still stands, the doors are still sturdy, and even after Aife has fallen, the library is still a safe place."

Mawr smiled at that. "A safe place. I like that."

The Shadow Wolves led their way around Mawr's pedestal and trotted up to the library's entrance. They had indeed gotten rid of all the books and what remained of the bookshelves had been tossed into a corner of the room. They looked badly damaged, but they would be perfect kindling for a fire. She didn't want to do that in front of Mawr though, not yet at least.

Shaleigh kept an eye on her friend as they walked. She didn't want him to get upset stepping into his old library and finding his precious books destroyed. It took him a moment to build up the courage to look up at the walls around him, then his mouth dropped open.

"Can you see the place okay?" she asked.

He nodded. "I forgot what it looked like when it was empty," he whispered with awe in his voice. "I forgot that it was empty at the beginning. I was so young then, maybe only a few months old when they finished building it. I felt so small inside, like the whole building ate me up like a whale. Now it seems huge again, like before."

She waited for him to continue, but he didn't, only

turned in circles and continued to stare. He wasn't even kneading his paws into the flooring. "Mawr? If you're not okay, just let me know."

He gave a sweet smile. "No, I'm just remembering. Many of the books they started with were copies from the Sanctuary. They needed something for people to read at first." He walked over to one of the walls beside an old, fallen fireplace. "This was where they gave me my first tasks. This was where they made me a Guardian." He beamed with pride, his large tail swishing back and forth so hard that Shaleigh had to step aside to keep from getting smacked.

"Was it fun?"

He shook his head. "Oh no, it was terrifying! I was afraid I was going to make a mistake." He looked down at his front feet. "It sounds kind of silly now, I guess, but I was afraid I was too heavy to even step in here. I thought I was going to break the new flooring. You see how clumsy I can be. I didn't want to break anything on my first day!"

Shaleigh went to reply but saw something glinting on the mantel of the fireplace, almost unrecognizable from the dust and cobwebs that had fused it with pieces of fallen stone. She walked over and pushed aside the rubble and picked up something thin that stuck out. More dust and dirt fell away, and Shaleigh began to recognize the shape.

"Mawr..." she whispered. "Mawr, come here!"

He hurried over and leaned down to see. "What did you find?"

Shaleigh knocked the item against her legs, throwing clouds of dust and dirt into the air. "They're glasses!"

Mawr gasped. "Wait, really?"

She cleaned the glass on her dress. The lenses appeared to be welded into the frames and were far too big for a human head. "I'm pretty sure they're yours! Here, hold on."

She straightened them out so they were even and Mawr put his head down so she could reach him. She placed the silver glasses on his nose and pulled the earpieces back. Each hook wrapped securely around each of his big ears, clearly made just for his head—the metal frames were tarnished and had certainly seen better days, but they fit perfectly.

"It's them!" Mawr cried, giving a small jump in the air. "You found them! Oh, I don't know how they got there or how they even lasted all this time. I can't believe it! Thank you, Shaleigh!"

He came over and nuzzled her arm, rubbing her skin a little too hard but she laughed. "You're welcome! There's no way you would have been able to find those. They were too well hidden!"

Mawr gave another leap and she had to put her hands out to calm him down again. He gave a sheepish smile and brought his big feet together. "Sorry, I'm just so excited!"

"I know, but we have to be careful. The Pello Pines are everywhere, and I don't trust that any place is completely safe."

Shaleigh glanced to the Shadow Wolves to see them watching, mostly curious but some were clearly not impressed.

Mawr looked at the remains of his library for the first time in several hundred years. "Oh wow, it's much dustier than I realized! And that hole in the roof is in the center of the room! No wonder the books couldn't last."

Shaleigh turned to see the leader motioning for her near the entrance and whispered to Mawr, "I'll be right back, okay?"

He nodded, keeping an eye on her as she walked over to the leader and gave him another curtsy. "Sorry, he... found something he lost."

"I see that," the Shadow Wolf huffed. "Regardless we have a place for you to sleep for the night that's big enough for your stone companion, too."

He led the way to the back of the library; Mawr followed but kept his distance. Here the ivy had run through the windows and made intricate patterns up to the ceiling of the domed building. There was a blanket that had been dropped in a corner and Shaleigh had never been so happy to see such a dreadful bed.

"Thank you," she whispered. "I mean it. You all deserve to be treated better than I've treated you."

He let out a long breath before replying, "You're right, we do deserve better. We're not mindless beasts." He glanced to Mawr who was still wandering the perimeter of his beloved empty library. "We aren't what people think we are. Like him, we merely long for home and freedom."

Shaleigh nodded. "Thank you for allowing us to share your den for the night."

"Any enemy of Keriam's can at least be tolerated for one night," he said, giving a little laugh before trotting off to the opposite corner where his fellow packmates were waiting. She saw the little nests of grass and leaves they used for their own bedding.

As Shaleigh watched him retreat, she felt the fear and adrenaline start to melt away. She was safe now, at least for the moment, and she could finally sleep without worrying about Mawr. She was also hungry, thirsty, and smelled terrible, but at least she had a bed.

The others were still out there somewhere, hopefully alive and safe, but she was so exhausted she couldn't think on that now. Her mind would run in circles all night if she let it. Instead she laid down on the blanket that smelled of dirt and curled up her arm to use as a pillow. She hadn't even realized she was starting to doze off until she felt Mawr behind her, purring. Sleepily she reached out to stroke his nose and felt his purrs rumble the ground. Finally, she fell into a deep sleep with Mawr as her watchful guardian.

He might not be the Guardian of the Library of Aife any longer, but he was her Guardian, at least for tonight.

RESCUED

Colin

Colin watched in horror as Shaleigh was pulled away from their group, then felt himself start to lose hold of Mawr's stone fur. He adjusted his grip, trying his hardest to hold onto his friend: Mawr turned his head to look at him, his eyes wide and terrified, before Colin lost his hold and Mawr fell away in a blur.

Dark shadowed trees whizzed past them, and the jagged movement made Colin dizzy. He stared at where Shaleigh and Mawr had fallen, frozen and terrified. What happened to them? Why had they slowed down to begin with? His mind whirled with questions, heedless of the fact that they were hurdling off course with no steering.

A branch smacked his right hand, which was holding onto air. He cried out, and that was the final strike. The circle they began with was shattered, and he, Teagan, and Talek were flung outward in all directions.

He was spinning; Colin tried to get his bearings, to figure out which way was even up. A tree limb scraped at his cheek, then another slammed against his left calf. The shock of pain forced him to alertness.

While he wasn't a true soldier, he still remembered his years of training in the military of the Garden. Pulling himself together, he spun around using his tail and let his body go limp. Instead of just falling helplessly, he needed to use his brain. He needed to be alert to anything that he could use to stop his momentum, otherwise something else would stop it for him—and he might not survive that.

A large trunk appeared in the distance, approaching far too quickly. With a growl he flung out his arms and legs, his claws extended, and grabbed hold of the trunk like a lifeline. He dug in, but with the momentum, it took a while to stop. Pain ripped through his fingers and up his arms as his body swung around the trunk and he finally stilled, clinging to its side. His teeth were clenched tight and his breathing was ragged.

Hot liquid spilled down his fingers, and he wondered if he had ripped his own claws off. He looked at his hands, noticing that he was shaking. Swallowing at the dryness in his throat, he tried to slow down his heart.

His fingertips were covered in blood. It even smelled like blood. But he didn't feel like he was bleeding . . . It couldn't be his. Before he could fully understand what he was seeing, his body slipped. He gripped his claws deeper into the bark, but gravity took hold and he fell down the length of the tree, drawing his claws down the trunk as he fell, trying to keep from falling too quickly. He heard a high-pitched shriek that made his ears hurt and he hunkered his shoulders up to try to drown out the sound.

"What is that?" he muttered to himself as his feet finally hit the ground.

He clung to the tree, gasping for breath. The air was crisp, and he shivered as the adrenaline left him.

The shrieking continued, and he wanted nothing more than to cover his ears from the sound. He dislodged his claws from the bark, but the shriek peaked in intensity as soon as they came loose—Colin stared down at the red tinted and matted fur on his fingertips.

The blood had come from the tree bark, he realized then. It was spilling out from the gashes he had made when he fell, pooling down the side of the tree along the dark bark. His mind couldn't make sense of it. His body trembled from head to toe as he lowered his gaze, following the blood as it pooled by his feet where it stained a pile of dried leaves a dark crimson.

The tree was bleeding.

He swallowed again at the dryness in his throat, trying to stop from trembling, trying to get his breathing back to normal. This was dangerous, this was bad, this was not good, but he couldn't figure out why.

Slowly he looked up the side of the tree, up past the long gashes he had made when he fell, up to the half-moon cuts he had made near the top—it looked like a raw, open wound. His mind started ringing in warning.

He needed to run.

All the hair was standing up on the back of his neck, but he couldn't move—

Why was the tree bleeding?

Trees weren't supposed to bleed. It wasn't possible. Trees didn't do that.

A dark shadow darted in his peripheral vision, jerking forward like a snake, and Colin's instincts kicked in. He darted away from it with a gasp, his claws splayed out ready to strike. He turned to look at the long shadow that appeared more like a vine than a snake. As he stared at it, trying to figure out what he was even looking at, something long and thin grazed just past the fur of his cheek.

He jumped back again. Was it a serpent? His mind wracked through all of the books he had read in the library but he hadn't read many on animal life in the Slumbering Forest. He had focused more on history than on wildlife, and now years later, he was sorely regretting that decision.

Something cold and wet touched the fur on the back of his left hand and he jerked away again, spotting another tendril moving closer to him. A trained soldier might not have the reflexes he did, but as a half stoat or *stoatling* as he preferred to be called, he was fast. It was one of the few benefits he had over his fellow soldiers in training. He wasn't strong, he couldn't take a hit, but he could dodge and avoid for longer than the others could— nobody had wanted to be his sparring partner.

More tendrils came at him from all around. There had to be six of them total. Colin thought back to those sparring matches when he would sometimes take on ten soldiers at once. He leaped and rolled, twisted and ducked, using all his best methods to keep them from getting near. The problem was because he was so focused on dodging them all, he couldn't escape easily. He had to take what little ground he could as he avoided the tendrils. It didn't help that his body was already trembling from the crash. He was trying to focus, but physically he was reeling. Finally, he got far enough away that the tendrils couldn't reach him, and he paused in a patch of sunlight.

Breathing hard, he stood up straighter, wearing a smirk. "Looks like it's just not your day, is it?"

Then the ground shook beneath his feet.

He shot his back foot out to keep his balance, but instead tripped over a root that he swore wasn't there before. He tried to get up, watching as another root emerged from the ground beneath him and clamped down on top of his ankles.

His eyes went wide. "No way," he whispered. "That's not fair!"

More roots emerged from the ground, cracking the dry soil and reaching out towards him. The tree that he had cut up, tilted to the side, then tilted to the other side. It was walking, he realized.

The tree was walking toward him.

He could see a better outline of the tree now, especially as it approached. Its tendrils hovered out over the ground, reaching for him. As it passed through the sunlight, tiny little barbs beneath the leaves on the end shuddered. It was horrifying to look at, but also fascinating, too. Colin knew he ought to work on freeing his legs, to see if he could slip them out, but he also couldn't look away from it.

Was this what Mawr had been warning him about?

Was this what a Pello Pine looked like? It was no wonder the City of Aife had fallen to them. Half of their forces probably didn't notice they were dinner until it was too late. Captain Briar would notice, for as monstrous as she could be in her own right, she wouldn't let herself be taken out by a Pello Pine, even if they did look like they came out of a nightmare.

He tore his gaze away from the tree and down to the roots at his ankles; he dug his claws into the root on top—blood seeped up between his fingers and the shriek came again.

"Don't like that, do you?" Colin cried, digging his claws in again, and kicking upward, trying to loosen his feet. The root loosened and cracked, and eventually slid back down into the dirt.

The Pello Pine screamed, again.

Colin scrambled to his feet and was about to turn around to run when something dug deep into the back of his neck . . .

He gasped, shaking from head to toe, his heart pounding in his chest. He tried to move forward, wincing at the barbs pulling at his skin, digging deeper as he squirmed. Now it was Colin who screamed as warm blood dribbled down the back of his neck and into his fur; he stumbled down to one knee. The dried leaves crunched beneath his weight. The barbs at the back of his neck went with him, this time not adding to the pain. It didn't mind if he fell to the ground, but it didn't want him to leave.

The tree waded closer, moving slowly through the soil and churning up the ground as it approached. Then he saw the other tendrils creep forward. Colin glanced up to the tree, wincing at the throbbing pain in the back of his neck. He looked around at the other trees and noted that they looked similar to this one. Were they all Pello Pines? Had Colin truly landed in the middle of a grove of them?

He really did have the worst luck.

The other Pello Pines still had black blobs that covered their lower halves, as though their feet were stuck in tar. Still he saw they had tendrils too, floating over to him as though hoping to just get a taste.

The tree's shadow fell over him as it eclipsed the sunlight that had been pouring into the clearing.

Colin tried to pull away again, but the barbs threatened him with a slight tug. He was afraid if he pulled too hard it would make him bleed out. A wound like that out here meant a very gruesome death.

He looked around to see other vines hovering over the ground like insect feelers, all six of them belonging to this single Pello Pine coming for him. He swallowed down the lump in his throat and tried to ease the pit of terror that took hold of his gut. Staring up at the terrifying tree that he had heard so much about, staring at the monster that had given the Bloody Forest its name before they had been trapped in slumber, Colin understood why they were feared.

A single tree, that was all it took to get rid of him.

He thought of the people of the Garden, the people down at the Pasture who only had gardening tools. He thought about the librarians who had kept the books safe for so long and had offered him shelter when he had nothing. He thought about the children that pinched his ears and liked to play with his tail. He thought of the shopkeepers that used to shoo him out of their stores for being an eyesore. None of them had a chance against a whole forest of these monsters.

Even Captain Briar for all her skill and tactics would be hard pressed to take out one of these on her own. And Madam Cloom foolishly had put all her faith into him: What good had that done? He had forgotten he even had the damn letter until he was in the presence of Tanwen.

His tail swished nervously as four more feelers brushed against him, searching for the best places to feed, looking for weak spots through his thick fur.

It was when he thought of Mawr that tears started to run down his cheeks. If Colin died, Mawr would be broken all over again. The poor guy couldn't take it, he was too kind to be in a war. He was too good to fight these kind of nightmare monsters. Colin couldn't imagine what his friend must have felt cowering inside the Library of Aife and listening to everyone he ever knew get slaughtered by these things. Knowing that the Pello Pines had taken another of his friends would completely ruin him.

Colin felt another series of nails jab into his wrist, right where it had tried to latch on earlier. He felt the pain surge in his veins as it started sucking at his blood instantly like a giant leech. He couldn't help but whimper.

"I hope they burn your whole forest to the ground. I hope you all get turned to ash," he whispered. He didn't know if Pello Pines could hear or even talk—it did seem like it understood him.

The barbs in the back of his neck twitched slightly, sending a new jolt of pain through his whole body. The creaking of branches above him sounded like crude laughter. "I hope they chop you down and build a new Garden out of your corpses."

Another feeler came over and hovered just under his chin.

"So, this is your plan, huh? Tear out my throat so I can't talk back." He gave a crazed grin. "I admit you wouldn't be the first to want to shut me up."

~

DESPITE HIS BRAVADO, Colin was terrified. The Pello Pine had complete hold over him, and worse yet, it seemed intent on silencing him before it killed him.

Against his throat, he felt the tendril shifting through his fur, still looking for a soft spot to strike. He braced himself for the inevitable pain that would surely kill him. Hopefully it would kill him quickly and end this torture.

Instead it placed the smooth side of its tendril under his chin and lifted his head. Colin tried to fight it, but for such a small, thin limb, it was surprisingly powerful. The barbs that were dug into the back of his neck pulled down to have him to look up: It wanted him to see it in its full terrifying glory. It wanted him to see what was about to kill him, forcing him to look up at its branches high above. Up in the canopy, it actually could have been a normal tree. It had bright green leaves at the top that browned further down on its trunk.

What truly caught Colin's attention was beyond. He could spot patches of cloudy sky between the gaps of its dark limbs and the canopy it formed with other Pello

Pines. The clouds had parted in one space, and he saw the blue sky. Oddly enough it made him calmer.

It was strange, the sky here always looked so much bluer than it did in the Human World. Almost like a bird's egg. It was a lovely color, and he regretted that he had never really appreciated it before. Why not? He had plenty of days he could have spent staring at the sky, appreciating all it offered, but he hadn't really looked and appreciated it since he was living on the streets of the Garden. Ever since, he never allowed himself the time to look, never thought it was worthwhile. It always seemed like a waste, but it wasn't, was it?

It was beautiful.

The barbs in his wrist dug deeper, dragging only a centimeter or so through his skin, but it felt like fire; Colin cried out, and the branches above shifted with laughter.

"You really don't like me talking back, do you? But you also don't like me ignoring you." He gave a hoarse laugh. "You want me to shut up and die quietly, am I right?"

He shuddered as it drew more blood from his wrist and the pain shot up to his elbow. He bit his lip to keep from screaming. He didn't care if he was about to die, he would be as much trouble as possible. The giant tree was going to regret choosing him to be its meal today.

"I wish Master Teagan hadn't shown you any sympathy," he said through gritted teeth. "I wish he and Master Cathal had burned this whole forest to the ground. You don't deserve mercy."

The barbs in the back of his neck pulled down, forcing his head upward again. His neck arched to the point that the muscles hurt, and he winced. The tree gave a wail like a low-pitched screech owl. If he was good at anything, it was at making people angry, and it seemed to be true for Pello Pines, too.

Colin tensed, feeling the tendril in front of him against his neck, moving through his fur once more. It wouldn't be so bad if the tree made it quick. It would be so much easier if it just did its deed and was done with him. Instead it liked to play with its food, to make its prey suffer.

And that was the worst part. The knowing and the waiting, being a puppet for something that you couldn't even negotiate with.

It planned to take its time, but Colin didn't care any longer. He was going to make this thing hate him by the time it was done.

He swallowed again, his eyes wet with tears, and felt the barbs scrape against his exposed neck. It wouldn't be long now—"I hope you choke on me," he hissed, his voice breaking from nerves.

He heard something move toward him, maybe some carrion bird here to take care of the scraps after the Pello Pine drained him dry. He didn't know anything about the area, but he had traveled with Mawr for days. Why had he never asked him? Why did it take him dying by the blood-thirstiness of a Pello Pine for him to think?

Colin squinted his eyes shut tight, squeezing out tears that fell through the damp fur on his cheeks. The tendril against his neck froze and a horrible screech filled the air. The barbs in the back of his neck pulled away from him, slipping cleanly out of his skin like dozens of needles all at once.

Colin collapsed to the ground, placing a hand to his throat—the Pello Pine hadn't torn it out. He was still alive. He was bleeding from the back of his neck and from his wrist, but he was alive.

Putting pressure on his wrist, he looked up to see Master Teagan standing before him, facing the Pello Pine. He had his hand held out to keep the tendrils at bay.

"Master Teagan!" he cried.

He felt hands prod at the back of his neck and turned to see Talek.

"Are you alright?" Talek asked.

"Yeah," Colin said, his voice breaking. "I am now."

Talek helped him to his feet and they backed away from the Pello Pine. Talek watched the ground carefully, clearly used to the tricks that these trees used to assault their prey.

"It was going to kill me; I couldn't get away."

"I know, but it's alright now. Teagan has it."

Once they were far enough away, Colin looked back to see Teagan had a tendril clasped in either hand, but the other four were coming up behind him.

"Teagan, watch out!" he cried, lurching forward but Talek grabbed hold of him and pulled him back.

"Calm down, he knows what he's doing."

Colin was only partially listening, he tried to pull away from Talek again, but was still too dazed to do much. The four tendrils went for Teagan, aiming to latch onto the back of his neck like they had Colin. If all four of them did, he would surely be dropped in an instant: Instead though the barbs scraped back and forth against his skin.

"What's happening?"

Talek had an arm under his and around his shoulder to keep him still. "He has Tanwen's gift, remember? He has the protection of her skin, and since Pello Pines are made of her magic, it can't possibly break through it."

Colin watched in awe as the barbs attempted to break through his skin again and again, but they couldn't; it was as if Master Teagan's skin was made of armor.

Then the unexpected happened: the Pello Pine started to pull away. It gave a hesitant shriek as it curled some of its tendrils back against the trunk. The roots started churning it backwards in the soil.

Teagan still held onto two of its tendrils, speaking to it in a low voice. Colin could just barely make the words out —"You know who I am, don't you? You remember me?"

The Pello Pine gave a low, short shriek, pulling at its tendrils, panicked.

"You remember my Master, too, I take it? We put you to sleep before."

It gave another pitiful shriek. What was it like to be put to sleep for such a long time? Did they dream during that time? Did they think of the faces of the ones who did it? It sounded like such horrible existence that he almost felt bad for his earlier insults wishing that the forest was burned down.

"I thought you would. Tell the others not to harm any of my friends, or else I will put you all to sleep again. You shall not eat any humans or beings in this forest, understood? Oh, and if you see a large stone lion, you must leave him alone as well."

The Pello Pine gave a pitiful shriek again, desperate to pull away, and Teagan was beginning to lose his grip.

"Do I have your word or do we need to use force? I would hate to have to finish the job that Colin started."

It gave another wail, louder than before, clearly terrified.

"Good," Teagan said and let go of the tendrils. The Pello Pine pulled away and thundered through the soil in its desperation to escape, far faster than it had when it was trying to eat Colin.

Teagan came over to join them, his arrogant smile fading to reflect how he truly felt: harried and frightened.

"That was too close for comfort," Talek whispered, taking a deep breath. "Somehow I don't think all of them will be so easily persuaded."

Colin slipped free of Talek's hold and darted for Teagan, wrapping his arms around him. "You saved my life! Thank you so much, boss!"

Hesitating, Teagan slowly wrapped an arm around Colin and gave him an awkward hug. "I'm glad you're alright. I was afraid we had lost you when you fell."

"I thought I was a goner," Colin muttered, tears rolling down his cheeks as the fear and the terror finally flooded through him.

"You were difficult to find," Talek said. "I knew you couldn't have gone far, and then we heard the shrieks from the Pello Pine."

Colin pulled away finally and wiped at his nose.

Teagan smiled down at him with a hand resting on his shoulder. "Are you truly alright?"

He nodded, trying to get his voice under control. "I don't think you understand how close I came to death, is all."

A sadness came to Teagan's eyes, as though he was remembering something, and he gave a short nod. "I can understand how that feels." His eyes went glassy and he took a deep breath. "But you're well. It seems like it drained you some, but you should heal. Talek, did you check—"

"Yes, the wounds are just pin-pricks for the most part. They'll heal in a little bit; you shouldn't have to worry about bleeding out or anything."

Colin rubbed both hands over his face, ruffling his matted fur. "Thank you both for saving me. Talek, you, too. Sorry I tried to get away from you, but I thought Master Teagan was..."

Talek smiled. "Fortunately we still have our gifts, and Teagan has some reputation with these trees."

"*Some*," Teagan insisted, lowing his voice. "Don't forget, all of the Pello Pines can hear us unless we keep our voices low, so let's please do that. I doubt my empty threats alone will stop them, but hopefully it will buy us enough time to be able to find the others."

Colin's eyes went wide. "Shaleigh fell first, I watched her! Then I saw Mawr fall away, he looked so scared. I can't imagine how he's doing in this place by himself. We have to find him!"

Teagan looked to Talek, "Do you think you can?"

Talek gave a nervous laugh. "I think I can try. This

forest is enormous, and Tanwen's magic is everywhere. She's in the ground, the trees, even the air. It's over-whelming at times."

Colin studied him for a moment, noticing his pursed lips, his worried face. "You're afraid, aren't you? Why?"

Talek turned to him and blinked. "I'm afraid I'll lose myself looking at that world. There's so much, and it's so beautiful. Sometimes it's hard to leave it."

"We wouldn't let that happen," Colin said.

"Yes, but... sometimes it pulls me in and won't let go." He put a hand to his chest and Teagan reached over to take his other hand.

"It's alright, we're all coming to terms with our gifts. Each of them have their own challenges."

Colin smirked, eager to change the mood. "I don't know, boss, yours seems pretty helpful!"

He arched an eyebrow. "I'm not your boss anymore, Colin." He turned back to Talek. "Perhaps if we found a safe place for you to commune, it would be easier. I know it was nerve-wracking last time. We heard the Pello Pine shrieks, but they seemed to come from everywhere."

Talek gave a sheepish smile. "It was not the best place to practice, no."

Teagan turned to Colin with a mischievous smile. "How are your legs feeling?"

Colin hopped from one leg to the next. "I might be a little slower. Are we traveling?"

Teagan nodded.

"I don't know, boss," Colin said, glancing around them. "The last time we tried to go really fast, we all ended up pinwheeling off—I don't think that's a good idea."

"It's safer," Talek countered. "Anything is safer than traveling on foot. I don't want to have another close call, do you?"

Colin sighed. "No, I don't. But I don't know if it'll even work without all five of us."

"It should," Teagan said. "If I was able to resist the sting of a Pello Pine and Talek was able to use his sight, you should be able to use your speed. I say give it a try. The worst that happens is we tumble down a cliff or something."

"Oh, is that all?" Colin rolled his eyes.

"Whatever we do, we need to hurry," Talek whispered.

Freezing at his words, Colin turned to look around. The trees were still but the forest was deathly silent—no forest should ever be so quiet. Most of the trees around them had black bulbous masses still clinging to their bases, but they could break free at any moment.

"I didn't see anything," Talek added. "I just don't like being out here in the open like this. We need to keep moving. The longer we stay still, the more chances we have at Pello Pines finding us."

Colin frowned. But where was a safe place to go when the entire forest was overrun with Pello Pines? He thought back to what he had seen when he would fly over it on his flying bicycle with the people he had kidnapped from the Human World. That thought made him feel guilty all over again, so instead he thought back to the maps he had studied when he was in the Library of the Garden. He loved looking at the old maps. He thought modern ones were boring because everyone knew them.

He remembered studying the map for the Slumbering

Forest often, mostly because his friend Finn was planning to live there. He had the crazy notion that if his friend ever got into trouble he would've been able to go find him and save him; of course that had never happened. Colin did remember the general layout of the forest though, the boundaries, the landmarks, and the cluster of safe places that existed—they were sparse and spread out.

Turning around in circles a few times, he studied where the sun was in the sky, until he was facing the direction he thought would lead to safety. He hoped it would at least. "I think this path should lead us to where the Pello Pines don't live anymore. Or at least they didn't."

Teagan gave a wide smile. "Excellent! I knew you would come up with something."

"You were the one who took care of these woods last time, I'm surprised you don't know this place better than me."

Teagan glanced away and put his hands behind his back. "Most of the work I did was on weather control and spreading Daegonrúsc plant seeds. Despite that crude threat I made earlier, I didn't interact with many Pello Pines before. There were a few I had to keep away from Master Cathal that tried to harm him, but for the most part, I was focused on the bigger picture."

Talek looped his arm around Teagan's. "In other words, he was too busy trying to protect his boyfriend than figuring out the lay of the land."

Teagan's eyes went wide. "That's not what I meant!"

"See you just have to learn to read in between the lines, Colin," Talek said with a smile, tapping his nose. "Especially around Teagan."

Talek and Colin both laughed.

Teagan was clearly annoyed but gave a little laugh all the same. "I suppose you're right to some extent."

Talek took Colin's hand in his. "You want us to follow that path and see what we can find?"

"I think that's right," Colin muttered. "I remember a big area roped off in that direction, though I don't remember where."

Talek nodded. "I think I know where you mean. Just a moment." Talek wet his lips and stared off in the direction that Colin planned to go, and his body went still. After a moment, his eyes clouded over and his fingers went cold. Colin shivered, but didn't let go.

Talek's breaths were short and shallow and he spoke in a daze. "Yes, that's the direction."

"Of what exactly?" Teagan asked. "You two are being far too cryptic for my taste."

"Somebody gets a taste of his own medicine for once," Colin teased.

"The City of Aife," Talek whispered. "At least what's left of it."

TRAVELING with three wasn't nearly as fast as traveling with five. Instead of forming a circle, it was more of a triangle. Colin didn't realize how much Mawr and Shaleigh helped them travel until they were gone. Instead of moving seamlessly across long distances with ease, they flew off course regularly. Of all of them, Talek seemed to suffer the most from it.

The gift that Tanwen gave Talek was meant to help him see her magic and peer into a world that was normally invisible. As he explained it, when they came to the Slumbering Forest before, all he had to do was work a map out in his head and they passed along it without trouble. Now he was a navigator working on choppy water. Without Shaleigh, their boat had nobody to steer the ship. Every time he tried to gauge the path, they got diverted down the wrong direction or they were thrown from their circle entirely. Fortunately, they couldn't go too fast, so they weren't separated or injured like last time, but after the third time of being thrown into the bulb of Daegonrúsc, Colin was getting sore and annoyed.

Colin pushed himself up off the ground with a groan. "That one hurt," he grumbled, shaking off the dirt and leaves that were stuck to his fur—he always seemed to land face down.

He looked around, not wanting to chance angering another Pello Pine, and wiped some sticky gunk off his cheek, realizing it was part of the bulb from a dying Daegonrúsc. He sighed, unable to rub it off completely. "We can't keep doing this."

"I agree," Teagan whispered as he limped over. He must have hit his foot on something in the fall. "I don't even know what happened this time. I didn't see any tree in the way." He glanced to Talek who stepped up to join them, rubbing his shoulder. "Unless you got distracted again by a rock."

"I thought it was Mawr that time. I didn't want to leave him alone in this place if it was." Talek was looking around them, as though searching for something.

Teagan grew silent at his words then gave a frustrated nod.

Colin rubbed at the crick in the back of his neck. "So, why did you stop this time?"

"I heard a scream," Talek said in annoyance.

"A scream?" Colin asked, looking around. He strained his ears, now noticing the sounds around them instead of being distracted by his sticky fur.

"Who was it?" Teagan whispered.

"It sounded like a woman."

They all went silent. The unspoken fear hung in the air between them, clawing at their minds like a thick humidity. Was it Shaleigh? Did the Pello Pines get her before they could find her?

Colin's tail swished back and forth. Then he caught something, not a scream like he was expecting, but something that made his heart race. He smelled blood. He held up a hand to the others and turned to where the scent was strongest. The blood was fresh, so it probably wasn't a carcass.

"What is it?" Teagan asked.

"Blood."

Talek's eyes went wide.

"I need to go check," Colin whispered, but Talek stepped forward.

"No, wait. I want to try to see it first, just to make sure. I don't want you walking into a trap." He held a hand to the side of his face and closed his eyes. He looked strange when he did because the black scales around his eyes looked like a single mass. Colin was still getting used to how he looked; his white hair looked even brighter in the dwindling daylight. When he opened his eyes, they were frosted over with white, making him look more like an animal and Colin couldn't suppress a shudder. It wasn't like he hadn't seen it before, but it was still creepy to watch. The utter silence of the forest didn't help.

After a few seconds, Talek shook his head. "I can't," he said in distress, clutching the side of his head. "It hurts my head too much."

Teagan put an arm around him. "It's alright, you tried. You've been using that sight all day."

Colin frowned. He hoped that Talek taxing his mind this much wouldn't bring the Madness back. He had no idea if the Madness was gone for good, or if it could creep back in again. Teagan gave him a worried look, and Colin wondered if he feared that too. They had no idea how these gifts were going to affect them in the long term, and Talek had a history of not dealing well with stress.

"Let me see if I can find out where it's coming from. If I can smell it, then it has to be close."

Talek gave him a pitiful look. "But Colin, if it's her, then—"

"Then I'll let you both know. Look, I'm a Seeker, remember? It's kind of my job to find things."

"It hasn't been your job for a long time," Teagan said with a gentle smile. "If you wish to try, just remember what I told you—Pello Pines hunt based on movement and sound. If you don't step carefully and make too much noise, they will find you. I may be able to take out one of them, but if there are many..."

Colin nodded. He didn't need to explain the rest.

"Don't worry, I'll be careful, boss. And you two be careful. Don't let anything sneak up on you while I'm gone."

"If you aren't back soon, we will come looking for you," Teagan insisted.

Colin gave a salute, an old gesture he hadn't used since training, but somehow it seemed appropriate. The look of concern on Teagan's face told him he probably shouldn't have done it, but he turned away and headed into the woods before he could say more.

Being a stoatling, Colin had a very good sense of smell, but he rarely had to use it in his job as a Seeker. Mostly he worked more like a detective, following clues, finding friends of the target, casing the homes and interests of his targets. He sought out times when his targets would be alone or outside by themselves, that was the best time to take them by surprise. He rarely had to use his sense of smell, and he admittedly wasn't very good at tracking, but he had to try. He had to make sure it wasn't Shaleigh.

He walked with barely a sound through the woods, sidestepping roots poking out of the soil. He paused for a moment, sniffing the air. The wind was picking up, and the floral scent it carried hid the blood he was trying to track. He waited, his tail swishing back and forth as he watched for any approaching Pello Pines. Then the wind died down again, and he caught the scent again, stronger. He was getting close.

He maneuvered around a few more Daegonrúsc husks before he found the first alarming sight. The sun was halfway down the horizon when he spotted a dark shadow of something up ahead. As he went around the Daegonrúsc, he realized there were several of them.

Barely wanting to breathe, he moved closer. Pools of wet blood glimmered in the fading sunlight, settling into the dirt. Colin put a hand to his mouth as he realized that he was looking at the bodies of Shadow Wolves.

Swallowing down the dryness in his throat, he wondered why the Pello Pines hadn't come to feed from the bodies, but whatever had killed them hadn't made enough noise or vibrations to alert them . . .

He felt a familiar brush against the back of his neck and had to refrain from jumping or screaming. Sure enough a tendril from a Pello Pine was reaching for him from above, only it was straining to reach him. Trying to catch his breath, he realized the tendril was attached to a Pello Pine that was still trapped—most of them were still trapped. The distant Pello Pines might not have felt the reverberations that these bodies had made, but these had and were trying to feast.

He took a deep breath and tried to calm his nerves.

"Who's there?" a woman's voice asked, and Colin looked around wildly. He didn't see anyone.

"I warn you, I'm armed," she added, and Colin recognized the voice.

Stepping cautiously over the bodies, Colin reached another cluster of Daegonrúsc bulbs growing far closer together. He stepped around them carefully, following the bodies of the Shadow Wolves and keeping an eye out for more tendrils.

Then he saw her.

Captain Briar had one arm up against the husk of a Daegonrúsc, her other hand held a bloody dagger—that arm was soaked in blood. Her face was a mess of cuts and bruises, and her dark hair was unkempt and matted. He hoped that none of the blood covering her belong to her. Usually dressed in armor, even when she was in hiding with Madam Cloom, it was unsettling to see her dressed in mere rags.

When she spotted him, her entire body went taut: "Colin?" she asked, her voice sounding much smaller than before. "Is it really you?"

"Captain?" Colin asked, inching forward.

The hollow look in her eyes diminished when she smiled. He had hardly ever seen her smile. "Wait, why are you here?"

He snickered and shook his head. "I think I should ask you the same thing." He looked around. "There aren't any traps are there?"

"No, I already killed the curs that damn Magician left behind to kill me. They thought they had taken all my weapons, but this isn't the first time I've been left to rot."

Colin went over to look at the thick chain that bound her to the tree. It was tied tight around her wrist. The skin around the links looked red and purple from bruising.

"I thought about getting rid of it," she said, her voice wavering. "But I didn't think I would make it far with the trees."

He licked his lips and nodded. It was so difficult even imagining having to make a decision like that, but of course the Captain did. She wasn't as squeamish as Colin would have been—he set about looking at the chain.

"There has to be a lock or something," he muttered.

"I tried to cut it with the knife," she said, shaking her head, "but it didn't work. The chain is too thick."

She was right, Colin had only seen chains like this used on boats in the shipyard. He circled the trunk of the tree with caution, watching out for more of the tendrils to take him by surprise. He spotted the deadbolt used to secure the chains. "You're lucky, because I used to break these things all the time when I lived on the street. Breaking into storage crates sometimes gave me enough food for days."

She gave a hoarse laugh. "You're saying I should be glad you were a pickpocket?"

He pulled out his own small dagger and started working on the lock, looking for the trigger mechanism inside. They were all different, but he knew the few types that were used in the Garden and he doubted that Keriam had bothered finding something fancier. Finally, he found it and did his fancy two jerk movement that elicited a click from the lock. The chains fell away, and Captain Briar let out a groan as she slowly lowered her arm down and cradled it against her chest. She knew better than to try to use it right away and Colin didn't want to imagine what it felt like.

"You know," he said as he came around the other side of the Daegonrúsc, "most people would either tie you to a tree or feed you to the wolves, not both."

"I guess he knew I was a special kind of trouble." She shrugged. "But, thank you. I would've died out here if you hadn't shown up."

"I'm not here by myself," Colin added, remembering suddenly that she might have some issues with her old boss and a prisoner that she had beaten up in a jail cell back in the dungeons of the Garden. He hadn't even considered whether it was a good idea to free Captain Briar or not as she was trussed up against a tree to die—it was simply the right thing to do.

But she was no longer a Captain, Teagan was no longer a High Faerie, Talek was no longer a prisoner, and he was no longer a Seeker. They were simply four survivors trying to take down a violent Magician.

He crouched down beside her and reached an arm behind her to help her up. They took a step or two and Colin already could see that Captain Briar had trouble walking, let alone stepping carefully. She was too hurt and too exhausted, and he wondered how long she had been out in the woods watching three Shadow Wolves rot.

"This isn't going to work," he sighed. "I'm going to have to carry you."

She furrowed her brows and it was good to see a flicker of his old Captain again. "Carry me?"

He nodded. "Look, no offense, but you're walking so heavily that every Pello Pine within a mile is going to want to visit. Not to mention that you're bleeding and barefoot. We have to step carefully to keep them from knowing we're here."

Her mouth dropped at his words and she looked up to the tall trees above them, their branches already dark against the evening sky. It was as if for the first time she understood how dangerous this place was and Colin couldn't blame her for being overwhelmed in that moment. He had that same realization when that Pello Pine nearly bled him dry earlier.

"It isn't far," he added, and his words pulled her attention back to him.

She blinked then gave a short nod. "If you think you can."

"I've carried Shaleigh more times than I'd like to admit, including the time I kidnapped her. You're not wearing your armor now either, so that helps." He turned around and crouched down in front of her, swishing his tail out of the way. "Climb on. It's easier this way."

"I'm not a teen either," she grumbled. "Okay, I hope you know what you're doing." She climbed onto his back and wrapped an arm around him. He picked up her legs and got to his feet with a grunt.

"I need both arms, Captain."

"I was trying not to use it," she whispered and shifted her hold so that she held onto his shoulders with both hands instead.

"Alright," he whispered. "Here we go."

He readjusted his hold on her, and then started back, retracing his steps from before. Whereas every footfall Captain Briar had made could be easily heard over the wind, Colin's footsteps were so light, it was more like he was floating across the ground than walking on it.

"I hate to say it, but you were right."

He grinned. "A complement from the Captain? I'll take it."

She snorted. "Don't get used to it."

He squeezed around more bulbous Daegonrúsc and stepped around the three dead Shadow Wolves. The sun had set quicker than he expected, and the tall Pello Pines were dark shadows all around them.

"I'm going to take a detour from last time," he whispered. "One of those tendrils nearly got me before, and I don't want any of them getting hold of you."

"From the trees?" she asked.

"The Pello Pines—that's what all of these are, but they're stuck in place by the Daegonrúsc."

"I appreciate that," she muttered.

He gave a wide berth to the tendril which still stretched out toward them as they passed, the leaf at the end like a hungry mouth.

Reach, grip, release.

Its tiny spikes caught the dim moonlight as it waved toward them. "Those," he said, "you have to watch out for. They're what can kill you if you're not careful. Didn't you see them when you came down here?"

He could hear the awe in her voice and felt her lean up to see the full tree above—"All of these have those...things?"

"I'm afraid so. Kind of creepy isn't it?" He waited a moment before adding. "So, you didn't see them?"

"I was blindfolded. He didn't want me finding a way out once he put me here. I think they were afraid I would find a way back to the Garden and start more trouble."

"I imagine you're good at that." He passed through another group of Daegonrúsc and turned back toward where he had left Teagan and Talek.

"Enough that he wanted to get rid of me, but I'm feared enough that he didn't want to be the one to do it."

Colin laughed. The Captain was so much better to be around when she wasn't giving orders. He wondered if she had been violent before because of the pressure Madam Cloom put on her. He had a better understanding now of how stress could make someone lash out: He had watched Talek break when they visited the City of the Fae and then went on that terrifying journey through the branches.

"I think you'll be surprised with who I'm here with," he declared as he approached the clearing where he had left the others.

"Probably your lion friend," she said. "You two seem inseparable."

He felt a pang at her words as they entered the clearing and stopped. "Where are they?" he muttered. "They promised they would be careful!"

The Captain was silent on his back as he turned and searched the dark forest for any sign of them. Panic slowly built up within his stomach turning it into a knot.

He looked up in the branches, wondering if one of the Pello Pines had gotten them. He looked down at the soil, wondering if they had been dragged underground some- how. The knot in his stomach seemed to rise to his chest as his mind rushed to the simple fact that he was here by himself with a very injured Captain Briar.

Why would they leave him? What if they were attacked by another Pello Pine? How was he supposed to survive with an injured Captain?

His mind went down a tunnel of options, all of which were more anxiety inducing than then next.

"Are you sure we're in the right place?" Captain Briar asked calmly.

"Yes," he said. "I rammed my face against that Daegonrúsc, and you can still see the imprint of my cheek on it. Also, I'm a Seeker, if I can't find my way back to where I started, I'd be pretty terrible at my job." He was panting, his breath coming too fast, and he knew that wasn't good, but he couldn't stop it.

"Calm down," she ordered, keeping her voice low but powerful all the same.

Colin froze and nodded, taking deep breaths to calm himself until he gave a nervous laugh. "All you have to do is give that tone and I snap back into being a recruit again."

"Good," he could hear the smile in her voice, "because this is not the time to panic. If you don't see their bodies, then they're likely still here somewhere. Stop letting your emotions get in the way and stay focused."

He nodded again, taking a few more deep breaths. His panicked brain wanted to argue that she was one to talk about not letting emotions get in the way, but he realized that it didn't matter. Regardless of what happened in the past, he needed her guidance right now, and they both knew it.

They needed each other.

"Alright, think," the Captain said. "Did you all have any backup location in case this one was compromised?"

"No," Colin said. "I didn't think of that."

"Hm."

He could hear the judgment in her voice, and snapped, "I'm the only soldier here and they're not used to that sort of thing."

"That doesn't matter. You have to always handle each situation as though it could turn deadly at any time, especially in such a dangerous environment." She sighed. "But it's alright. It's too late for that now. Perhaps we can retrace our steps and see if there's any sign from them."

Colin nodded, refraining from giving a salute, and turned to head back from where he came.

"Colin, over here!" a voice hissed before he had taken a step.

He spun around and saw in the distance that Teagan and Talek were cautiously making their way closer. He let out a shuddering breath. "Why did you all leave? I thought you were dead!"

"Shh, keep your voice down," Teagan demanded. "We had to move because a Pello Pine came very close. Then it went off in that direction." He pointed to the path that Colin had just traveled.

Colin shuddered.

"We need to move," Captain Briar said, and there was no question in her voice.

"This way," Talek said, looking between Colin and the Captain as though just realizing she was there. He frowned briefly before leading the way back to where he and Teagan had come from.

As they walked, Colin could hear the sound of dirt being pushed aside somewhere in the darkness. It was a Pello Pine, and the sound was coming from behind them, possibly from the clearing they had just left. Had he made too much noise in his hunt for his friends? Had they raised their voices or made some kind of vibration? He had no idea, but he was shaking from head to tail as he followed Talek's lead.

～

THE PELLO PINES thinned out more as they walked through the forest. Colin was grateful that Teagan and Talek were with them; they knew how to walk quietly without him having to ask. He couldn't hear the Pello Pines churning through the dirt anymore, but that didn't mean they were safe.

Night descended quickly and they had to slow down. Normally Colin liked being out in the woods at night, but this forest was different. Walking through the cold wind, trying to stay as quiet as possible, and listening to the absolute stillness was difficult. He had to resist the urge to crack a joke to lighten the mood, but he knew better.

His arms were starting to shake under Captain Briar's weight. He didn't want to say anything because he didn't want to embarrass himself in front of the Captain. Even though they didn't always agree on things, he still respected her. He didn't want her to see him as weak or untrained. He didn't want to confirm the stereotype that soldiers of the Garden had about Seekers: that they weren't well trained. He knew she wasn't really a Captain anymore, but he still didn't want her to see him like that. He wanted to impress her.

However, he knew he couldn't keep up the show much longer. Despite his pride, he knew he hadn't fully recovered from the Pello Pine attack earlier, and the wound on his wrist was starting to open. He was afraid if he didn't say something soon, he would either leave a blood trail through the forest for something to follow them, or he would pass out. Either option would end up being super embarrassing.

Just as he was about to say something, Talek came to

an abrupt stop. He put a hand to his temple and turned his head slowly.

"What is it?" Captain Briar whispered, and there was something encouraging about the fact that she, not Colin, was the one to break the silence. She could probably tell just how close she was to being dropped onto the forest floor based on how much Colin's arms were shaking.

Talek turned and put a hand out. "That's where we need to go." He started to head forward, but Colin interrupted.

"Before we run off again," he said, "can one of you help me?"

"What is it?" Teagan asked,

"He's about to drop me," Captain Briar said with amusement and Colin cringed.

Teagan turned to him with concern. "Oh, Colin. You should have said something. Here, let me help."

He stepped behind Colin as the Captain muttered, "I wish I could help. I hate feeling so useless."

"Nonsense," Teagan muttered, picking her up and holding her in his arms.

Colin felt the blood rushing to his arms instantly. It took a few moments for him to be able to straighten them out again. He groaned as he brought them forward, feeling the pain in his joints. "I'm sorry, Captain. I tried."

"You did your best," she said with a nod, then turned to Talek. "Where exactly are we headed?"

"To a safe place," he stated, crossing his arms.

"Are you not telling me because you don't trust me?" she asked with a slight smile. "Or is it because you don't like me?"

"A little of both if I'm being completely honest."

Colin sighed. Were these two really going to fight in the middle of the Slumbering Forest? He had hoped they would understand the situation and not cause waves considering they could be killed at any moment.

"Look, we don't have time for this," he said, rubbing at his shoulder to ease the ache. "We need to keep moving. I feel like we're too out in the open here."

Talek sighed before walking up to the Captain. "Look, I've been through the Madness and somehow I survived and came out the other side. I know you don't like me, and I destroyed your city, but—"

"But you want me to forget and forgive," she said with a cold glare.

"Please," Talek whispered. "I am finally reunited with the one I love. Please don't ruin that for me."

"Talek," Teagan muttered with affection in his voice.

Her gaze softened at that and she lowered her eyes. "Yes, I suppose you have."

For the first time, Colin wondered if the Captain had anyone in her life. She never mentioned anyone, but she never denied it either. In fact, whenever it was brought up, she usually got angry. He had never seen her grow compassionate like that before. Had she lost someone in the Garden when it fell? The thought made his heart ache. He wondered, and not for the first time, on how little he knew about the people he had worked with every day.

"Alright," the Captain stated, clearing her throat. "You and I will call a truce for now, but mostly because we're in a dangerous place here."

Talek nodded. "Agreed."

The Captain held out her bruised hand and Talek took it. Then she pulled him forward so he and Teagan both stumbled closer. "I will keep this truce for now, Talek, but I swear if you try to backstab me like you did before..."

Teagan stepped away, forcing her to let go. "That's enough," he said. "You two can work out your differences later, but neither of you are in any shape to be exchanging insults—Captain, please control yourself."

She huffed in response.

Teagan turned to Talek. "Do you think we'll get to a safe place tonight?"

"I think we're very close," he said. "The lake is just beyond that hill. We should at least have some shelter to use, though I'm not sure if we'll have much else."

"As long as there's a place to sleep, I don't care what it has. I don't need an inn; I just need to not be carried like I'm an invalid." Captain Briar growled.

"Would you prefer to walk then?" Teagan asked.

She sighed. "Let's just keep going."

Colin's arms felt better already, but the wind felt far colder when he wasn't carrying someone on his back. There was a flowery smell that came and went, and just knowing that there were plants out there that weren't Pello Pines made Colin unexpectedly happy. At least there were some places in the forest where normal plants grew.

As they peaked the hill, Colin had to wrap his arms around himself because a large gust of freezing wind blew past them, ruffling his fur and making his teeth chatter. He didn't know how the others could handle it, especially Captain Briar in her old rags. And he even had a built-in fur coat.

"Down there," Talek said. "There's the lake that I saw earlier." There was a giddiness in his voice as though he hadn't been entirely sure that the lake would actually be there. It reminded Colin that they were all still working with their powers, and they were still learning.

"Do you think the water is clean?" Captain Briar asked, a glimmer of desperation in her voice.

Colin glanced to her; she was arching her head, trying to get a better look at the lake. He noticed for the first time that her lips were dry and cracked. She had to have been out there all day if not longer.

"To be honest, I don't trust any water out here," Colin said. "Look at the Pello Pines trees. If they're this bad, there's no telling what's in the water."

"We're near the City of Aife," Teagan added. "It might be clean."

Colin glanced to him. "Yeah but that's been abandoned forever."

He rolled his eyes. "A long time, certainly, but not forever. I was there, remember? I think there was a well."

Talek led them down through the trees and Colin couldn't help but smile as he saw the moonlight reflected on the surface of the lake. Talek was just passing it by and so was Teagan with Captain Briar, but Colin couldn't help but stop and take a closer look.

The cold wind swept across the water and made little ripples which cut through the reflection of the moon on the surface. He breathed in the cold air and allowed a shiver to go through him. It was absolutely beautiful. He wished he could just sit by the lake and doze off by a night fire and listen to the lapping waters all night. He wished he had such beauty in the Garden growing up. He would have spent days just watching the water of the lake at night.

"Colin?"

He turned to see Talek standing there, a quizzical look on his face. "Are you alright?"

"Yeah," he muttered. "I guess I got distracted."

There was sympathy in his eyes, but his voice was urgent. "There is no time for that. We need to get inside before anything tries to attack us out here."

"Do you think they would come here?" Colin asked, not able to quite imagine the Pello Pines cutting through the soil to reach them.

"Do you think they wouldn't?"

Colin sighed. "Right, sorry."

Talek put a hand on his shoulder. "Don't worry, we should be safe here."

They walked back over to join the others near a large wall of hedges.

"This is a heck of a time to go sight-seeing," the Captain said with a smirk.

Teagan rolled his eyes. "I'm afraid the path inside is too narrow for me to carry you, Captain."

Her eyes went wide, "Wait, what?"

"If you're able to antagonize Talek *and* Colin, then I think you should be able to walk on your own." Teagan put her down on her feet. She was shaky and leaning heavily on him, but she was able to stand.

Colin couldn't suppress a chuckle. The Captain glared at him. "Colin, enough of that. Get over here and help me."

Falling back into his old training, he jogged over to help her. He offered to carry her again, but she shook her head. "No, just let me walk by you... please." She leaned heavily on him, but he didn't mind. Even getting a scrap of an apology from the Captain was more than he ever expected.

Teagan smiled. "See? Was it so terrible to be a little kind?"

She sighed, "I didn't miss your cheekiness, Teagan. Not at all."

GAINING TRUST

Shaleigh was awoken by Mawr's pleading voice, "Shaleigh, please wake up! Oh gosh, please!"

Her eyes shot open as she looked up at him. The first thing she noticed was that his glasses were rattling on his nose. If they were his old glasses, they would have fallen off. Her heartbeat sped up at the sight of his worry. Her hands shook as she pushed herself up to a sitting position, adrenaline pouring through her—"What's wrong, Mawr? What happened?"

"It's the others!" he cried, glancing over his shoulder and kneading his paws, digging his claws into the floor. That's when Shaleigh knew that it was serious. She didn't know who he was talking about, but Mawr would never intentionally damage the floor to his precious library.

She climbed to her feet, stumbling a little as her body recovered from the stiffness of sleeping on the floor, and hurried after him as he ran across the barren library toward the entrance. She glanced around but didn't see any sign of the Shadow Wolves. Had they left as soon as she had fallen asleep, or had something else gotten their attention? That made her worried.

Rushing down the library steps and around Mawr's pedestal, Shaleigh saw the Shadow Wolves at the far end of the path. Even from their distance she could see their aggressive stance. They were near the hedge wall close to the entrance.

Her first thought was a Pello Pine.

"What happened?" she asked again, hoping Mawr could explain.

"The Wolves are angry! I should have come to get you sooner, but I didn't know things would get so bad so fast."

She loved Mawr to death, but sometimes when he panicked, he had a hard time explaining things.

When she passed the second fountain, she finally could see that the wolves were in a semicircle formation around the entrance. Then she spotted what had them so agitated and understood why Mawr was so frightened.

There stood Teagan and Talek: both looked terrible, partially covered in dirt and grime. Both were unarmed and had clearly not known anyone was in the ruins any more than Shaleigh and Mawr had when they first arrived.

Teagan and the leader wolf were both talking at each other at the same time, each trying to drown the other out. The result was that the other wolves were on the offensive, snarling with their bright red eyes, looking ready to pounce.

"We mean you no harm!" Teagan snapped. "We didn't mean to disturb you!"

"I swear I had no idea there was anyone here," Talek said more to Teagan than to the wolves.

"You're both mad if you think we'll let Keriam's pet Faerie into our home!" The leader wolf roared. "You were both probably sent here to spy on us, weren't you? To feed us some of your nasty Scáil from your high and mighty Faerie city!"

Shaleigh had to stop this. Her friends were about to get ripped to pieces. She had worked so hard to gain the trust of the Shadow Wolves—stepping forward meant that trust might be broken. She clenched her fists, fully knowing that she could get caught in the crossfire but rushed forward anyway.

"Shaleigh!" Mawr squeaked at her from behind, but she didn't look back.

"Stop it!" she cried.

Teagan looked her with wide eyes. "Shaleigh, you're alive!"

Talek smiled at her, placing a hand to his chest. "We thought the Pello Pines had gotten you."

She gave them a quick smile before turning back to the Shadow Wolves. The leader cocked his head to the side while the others yipped in confusion.

"You know these Faeries?"

"Yes," she said. "They're my friends."

He snarled, looking at her then at the others. "Then you were part of this trick, too? I hadn't expected that, Human girl. Here I thought we could trust you."

"No, there is no trick! We're here to stop the Pello Pines from destroying the Garden and to get rid of Keriam."

The leader leaned his head down and snorted into the dirt. "You're telling me that the Faerie who willingly went into a pact with Keriam is now trying to kill him? With all the power that comes with it?" He glared at Talek. "He must be quite a fool indeed."

She shook her head. "It's complicated, but—"

"I too was an unwilling puppet," Talek muttered, drawing all of the wolves' gazes. "I didn't want to work for him, but he promised me that he could help me, and I was fool enough to believe him."

"He keeps us as his pets and executioners," the leader growled, baring his teeth. "We're nothing more than beasts to him."

"And I was nothing more than a tool." Talek added, staring intently at the wolf. "My love was killed at his hands, and I have sworn myself to avenge him."

Shaleigh glanced over to him, trying not to show her shock. Even Teagan looked surprised by his assertion. It wasn't wrong, but it wasn't completely right either. If anyone had a right to kill Keriam, it was Talek, but it wasn't like his love had stayed dead . . . He was standing right beside him.

Teagan reached over and took his hand and Talek lowered his gaze as he added, "I have not forgiven him for what he did to me or him. I will not let him go unpunished for his acts."

The leader watched him, sizing him up like a predator analyzing a fellow carnivore. Shaleigh wasn't sure if he was trying to decide if Talek was right, or if he and his small pack had a chance of killing them all.

"If you're having trouble trusting them," a woman's

voice said from the other side of the hedge entrance. "You're really not going to like me coming inside."

Instantly the demeanor of the wolves changed. They pushed their shoulders up and bared their fangs.

"Captain Briar," the leader snarled.

She came through the entrance, leaning heavily on the hedges; Teagan and Talek stepped aside for her, and Shaleigh saw Colin peek his head forward, looking terrified.

"Yes, it's me." The Captain grinned, seeming to relish the hatred aimed at her, but there was a desperation in her eyes too. "I knew you had to hate me more than a couple of Faeries. I'm glad to see you didn't disappoint me."

"Looks like they brought us some fresh food!" One wolf laughed. "Maybe she's a peace offering."

"Absolutely not!" Teagan scoffed. "We rescued her from certain death at Keriam's hands."

The leader approached her. When Shaleigh tried to step between them, the Captain put out a hand. "No, I've had this coming, Shaleigh. Let me handle it."

Shaleigh took a deep breath. If the others looked rough, the Captain looked half dead. She looked like she had been tortured. She was covered in cuts and bruises, and the rags she wore had bloodstains in places. She pressed her back up against one of the hedges as the leader came to her, growling deep in the back of his throat.

The Captain lifted her head, taking deep breaths as saliva dripped down the wolf's chin.

"You smell like you've slain my kind recently," he snarled.

"I had to," she snapped. "They were going to eat me. And if they had, the Pello Pines would have eaten them. Keriam didn't exactly tell them that part though, and they weren't smart enough to ask."

"You've killed our kind for years," he continued. "I've watched you gut my brothers, behead my sisters, and celebrate the slaying of both my parents."

She shook her head. "I'm sorry. I had no idea you were under Keriam's control. I was just doing my job."

The wolf snapped at her and she fell back, losing her footing and landing hard on the ground with a wince.

"Your job was to kill my kind?" he hissed. "Your job was to take glee in the murder of my family? How dare you claim it was your *job* to treat them like trash."

"I didn't realize they were being controlled! I didn't know they weren't beasts because that was all that they seemed to me! How was I supposed to know? How was I supposed to see that?"

The leader took a step back as the others closed in behind him. "My family," he whispered. "My family is dead because of you."

"No," Shaleigh whispered. "Your family is dead because of Keriam. He's the one who took you away from your home and left you in the Slumbering Forest. He's the one who had you attack the walls of the Garden every night. He's the one who really killed your family. Captain Briar could have died if she hadn't killed them, and so would many others."

"But they were my family!" The leader whimpered. "I

loved them." The other pack members hung their heads, one threw his head back and howled up into the black sky.

Shaleigh watched them with empathy. Keriam had ruined the lives of many, but he had murdered so many more on his quest for power. As much as she and her friends had lost, many had lost more, and it hurt her heart to know that.

The leader stiffened and turned back to the Captain. "Answer me this, oh Captain of the fallen Garden, why did you relish it? Why did you take such joy in the slaughter of my kind?"

Captain Briar hung her head, and there was no arrogance or pride in her face, only regret. "I didn't see them as anyone's kind. I saw them as beasts bent on devouring as many as they could. I saw them as a virus that needed to be wiped out." She held up a bruised and bloodied hand. "I'm sorry. I guess I've always taken my anger out on my enemies, but that only leads to more death, doesn't it?"

"We were all trained to do that," Colin muttered. "That's what you do as a soldier of the Garden."

The Captain shook her head. "It doesn't matter, Colin. The Garden is gone, and I can't use that as an excuse anymore."

The leader snorted. "Your kind are not the smartest I've known, but at least you do learn eventually."

For all the Captain's experience, for all her training, and all her ferocity and tactics, it did no good if she wasn't fighting the real enemy and Shaleigh understood that, she felt the same way when Keriam used her to destroy the Garden. Keriam had used her arrogance and desperation against her. She was a pawn just like everyone else was, and realizing it was sobering.

They had all been fooled by Keriam. The Captain had been taken in with her bloodlust and fear of Faeries, Teagan was too drunk on power to notice the bizarre appearance of the Shadow Wolves, Talek was an easy target due to his pining for Teagan, and Madam Cloom was so determined to stay at the top that she hadn't bothered to worry about some beasts in the forest. Colin merely did as he was told and tried not to think too much about what he was doing. The Shadow Wolves were promised the impossible and in exchange were given servitude. Shaleigh herself was promised the only thing she wanted at the time—to go home.

All of them had been abused and mistreated.

All of them were a means to an end in a chess match they didn't even realize they were part of.

Shaleigh felt an anger rising in her, an anger smoldering deep down that she hadn't felt before. It wasn't out of rage or fear, it was born out of the need for justice, and it was so hot that it made her eyes burn.

Beside her Mawr pushed his head into her hand. She turned to see him crouched down with his belly on the ground, nuzzling her hand for comfort. He didn't have to say a word for Shaleigh to know how he felt. He didn't want to see anyone killed any more than Shaleigh did, especially knowing that Keriam was still out there, not feeling the weight of his wrongs like the Captain did. They shouldn't have to suffer for his atrocities.

"Will you kill me then?" the Captain asked. "Will you add me to the other dead out in the woods?" Her eyes were wild as she took a deep breath. "If you do, all I ask is that you do it quick, because despite my bloodthirst, as you've called it, I always took them out quickly. I never let them suffer. Call me a monster for slaying them, but if they were killed by my blade, I did my best to minimize their suffering."

The leader looked to the others of his pack, meeting each of their gazes in turn. "If any of you wish to kill this Captain, you have my permission."

The Captain wrapped her hands around the branches of the bush.

"Shaleigh," Mawr whispered, and she wrapped an arm around his muzzle as he shut his eyes. Teagan and Talek came around to stand with them, and she met Talek's eyes with terror. What could they do to stop it? Could all of them together take on a pack of Shadow Wolves? The odds were too great that one of them would be hurt, or killed, and then what would happen to Keriam? Would he go on to destroy more lives?

"However, I do not think it is a wise decision. She was quite a force against our kind and perhaps she will be useful against the Magician as well." The leader stepped away from the Captain, allowing the other three wolves to approach her.

Colin tried to push his way forward to try to prevent them from getting near her, but the Captain held up a hand again. This time Shaleigh could see it was clearly trembling.

"No, don't do it, Colin. That's a direct order from your Captain."

Colin froze and balled his fists. "I didn't save you just to let you throw your life away!"

She gave a weary smile. "No, you saved me so I could choose what to do with it."

Colin sighed and turned away; Mawr whimpered into the ground.

Shaleigh felt Teagan's hand come to rest on her shoulder and glanced to him. "I can't let this happen. I can't just stand here and watch them kill her."

"If this is what she chooses, you should let her make that choice."

"Why? It's stupid!"

"No, she wants an honorable death that has meaning. A poor death would have been dying on the side of that tree that Colin saved her from: She feels useless and perhaps feels this is an appropriate end. You cannot take someone's death away from them if that is what they want."

Captain Briar closed her eyes as the wolves leaned in close. They weren't snarling and snapping at her like Shaleigh had expected. One of them snorted in her face before walking back to sit with its leader.

The Captain flinched and squinted her eyes open. "What?"

Another one leapt up on her stomach, knocking the wind out of her as she fell onto the ground, before turning around and leaving. It reminded Shaleigh of what a big dog might do more than a wolf.

The Captain stared after it with growing anger, gasping for breath. "What was that about?" She looked at the last one warily, with confusion. "What about you? Do you plan to take this seriously?"

It was the angry one from earlier. He was the one Shaleigh feared would actually kill the Captain. He gave a hissing laugh as he turned around, lifted a back leg, and peed on the Captain's leg before walking away.

"Really? Come on!" she cried, pushing herself to the side and shaking her leg. "I thought you planned to kill me, not urinate on me!"

"What do we look like, wild dogs?" The leader said through a deep laugh. "You clearly wished for us to kill you, to put an end to your humiliation, but this is the true punishment for you. And once you decide you actually have something to live for, you'll rise to greatness again." His eyes narrowed. "When you do, you best remember that all four of us spared your life this day, Captain."

She stared at him with open fury. "This is outrageous."

The leader laughed again. "You prove with your anger that this was the right decision. Now, if your friends truly like you, there's a lake out front to bathe in. You'll need that before you're permitted to enter our den."

With that, the Shadow Wolves trotted back to the library, yipping and laughing along the way almost like hyenas.

Shaleigh put a hand to her chest; her heart was still racing. She had prepared herself for a slaughter, not whatever had just happened. "I did not expect that."

Talek laughed. "I think we really don't know much about Shadow Wolves at all. I actually feel terrible that I've never gotten to know them, they have a first rate sense of humor."

The Captain slammed a fist into the ground, shaking with fury and Shaleigh stepped closer to her. "Do you want some help cleaning up? I don't mind."

The Captain just stared at her, before snapping, "No, I can make it myself."

"Are you sure?" Colin asked.

"Just be quiet and leave me be for a bit, Colin." She pulled herself up to her feet slowly. "Go bed down. I'll...I'll be back in a few minutes." With that, she limped her way out of the entrance and toward the lake.

"Should we be worried about the Pello Pines?" Colin asked, turning to Teagan and Talek. "I mean, it's not a long walk to the lake, but still."

"If you want to risk her wrath, then by all means." Teagan shook his head with a smile. "You're probably right, it's a good idea, but just be careful."

"Yes," Talek added, "her wrath almost competes with the danger of the Pello Pines."

"Here, I'll come with you," Shaleigh said. "I've fought one off by myself, I could do it again if I had to."

Colin's eyes got big. "By yourself? How did you do that? I would have been a goner if these two hadn't found me."

"I used my gift," she said with a smile, then turned to Mawr. "Can you take them to the library while I help with Captain Briar?

"I can do that," he said, before coming over to nuzzle her. "Just be careful, please! I don't want anything to happen to you. I've had enough terror for the day." Then he went over to rub on Colin and head-butted him in the stomach. Colin huffed but put an arm around Mawr to rub on his fur.

"I missed you too, buddy. I'm glad you're safe."

"I thought you were dead," Mawr squeaked. "I thought Shaleigh and I were the only ones left in the whole forest."

Colin scratched him under his chin. "You're not, okay? We're together. And remember what I said, as long as we're together, we can get through this."

Mawr blinked at him. "But we won't be together. You're going out to the lake to—"

"You know what I mean. We won't be long, I promise."

Clearly Mawr didn't fully believe his assurance, but he gave Colin a rough lick before turning to lead Teagan and Talek to the library.

Once they were out of sight, Colin turned to Shaleigh. "You ready to see how she's doing out there?"

She gave a long sigh. "Somebody has to check on her."

COLIN INSISTED on going first as they stepped through the gap in the hedges and out into the open. The wind was still cold but had thankfully died down from earlier when her teeth had been chattering; Shaleigh shivered a little. After all the outrage and discussion inside the hedge wall, it was strange stepping out to the silence of the forest. It was dark, but the starlight and crescent moon provided enough light in the clear path down to the lake.

Together they walked down toward the lake, looking for the Captain. Their footsteps sounded so loud in the quiet. Tall grasses along the edges of the path swayed in the wind and the crickets had even died down. There was a threatening electric energy to the air despite there being no clouds in the sky.

Shaleigh couldn't shake the feeling that they were noticed. She looked around at the trees in the distance. These trees weren't Pello Pines, but beyond them she knew the forest was full of them. "Stay close, Colin," she said, keeping her voice low.

Colin glanced to her, slowing as he looked around. "I don't hear any of them around. We should be safe here."

She shuddered. "I guess I'm just on high alert right now."

He gave a knowing smile. "It's okay, we all are."

As they neared the lake, she spotted the Captain who had made it down to a boulder near the lake, not too far from the bush where Shaleigh had once come onto shore. She was leaning her head and arm against it, staring down in the dirt--Shaleigh couldn't tell if she was exhausted from her trip down, or if she was crying.

"Captain?" Shaleigh whispered, feeling the need to keep her voice down out of respect.

The Captain jumped and turned toward them with fearful eyes. "What's wrong?" her hand dropped to where her sword used to be on her hip, but she had no weapon.

Colin put out his hands. "Nothing's wrong," he said. "We just wanted to help. You were pretty badly injured, and we were worried you would get attacked out here."

She gave a weak chuckle. "I'm pretty sure I would notice if a Pello Pine was sneaking up on me, but I appreciate your concern."

The Captain might notice out near the lake, since they

were so far from the tree line, but Shaleigh knew there was no way she would be able to escape. She had seen how fast the Pello Pines could move, and how slowly the Captain limped away earlier. Surely the Captain knew that too.

As Captain Briar turned back to the water, Shaleigh could tell her cheeks were wet—she had been crying. Shaleigh couldn't help but feel bad for the woman, brought so low when she had once been such a fierce and independent person. Someone who had her faults, her flaws, her prejudices, but had thought she was in the right. It had to be gut-wrenching to realize that she had truly been in the wrong.

Shaleigh understood that though. She had been there herself not too long ago.

Colin went to take one arm and Shaleigh took the other. Captain Briar looked at Shaleigh with such a pitiful expression. She didn't resist their help, but Shaleigh could tell it hurt her deeply to have to accept it.

Captain Briar sighed. "You two don't have to do that."

Colin smirked. "You know, we'd get a lot farther if you would quit complaining and let us help."

The Captain sighed again then nodded.

Together Shaleigh and Colin helped the Captain reach the edge of the lake, where they helped her sit down on the ground. Immediately the Captain sat back with her arms behind her and took deep breaths of the cold night air.

"You okay?" Shaleigh asked, squatting down beside her.

"How the hell did I get here?" she asked, her voice cracking. "How did I go from being a respected leader to this pathetic, beaten mess? Even the Shadow Wolves mock me."

Shaleigh glanced up to Colin–he looked both concerned and bewildered. How were they supposed to console her? There was a time when both of them would have been locked up in the dungeons for their actions, but here they were helping her wash off Shadow Wolf pee.

"Things change," Shaleigh whispered as she went over to cup some of the cool lake water in both hands. "The Garden doesn't exist anymore. I know I'm partly the cause for that, but I've come to realize that if it wasn't me, it would have been someone else. Madam Cloom had too many enemies, Talek was too determined, and each time they kidnapped someone from the Human World, they made a new enemy."

The Captain shook her head. "But the prophecy said—"

"Oh, come on, Captain!" Colin snapped, smacking the water and making Shaleigh jump. "We both know the prophecy was only put into place to give an excuse for some regular bloodshed. Master Cathal wasn't ever going to be reincarnated, and Madam Cloom wasn't ever going to give up her power. It was all a charade, a hoax, and you and I were just the gears in it all."

Shaleigh stared at him: Colin was looking down into the lake, his tail swishing back and forth behind him. She had never seen him so angry, and his outburst took her completely by surprise. Then again, she didn't know yet what all he had been through. He had mentioned nearly getting killed by a Pello Pine earlier.

Captain Briar shook her head, breaking the silence as she said, "I had no idea you were a skeptic, Colin."

"Sorry, Captain," he huffed. "I guess I've had a lot of time to think about my job as a kidnapper. I'm pretty disgusted with my part in all this."

"Kidnapping is a bit of an extreme take on it, but I see your perspective."

Shaleigh shot her a glare. "An extreme take? I was kidnapped from my home. I didn't ask to be part of any of this, but here I am trying to fix my mistakes." She inhaled sharply. "I got the chance to go home before, did you know that? I was given the opportunity to choose to leave all of this mess behind and go back to my family and my friend. I haven't even gotten the chance to graduate from high school yet!"

Colin stared at her with regret; her words had hurt him. She let the water drop from her hands and clasped her knees, staring at the mosses around her feet. She couldn't look at the Captain's face right now. If she did, she would do something she would regret. There was a time in her life where she would just do what she wanted and not care about the consequences, like the time she threw her drink in Red Dawkins's face.

She was a different person now, and even though she couldn't always control her anger, she could control who it impacted. She was out here to help the Captain to deal with her wounded pride, not to let her own demons out. She squeezed her eyes shut against tears, taking deep breaths to calm down.

Shaleigh felt Colin's furry hand on the back of hers and opened her eyes to look up at him. He was seated across from her and he gave her a sad smile when their eyes met. "It's okay to be angry," he said. "You have every right to be."

"I'm sorry. I thought I would be over it by now. I thought I would have gotten this all under control, but apparently not." She wiped her eyes with the back of her hand and looked up at the dark trees around them. "This isn't at all where I thought we would be. I thought once we were given these gifts, we would be able to come here and really make a difference. I thought we would come to this forest and somehow prevent the Pello Pines from hurting people."

She looked down at her palms, the tiny little scales were hardly noticeable in the dim moonlight. "We have no idea where we go from here…I always thought that going home would happen eventually regardless of who I helped along the way, but now I wonder if I'll ever get the chance to go home again."

She wiped at her cheeks again, avoiding his gaze.

"I'm sorry," Colin muttered. "I shouldn't have said anything about the kidnapping."

"No, my head's just been in so many places lately, that I've been afraid to think too hard about things. I have to though, don't I? If I never get to go home, I have to accept that. I don't have a choice."

"Who told you they could send you home?" Captain Briar asked. There was no anger or sorrow in her voice any longer, only the weighted voice of authority, and Shaleigh turned to her. Her gaze was focused, intense, and Shaleigh wondered if she had said something that upset her.

"The Magicians at the Sanctuary," she answered. "They said they could send me home."

The Captain smiled. "That's easy then. Once we tame the Slumbering Forest and get rid of Keriam, my troops can escort you to the Sanctuary where you can go home again."

"That's assuming we can do both of those things. Besides I don't think they want me back there. I kind of burned down their home."

"Keriam did that," Colin corrected, dumping water over the Captain's legs. "You were trying to save people. Get the facts right."

"You mentioned you had gifts, what exactly are those?" The Captain's question left no room for uncertainty.

Shaleigh almost answered, but then caught herself and looked at Colin. Should they tell the Captain what they were given? Was it a good idea? None of them had discussed how they were going to explain themselves to others. She should have asked back at the campsite the night before.

Colin shrugged, just as uncertain as she was.

The Captain looked between them both, a smile pulling at her lips. "Is it a secret?"

"No, not exactly," Shaleigh muttered, letting out a deep sigh. "I guess it's okay to tell you. We didn't say we *couldn't* tell anyone about them."

"I think we're still getting used to having them," Colin added.

So Shaleigh gave the Captain an abridged version of the events on the Peak of Gwern. She told her about their trip up there, Talek's Madness, the dragon's ferocity but also her surprising understanding. Tanwen, too, was against the deeds that Keriam was taking, and when Shaleigh mentioned that Keriam was immortal, Captain Briar's dark eyes went wide.

"He's *immortal?*"

Shaleigh nodded. "That's why she gave us these gifts." She held her palms out so that the Captain could feel the scales on her skin. "She wants us to take him down because the magic he's wielding isn't permitted in her land."

The Captain dragged her thumbs over Shaleigh's palms in the opposite direction of the scales. "I feel them," she muttered in awe.

Shaleigh proceeded then to explain each of their gifts, as best as she could—words didn't always work well when describing feelings. Colin also explained about the traveling difficulties they struggled with without Shaleigh and Mawr being present.

"So, you have to work together to have the strongest outcome," the Captain summarized. She had a hand to her chin, Shaleigh could see the gears in her head working.

"We have all these abilities, but to be honest, we don't know what to do with them. We barely figured out how to travel here." It was actually such a relief to tell someone else about these problems, especially someone who hadn't been with them at the time. Shaleigh just had to hope that pulling in a new perspective would help them figure out how to handle these abilities.

"What you need is an advisor," the Captain said with a gleam in her eye. "Fortunately for you, I have years of tactical and strategic experience at Madam Cloom's side.

My first thought is that you all are thinking too small. You need to think bigger that just darting through places... that's the most basic use for such a wonderful magic."

"Hey, it was the first thing that came to mind, okay?" Colin shrugged. "I think we're all in shock that we can even do these things."

The Captain waved his concern aside. "Yes, I understand that. That's to be expected with the stress you all have been under. You haven't had the ability to recover and wrap your minds around the full potential that you have." She gave an infectious laugh

Shaleigh gave a worried glance to Colin. She worried that maybe it hadn't been a good idea to tell the Captain everything without consulting with Teagan and Talek, but then again, they clearly needed help. For all of the Captain's shortcomings, she was indeed an excellent fighter... when she wasn't distracted by her own prejudices and hatred.

"Do you two realize how lucky you are that I'm here? I could have been killed so many times in the last few days, and yet, fate has brought me to you all. I thought I had been abandoned completely, that this entire journey was a penance for my actions over the years, but now I see I merely have a new purpose. My body may need to recover, but you all need vision. You need an advisor, a strategist," she smirked, "maybe even a coach at your side."

Shaleigh pushed up to her feet. "I'm glad you're feeling better, *coach*," she started, "but can we discuss this indoors? The wind is starting to pick up again."

The Captain blinked, seeming to realize that it was getting colder and that her feet were now soaked from getting washed; she gave a little shiver. "Yes, good point. Let's head indoors."

Together Shaleigh and Colin each wrapped an arm around her and helped her back toward the hedges around Aife.

"I sure hope the others are okay with us telling you about all this," Colin muttered. "Master Teagan is going to have my head otherwise."

The Captain shrugged. "If he does, he's going to have a hard time handling the forest or Keriam. He needs you. You're probably in the best position of your life, to be honest."

Shaleigh appreciated the Captain's enthusiasm, but she hoped that in their attempts to help her that they hadn't unintentionally given her false hope. Captain Briar might think that all they needed was vision and strategy, but Shaleigh was pretty certain there was more to it, especially after learning about their mishaps after she and Mawr weren't around.

They still had a lot of work ahead of them.

WHEN THEY GOT BACK to the library, Shaleigh saw that the Shadow Wolves had already bedded down in their corner. Teagan and Talek had found a spot near where she had slept earlier, and there was a firepit that had been setup in the middle of the room beneath the hole in the ceiling. Pieces of bookshelves were burning, making a nice warm fire, and Shaleigh couldn't help but smile as they approached it.

"It's so warm!" she cried happily, holding her hands up and enjoying the feeling of her skin slightly baking.

"This is much better," the Captain agreed.

Mawr walked toward them, looking ashamed. "Shaleigh, I saw the damage I did to the floor earlier. I'm so sorry! I didn't even realize I had done it."

It took a moment for Shaleigh to realize what he was talking about. Then she remembered him kneading his claws on the floor when he woke her earlier. "Mawr, it's fine. We have a fire going right here--this floor has seen better days."

He came over to her side. "Do you all need help?"

"I'm fine," the Captain grunted before sitting down on the ground near the fire. It was awkward with both Colin and Shaleigh helping her, but clearly it was still rough on the Captain. She was struggling more than she let on.

"Do you need any more help?" Shaleigh asked.

"No. I'll just sleep here by the fire tonight, that works well for me."

Shaleigh nodded then went to her own bed, yawning as she got near it. She passed a makeshift bed for the Colin; it looked like Teagan and Talek had found some old stashes of clothing throughout the city. Teagan had an embroidered green and blue blanket of a forest around his shoulders that reminded her of the quilt that she had seen in her bed chamber back in the Garden. It had different colors and it wasn't nearly as detailed, but it was still unsettling.

She pulled up her own blanket as she laid down, thinking back to that night in the High Castle. She remembered Teagan's questioning look that maybe she was a reincarnation of Master Cathal. Things had changed so much then.

Mawr came around behind her, laying down close so she could feel his purrs rumble through the floor.

"You always help me sleep better," she said with a smile.

"I'm glad," Mawr whispered. "I'll be here all night for you."

Teagan and Talek both went to the Captain and after a brief whispered discussion helped her to her own makeshift bed. Now that Shaleigh was watching, it was clear that the Captain was in pain. She didn't like to show it, but Shaleigh noticed the way she winced when she laid down.

Colin went over to them, shaking his arms out. "Can I do anything to help?

"It's just bruising," the Captain grunted. "I'll be fine, just let me rest."

Talek snickered and shook his head in disbelief, returning to his own bed. Teagan nodded before he and Colin walked over to Shaleigh. Teagan furrowed his brows and steepled his hands together. "She looks even worse than before. Colin, you could have carried her on your back like earlier."

"I'm sorry, boss, my arms are killing me. I couldn't have picked her up even if I wanted to." Colin rubbed at his arms, clearly upset that he had let him down. She couldn't let that stand.

"You know you could have come and helped us, too," Shaleigh pointed out. "You carried me through those tree-tops, you could have carried her easily."

Teagan huffed and Shaleigh knew she hit a nerve. He and the Captain had never seen eye to eye, and she wondered if that was going to be an issue if Captain Briar came up with a good strategy. Would they butt heads still even after so much had happened? Surely, they could put their pride aside to take down a shared enemy.

Colin sighed and headed over to his own bed.

Teagan stiffened and turned toward him. "I didn't say you could leave."

"I didn't ask, boss," Colin muttered. "Goodnight."

Shaleigh waited a moment, seeing the way Teagan deflated, hurt. "He doesn't work for you any longer. Nobody does, remember?"

"I know, I just..." He gave a weary sigh. "I don't know. At times it feels like hardly any time has passed at all, and at other times it feels like years." He put a hand to his head. "Sometimes I feel like I should be the High Faerie again, and then I wonder if perhaps you and I are still stuck in the Masked King's realm." He gave a nervous laugh. "Then again, I wonder if I am dead and this is a sort of purgatory."

"You've been through a lot," she said, nodding in understanding. She would probably never forget his empty eyes staring out over the fire light when he was a walking corpse. A shudder went through her at the memory. "We all have. All of those things did happen, but that's not who you are now. That's not where we are either. We all need to work together, not as a boss or a competitor, but as a team. That's the only way we're going to get out of this alive."

His gaze fell. "Death was... horrific." He swallowed and

she could see the pure terror pass over his gaze. As bad as the experience had been for her, she couldn't imagine what it had been like for him. "I don't want that to happen to any of you. As we go out to face Keriam again, or those blasted Pello Pines, I worry every time that I will lose one of you. I just don't know if I can stand it knowing now what it feels like."

"You can't control what happens. We're all here because we want to fix all of this." She pulled her blanket up to her chin to fight off the chill. Mawr shifted closer behind her. "You don't control life and death, Teagan."

"No, but sometimes I wish I did." He gave her a bitter-sweet smile, "Goodnight, Shaleigh. Thank you for helping me keep my head. I don't know what I would do without you."

"You'd get by fine without me," she said with a smile even though her eyes went misty at the thought.

He turned toward Talek's bed, and Shaleigh felt the words come suddenly, afraid she might not get the chance to say them again if she didn't say it now. "I love you guys."

Teagan glanced back to her.

"I love all of you. You're like a family to me, and I never really had a family before."

"I'm afraid you have quite a dysfunctional family."

Shaleigh couldn't help but laugh.

SHALEIGH AWOKE to her stomach growling and the scent of seared fish in the air. She had to work to open her eyes, and winced at the brilliant sunlight that streamed in through the open windows. Through narrowed eyes, she noticed that the window frames were carved into the stone, and in the morning light she could see details she hadn't noticed at night: there were deep spirals of ivy interwoven with each window. Actual ivy had spilled in through the windows and wavered in the breeze. Shaleigh smiled as a ladybug crawled along one of the vines, bouncing in the breeze.

Ladybugs were supposed to be good luck--Shaleigh couldn't remember where she had heard that before, maybe something her father had said once, but it felt true. She felt optimistic for the first time in a while. She listened to the low murmurs of Teagan, Colin, Mawr, and one of the Shadow Wolves, and felt strangely content. Maybe it was the sleep, maybe it was knowing that so many of her friends were nearby, maybe it was spending the evening in a building for once. Either way, she couldn't refuse it.

The blanket she had been given was thicker than what she had used to sleep on before, and she cocooned herself underneath it, watching the ladybug crawl along the ivy, following the spiral. She wished for such a simple existence. She wished all she had to worry about was what stem to walk on next. Instead she knew the path ahead would be difficult; there was still so much to do.

"Are you awake?"

She turned to see Talek crouch down beside her. "Mostly," she said with a yawn.

"I thought you would like some food." He handed over

a slab of wood with a fish still sizzling on top. He also put down a clay cup of water.

Normally she would never have wanted to eat fish first thing in the morning, but she was so hungry it didn't matter. "Thank you!" She sat up and picked up the water first. Her mouth and throat had been dry during the night, but she hadn't really thought about how little she drank the day before. Her lips were parched, and the water was warm but refreshing.

Talek said, "I know it's early yet, but there was talk of putting together plans. I thought you needed to be part of that."

She downed the entire cup of water and sighed. "Yeah, thank you, I wouldn't want to sleep through that." She started picking at her fish as Talek went to fetch her more water without her even asking. He soon returned with a full bucket from the well and a freshly filled cup.

She took another long drink, watching as Talek sat down in front of her with his legs crisscrossed. When he put his hands on his knees, she arched her eyebrows at him. "Uh oh, what did I do?"

He smiled. "Aren't you the guilty one?"

"I just know that move. It reminds me of Teagan. He gets that same look in his eyes when he's about to break some bad news. I'm surprised at how alike you two are."

He blushed a little and lowered his gaze. "We lived together for centuries, it's impossible not to pick up on a partner's habits."

"Fair enough," she said. "So, what am I in trouble for?"

He grinned and shook his head. "You're too perceptive

for your own good." He cleared his throat, continuing, "I heard you told the Captain about the gifts from Tanwen?"

She sighed. "There it is."

"I don't mean to offend, but she mentioned it with such zeal earlier, I was concerned." He put a hand to his chin. "Colin said it was your idea, so I thought I'd ask why you decided to share."

Shaleigh gaped at him. "He did not! That little stinker threw me under the bus."

He squinted at her. "Under the bus...?"

She shook her head and took her last bite of fish. "We both decided to tell her. Well, we didn't really decide, it just sort of happened." Talek stared at her without a word, so she continued, "She appreciated it. I think she wanted a reason to feel useful again. So really it didn't just help us, it helped her, too."

Talek laughed, slipping a hand over his mouth. "I'm sorry, I can't keep this up. I just wanted to see how you would react!" He giggled again and Shaleigh threw her blanket at him.

"You little weasel!" She laughed. "Here I thought you wanted to be nice and get me food!"

"I did! I just wanted to play a bit of a joke as well." He gave her a sly smile as picked up the bucket and empty dishes.

"I'm going to have to watch you. You're worse than Teagan."

"I'll take that as a complement." He gave a short bow. "Speaking of, he found an outfit for you in some old crates. I have no idea how warm it will be, but it has to be better than the rags you're wearing."

Before she could retort, he walked off toward the center of the library where the fire was still going, and several Shadow Wolves were munching on plates of their own fish.

She noticed the pile of clothes beside her, wondering when Talek had left that for her. How had she missed him carrying it? Looking down at herself, she grimaced. Her own dress was frail and grimy from rolling around in the mud. There were a few places where it had been singed at the Peak of Gwern, too.

She began to sort through the clothes; Teagan had found her a long-sleeved linen dress, a wool dress, a leather coat, and some linen pants. She picked up the pants and got to her feet, checking the length. They were clearly for a man, but she didn't care. She was just happy to have pants again, even if she did wear them under the dress. Rubbing the fabric between her fingers, she marveled at the texture. They looked far too new. The style was definitely old-fashioned though, not like anything she had seen worn in the Garden.

She went into the corner, far away from onlookers, turned her back to everyone and quickly changed, leaving her old, grimy dress on the floor. The clothes felt like they were new, not even worn, and the detail was incredible. The same ivy design work she had seen on the window frames was reflected on the pants and the dresses. These were clearly made in Aife, but she had no idea how they survived for so long untouched.

The linen dress went on first, she knew that from years of studying the fairy artwork her father collected. They always wore underclothes. She pulled on the wool dress next, having to flatten out the bunching before getting it to fit properly. The pants were thin and too long for her, but that didn't matter. She folded up the bottoms into cuffs and then slipped on her sandals again. She felt so much warmer and more comfortable.

Then there was the coat. It was brown leather, with more ivy designs etched on the front, around the arms, and down the back. It was gorgeous and not something Shaleigh would ever choose for herself. The inside was lined with a dark red fur that was definitely real. She wasn't sure what kind of animal it came from, but it was beautiful. She put it on, thrilled to discover that it fit. Trust Teagan to find the only secret clothes stash left in the ruins of Aife. He probably tore several buildings apart looking for something decent to wear.

She went to join the others near the fire, beneath the hole in the dome overhead. Hidden in the little alcoves high above, she could hear birds chattering. She could even spot a few tiny nests tucked away in the corners. Aife, it seemed, hadn't been completely abandoned.

As she approached, Shaleigh noticed that Captain Briar was on her feet and had a walking stick that someone must have found for her that she was using as a cane. She leaned heavily on it, but Shaleigh was happy to see she was standing. She would never admit it to the Captain, but she had been worried about her last night. Between the confrontation with the Pello Pines and the whole embarrassment with the Shadow Wolves, Shaleigh hadn't been sure if she would be up at all today. Thankfully she was, and it looked like Teagan had found a warm dress for her, too: It was strange to see her in anything that wasn't armor.

Shaleigh saw that Teagan and Talek had coats similar to the one she wore--leather engraved with ivy and lined with fur. Talek's even had a fur collar. Colin had also gotten new clothes; he wore a fur lined vest.

"Look who's awake!" Colin grinned, sipping from his own clay cup.

Shaleigh gave Colin a smile before turning to Teagan, "Where did you find these clothes? They're gorgeous! I know you didn't go by the Garden to get them."

He smiled. "I'm glad you like them. Based on Mawr's account, I assumed there had to be something useful left since the final battle was so sudden. Fortunately, the tailor who made them had hidden them and many others in a protected chest. I'm sure they thought their works would be safe after the battle...though they likely never expected them to last quite this long."

Colin mused, "I wonder what other hidden treasures are around this place."

Teagan clicked his tongue. "I don't think it would be wise to get carried away. We're encroaching here as it is." He turned to Shaleigh with a smile. "I told Talek not to give you trouble, but it seems he has little restraint. We'll have to work on that."

Talek laughed, standing on the other side of the fire. "You say that like you're my tutor and not my boyfriend."

"Considering your trust in strangers, I'd say you definitely need a proper tutor."

Shaleigh couldn't suppress a grin as she held up her

hands. "Alright you two, calm down. I'm glad to see every-one's in high spirits at least."

Colin scooped up another cup of water from the bucket. "Hey, we lived, I think that gives us reason to celebrate."

There was a clatter behind her, and she turned to see that Mawr had brought more kindling in. She recognized them as pieces of the bookshelves from the corner–that had to be difficult for him.

"I wish we could just stay here," he muttered. "I know we can't, but I wish we could. I forgot how nice it was to look at my library."

Shaleigh went over to put a hand on his shoulder. "Maybe after all this is done, we can come back again to visit."

He blinked at her, his brows furrowing. "No, I think it would be far too dangerous."

She kissed the stone fur of his cheek. "If we can do it safely, then I promise, we'll visit again." She felt a tight-ening in her stomach at her words and wondered if they would be able to visit. Was she giving her friend false hope? She didn't want to mislead him.

Teagan gestured to Shaleigh's clothes, commenting, "I'm glad you like those. I was told that you nearly froze to death on your trip here." He smirked and Shaleigh glanced to Mawr who gave a sheepish grin.

"I told them. I didn't mean to, but it just kind of came out."

"It's okay, I said things too without thinking yesterday. It's nice to be warm, I was afraid—"

She was cut short by a loud smack and turned to see

Captain Briar slam her walking stick into the ground again.

"We were discussing strategy," the Captain snapped, and the convivial mood vanished. Clearly, she wasn't in the mood for morning pleasantries. "I was told of your gifts last night. They were given to you by the dragon, Tanwen. Based on what I know of each of your abilities, I think we should be able to take care of the Pello Pines relatively easily. Based on Teagan's story," she aimed her walking stick in his direction, "it sounds like we should be able to frighten them. But I'm still learning." She turned to Shaleigh, "I need to know what you experienced out there. What have you learned of our enemies? You and Mawr had your own experiences, but he didn't mention that he ran into any trees."

Shaleigh blinked at her, surprised by her sudden demand for information.

"If I ran into any Pello Pines, I didn't see them," Mawr said, hanging his head.

Shaleigh gave him a pained glance. "No, that's a good thing." She turned back to the Captain and took a deep breath.

It was strange to be addressed as an equal by the Captain when just a few days ago the woman had been talking down to her and acting like she wasn't fit to lead. Here in this abandoned library that felt almost like an old church, Shaleigh felt the weight of that responsibility heavy on her shoulders. It was strange how she used to want that respect, but now she understood that it came with the price of potential failure.

She crossed her arms, listening to the birds chatter up

above. Mawr stayed at her side, leaning over to lick her arm in support as she thought back to her fight with the Pello Pine. She remembered how terrified she had been: It was surprisingly fast. It reached her so quickly, and dug its barbs into her skin, and then when she got free and tried to escape again, it tried to slam her into the ground.

"I think they first try to drain a victim, and when that doesn't work, they try to smash them." Mawr whimper at her side and she put a hand on his mane. "I'm sorry, I know this is difficult. Do you want to step outside for a bit?"

"No, it's okay," he said looking to her. "I'm braver when you're with me."

The Captain cleared her throat. "Alright, so we might assume that their general strategy is to bleed their victim first, then if that doesn't work, they resort to their strength and their height. I don't think anyone else has gotten to that second tactic yet. Anything else?"

Shaleigh turned her gaze up to the rafters, to the flapping of wings and the chirping of birds. She pulled at her memory. Something else seemed important, but she couldn't quite put words to it.

"Their bark is very fragile," Mawr muttered.

Captain Briar narrowed her eyes. "I thought you didn't see any others."

He shuffled in place, and Shaleigh stroked his mane to help with his nerves. "Not yesterday," he whispered. "But I saw a bunch of them a long time ago."

Talek lowered his eyes. "I can't even imagine what that must have been like."

"You know you don't have to talk about it," Colin said,

putting down his cup. "If you don't want to talk about it, we all get it."

Mawr took a deep breath. "No, I need to. If we want to fight them, you need to know." He shuffled again and pranced in place, but Shaleigh noted he was careful not to pull out his claws and tear up the floor like he had the night before.

Nobody said a word. Everyone gave him the space to talk.

"I remember that swords were used on them, but it was difficult to make a complete circle around their trunk. That's what they had to do to kill them. But they had to get really close. Hardly anybody could, and even if some did, they usually couldn't do it for long without getting caught by one of their vines."

Shaleigh nodded, "Their bark is really thin; I remember that now. I was able to hurt one with my palms. It was trying to drop me on the ground to kill me, but I stopped it."

"They bleed too," Colin said, his tail swishing behind him. "I clawed one up, and that's why it was so angry with me. I didn't even think to make a full ring around its trunk. That does makes perfect sense; they are trees still after all."

Mawr nodded. "They knew how to kill them, they just couldn't. And there were so many." He lowered his head. "I'm sorry, I think that's all I can talk about for now."

"Thank you," Shaleigh said, hugging him tight around his neck. "You're always such a great help, you know that?"

"I want to be," he whispered. "I try to be, but some-times it's just too much."

"I completely understand." She went around and readjusted his silver spectacles on his ears. "There, is that better?"

He nodded and licked at her hand.

"So, we know that they try to feed first, which is in many ways their downfall—and they can't feed from Teagan or Mawr. They have to get close to us in order to attack us. That's good. That means that if they try to get close, we can hurt them. It just doesn't help the group as a whole. We need to have a plan to truly make them terrified of coming after us, of coming to the Garden. And I think the best bet is that little trick that all of you do together."

Colin gave a nervous laugh. "You mean you want us to travel around a bunch? I don't really see how that's intimidating."

She glared at him. "Yes, but instead you make a show to the Pello Pines. You demonstrate your power and prevent them from wanting to attack you again." She shrugged. "The only difference is instead of traveling quickly, you kill several of them quickly as an example."

Colin's eyes were wide. "Oh, is that all?"

Mawr shook his head. "I don't know about that. I don't like killing."

Teagan stepped forward with a stern gaze, "Yes, but if they're trying to kill you or your friends, that might be the only option. I've seen how powerful a demonstration like that can be. It's a good idea, but I worry that it will only permit a brief window. What's to keep them from attacking again and again?"

Captain Briar turned the walking stick in her hands,

pulling at the loose bark and removing the final dried up leaves from the shaft. "When I was a child, my family's kingdom used to be where the Pasture is today. All of that land used to be ours before a Faerie burned it to the ground." She shot a cold glance toward Teagan and Talek.

"Keep your accusations," Talek huffed. "We weren't the ones to destroy your homeland. If you want us to entertain your ideas, you'd be wise to keep your biases to yourself."

The Captain sighed. "You're right, I suppose." She cleared her throat again and gripped the walking stick harder. "My parents had found a way to sate the needs of the Pello Pines, to keep them from venturing into Briar Kingdom." She paused. "We used to feed them."

"You fed them?" Shaleigh asked, putting a hand to her throat at the imagery that came to mind. "You fed them people? Surely not."

Captain Briar shook her head. "No, animals. I remember helping to carry a cluster of rabbits over once. Sometimes there were dogs, other times cats. I was too young to be permitted to watch, but I wanted to."

Shaleigh swallowed down the lump in her throat. "That sounds horrible."

Teagan snorted in disgust. "Yes, and it could have encouraged them to multiply...which is likely why this forest is so enormous now. It likely helped to keep Briar Kingdom safe, but it could also have contributed to Aife's destruction."

The Captain frowned. "I hadn't considered that."

Shaleigh took a deep breath and shook out her arms, trying to rid herself of the image of a whole city sacrificing hordes of innocent animals to this gruesome forest. "Let's get back to the first plan. Assuming that one show of power isn't enough, we'll need to perform it often, I guess. I'm pretty sure we can do that without sending animals in to be slaughtered."

"Yeah, but we're still killing a bunch of Pello Pines, is that really better?" Colin asked.

The Captain snarled, "Killing them is probably the only way to get their attention. Besides, that idea is not viable long-term."

"Why is that?" Shaleigh pressed. "We just keep doing it every week or month or year or whatever. That's not a problem."

Captain Briar stood up straighter. "Well first of all, *Chosen One...*"

Shaleigh flinched.

"You are heading back home after all of this. You don't intend to stay here. So, what happens then? You go back to your boring little life and the people of the Garden get slaughtered? You once again cause the destruction of an entire city?" She smirked. "And they call me bloodthirsty."

"That's enough!" Teagan snapped. "How dare you try to guilt her into doing something she doesn't want to do. She didn't want to be here, and she shouldn't have to mold her life around our problems. We can't keep blaming Humans for everything that's wrong in this land."

"All I'm saying is that she put the entire population of the Garden at risk before, what's to say she doesn't do it again? Everywhere she goes, trouble follows, so what's to say this won't be any different?"

Colin shook his head, "I can't believe you're saying this. She helped you last night! She stood up for you!"

The Captain crossed her arms, "I'm merely stating the facts."

Shaleigh stepped forward, strangely calm and focused which was bizarre. Usually she would be boiling with rage when getting pulled into a fight, but for some reason she could clearly see what the problem was here, and it wasn't her. "I think you're jumping to conclusions, Captain, and I think you're not in the right frame of mind to be a strategist or an advisor here."

"What did you say?" Captain Briar growled.

"You don't know how this is going to work. You have no idea how the Pello Pines will even react. I'm sure they loved getting rabbit dinner occasionally from your kingdom, but their attitude might have changed since then; they've been asleep for centuries. Some of them still haven't escaped from the Daegonrúsc, and I don't know how many of them will survive. We've faced a handful or two of them as a group, but there are many more out there that haven't moved.

"It's been what, a week now, and they still aren't free? Can they survive that long without food? There's no telling. I say we do what we can to intimidate them away from the Garden. I'll admit, that's a good idea, but we need to keep our sights on the real threat. It isn't Teagan or Talek, and it isn't me, it's Keriam. He's the one behind all of this. He's the one who left you for dead."

The Captain trembled for a moment, holding onto the walking stick to keep her balance. "I realize that," she said through clenched teeth as her eyes filled with tears. "I know all of that."

Shaleigh stepped closer to her. "Then what's the problem? What are you afraid of here that you're throwing anger around at all of us like we're the enemy?"

The Captain lowered her gaze and a tear slipped down her cheek.

"It's okay," Shaleigh pressed, stepping close enough to put a hand on the Captain's. "You can talk to us. Please. What did he do to you?"

She let out a shuddering breath, and her face scrunched up with worry. More tears fell before she put a hand on top of Shaleigh's. "He wanted me dead, but he still has Geneva."

"Madam Cloom?" Colin asked, his voice hollow.

She nodded. "Keriam carved her a new mouth."

Shaleigh felt a shudder go through her at the memory of Madam Cloom losing her mouth when Talek entered the throne room . . .

Captain Briar looked up to the dome above their heads. "She was so weak. She hadn't eaten or drunk anything for days. Then he strolled in like he knew we were there the entire time. He has followers now, people who work for him, including the minotaurs."

"Not Graddic." Teagan insisted. "He can't be under his control. He would never—"

The Captain shook her head, interrupting, "Keriam carved Geneva a mouth again. It was... horrific. She told me to run, but I wasn't fast enough—the minotaurs got hold of me. I have no idea if Graddic is on her side or not, but Keriam does have several minotaurs. They're known for guarding him and patrolling with the Shadow Wolves." She met Shaleigh's gaze, her eyes red and tired. "Keriam had her taken away. Shaleigh, she couldn't even sit up on her own. I barely survived the beating they gave me. I don't know what they're going to do to her."

Shaleigh pulled her into a hug, something she never thought she would do, but the Captain needed comfort, even if she fought it the entire time.

After only a short moment, the Captain pulled away and wiped at her eyes. "I'm sorry. You all are right; I spoke out of place." She swallowed back more tears.

"I'm so sorry," Talek said, putting a hand to his mouth. "I'm so very sorry for everything."

Shaleigh turned and looked at all of them. "No, we can't think like that. Remember, we're not at fault–Keriam is. He made promises that he never intended to keep. We've been played by him for far too long." She took a deep breath. "Talek, you aren't responsible for Madam Cloom. Keriam pushed you to that. The same goes for you, Captain."

The Captain gave a short nod, keeping her eyes downcast. Talek pursed his lips and crossed his arms. Teagan stepped over to put an arm around him. Colin had a hand over his mouth, clearly horrified, and Mawr had his head lowered. As terrible as Madam Cloom was, the imagery conjured by the Captain's words haunted all of them. In unspoken words they all agreed that she didn't deserve that.

"We're all in this together. We're all fighting together. We need to focus on the real enemy here, not us, but Keriam."

The Captain cleared her throat and stood up a little straighter. "Unfortunately, I have no idea how to even start. Every strategy that Madam Cloom and I came up with failed. Every approach we took he somehow knew. I don't think he can't read thoughts, but it certainly felt like it sometimes."

Teagan nodded. "Captain, you have made a clever premise of starting with analyzing our enemy, like with the Pello Pines, so why don't we do that with Keriam? You may have been thwarted by him while undercover in his city, but fortunately Talek knows him better than any of us. Perhaps you can shed some light on him, love?" He gave Talek a squeeze, adding, "If you feel up for it."

Talek gave a warm smile, but before he could say anything, a gruff voice echoed through the chamber–"He's not the only one."

Shaleigh turned to see the Shadow Wolf leader sprawled out against the wall. She hadn't even noticed he was there. He got to his feet, gave a toothy yawn and trotted over. "We know his faults, we know his pride, and we know his allies. We've been with him for a long time."

Talek smiled bitterly at that. "Longer than even I?"

"Aye," the leader said. "Longer. I don't think you were there when he begged for immortality, were you?"

"You were there for that?" Colin blinked. "I can't believe he was stupid enough to bring anyone with him for that!"

The leader gave a rough laugh. "You underestimate his pride. I wager it'll be his ultimate downfall if fate is kind. He wanted to show off, even if we were an unwilling audience."

Talek narrowed his eyes. "It was in the land of Ciar, wasn't it? With the Dragon of Darkness?"

"So, you do know where he got it. I'm impressed, but I guess he spoke with you at length." When Talek didn't respond, the Shadow Wolf continued, "It was indeed in Ciar, my homeland in fact. I was scared; my pack was terrified. I could smell their fear even under the control of that blasted Scáil leaf.

"Keriam for all his supposed intelligence was too stupid to be scared. Some King had told him the dragon could grant him anything he wanted, and he believed it. He thought that Bāhv, the Dragon of Darkness, would instantly see his value and worth. He thought it was impossible for him to be refused immortality, and I hate to say it, but his arrogance paid off."

He sat down with a huff. In the light of the day, he didn't look nearly as dangerous. His eyes glowed a faded red and his fur looked more gray than black. He purposefully kept his gaze away from the bright sunlight coming in through the doorway and she wondered if it was dangerous for them to go outside, or at the very least painful.

"What did he promise Bāhv?" Talek urged. "What did he say he could provide? I'm dying to know. That could be the key."

The leader ignored him. "My pack had to be his eyes when he delved down into the deepest cave to find her. She thrives in the darkness, and at some depths, the silence is nearly unbearable. It was so dark at one point, that even we couldn't see, but we could hear plenty. She smells like old bones left out too long in a hot, dry desert;

Keriam screamed when he met her. But her laugh, aye that was a wicked magic. The sound of it will stick with me forever. It still haunts my nightmares." He shook himself and looked away.

"You didn't answer my question," Talek said, impatience working into his voice. "What did he promise her? I need to know. Not only for ourselves, but also for Tanwen. She considered his immortality to be blasphemy in her eyes. A gift from another dragon brought to her land made her quite irate."

"I bet it did. It warms my fur to know that another dragon wants him dead. Serves him right for meddling in things that ought not to be meddled in. He would have promised her anything, he was that desperate to outlive and destroy his enemies..." He paused.

"He promised that he would give her something that she had craved her entire life, a being who had a foot in two lands at once, someone who was part of multiple worlds. She loves her darkness, you see, and she is devoted to her land. But she wanted to see the world outside of it even though she doesn't want to leave it. Now I might not be a strategist like some of you are, but I'm pretty sure someone here fits that description..."

All eyes turned toward her.

Shaleigh gaped at him. "Me?"

THE PRICE OF IMMORTALITY

"I don't understand," Shaleigh said as panic built in her chest. "Why would a dragon want me? I never even asked to be here."

The Shadow Wolf just chuffed a laugh. "I don't think she cares about that."

Talek stepped forward. "No, that can't be right. He wanted me to kill her on sight. I remember that much in the library in the Garden. He wanted me to kill Colin first, and when I refused that, he wanted me to kill Shaleigh."

Shaleigh shuddered, and Talek put his arm around her shoulders.

"Aye, that used to be his plan, but he changed his mind. You see, the Garden has plenty of people who have lived in two worlds; Keriam sent troops to deliver them to the Dragon of Darkness the first day he took power. My kind went with them, and we were the only ones that returned. The dragon killed all of the humans including the ones sent as payment. They were too soft, she had said. She

255

wanted someone who had truly lived, someone who had no fear."

Shaleigh felt her pulse pounding in her ears as Talek removed his arm and stepped away.

Talek took a deep breath. "I vaguely recall that. They returned the day we were set to head out. I knew Keriam was angry, but I couldn't figure out why." He put a hand to his forehead. "My memory is so skewed from that time. It's hard to remember details like conversations, but I do remember seeing the Shadow Wolves, run ragged and panting for breath from Keriam's demands. They didn't survive, did they? Keriam's mind control forced them to run to the point of exhaustion."

The leader nodded. "They did, both were my nephews. They were a strong pair; they didn't deserve that."

"Logically it doesn't make sense." Teagan scowled, pacing back and forth, his fingers drumming against his legs. "Why would he trap her in the Sanctuary when it was burning to the ground if he needed her to complete his promise? It's very unwise to cross a dragon to begin with, but to fail over and over again... He truly is courting death. They could send a fireball to smite him if they wanted. He's more of a fool than I ever realized."

Talek put his head back, squinting. "No, remember, the Dragon of Darkness has no reach here. Only Tanwen does, and I get the impression they don't talk much."

Shaleigh shook her head, trying to wrap her head around it all. "We barely survived the encounter with Tanwen, I don't think I want to meet another dragon. Especially not one in a deep, dark cave that has a history of slaughtering humans."

"I agree," Mawr muttered. "That sounds terrifying!"

Shaleigh rubbed her hands together, lost in thought, and felt the scales on her palms rub together. In many ways she not only had a foot in both worlds, she was part of both worlds now. Even if she went back home, she would still bear the mark of Tanwen on her skin. Holding her palms up, Shaleigh looked closer at the scales, thinking of what the Shadow Wolf had said about Keriam's scream in that dark tunnel.

He had kept his composure the entire time until he had gotten to that depth and spoke with the dragon herself. He might not fear any of them, even the Pello Pines, but he did fear a dragon's wrath. There was no telling how many more people he had sent to the Bāhv, how many people he had slaughtered in his vain attempt to sate the dragon's anger. His mere presence was seen as an abomination on this land, and the more she learned about what all he had done to reach where he was, the more she agreed that they had to not only stop him, they had to get rid of him. He was too dangerous.

"Tanwen sent us to get rid of him, she gave us these powers to remove him from her land."

"Like a pest," Colin added with a nervous laugh. "I hate to say it, but I don't think going really fast or killing Pello Pines is going to frighten him. He's got no problem sending innocent people to be killed by a dragon—there's no telling what he'll do. How many has he got under control now, do we know that?" He was met with silence, and he groaned. "If he's got minotaurs like Graddic under his thumb, we're going to have a tough time."

Shaleigh turned to him. "We have an edge here. We

have Tanwen's power at our fingertips, all five of us. We have her blessing to do whatever it takes to remove him from power. What does he have now?"

"An army of Shadow Wolves," the leader snarled. "My kin."

Shaleigh gave him a sympathetic look.

"Mind controlled servants," Teagan muttered. "How disgusting."

"A frightened populace," Talek added. "Not just in the Garden either, we can include the Sanctuary as well."

"His own magic," Mawr said. "I don't know what all he can do, but it seems scary enough to me."

"Okay," Shaleigh said. "He doesn't have a Faerie Pact anymore, not a full one at least."

"True." Talek nodded. "We're close enough to the Garden that I can feel his presence and his intents, but I don't feel the urge to assist him or even to go to him like I did before. That's quite a relief."

"Most of it is fear, really," Colin said as he stared up into the dome above their heads. "He controls with fear. If you get in his way, he either kills you or sends you off to be eaten by a dragon. Everyone is scared to go near him."

"Okay so here's a thought," Shaleigh started, plotting aloud, "Talek, you can pretend to be his loyal servant again. Somehow you recovered from the Madness after Teagan died, and were forced to return to your master."

Talek winced and she knew she had misspoken. "I consider myself a decent actor, Shaleigh, but I'm not that good. He would see through me, and you all would be handicapped."

"Yes, that's a terrible idea." Teagan stepped closer to

Talek's side. "I won't put him at risk again on his own. I know it would be easier if we did, but we don't fully understand the Faerie Pact that he's bound with still. I would rather him be among friends instead of near an enemy, especially after all we've been through." He reached over to take Talek's hand, and they exchanged a glance.

"Yeah, you're right," Shaleigh admitted. "I'm sorry, I'm just trying to think. We should be able to come up with a plan to use our gifts to take him out, but I'm running out of ideas."

"What you need," Captain Briar said with a smile, "is vision. If this fool is frightened of dragons, why don't we bring one here?"

"You mean summon one?" Mawr squeaked, backing up and knocking the bucket of water over. "To the Garden?"

The Captain shrugged. "It doesn't have to be the Garden; it could be anywhere. We could do it in the Slumbering Forest for all I care. You have her gifts, that means she probably knows what's going on."

"But she said she couldn't leave her volcano," Mawr whispered, crouching down to the ground. "Don't get me wrong, I'm a big fan, but I think seeing her once in my lifetime is good enough. She belongs in her home in the volcano, not here."

"But," Teagan said with a sly smile that put Shaleigh on edge, "Keriam likely doesn't know that. I get the impression he doesn't read many books on the behaviors of dragons. Most are written about how close someone came to being eaten by one, not about where they are permitted to roam across the map. I like your idea, Captain, even if it does need some work."

The Captain grinned. "Like I said, you all need some creative vision."

"So, what, we just pretend like we're dragons or something?" Colin asked, rubbing at the fur on his head.

Shaleigh licked her lips. "No, we pretend like she's here. We summon an image of her the same way we moved quickly through the forests and down the mountainside."

"Traveling is very different from conjuring up imaginary dragons," Talek sneered. "I'm not opposed to trying, but I'm not sure if it'll work. We failed at even getting through this forest, if you all remember."

Shaleigh held up her hands, palms out for the others to see. "We can change things. Our powers are about more than just traveling. I made my scales small when she gave them to me just by concentrating on it. I willed them that way, and so that's how they appeared."

Talek reached over to take her hand and rubbed his thumb over the scales. "That's fascinating. I would love to try that myself, not that I don't appreciate my new look, mind you, but the ones on my eyelids are a little uncomfortable." He put a hand to the large, thick layer of scales on his eyes.

"If we do this, you'll be a key member," she told him. "You control sight, so you would have to pull a clear image of her up in your mind that would have to be believable."

He furrowed his brows. "She was in my mind for a long time. She was fixing things, sifting through things—— I don't think I could forget her even if I wanted to."

Shaleigh turned to the others. "Teagan, you're resistant to the Pello Pine thorns, right?"

He arched his eyebrows. "The barbs? Yes, they couldn't get through my skin."

"I made one of them bleed with mine."

Teagan narrowed his eyes at her. "I see what you're saying, but those are individual examples. We don't know if we have that ability as a group."

"We won't know until we try," Colin quipped, coming over to stand beside Shaleigh. She gave him an appreciative nod. "Besides, boss, you didn't know you could turn me into a stoat until you tried."

Teagan rolled his eyes. "Yes, but that was a different kind of magic. I had to work within the box that Madam Cloom gave me, but I worked mostly alone. I'm not used to having to..."

Talek casually picked up his hand and kissed his fingers; Shaleigh chuckled as Teagan went bright red. "You're not used to having to rely on others," Talek stated simply. "That's fine, it's pretty obvious."

Teagan briefly looked offended, then sighed. "I suppose it is arrogant of me, isn't it?"

Talek nodded. "I mean, I think it's folly too, but if we're all willing to give it a shot, it can't hurt. You were always the realist, and I was always the idealist."

"I don't know about that, but I think it's the smartest option we have available."

Shaleigh turned to Mawr, who was a little farther back from the group. He had his head down and was staring at the floor, deep in thought. Shaleigh went over to him—"Are you alright?"

"I don't know," he lamented with a frown. "I've seen Keriam angry before, Shaleigh. He's very frightening. I know we all want this to work, but what if it doesn't? What if he takes control of Talek and prevents him from helping us? What if he isn't fooled by a fake Tanwen?"

"I'm worried about all these things, too," Shaleigh admitted.

He blinked at her, his dingy silver spectacles catching the sunlight reflecting on the old library floor. "Really?"

"Yes, but I can't answer any of these questions unless we try."

He looked down again. "I just don't want anyone to die again. I can't stand it."

She rubbed his mane, glancing unconsciously over to where Teagan and Talek were flirting quietly together. She still remembered all too clearly what her friend had looked like when he died, and how he looked when he was undead as well. She understood Mawr's discomfort, his fear, and his confusion. She felt the same way, but she knew they had to press forward. Even the Shadow Wolves couldn't live here forever, and they made a promise to a fire dragon.

"We'll practice first," she stated, the idea spreading in her mind. "Here in Aife where it's practically deserted. We'll see if we can conjure her likeness and the Shadow Wolves can tell us how real it is."

Mawr looked up at her, his eyes searching, "Do you really think we have a chance against him? I know we have magic he doesn't, but Keriam has centuries of experience wielding magic. We just got ours."

Shaleigh stared into his eyes, wishing she could lie to

him, wishing she could say something to give him confidence because she hated to see him worry. "No," she stated with a tremble, "but we don't have any other options and we're running out of time."

~

SHALEIGH PULLED her coat closer as she stepped out of the library. Being inside had prevented much of the wind, but now she was very glad that Teagan had given her a coat.

She took a deep breath and looked around at the remains of Aife. There was a clearing up ahead between two of the fountains—the three children and the woman who would normally be shooting water up from her fingertips.

"Where do you want us?" Colin asked at her side, practically bouncing on his toes.

"Eager to get started?"

"No, just eager to get this over with."

Shaleigh went down the steps then heard a snarl from behind. She turned to see a pair of red eyes staring back at her from a shadowed corner from inside. "I'm assuming you want us to stay here."

"Yes," she said. "Stay inside, we'll try to send the dragon in to see you."

Talek stepped outside, eying the entrance, the steps, and Mawr's pedestal. "I didn't realize that our Tanwen illusion would need to move," he muttered to himself.

"We need her to look realistic. How else is she supposed to fool Keriam?" Teagan asked. "Come now, you have an excellent eye. You'll have no trouble with it."

Talek huffed, "Drawing pictures of someone I love is very different from remembering where steps are. Do we really need to have her go up these steps? Isn't there a ramp somewhere?"

"Okay, that's enough," Shaleigh called to them, and motioned for them to follow. "You won't have time to study the landscape with Keriam, so you don't get to study it here either."

"Then how am I supposed to picture it? You said my task was important, not impossible."

Mawr stepped out and down the steps with practiced ease. "You have to believe in yourself," he said.

Talek shook his head, "You say it like that's easy."

Between the two fountains, Shaleigh took Talek's hand then placed a hand on Mawr's flank. The others took her cue and took hands as well. Captain Briar stood at the top of the stairs of the library, watching from a distance. She was studying them and Shaleigh felt a restlessness building like she was getting ready to take an exam, only there was no studying, just experimenting.

"Okay," she said. Judging by the looks that the others gave her, the confidence she wanted to feel wasn't in her voice. She breathed out slowly, trying to calm her nerves, but her mind just circled the possibilities over and over again. "We need to think of Tanwen."

Talek smirked. "That's not very specific."

"Okay," she said again, her mind drawing a frustrating blank. "We need to think of her standing."

"Oh boy..." Colin muttered.

"Let me try," Mawr urged, his voice soothing and not at

all plagued by anxiety like hers was. She glanced up at him, both shocked and proud of his confidence. "I want everyone to close their eyes and hold on tight. We're going to think of the dragon Tanwen. Not with her fiery claws or great wings, but with her lava skin and deadly smile."

"And those eyes," Talek offered. "Who could possibly forget those?"

That's when Shaleigh pictured them clearly in her mind, Tanwen's white eyes staring back at her, seeming to stare straight through her. Her eyes were swirling and always moving, as though barely containing the power and energy within. She thought of the dragon probing her mind, pushing around her thoughts, and pouring over her past.

"Okay," Mawr continued in his calm voice. "Now Shaleigh, I want you to imagine her walking into the library."

"From where?" she asked, mostly because she couldn't snap her mind away from those eyes that she remembered so clearly now.

Mawr paused for a moment with indecision and the image flickered. "From the entrance near the hedges."

Shaleigh concentrated on Tanwen's eyes again and the image flared back to life in her mind. She imagined Tanwen walking out of the bushes, but the body was hazy. They had to get her to the library, up the stairs, inside so the wolves could see her, but it was difficult. Shaleigh was having a hard time picturing everything.

"Stop," Talek urged with worry.

Immediately Shaleigh let go of the image and opened

her eyes. They were all breathing hard and Talek had a hand on his temple, his eyes pinched closed.

Mawr turned to look up toward the library. "Excuse me but did you see anything?" he called.

The Captain was limping toward them, leaning heavily on her walking stick. She was already past one of the fountains. "I saw something!" she called back excitedly.

"That's promising, I hope," Talek muttered.

"I saw a pair of eyes," Captain Briar said, smiling at them like that was absolutely incredible. "I saw them come from the entrance at the hedges and float over to the pedestal."

"Only eyes?" Shaleigh asked in exasperation. "That was supposed to be her entire body!"

The Captain's smile faded. "That's all I saw."

"This won't work!" Talek cried. "It's too much. There's too much going on with her. I can't possibly imagine everything moving at once. There are too many pieces that get lost."

Colin was watching all of them, his tail twitching in thought. "What if we each take a part of her?"

"What do you mean?" Shaleigh asked him.

He shrugged. "Divide and conquer. That's from the Human world, right? You divide a people and conquer them?"

Shaleigh winced. "I like to think it was talking about boats more than people, but sure."

"I can get her movement," Colin said and looked at each of them. "I remember that really well. She walked like the ground obeyed her."

"Her gaze," Talek whispered. "I remember that all too well."

"She was patient too sometimes," Mawr said. "I can be her patience."

"I don't think Keriam needs to know about her patience, big guy," Colin added.

Mawr shook his head, "No, I think that's the best part! If we're going to portray her like this, we need to do her justice."

"I'll take her voice," Teagan said, his gaze downcast. "It drew me back here when I heard it. It *compelled* me." He put a hand to his chest to where the fireball had blasted through him. "I don't think I'll ever forget that."

"What about you, Shaleigh?" Mawr asked, turning toward her. "What will you take from her?"

"I don't know," she sighed. "I was going to take her eyes, but I think Talek already got that one."

He chuckled at her side. "And I'm not giving it back."

"I know, I just don't know what else I can add."

"Be her ferocity," Talek said. He stared at her with frightful determination. "Be her malice. Keriam only respects what he fears. If looks alone don't intimidate him, you can demonstrate her power."

Shaleigh nodded, realizing what that would mean, what she would have to do. This wasn't about smoke and mirrors, this wasn't a fake performance to scare Keriam off, this was a distraction to kill him. She would be the one to have to do it because only she would have that power. She couldn't falter. If she did, every one of her friends could die.

She looked around at the group of them. Colin was

trying to convince Mawr to change his focus. Teagan and Talek were both planning their approach like preparing for an act on a stage... Only this wasn't a show. This was real and their practice now meant life or death.

She felt her hands start to shake and took a deep breath. She didn't want to see any of them hurt, she wanted this to be quick and easy, but she knew deep down that wasn't likely. Keriam might not know what was coming for him, but he was a cruel man. He didn't even have respect for his own bound Faerie.

"Shaleigh, are you alright?"

She turned to Mawr, realizing that she still had her hand wrapped in his stone fur and he must have felt her shaking. "I'm just... preparing," she said finally, not sure what she could say to really describe how she felt.

"Do you think you're ready?"

She closed her eyes for a moment. She had never killed anyone before. She had come close in the Games on top of that stage, but even then, she never expected to win. Her whole strategy was how to lose without getting killed in the process. It was different now. Now she might have to kill someone on her own, and it would be on her hands, no one else's.

"I don't know," she whispered. "It's weird, I used to think it was crazy that they thought I was a reincarnation in the Garden, but here I am fighting off Pello Pines and trying to save the Garden."

Mawr leaned in close. "Do you think you are that magician's reincarnation?"

She shook her head, choking out a laugh. "No, but I think I understand him better." She stepped away and shook her arms out, trying to get herself ready again, trying to focus.

"We don't have to do this if you don't want to," Mawr said. "We might be able to find another way."

"No, we don't have time for that, remember? We have to try this." She turned to the others. "Are you ready to try again?"

Colin turned away from his conversation with Captain Briar. "Ready as I'll ever be," he said.

"I'll let you know what I see this time," the Captain said.

Together they all took hands, or gripped fur, and tried again. This time Shaleigh wasn't distracted by Tanwen's gaze. This time she imagined the dragon's power coursing through her body. She imagined the heat of the molten lava of her skin, the quick whip of her tail, her great wings, and compacted them all down like she had seen Tanwen do before she took the shape of a woman.

Oddly, this time Shaleigh felt compelled to open her eyes, so she did.

She was no longer seeing through her own eyes, but instead from a person standing at the gap in the hedge wall. She looked to her side and saw each individual branch; she could count the leaves on one just above her head. She was taller than normal and as she walked forward, she felt the earth reach up to meet each step. She noticed Captain Briar, gaping, but Shaleigh was careful not to look her in the eye.

She gave a sly smile and approached, moving far quicker than normal and darted across the empty space with alarming speed.

The Captain was so startled that she lost her footing, lost her walking stick, and fell down hard onto the ground.

"Oh!" Shaleigh cried out, breaking the spell and gasping in surprise. She felt Talek jerk as she opened her eyes and heard Mawr moan. She was back in her body, back to being her normal self instead of inhabiting the form of the powerful dragon.

Captain Briar was laughing as Shaleigh broke free of the circle and ran over to her. "I'm so sorry!" she said as she picked up the walking stick and helped the Captain back to her feet.

"Don't be!" she cried. "That was exhilarating! For a moment there I thought you all had accidentally summoned the dragon here—I'm glad I was wrong. I had no idea she was so fast! And those eyes!"

Talek had a hand to his forehead. "I forgot who I was for a moment. It's so very strange to lose yourself inside of someone else like that."

"It kind of reminded me of being a photographer. You get used to looking through the lens and you forget that that's not how you normally see the world."

"That was amazing!" Colin laughed. "We did it! We all worked so well together!"

"I tried to be her kindness this time, and I'm glad," Mawr added. "If I hadn't thought of how much I liked the Captain, she might have attacked her."

"I wouldn't have," Shaleigh insisted, but even as she said it, she wondered if it was true. Had Mawr held her back from hurting someone accidentally? Could that even happen when they were in that form? Of course, it could.

They might have embodied Tanwen the dragon here in Aife, but none of them could control the ground to rise up to meet each step.

Did Tanwen realize she had given them such grand power, or had she underestimated them and assumed they wouldn't even try?

Colin's comment jerked her from her thoughts. "Hey Talek, what are the odds Keriam wets himself if we do that to him?"

Talek grinned. "Very high, and I'd pay money to watch it."

"We have to be careful," Shaleigh said giving the Captain back her walking stick. "I don't want to accidentally hurt the wrong person when we're doing that. I didn't realize that I would have so much control over her."

"You wield her power," Teagan said, coming to her side. "She is a dragon; therefore, she is made of pure magic. By carrying her power, you channel her essence, and judging by the scare you gave, you must have been very realistic."

"That's good," the Captain said, wiping off her rear. "It goes to show that as a team you all are far more powerful than you realize. You just need to practice." She took hold of the walking stick with both hands. "Fortunately for you, I'm used to handling trainees."

"We don't have weeks though, Captain," Teagan stressed. "We barely have hours."

"That's right." She nodded. "We have today, and only today. Get back over there and get in formation. We're going to practice this together until it's good enough to fool even a dragon."

"But there's only one dragon in the land," Mawr said plainly. "There used to be more, but they disappeared and—"

"First rule of training," the Captain called, interrupting him. "No history lessons. We're staying focused on the task at hand. If it isn't about how to properly portray a dragon, we don't need to hear it."

Shaleigh went over to put a hand on Mawr's flank. He leaned over to whisper in a voice that was loud enough for everyone to hear, "It's true though."

"I know, Mawr." Shaleigh grinned, preparing for another round. "You're right."

THE WIND GOT COLDER the later it got, but it was strange because when in the form of Tanwen, Shaleigh couldn't feel it very much. She knew the wind was there and knew it was cold, but it felt very distant. Throughout the day as she took on Tanwen's form again and again, she learned to pay more attention to those distant feelings, because she understood those feelings belonged to her actual body–Captain Briar made sure she understood that when she had tripped her earlier. It took Shaleigh by surprise, and she couldn't get out of the trance in time to catch herself.

She scraped up her knee and the Captain sneered, saying, "Good. Hopefully the pain will keep you more grounded."

At the time Shaleigh was angry, but now she understood. The pain did help her get her bearings, to keep her connected to her body. And after more practice, she could handle getting tripped, getting smacked on the arm by Captain Briar's walking stick, and she could even do minimal talking in her normal body without giving anything away in Tanwen's form.

As for the form itself, Shaleigh enjoyed controlling it more than she let on. Tanwen roamed around fountains and peeked into the abandoned buildings. She wandered within the library for most of the late afternoon, walking over to each of the Shadow Wolves and allowing herself to be sniffed. It was important that Tanwen smelled like a dragon, which was difficult since none of them really had registered her scent on the mountain.

"You might not smell her much," the leader insisted, "but my brethren would. And right now, she smells like you."

That wasn't comforting. It didn't help that the Shadow Wolves had never met Tanwen, so as a group they had to come up with a unique scent.

At the volcano, all Shaleigh remembered was the smell of ash and sulfur all around them and sometimes the searing of flesh like when her leg was burned. However, they wouldn't have the smells of a volcano to hide behind when they approached Keriam. They were going to be near the woods or near the grassland where the Games had been played, so Tanwen had to have a very different scent.

They had decided as a group on the smell of charred wood, and that helped. They all knew the smell of a campfire... and the smell from the fire that burned down the Sanctuary.

"That's much better," the leader said as he sniffed Tanwen near one of the fountains, standing up on two legs to get closer to her. It was dark enough now that the wolves could emerge from the library without potentially catching aflame.

The leader reached a paw out and touched her arm, then whimpered and pulled away quickly; Shaleigh felt her concentration waver.

"What's wrong?" she asked at the same time that Tanwen did. Wincing then as the walking stick rapped against her leg.

"Either you talk or Tanwen does, never both at the same time," the Captain lectured.

"Sorry," Shaleigh said. "I was just worried about him. Did we hurt you?"

"It's fine," the leader said with a raspy laugh. "Your skin is warmer than I expected. Just scalded my paw a bit is all. That's to be expected, but I had to see if she was truly solid. If you can keep that heat going, none of the wolves will be able to get near her."

A sinking sensation came to her at the realization that Keriam might not be her only target. She might also have to kill Shadow Wolves, several of them. Was she ready for that, knowing that they were being controlled against their will just like these survivors were?

"Focus," the Captain demanded.

Shaleigh snapped her attention back to the form of Tanwen. Her head throbbed at the center of her forehead, it had started about an hour back, but she had to ignore it. They only had a day to prepare, only a day to go up against a Magician who had centuries of experience, only a day to get Tanwen the dragon right so they had a chance at victory. If they failed, there would be no second chances... She pulled her rambling mind into check. It was difficult to do when they had been at this for hours, but she knew it was necessary.

Looking through the eyes of Tanwen, Shaleigh walked through the empty walkways of Aife, ducking beneath vines and reaching out to touch statues. With concentration, she could control the heat of her body. She could make herself look more human and less fire, or vice versa. She had at one point turned the body into an inferno and had trouble putting it out in time.

The form of Tanwen put out her hand, formed a ball of fire in her palm, and flung it at the ground. The molten lava splattered outward as it hit the ground, leaving behind a black scorch mark in the soil and killing the grass where it landed. A sudden surge of guilt went through her and she waved her hand over it, watching the remains of it return to her hand and then disappear in her grip. She knew without asking that was Mawr's doing. He had gotten much better at not only encouraging good behavior but enforcing it.

They had all gotten better.

Colin controlled Tanwen's footsteps and movement, making her move in fluid steps across all kinds of terrain. He struggled with the steps of the library at first, but eventually got it figured out.

Teagan had to work with Shaleigh to control her heat levels, her physical form, and to make her body leave impressions in the earth.

Talek gave the intensity to her eyes and allowed her to

see, and indeed, Shaleigh noticed that none of the Shadow Wolves could look into her gaze for long.

And Mawr gave her the sympathy and a dash of humanity which made her seem all the more real. Each time he pushed for an action; they all felt his warm presence.

They each had a role to play, and so did Shaleigh. She had to manage them all. She had to control every aspect of them and know when was best to allow each one of them forward. She also had to control Tanwen's voice, her words, her mannerisms. She put the final touches on the facsimile, and it was exhausting work.

They had been at it since morning and the sun had just dipped under the horizon. Even though they had taken a few breaks throughout the day, Shaleigh felt wiped.

She heard Tanwen turn to the Captain, saying, "I think we're done for the day." After the words were spoken, she could feel the relief from the others. They were feeling just as exhausted as she was, though none of them had said a word. She had Tanwen give a small smile, adding, "We're all exhausted."

The Captain was sitting on the edge of a fountain. The walking stick had helped for the first half of the day, but by nightfall she was clearly too tired for it. She licked at her lips and turned to meet Tanwen's gaze. Unlike the Shadow Wolves, she didn't flinch under the weight of her eyes. "Are you all certain? Tomorrow there is no practice. Tomorrow, he and anyone who would kill you is disposed of."

Shaleigh stepped out of Tanwen and felt the others pull away as well. Colin gave an audible groan and Mawr flopped down on the ground. "I think it's as good as we can make it," Shaleigh admitted. "We can only do so much."

"I agree," Teagan said, going over to sit down on the fountain next to the Captain. "This work requires a good amount of mental concentration, and while I'm used to dealing with that, I rarely worked at it for so many long hours, even when I was High Faerie." He smiled over to Mawr and Colin. "I have no idea how you two are handling this so well."

Colin gave a tired laugh. "We aren't. In fact, my head hurts in places I didn't even know it could hurt."

"My whole body is vibrating," Mawr muttered, not wanting to get to his feet. "I have to remind myself that we don't get earthquakes in Aife."

"That's probably because your entire body is being used as a conduit," Talek said, staring at Mawr with sympathy. "At least for us, only our heads can hurt. This must be quite uncomfortable for you."

Teagan nodded. "I certainly am glad that Shaleigh has already had a bout of magical sickness because this certainly would have triggered it otherwise."

Shaleigh joked, "I think I've finally got my sea legs."

The Shadow Wolves returned then with a few more small fish from the lake, so Teagan offered to cook up a stew for everyone: They lumbered as a group back into the library, weary and dreading the next day.

As Teagan worked on the stew with Colin's help, the Captain spoke with the leader of the Shadow Wolves in private. Shaleigh found herself settling down in a corner with Mawr and Talek, all three of them tired and trying to keep warm.

"What do you think our plan will be tomorrow?" Shaleigh asked, glancing between the two of them. "Do we just head over to the Garden with Tanwen's form and try to kill Keriam?"

"I hope so," Mawr said. "I hope we can do it quickly. I don't want anyone else to get hurt."

Shaleigh reached over to pet his mane. "You're worried about the ones he's mind controlled, aren't you?"

Mawr nodded. "I don't like the idea of him sending people from the Pasture to the Dragon of Darkness. I worry how many of them have gone already. And I don't know what I'll do if one of the nice Librarians tries to attack us. I don't think I could hurt them. They're so very sweet normally, and I don't think they would like working under Keriam at all."

"If Keriam is throwing Librarians out to fight us, then we at least know we're winning," Talek joked. "The only ones who I fear will be caught in the cross-fire are the Shadow Wolves who belong with their clan. I know they've given us permission to protect ourselves in the event that we must fight them, but that won't end well."

Shaleigh's gaze shifted over to the leader, sitting on the ground beside Captain Briar. The Captain looked concerned and it made her uncomfortable. "I still don't understand how Keriam got the Captain out here in the woods with those Shadow Wolves. He can't control the Pello Pines, can he?"

Talek shook his head. "No, but you don't know how many Shadow Wolves died in the process. The Captain had been unconscious for that trip and was lucky to survive it." He held up his arm, and the black ribbon on his wrist fell slightly. "Even though I am not at his side, he wields more power because we are still in a Pact. It's likely he picked up some spells while in the Sanctuary to send a group to a random location in this forest."

"Why don't we just cut it?" Shaleigh asked. "We could break you of the Pact and make him lose power."

He shrugged. "We don't have the proper scissors… Not only that, but if we do cut it, he'll know that I have willingly left his side. Should I die while under the Pact, he would know that, too. It's very different."

Shaleigh reached over and took his hand and squeezed it tight. Talek stared at her in confusion.

"Look, I don't like you talking about dying, okay? We finally got you back from the Madness, I don't need you dying on me."

He squeezed her hand back and gave a nod before dropping his gaze to the ground and pursing his lips. "To be honest, I don't entirely know why you trust me. Part of me expects that once this is over, once we defeat Keriam, that you and I will go back to being enemies."

"Why would you think that?" she asked. "I've stayed by your side this entire time, and I don't plan to leave anytime soon. Sure, you've made mistakes, but so have I."

"Yes, but my mistakes were terrible," he said, a hardness coming over his features. His lip trembled. "I used you to get access to Teagan. I manipulated you both in these woods mere days ago. I lied to you about who I was and where I came from, and yet you still trust me. Why?"

"You're not a bad person," Mawr said, surprising both

of them. "You think you are, but you're not. You wouldn't have been so sad about Teagan if you were a bad person."

Talek's eyes went glassy with tears. "How can you possibly know that? I killed all those minotaurs, Mawr. You saw that with your own eyes."

He nodded, his dingy glasses glinting in the firelight. "Yes, but you didn't want to. You did what Keriam wanted. And when you did have control, you only wanted Teagan to be happy. You love him, and if you can love like that then you aren't a terrible person. You can't be."

Tears fell and Talek looked away. Shaleigh reached over to put an arm around his shoulders, and Mawr, purring, cuddled closer to them both to lend his warmth.

"Thank you," Talek whispered, wiping at his cheeks. "I thought maybe this would all be temporary, that you secretly hated me this entire time, ever since we sought out the dragon."

"We don't hate you," Shaleigh said, giving him a hug. "We all make mistakes. You trusted Keriam, he used you, and then I trusted you and you used me."

That made him cry harder.

"And it's okay because that isn't us. That wasn't you, and it wasn't me either. We were trying to do what we thought was right. We were trying to help the people we cared about, and Keriam used us both."

"You're right," he said, finally getting his tears under control. "Thank you for understanding. Thank you for listening to me and putting up with me."

"That's what friends are for."

❧

Morning came far too early for Shaleigh's taste. The humidity in the air indicated that the sun must have just risen as it seeped into the room.

Then Captain Briar was poking at her with a walking stick.

Shaleigh turned over to look at her with bleary eyes.

"Wake up," she said. "We need to plan."

There were dark circles under the Captain's eyes as though she hadn't slept at all that night. Shaleigh pushed herself up from her blanket.

Mawr, who was still lying down beside where she had been sleeping, started purring when she got up. "Should I come with you?"

Shaleigh glanced over and saw that Colin was curled up asleep on his back. She smiled, whispering, "No, it's okay. Let him get some more sleep."

He nodded and watched as she stretched and yawned. "Good luck," he said as she stumbled off to follow the Captain. She turned slightly and gave him a sleepy thumbs up.

Captain Briar led the way over to the Shadow Wolf leader who waited in a dark corner away from the other Shadow Wolves. Shaleigh knew that whatever plan they were going to discuss wouldn't be good. Otherwise they wouldn't have stayed up all night devising it.

Shaleigh pulled her jacket closer around her. "What's wrong?"

"Nothing's wrong," the leader snarled. "We simply need to let you know the plan since neither of us will be with you to fight the Magician."

That made all the exhaustion seep out of Shaleigh's

mind in an instant. "Wait, what? I thought you were both going to be with us."

"We can't do that," the Captain stated. "First of all, the Shadow Wolves can't travel during the day, and it's too dangerous to travel at night—as you know."

Shaleigh stared at her with wide eyes. "But this place means death. There isn't enough fish in that lake for anyone to subsist on forever."

"We knew that as soon as we arrived," the leader scoffed. "Besides we have no interest in being forced to work alongside Keriam again. We'll take our chances here."

"You don't think we can do this? We haven't even tried yet."

"Look, child," the leader started without looking her in the eye, "we had to work alongside Keriam for so many years. My kind live like Faeries in Ciar, we live very long lives. I'm tired. I don't want to have to see that man's face ever again, and I can guarantee the others don't either."

Shaleigh started to speak, but the Captain held up a hand for silence. "I obviously can't join you because I'm too much of a hindrance. But that doesn't mean we're staying here forever. Once I'm healed up, we're going to try to make a run for it north. Which is why you all need to be ready to fight Keriam on your own."

Shaleigh looked between the two of them, her mind slow to grasp what they were saying. She turned to the leader first. "But you all know the ins and outs of the Garden, the way Keriam has it now. You know the routes, the routines, the weak spots. We need you there!"

He shook his head and gave a grunt. "No, you don't.

You all have the power to take out Keriam, that's real magic. He'll never expect it... But if my kind get one whiff of us then the rouse is up. They'll know something is wrong."

Shaleigh turned to the Captain, feeling the panic settle in as her chest again. "We can't do this without you. We're not soldiers, we only got a day of practice! How are we supposed to do this without you?"

Captain Briar put a hand on Shaleigh's shoulder. "That's not true. Colin is a solder and Teagan helped to lead the army when he was the High Faerie in the Garden." She gave a smile that was supposed to be encouraging., but instead just looked sad. "And look at Talek! He was at Keriam's side, strategizing with him. You're in good hands with a strong team."

"We can create an illusion, that's it. Just a bunch of smoke and mirrors. How can you expect us to take Keriam down without your help? What if his Shadow Wolves attack us while we're trying to concentrate? Who will protect us when we're vulnerable? What if the Pello Pines attack?"

The Captain glanced to the leader and a flicker of doubt went across her face.

Shaleigh narrowed her eyes. "You're scared, aren't you? That's the real reason."

The leader lowered his gaze, saying nothing.

"No," the Captain insisted a little too quickly, but she couldn't quite keep her voice from shaking. "That's not it at all. We've both assessed the situation and decided that our joining you would only impede the mission."

Shaleigh saw beyond her words. She saw the small

tremor in the Captain's hands, the hint of terror in her eyes. And for all the ferocity the leader and his few pack-mates showed when they arrived, he hung his head now. He couldn't even bring himself to look at her.

"What has Keriam done to you two? He's broken you both down, made you terrified. You should be at our side fighting him, not risking your lives alone in the woods."

"It's complicated," the leader grumbled. "You wouldn't understand all the atrocities I've seen. You've only been dealing with these struggles for what, a week or two? I've dealt with Keriam's control for almost my entire life. We were barely more than pups when he captured us and brought us here. You and your people have strength, determination, and the magic of a dragon on your side. We had none of those gifts and we struggled because of it.

"My pack and I wish you well and offer you any assistance you need, but do not ask us to go back to that cursed land. We can't return and see our brethren used in such a degrading manner." He hung his head again and slowly lowered himself onto the ground.

For the first time since she met him, Shaleigh could see the years weigh on him. His bones cracked as he moved, and what she might have mistaken for a snarl was actually a grimace of pain. Keriam had killed many, but his unwilling supporters were put through more pain and torture than she realized.

"I can't go back there either," the Captain said, her voice soft. "I barely made it out alive last time. I under-mined the man for days while I tried to help Madam Cloom. We rescued Colin, set his leg, and nursed him back to health, all under the nose of Keriam. I didn't realize he was letting us think we were hidden. How could I have known that we were still part of his game?" She grunted and shook her head, her body shaking. "Now he has the only person I ever loved, and you're the only chance she has left."

"That's not fair," Shaleigh snapped. "You can't put that on us."

"This world isn't fair, Shaleigh. Look around. Do you think the people of Aife thought it was fair when they were ripped from their homes by Pello Pines? I don't even know if Geneva is alive right now and I hope by my ancestors that she isn't. I hope she's dead already, because I don't want to imagine what Keriam is doing to her." The Captain put a hand to her chest, continuing, "I'm trained for combat, I'm trained to withstand pain, she is not. Trust me, if I thought I would be some good at your side and not a hindrance, I would. This isn't easy for me."

Pursing her lips, the Captain glanced away.

Shaleigh saw that she leaned heavily on her walking stick, the daylight behind her accenting the dust in the air and making her look almost like a statue for a brief moment. Shaleigh had the horrible realization that Captain Briar might not ever escape the library of Aife, that she would perish here, and she couldn't let that happen. She couldn't let someone who had fought so hard be killed by abandonment.

Taking a moment to let her own anger cool, she watched as the leader got to his feet and trotted away without a word: which seemed to be more his custom than out of rudeness.

Finally, Shaleigh chose her words carefully because

she didn't want to lose the Captain's trust because of her own fear at what was to come. "I didn't realize you loved her."

The Captain swallowed hard and gave the smallest nod. "I admired her. I always did. I loved her mind, I think, and I never had the courage to tell her."

Shaleigh winced. "I'm so sorry."

She sighed. "No, that's my fault. Even if she was here now, I doubt I would have the guts to say it. We lived together for a solid week and I kept my mouth closed. I didn't want to risk it. If I lost her..."

Shaleigh tried to consider what it was like living in the rubble left behind in the Garden, under the all-knowing eyes of Keriam and his mad Faerie. Even after they rescued Colin and plotted to undermine Keriam, Madam Cloom had no mouth. Each day she got weaker and each day Captain Briar prepared for the worst. By withholding her feelings, perhaps the Captain wanted to protect her from further grief and protect herself from losing a loved one.

"I'll do my best to save her if she's alive," Shaleigh said. "But I'll admit I've never liked her much. She would have had me killed, you know."

The Captain nodded. "Yes, but isn't that what her people wanted? Wasn't that expected of her?"

Shaleigh shook her head. It wasn't the first time she had heard that excuse, but it still shook her to hear it about Madam Cloom of all people: She was the person who ordered Shaleigh be kidnapped, who threatened to have her killed, who would have had Talek killed. However, she couldn't deny the pain in Captain Briar's eyes or the support she had given them. Without her help, Colin might not have lived. They also would have missed out on the Captain's guidance while training.

Shaleigh gave a heavy sigh. "You've helped us so much and I appreciate that. I'll do my best."

Captain Briar blinked and gaped at her. "You will?"

"Just to be clear, I'm not doing this for her. She wanted me dead. I remember her rage at the top of High Castle before Talek appeared. I think she would have killed me that day."

"She's ruthless," Captain Briar said with a small smirk. "I agree, but it's also why I love her, I think. I admire her drive."

Shaleigh chuckled. "Well her drive was going to have me killed, and I can't forgive her for that." She held her arms out, adding, "And all this talk may be for nothing. I might get there and... find out I'm too late. But if I'm not, then I will help her because you love her."

Captain Briar suddenly fell to the ground, her walking stick clattering to the old Library floor. Shaleigh for a brief moment thought she collapsed but realized she had fallen to one knee before her.

Shaleigh took a step back. "What—?"

"Thank you, Shaleigh," Captain Briar said in a wavering voice. "I didn't expect you to want to help me or her after everything. I'll fight harder knowing she might be waiting for me somewhere. I... just have one more request to make of you. You can tell me no, and I'll understand, but I have to ask it."

Shaleigh braced herself, her mind flying into a million directions. Her hands felt cold at her sides. "What is it?"

The Captain looked up at her with red-rimmed eyes, her lips trembling. "If Geneva is suffering, if she is in terrible shape, please help her escape it."

Shaleigh's mind went blank, not wanting to process the meaning of those words at first. "What?"

"Geneva is a brilliant but prideful woman. If her body or her mind have been ravaged, please help her pass as respectfully as possible."

"*What?*" Shaleigh asked again, louder, as her mind tried to catch up with her mouth. "I can't do that. She isn't an injured horse or something, she's a person, Captain." She looked around with wide eyes, seeing Mawr watching from the corner of the room, seeing Teagan walking slowly toward them. But the otherwise empty room could not give an answer to an impossible request. "I couldn't even do that to a horse let alone a person. I'm sorry. I know you want me to help, and I'll try to save her if I can, but I can't do that."

The Captain pursed her lips and a tear streaked down her cheek. "I hope you don't have to consider it then," she said with a sad nod. "Forget I ever asked."

Shaleigh nodded, but she knew very well that there was no way she could forget a request like that. Yes, she despised Madam Cloom for everything she did; she hated the woman. But for all her abuses and threats and insults, as soon as Talek took away her mouth in his Madness, Shaleigh felt pity for her. A part of her understood why Captain Briar admired her, even though she knew how terrible the woman was. She too had been intimidated and impressed by her once upon a time.

But Shaleigh could never kill Madam Cloom. Even if

she was on the brink of death, she doubted she could bring herself to do it. Even through the guise of Tanwen the dragon, she couldn't do that.

As Shaleigh stood there stunned, Captain Briar took her walking stick and picked herself back up. Vaguely Shaleigh heard Teagan stepping closer.

"Is everything alright?" Teagan asked, but Shaleigh couldn't look at him. Her mind was filled with too much to answer.

"It's fine," Captain Briar stated in a clear voice, as though she didn't have tears streaking down her cheeks. She brought herself up to her full height as she turned to face Teagan fully. "You need to gather your team, Master Teagan. Your mission today depends on daylight. Come nightfall, you'll have the Shadow Wolves contend with."

PART III
TAKING A STAND

SHOWING RESTRAINT

The sun was just over the horizon as Shaleigh stepped outside. The sky was a brilliant blue, filled with puffy clouds, and the scent of lavender was heavy in the air. Shaleigh breathed it all in, watching her friends as they descended the steps of the library. Colin yawned, scratching his fur as he made his way out into the sunlight and Mawr took each step down with practiced care. Talek was slower to emerge. Teagan moved to stand at her side, his hands clasped behind his back.

"I can't believe this," he muttered, breaking the calm. "They should be coming with us, they're our strategists. They are useless to us here."

Shaleigh winced. She knew Teagan was angry as soon as she gave him the news. He hadn't said a word, but she could see the shock and frustration on his face. She knew a discussion was coming, but it didn't make it any easier.

"I know, I told them that we needed them, but they said it was too dangerous. Captain Briar is too injured, and the Shadow Wolves are afraid their scent will be picked up. Not to mention they can't travel during the day."

"Too dangerous, they do realize they're surrounded by Pello Pines here, right?"

Shaleigh shrugged.

He huffed and glanced back to the library. "You and I haven't even been in the Garden since it was ransacked. The others haven't stepped foot in the place for days, there's no telling where the soldiers are stationed or how that city is being run right now. We have no plan on how to approach the damn place."

Shaleigh glanced over to see Talek had slipped past them and had joined Mawr and Colin near Mawr's pedestal. They were talking, but Talek kept glancing up to them, concerned.

"Teagan," she whispered.

"We need to talk with them, convince them otherwise. I can't believe they waited until now to tell us, and then they talk to you instead of me or Talek."

She narrowed her eyes. She wanted to ask him why he was so offended that the Captain would talk to her and not the others, but she could barely get a word in. He kept circling back to his own wounded pride instead of focusing on the situation.

She tried again, "*Teagan.*"

"I thought we were considered a team, and yet still she goes around me to speak to someone else." He huffed. "That's so typical of the Captain to—"

She raised her voice, interrupting with, "*Teagan.*"

"What is it?" he shouted back.

The conversation near the pedestal came to a halt as

the others looked up to them at the entrance to the library. She leaned in close to Teagan, careful to keep her voice low. "Keriam has Madam Cloom."

He blinked and swallowed down whatever retort he had prepared. "What do you mean he has her?" he whispered. "Where?"

"He has her captive, In the Garden. Captain Briar told me he took her shortly before she was left to die out here. Madam Cloom was still alive at the time."

Teagan gave a short nod, trying to grasp what it meant. "So, I assume the Captain believes that the ownership of the Garden is still in Madam Cloom's hands? That's interesting." He gave an annoyed sigh. "I don't see how that helps us right now, but that's interesting to know."

"No, you're not listening." Sometimes she wanted to pinch the man's ear. "He gave her back her mouth before he took her. I'm not sure if she can talk but it's very possible, he meant to keep her alive, and she's being tortured."

That brought him down a peg. He pursed his lips and looked down. "That's...terrible."

Shaleigh gave him a moment to let that sink in before she dropped the real shock. "Also, I should tell you that Captain Briar is in love with her, but please don't let the others know."

He laughed out loud. "That's impossible. No, you must be mistaken."

She leaned in closer and gave him the most serious expression she could. "I'm not mistaken. She told me that herself. And why is that impossible exactly? You don't think two women can love each other?"

He shook his head as the humor died on his lips. "No,

that's not why I said that, not at all. I see nothing wrong with two women loving each other. That would be rather ridiculous considering my relationship. My point is that Madam Cloom...said things to me before. I didn't get the impression she was interested in women."

Shaleigh put her fingers on the bridge of her nose to try to rid herself of the headache that was growing. "You know she can like both, right? Madam Cloom can like whoever she wants."

He sighed. "I suppose it's just difficult to see. I worked beside Madam Cloom all the time; I should have known everyone she was interested in." He squinted up at the hedge wall in the distance, adding, "But Captain Briar was her favorite guard, and they did spend a good amount of time together."

"Regardless of their relationship, Captain Briar wants us to try to save her."

Teagan was only partially listening as he said, "If there was something between them, that means the Captain should have forfeited her position to prevent any conflict of interest. Otherwise there would have been more than mere scandals, it would have meant several broken laws and a serious punishment..."

Shaleigh reached out and grabbed his hand. She had to resist the urge to shake him. She thought him dying would knock some sense into him, but apparently not. If anything, he was just as stubborn and obtuse as ever. "Listen to me, *please*. If Madam Cloom is in really bad shape—and Captain Briar seemed to think she very well might be—the Captain wants us to help her die."

His mouth dropped and his face went a shade paler.

"Oh," he whispered, finally understanding the gravity of what she was saying. It had nothing to do with political maneuvers, scandals, or what obsolete laws were broken, it was life and death.

Neither of them were very fond of Madam Cloom, but of their group, only she and Teagan had known her very well. Even though she had tried to kill Shaleigh, that didn't mean she wanted her dead. Even though she forced Teagan to stand and watch his Garden burn, Shaleigh didn't think he would be able to kill her either. Judging by his silence, he was struck with the same horrible decision that she was. Neither of them wanted this potential responsibility, but they had it, nonetheless.

"I don't think I can do that," he finally whispered, his gaze distant. "She was cruel at times, yes, but so was I. She and I weren't really that different." He thought for a moment then added, "I don't even know if Madam Cloom would want that."

"She might be dead already. I told Captain Briar that, and she knows it, too. But if she's not and she's in bad shape..." Shaleigh took a deep breath, trying to keep from shaking. "I don't think I can do it."

Teagan nodded, his eyes glassy. He swallowed back tears and took a moment to compose himself. "I don't think I could either. There was a point in my life when I could have and would, if given the chance, regardless of whether she was at death's door or not."

Shaleigh gave him a sympathetic smile.

"After going through it myself, I don't know if I would wish it on anyone. It's going to be difficult enough doing it to Keriam ultimately."

She narrowed her eyes. "You knew him before, didn't you?"

"Oh yes. He was always so jealous, always trying to prove he was more powerful than the others. He never had power himself, he was always forcing others to do his bidding. When we found out he had poisoned the well of a village with essence of the Scáil plant—they were treating him like a god. It was disgusting. I never thought he was worth thinking about then, and now here we are dealing with him again. Oh, how my dear Cathal would be furious at his actions." A tear slid down his cheek. He was trembling.

"I'm sorry," she said. "It's a bad time to bring all this up, but I wasn't sure when we could talk again."

He took a deep breath and wiped at his eyes. "No, it's not your fault. I think on that time and remember how much good we thought we were doing for the world, how much we wanted to help other people. Now I look around and see that everything we did was really rotten from the inside, spoiling everything from within. The Garden wouldn't last, the Pello Pines would wake, and he would ultimately perish. It was a dream too good to stay."

"You were happy though, right?"

He rubbed at his eyes again. "Yes, I was happy. I was free and respected, and I was in love again."

"Then it's okay. You loved him, he loved you, and you did your best. Sure, not everything worked out, but some really good things will come out of this. I think he would be really proud of you."

He closed his eyes for a moment, pulling himself together and pushing the emotion down. He swallowed once more before answering in a voice that didn't even waver, "Thank you, Shaleigh. I like to think he would be, despite everything."

She reached over and rubbed his arm, keenly aware that the others were watching. She didn't want to have to ask the tough question, but this might be the only time she could. There was no telling what they would encounter once they traveled. "What should we do about Madam Cloom?"

He licked at his lips, and the only trace that he was crying was a slight redness around his eyes. "I believe it doesn't help to worry about a problem if we haven't encountered it yet. I say we cross the bridge when we get there."

Shaleigh wanted to point out that they weren't talking about crossing bridges, they were talking about someone's life. But she also understood that Teagan was still recovering from everything and they were about to go into a dangerous situation. She didn't want to compromise his safety with too many difficult questions, and she had already pushed him enough—possibly too much.

"Are you two alright?" Talek asked, a hint of concern in his voice. He was partway up the steps and Shaleigh hadn't even known he was there, but she guessed that Teagan did. Mawr and Colin still stood by the pedestal, trying to look disinterested, but catching glances every chance they could.

Shaleigh squeezed Teagan's arm before releasing him. "Yes, just preparing ourselves, I guess."

Talek came the rest of the way up the steps then looped an arm around Teagan's. "Are you alright?" he asked, staring into his eyes. Shaleigh couldn't refrain from smiling when she saw how much Teagan relaxed when Talek came near. His facade cracked only for a brief moment before disappearing again.

"Absolutely," he said with more composure than Shaleigh felt.

"Good," Talek said with a knowing nod; Shaleigh knew he had seen that brief flash of weakness in Teagan's face. "Shaleigh, I think Colin is considering curling up on that pedestal to take a nap. Would you mind going on ahead? Teagan and I will be right behind you."

"Sure," she answered, grateful for the help. She wasn't sure if Talek was jealous of Teagan being with Cathal, but that was their problem to sort out.

Glancing back once she was down the steps, she saw Talek with an arm around Teagan's waist, and a genuine smile on Teagan's lips. Which was good—she had to keep an eye on them. For all their knowledge and prowess, they were the most fragile of their group. She turned to Colin who had already climbed up on Mawr's pedestal.

"It's too early to be fighting Keriam, isn't it?" Colin groaned. "Shouldn't we let him get some breakfast first or something?"

"I think it's best to catch him when he's unprepared, don't you?" Talek asked as he and Teagan joined up with them.

Mawr came over beside Shaleigh and nuzzled her. "I'm scared," he said.

She wrapped her arms around his muzzle and gave him a squeeze. "Me too," she whispered. "But we did really well yesterday, and you were incredible."

"Really?" he asked, pulling away. "I felt like I didn't do nearly as well as everyone else. We're supposed to be trying to attack him, not help him, but that's all I want to do when we're making the dragon."

Shaleigh grinned. "Making the dragon?"

Mawr nodded. "That's what I call it. Colin said I'm just scared to say her name, but I don't think that's a bad idea. If she controls all the magic in the land, she might be able to hear us, and I don't want to insult her accidentally. I don't want to make her angry, even if she can't come here."

She couldn't help but laugh. "I don't think she cares when she's so far away, but if it makes you feel better, I won't say her name either."

"Thank you, Shaleigh. I'm sorry I'm always so frightened of things."

"Don't apologize, your fear makes you stronger."

"Really?" He blinked at her, his worn glasses catching the morning light and exposing all the cracks in the frames.

"You're afraid you'll be too kind when we're fighting with Keriam the Cruel, even after everything he's done. I think that makes you stronger than any of us."

He licked at her with his stone sandpaper tongue.

She took a step back and placed a hand on his mane, taking some of his stone fur in her hand. She led them down to the clearing between the fountains. "Alright everyone, get in a circle."

Colin asked through another yawn, "Wait, so are we traveling then?"

"We're traveling first," she explained. "We might have

to make an example of the Pello Pines if we run into trouble, so wake up and get ready."

Colin's eyes went wide. "The Pello Pines?"

She nodded. "If we have to, yes."

"Good luck, all of you!" Captain Briar said, limping down the stone steps in the distance with her walking stick. "Remember: Concentrate. Believe in yourselves. Remember you have the advantage." She waved at them. "Hopefully we'll meet again soon."

"Wait," Colin muttered, "she's not coming with us?"

"It's a long story, Colin," Teagan said. "We'll have to explain later."

Shaleigh glanced to Teagan with a frown before turning to Colin. "She can't come even though she wants to. And I don't want anyone else getting hurt." He looked sad but nodded.

Mawr glanced back to her with a worried look. She gave him a reassuring squeeze before getting back into position.

Talek spoke up to get everyone's attention—"Stay focused, everyone. We need to work together to keep from getting separated, remember? If we can create a solid dragon, surely we can run through a few trees."

"They're nothing but a few trees, I like that!" Shaleigh grinned.

Colin laughed and shook his head. "A few trees, sure!"

Shaleigh continued. "Okay, let's focus on the path from the gates of the Garden at the edge of the Slumbering Forest. Where nighttime becomes daytime...or well, it used to. I don't want to go too far from the Garden."

"Where is that?" Colin asked. "I don't know the grounds outside of the Garden very well."

"Where we fought Keriam," Mawr stated helpfully.

"Oh, yeah, I remember that place. Gives me the creeps. Why are we going to a creepy place again?"

"That's likely where the Pello Pines are congregating if they want to attack the Garden," Teagan said with a glance to Shaleigh.

"Look, we have to go somewhere near the Garden. If we go to the Garden, we have to choose the Marketplace, where people could be controlled, the Pasture, where there's no cover at all, or the Games, where we're were sitting ducks."

Teagan frowned. "You make a good point."

Shaleigh nodded, pleased that he agreed with her strategy. "How does that sound, everyone?"

"It still sounds creepy, but I'm ready to kick some Pello Pine butt!" Colin cried, hopping from one foot to the next. "If they have butts!"

Shaleigh leaned over to Mawr, whispering, "Remember, your fear makes you stronger. Stay with us this time, okay?"

He glanced at her with big eyes. "I will, Shaleigh. For you."

She gave him a scratch of appreciation. "Alright. Talek can you see where we're going?"

Talek's eyes were already clouded over. "Yes, I do. I distinctly recall that clearing."

"Colin? Can you get us a path?"

"I'll try! Talek, you guide, and I can follow."

Talek gave a slow nod as Shaleigh added, "Teagan, keep us from getting hurt by any trees."

"The wrecking ball approach, I suppose. Excellent."

"Perfect." Shaleigh closed her eyes and felt their energies shift; a full day of practicing to create Tanwen's form made her attuned to their powers. Concentrating, she felt them all aligning before working together in blasts of color that formed a unified rainbow of movement.

Mawr's warmth was strong this time. He was determined to keep them together, which was exactly what they needed. Colin's excitement showed in their speed—even though they stumbled once, as though they took a hard turn on a slippery road, but Mawr kept them together and prevented them from being separated. Talek's path was clear ahead, a warm unseen presence on the forest floor, and Teagan made their team impenetrable by even the most determined Pello Pine they passed.

She was proud of them. They had all been through so much, but somehow, they not only learned how to use their powers, they could now control them. They didn't let their fear, or their sadness hold them back: they each threw themselves into the magic, allowing them to work together as a formidable, cohesive unit.

She only hoped it would last.

THEY LANDED in a flurry of leaves and dirt.

The air was filled with the sound of creaking wood.

Shaleigh opened her eyes and realized with horror

that they hadn't just landed near the awakened Pello Pines, they were right where they were all congregating—this was the front line of their assault.

The Pello Pines were in a panic. Branches were being swung back, colliding with other Pello Pines. Splintering wood and snapped twigs rained down from above and dirt was flung around as they tried to clamor away, but their tendrils tangled amid other tendrils preventing them from escape. The ground churned angrily.

It looked like they had come into the middle of a war zone. The Pello Pines pulled back, into a haphazard circle around them and grew still. They had been startled and frightened at first, but Shaleigh wasn't sure how long their shock would last before they realized they were prey. The morning sun didn't deter them, the cold wind didn't stop them, and it looked like there had to be dozens of them all around.

She looked around at the group and saw that even though they were all holding onto each other, they were looking around in a panic. Shaleigh didn't let go of her grip on Mawr, and she didn't let go of Talek's hand either.

"Stay focused!" she cried as the Pello Pines began to move hesitantly toward them again. She felt Mawr's fear, starting to light like an ember catching flame. "And don't be afraid! Remember we are strong together; we can stop them as a team! Close your eyes and focus on Tanwen!" She fought her own instincts and closed her eyes to concentrate.

"Let's set an example!" Colin cried.

Teagan grunted a response, Talek gave a cry, and Mawr shook at her side. She could feel the ground vibrate beneath her feet as the Pello Pines advanced, creating a mini earthquake.

The energy from her friends pulled at her, and just like in training from the day before, Shaleigh thought of what they had practiced: Tanwen the Dragon.

They birthed her in the center of their circle, and Shaleigh opened her eyes. She had Tanwen stand to her full height, and shifted her outside of their circle, darting toward a huddle of the Pello Pines. Many of them were closing in slowly, waiting for an opening, for a chance to attack. With Tanwen's eyes, Shaleigh could see they were starved for food, and it wasn't sunlight they wanted, they wanted blood. She saw their wilted leaves, the dry bark along their trunks, and their weakened tendrils that hovered around. Some of them couldn't even muster the energy to keep their tendrils raised.

Shaleigh smiled and Tanwen did as well. Raising her hands at her sides, she lifted two fireballs into the sky. The Pello Pines realized in that moment the danger they were in, and in an instant started scrambling backwards, leaving behind large trenches in the earth.

A fierce glee filled Shaleigh at the sight, at all of the Pello Pines being absolutely terrified of her presence. The flames in her hands grew as the heat started to make the dried magma of her arms melt. One of the Pello Pines was frozen not too far away on the other side of their circle, and Tanwen darted toward it in an instant. It wasn't as clever as the others. It was rooted to the spot, like it couldn't move. However she saw its roots aboveground, she saw it was just as mobile, and all Shaleigh could think was that it would be easy to get rid of it, to burn it down and hopefully burn most of the forest in the process. But as she lifted an arm, a change came over her.

It felt like a light filled her from the inside, soothing and cool against the heat of her body. The fire in her hands dimmed down to barely more than a candle before finally snuffing out in a puff of smoke. The Pello Pine finally broke free of its terror, and slowly dragged itself away. It wasn't that it was slow, Shaleigh could see spots of bright green on its branches. It was a young tree, and its roots weren't as powerful as the older trees. It had probably spent more of its life deep in slumber than it ever had awake. It might not have even remembered how to move properly.

Shaleigh let Tanwen's arms fall to her sides as realization struck her. She was about to burn a young Pello Pine alive, one that hadn't even attacked her. She was grateful for Mawr, whose warmth and kindness she would know anywhere.

Turning, Shaleigh saw that the other Pello Pines had departed back into the far reaches of the Slumbering Forest, the sapling limping along to follow them, not strong enough to churn up the dirt like its older brethren.

They were left alone in the wasteland of churned dirt and a strong wind. There was no scent of lavender here, no promise of calm and quiet.

Shaleigh had to quell the surging power within. It was difficult each time they formed Tanwen, but this was more difficult than the last. She wondered absently if this was what Teagan dealt with as High Faerie in the Garden, wielding such powerful magic every single day.

With a force of will, she pulled herself back and let

Tanwen's form diminish. She opened her eyes, her face wet with tears and her body drenched in sweat; Colin was panting on the other side of Mawr.

"That was glorious," Teagan muttered, his forehead gleaming with sweat. "They fled."

"They were terrified," Talek corrected him, holding a hand on his chest. "And rightly so. We nearly burned down the entire forest."

"I'm sorry." Shaleigh gulped down air, untangling her fingers from Mawr's stone fur and wincing from the abrasions on her skin. She had been clutching him so hard that her skin between her fingers was raw. "That was all me," she said. "I don't know what came over me."

Teagan clucked his tongue. "You make it sound like we made a mistake. We did it. We terrified them." He was rubbing his hands together. It looked like she wasn't the only one who had been holding on too hard.

"We nearly killed one of them that wasn't even attacking us," Shaleigh insisted. "That could have been bad. They could have retaliated. I wanted to make an example, but not like that."

Teagan rolled his shoulders, "Unbelievable. We did in an instant what it took Master Cathal and I months to do, and you think we were too harsh."

Talek shook his head. "I can't believe you still have a lust for power after all of this time."

"I don't have a lust for power!" Teagan shot a glance at him. "I'm merely in awe of the power we wielded."

"You should be in awe at Mawr's ability to hold us back from making a terrible mistake," Shaleigh said as she went over to put a hand on the stone lion's muzzle.

"Thank you, Mawr. I told you that you were the strongest of us."

Teagan sighed. "I don't understand."

"This power is greater than anything you or I have ever dealt with," Talek stated simply. "Remember that. Now if we wanted to burn down a whole forest we could. And everything in it. That didn't do so well for the Masked King, did it? Or Briar Kingdom?"

Teagan gaped at him with dawning realization. "I didn't mean... I wouldn't..."

"I know that, love, but you have to learn to restrain yourself. We could wipe out an entire species if we're not careful, you understand?"

Teagan stared at him, his face reddening with embarrassment as he glanced at each of them. "I'm sorry. To all of you, but especially to you, Mawr. You were right to stop us."

Mawr shuffled his paws in the dirt. "I just didn't want to hurt him. He looked just as scared of us as we were of him. I never thought I would feel bad for a Pello Pine, but I did."

Shaleigh rubbed at his fur. "You did well. Thank you."

He nuzzled against her.

Colin went over to one of the ditches, squatting down and looking at the soil. "How long do you think they'll keep their distance?"

"Probably for as long as they sense we're here," Shaleigh said. "So, let's make sure we keep stomping around to let them know we haven't left."

Shaleigh turned to the path toward the Garden. It was strange because the trees that had been here before, that weren't Pello Pines, had been completely uprooted or torn apart; the Pello Pines worked like giant bulldozers on everything they passed. They had destroyed everything in their desperation to reach the Garden, and that was terrifying. How many Pello Pines had there been? Had they broken through the gate? What defenses did Keriam have to keep them at bay, if any?

The unknowns felt numerous and Shaleigh felt her pulse quicken. "How did Keriam keep them back?" Shaleigh asked aloud. "What could he have in place to prevent them from assaulting the Garden?"

"I don't know," Talek admitted. "He had nothing strong enough to fend off an army of that size when I was with him. Though there were hardly any awake when I was last here."

Colin got to his feet. "Let's stay close in case they try again. I don't want us to get split up, we're a lot weaker when we're alone."

Shaleigh glanced back to him. "Do you think we should have Tanwen enter instead? Would that be safer?"

He shrugged. "I don't even know what we're up against at this point. The Shadow Wolves won't be out, but he has access to the army of the Garden and all of the people who live here. He could do anything he wanted with them."

Madam Cloom's face came unbidden to her mind and Shaleigh had to shake herself to get rid of the image. What would he want with Madam Cloom after all that time? Why not let her waste away and die? She wished she understood Keriam more. Yes, he wanted power and he had lied to get immortality, but there was a clear grudge, too. He couldn't just want the Garden, could he? It wasn't like he was putting statues of himself up according to Colin and Talek, not like Madam Cloom did.

She couldn't shake the feeling that there was more to it, but she couldn't say what. Especially with what Teagan had told her: he was jealous to begin with, but that was centuries ago. Since most of the people he hated were dead now, she wasn't sure what that meant. Even Talek didn't know his motives. That only made her more uncomfortable as they neared the entrance of the Garden.

It was clear that many angry Pello Pines that had passed the area from all the upturned trees and foliage. Great mounds of dirt were piled up all around and the destruction lasted far longer than Shaleigh expected. She could hear the roaring river much sooner than before, likely because there were no trees to dampen the sound any longer. It was incredible to see the destruction that the Pello Pines had caused—was it out of hunger, anger, or confusion from being asleep for so long that caused this? Did they target the Garden because they believed Master Cathal was still there?

Another plain truth was that the Garden was no longer hidden. Its high stone walls were clearly visible in the morning light. The gated entrance was closed up and the towers on either side of the gate held flag posts on top, but they bore no flags. Keriam had no symbol or army of his own, but he was quick to take down any symbol of Madam Cloom or Master Cathal. The tops of the walls were empty, too.

Keriam had no special weapon or magic spell to prevent the Pello Pines from getting through, he merely got rid of the bridge. The Pello Pines were earthbound and couldn't leap across the river to reach the entrance of the Garden. By getting rid of the bridge they prevented anyone from approaching the Garden from that gate, or so they thought.

Shaleigh walked up to the edge of the grassy hill that led to a sheer drop down to the river. The earth on the edge had been worn away and she couldn't get too close for fear of falling. The four pillars that had made up the bridge originally were still there, but the bridge itself had been completely dismantled.

"Do you think they did that before the Pello Pines awoke?" Talek asked.

"If they didn't, they must have lost a lot of people," she said, pointing to the edges of the hill that had been torn away by the Pello Pine roots. They must have been churning up the ground to reach the Garden, but their determination only made the gap wider by eroding the soil.

Despite not seeing anyone high up in the towers, Mawr still crawled along his belly for fear of being spotted. She wanted to comfort him, but he was also the biggest target out here, so she understood his worry.

"It's strange to see it," Mawr whispered, looking up with wide eyes to the towers. "It's much more intimidating when you look at it from out here."

"The amount of time it had to have taken them,"

Teagan muttered with a hand to his mouth. "With my magic I recall rolling the bridge out in a matter of moments, but I hadn't considered the work it would have taken to undo it."

"I'm surprised it didn't fall with the High Castle," Colin said.

Shaleigh looked up at the walls. "Me too, actually," she glanced to Teagan, "why is that?"

He sighed and a flush came to his cheeks. "I actually took great pride in creating the walls and bridges. It was a thrill to be able to create such things with a flick of the hand."

Colin smiled. "That must be it then! You enjoyed the castle walls and bridges, but not building High Castle." He wagged a finger at him. "If only you knew your enthusiasm meant so much."

He shrugged. "The magic knew my feelings even if I didn't. It's strange to think that I took such creations for granted. I would have tried to have more excitement for my creations if I knew they would have lasted so long."

Talek took his hand. "The structures you built were also your children."

Teagan rolled his eyes and Colin laughed.

"I suppose it does explain why I can't tap into any of my magic any longer. I don't want anything to do with him," Talek admitted.

Teagan sighed. "I think it's also different because I was in a Pact with the Garden, not with Master Cathal or Madam Cloom. I was tethered to the place, not the person. So even though I wasn't very keen on Madam Cloom, my magical abilities didn't waver because of it."

"Maybe Master Cathal was onto something, huh?" Colin asked with a sly smile.

Teagan's amusement faded. "It felt like a betrayal at the time. I felt like I had been conned, but I suppose it was clever in the long run." He arched an eyebrow. "For the Garden, not for me."

Talek changed the topic, asking, "So, if they're keeping out the Pello Pines, how are we supposed to get inside?"

"Do we need to?" Shaleigh asked. "We could just conjure Tanwen and send her through."

"But the Pello Pines," Mawr muttered, his ears flattening back. "If we're out here, they could come back."

Colin kicked at some debris. "That's a good point. I guess we could travel up to one of those towers."

Teagan glanced to him with concern. "But can we cross a river like that?"

"We crossed over lava flows; a river should be no problem." Talek shook his head. "But where do we go where we won't be seen? See, this is why I wish we at least had Captain Briar with us. She would know their habits, their shifts, where they had guards. When I snuck in before it took me days to figure that out. I needed that information in order to not get killed on sight."

"We don't have days," Shaleigh reminded him. "We only have today before we need to leave to prevent the Shadow Wolves from sniffing us out."

Colin ticked off on his fingers as he said, "So, we need to have a place where the Shadow Wolves can't reach us, we need a place where Mawr can't be seen, and we have to somehow get our dragon lady close enough to see and take out Keriam."

"What about up on the wall?" Shaleigh suggested. "They're clearly not guarding it now."

"True," Teagan said. "It would at least give us a good vantage point."

While they discussed options, Shaleigh noted that the sun was fully over the horizon and climbing steadily. The longer they took to decide, the less time they had. She thought about Captain Briar and the Shadow Wolves at how little food they had left. She thought about Madam Cloom in a jail cell, possibly dying. She thought about the people of the Pasture, sent to the Dragon of Darkness to be killed.

She started looking at the wall not as a girl from the Human World, but as an expert urban explorer who understood architecture instinctively more than the others did. They could do this. She had done this countless times with Kaeja and she could do it here.

"Alright," she said, cutting off Teagan as he spoke about what places he would protect if he was in Keriam's position. "I have a plan. Talek, I want us up on the wall, but not on the top. See if you can find a safer place beneath that but obviously out of sight."

"I'll try," he whispered, shutting his eyes tight. When he opened them, they were clouded over as he searched.

"Mawr, I want you to help us stay together. You need to believe in us so we can get in and stay hidden. We might find a place to hide that's out of sight, but that doesn't mean we'll be safe."

Mawr gave a slow nod, looking up at the castle wall like it was a monster all its own.

She put a reassuring hand on his side. "I know you can do this. You're the strongest one here, remember?"

"Thank you," he said.

"Okay, boss, what about me?" Colin asked.

Shaleigh couldn't help but smile at Colin calling her the same thing he used to call Teagan. It was bizarre being considered someone's boss. "You are going to give us speed. You're not going to think about the river. We've run over worse things, right? This will be no different."

He stared at her. "We can't fly though. That's crazy."

"Is it really? It seems like you've flown a bunch lately."

He groaned and shifted back and forth. "I mean, you're right. I guess I've had a lot of experience with it, but that's all Talek's fault that I do."

Fortunately, Talek was too focused to notice. "Sure, he is, but he doesn't remember all of that. You do."

Colin dragged his hands through the fur on the back of his head. "I hate it when you're right. Okay, if we can create a dragon lady, we can fly over a river, right? Right. No big deal. I can do this."

"*We* can do this," she reminded him.

"You're right, boss. *We* can do this."

She approached Teagan who stared at her doubtfully. "I know, you probably don't agree with this plan, but we need to get in there and find Keriam as quickly as we can. As long as we're in a safe and hidden place, we should be able to 'make the dragon' and take care of him easily, right?"

"No, I actually think this is a clever plan. A little haphazard perhaps," he added with a smirk, "but it's a solid plan. I don't really see my role in it though. We don't plan to go bursting through walls I hope."

She couldn't help but laugh. "No, I hope not. I need you all the same." She turned and held out a hand to gesture to the entire length of the wall, which went along the river and past a bend out of sight. Further down river she knew was the Marketplace where most of the people were likely hidden away, if they hadn't all been killed or turned into Keriam's servants against their will. "You know the structure of this place better than Keriam, better than the Shadow Wolves, better than anyone else. You built it all."

"Shaleigh, that was a long time ago," he scoffed. "You expect me to remember all of that?"

"I know that you remembered to keep the Slumbering Forest in check every day for centuries. You have a good memory, and I think especially when you're in there looking at the inside of these walls, you're going to know the best places to hide and the routes we need to block off to prevent others from finding us."

He pursed his lips and looked up at the walls with renewed interest. "You're right. I do know those paths. I built these walls to be a defensive structure, but also to house the guards in key places."

"Exactly," she said and grinned. "So, you know where the troops will likely come from."

"I do, but I'm not sure if they're still using those places. These are Lieutenant Varg's troops now. There are hidden tunnels, paths that go from the prison cells to the wall that were meant to be used during combat. I don't know if they've been used much since."

"They aren't being used," Talek said in a dazed voice. Shaleigh and Teagan both turned to him. His eyes were still clouded over but he had a devious smile on his lips. "I'm seeing them now, they're mostly abandoned, and probably the perfect place for us to hide."

Once Talek settled on where they were going, they moved away from the castle wall a good distance to be safe. Above them were a few remaining trees that weren't Pello Pines. Several of them had taken some bad damage around the trunks or been nearly stripped of their branches as the Pello Pines passed by, but they still stood.

"You all ready?" Shaleigh asked, putting a hand onto Mawr's side and waiting for the others to take their places.

"I don't think I'll ever be ready for this," Colin sighed. "Part of me thinks we'll get there and Keriam has a trap waiting for us."

"There's no trap," Talek insisted. "I looked it over thoroughly. You're just nervous at returning to the Garden again."

Colin hung his head. "I nearly got killed there last time, multiple times with Keriam. I don't know what it's going to be like this time."

"Worse, I would imagine," Teagan muttered. "Brace yourselves for anything."

Mawr swished his tail back and forth. "Stay strong, everyone. We're together at least."

Hearing the encouragement come from Mawr made Shaleigh feel like they really could do this.

They took hold of each other's hands and concentrated and slowly the world melted away.

PERHAPS IT WAS due to their nerves or their fear, but together they took off into the air faster than any of them expected. Colin was so determined to make sure they could fly and cross the river, that soon they were floating so high above the Garden that the fluffy clouds seemed dangerously close. Shaleigh could see the Pasture and the Marketplace like Madam Cloom had once shown her. After everything that had happened, those places still stood intact, at least from this distance. What she hadn't been prepared for was that the High Castle was gone. As soon as she realized it, she felt the loss in Teagan as he too saw it. It was a cold and heart-wrenching feeling and she wondered if his sorrow would undo the magic, sending them all plummeting to the ground.

Then she felt the warmth of Talek's path tug at them. He was urging them to focus on where he had chosen for them to go. Mawr's encouragement came flooding through them next, despite his clear terror at flying through the air, and slowly their group turned and floated down. It took longer for them to speed up again, the loss and heartache was palpable from Teagan. Finally, they began building up speed as they approached the ground.

They weaved around buildings, nearly colliding with a minotaur who was dragging something behind him. Shaleigh tried to see if she recognized them, but she couldn't make out any features. They took a hard turn as a troop of soldiers came out of an alleyway, zipped past behind some more buildings, and then took another hard turn as they got back on the path. They slipped into a shadowy hole in the wall and suddenly they were underground, passing through a series of catacombs that Shaleigh had never seen before. There were grates above their heads that made it look like it was part of a sewer system, but in fact it was an underground area for traveling. There were a few people who lived down here, some who must have discovered the tunnels and hid from the aboveground world. Shaleigh wondered if they were homeless like Colin had been.

Finally, they came to a stop between a pair of sewer grates that gave them enough light to see but prevented them from being seen by anyone above. Mawr barely fit in the low ceiling, so he had to lay down on his belly.

"Wow, that was a ride!" Colin whispered, trying not to get too giddy and laugh. "I didn't even know this place was here. I sure wish I had when I was a kid."

"It floods sometimes," Teagan said, a tremor in his voice. "It was meant for quickly moving soldiers from one part of the Garden to the next, not for living."

"I believe it," Shaleigh whispered, looking around. It smelled damp, with alternating smells of moss and mold. It was more aired out than she had expected an underground tunnel to be, but if it connected as many places as Teagan said, perhaps the people who lived down here maintained it. Farther down at a crossroads they passed, Shaleigh could see red arrows on the wall with words beside them, probably indicating directions where supplies were for soldiers in need.

"It's strange that these tunnels are open for anyone to enter," she said. "I would think they would lock them off so nobody would get lost down here and get hurt."

Teagan shrugged. "I mentioned that to Madam Cloom once and she said it wasn't worth the time. Once she made that decision, I honestly forgot about them for a while. Captain Briar was very good about stationing her soldiers at key places around the Garden, so these tunnels weren't as necessary as they once were. I imagine if Madam Cloom had remembered them when the Shadow Wolves started attacking on a regular basis, she would have had them destroyed or at least sealed off... So, I'm glad she too forgot about them."

"Where should we create Tanwen?" Mawr asked in a small voice that still seemed to reverberate up and down the tunnel. At the noise he made, he hunkered down closer to the ground. "Sorry," he added in a whisper.

"No, you're fine," Shaleigh soothed and ruffled his stone fur as she looked back and forth down the tunnel. "Should we make a scene and let everyone else see her, or try to take Keriam by surprise?"

"Take him by surprise," Talek said without missing a beat. "He's a coward. If he thinks he's being attacked by someone he can't immediately destroy, he'll flee. Especially if it's the feared dragon, Tanwen."

"Do you know where he is?" Colin asked. "Can we just have her step out of the shadows or something?"

"She's a dragon, not a ghost," Shaleigh said. "We have to make her act like a dragon if we want him to believe that she is one."

Talek closed his eyes for a moment, tapping his toe. "There he is. He's down in the dungeons of the High Castle." He shook himself and opened his eyes. "How fortunate to know those survived despite everything that's happened. I suppose you enjoyed building those too, love?" He asked Teagan with a sly smile.

Teagan avoided his gaze.

Colin's tail swished back and forth with excitement. "Perfect! We can take Tanwen down the stairwell and Keriam will be trapped. There's no way to escape!"

It seemed too easy, but Shaleigh couldn't explain why. She thought to voice her concern but knew she couldn't explain her misgivings. It made perfect sense, kill Keriam down in the dungeons where he had accidentally trapped himself. Take him out before he could harm more innocents. Take him by surprise so he had less time to prepare and defend himself. So why did Shaleigh have this nagging feeling that something was going to go wrong?

She tried to shake the dread that filled her. This was the only option they had. Everyone had done their job perfectly. They were inside the gates of the Garden, hidden and out of sight from everyone, and they were going to summon their version of a powerful fire dragon to get rid of the Magician in an instant. It was the closest they were going to get to a perfect plan of attack.

So why did she feel like this was a mistake?

CRACKING UNDER PRESSURE

Tanwen emerged. She got to her feet between all of them and crouched because she was too tall to stand in the tunnel.

"No," Shaleigh said, "we need her to be outside."

She felt Talek's searching as he tried to find a place to take her, and then Tanwen was in an alleyway, staring out at the mostly empty streets. It took a moment for Shaleigh to get her bearings. She could imagine what it would be like for these people to see Tanwen out in the daylight, with fire emitting from her hair, her intense white eyes, and her volcanic skin with bubbling magma beneath the surface.

"No," she said again, and this time it came out of Tanwen's mouth too as Shaleigh struggled to keep herself separate from the form. "Closer. We can't let the others see us. We can't let them warn anyone."

Talek was searching urgently again and her heartbeat picked up the pace. She felt Talek's rising panic, slowly slipping into her, before Mawr's cool calm came washing over them. Panic turned to determination, and she glimpsed brief flashes of the Garden as Tanwen's form was shifted between locations. A troop of soldiers marched up and down the main street as people ducked into their homes. Someone threw a rock at them, and the soldiers turned toward one of the shops, kicking down the door as a child screamed within.

Fear reigned supreme.

Then Tanwen was pushed to another location, and Shaleigh saw Graddic through Tanwen's eyes. He was picking through a huge pile of stone and shattered glass. He froze and turned around slowly, staring in disbelief. He met Tanwen's eyes and he gaped.

He couldn't even form a full sentence. "Who—?"

"Keep moving," Shaleigh said at the same time Tanwen did.

They took off again, bumpier than before. The embodiment of Tanwen smacked into something, it could have been a tree, or it could have been stone, it was difficult to tell since Teagan's resilience prevented Tanwen from being harmed by it. Someone cried out then was gone.

Finally, Tanwen stood in a chamber that Shaleigh remembered all too well—the Memorial Chamber.

When Shaleigh had been a prisoner before, she had spent a good amount of time there with Colin. That was their rendezvous point before venturing down to the dungeons, aided by his magical flute. At the time it held statues of the five magicians and a token statue for Madam Cloom. It was a place of pomp and reverence and almost reminded her of a church. Now it was barely recognizable.

Many of the walls had fallen and the ceiling was completely gone, open to the blue sky above. Large stones littered the ground, and the statues that had once stood were gone. It was difficult to tell if they had been hit with debris when High Castle fell, or if they were intentionally damaged.

Master Cathal's statue was missing an arm. He used to be wielding a great sword over his head, but now he stood before the black crystal vines, weaponless and vulnerable. Seeing the black crystals that made up the tendrils of the Pello Pines behind him sent a shiver down Shaleigh's spine.

She looked around at each of the statues, realizing they were all damaged, but noticed one was missing—where was Madam Cloom's statue? At first, she thought it had been relocated, but then she spotted its stand and plaque. Her heart pounded in her chest as she approached it; Tanwen's feet crunched down on glass. Shaleigh looked down to see the red crystal flowers that had been part of Madam Cloom's statue, decimated into a powder and littered around the room. Spread out from the statue, they reminded her of blood. All that remained was the plaque dedicating it to the Steward of the Garden, Madam Cloom.

She had no doubt that its destruction was intentional.

Shaleigh thought of Captain Briar then and her fear that Madam Cloom was being tortured if she wasn't already dead. She understood that fear now. Keriam hated them both. He had already left Captain Briar in terrible shape; what did that mean for Madam Cloom?

Mawr must have sensed her worry because a great wave of calm and love swept over her.

"Stay focused," she heard Teagan's voice back in her true body. "We have to get to the jail cells."

"This was as close as I dared without him seeing us," Talek added.

Shaleigh nodded and focused her attention back on the doorway. The doors were long gone, possibly pillaged or burned, but the door to the dungeon was still intact. Of course, it was, that was probably the first place Keriam had fortified. There were no guards that she could see, but they had to be careful.

Moving with the confidence and grace of a true fire dragon, Tanwen went to the door and reached out to the handle, but her hand couldn't grasp it: Door handles required far more focus than walking up steps or creating fire. She tried again, but her hand was limp and rubbery.

"Damn it," she muttered.

Shaleigh felt Teagan reach out and Colin, too, with Mawr's support, and suddenly all four of them were focused on the simple act of turning a door handle. It was such a simple motion but required more dexterity than they had expected. Talek kept watch for them, sometimes pulling Tanwen's gaze away, much to the frustration of everyone else. Finally, the doorknob turned and Tanwen stepped through, pulling the door closed behind her. Collectively, they breathed a sigh of relief.

Tanwen gave off her own glow as she moved silently

down the stairs. It felt like just yesterday Shaleigh and Colin snuck down and hid together, clinging to ceiling or walls. This time Shaleigh didn't hear any sounds ahead, and it was eerie. As they turned the corner, she half expected to see Captain Briar sharpening her blade while guards played cards at the table, but the room was empty. There were no weapons or armor. The table was the only occupant left in the room. Even the chairs had been taken.

I did this, Shaleigh thought suddenly. *I'm the cause for this place being destroyed, and for wrecking every single life that was part of it.* She closed her eyes and willed down the sadness that threatened to come forward. There was no time for that now, she needed to focus. Her friends needed her right now, and she wouldn't let them down again. She had already failed them enough. She felt the pinpricks of worry from the others but had Tanwen square her shoulders and head for the jail cells.

"What's that?" a man called and Shaleigh's heart skipped a beat—Tanwen froze in place. "You did a terrible job of helping Master Cathal?" There was a crazed laugh, "I would have to agree, old man! You're an unlucky fool." There was silence again, then a thud. "Why did he choose you when I was right there? Why did he want you by his side and not me?"

She felt Talek push ahead to see, his curiosity was overwhelming, and Shaleigh didn't stop him. Through Talek's sight she saw Keriam standing with his hands balled into fists at the far end of the jail. He was inside of one of the cells talking to someone, but the door behind him was wide open. Talek pulled back and she felt the struggle it took him to use his sight and keep Tanwen going. She hoped he didn't decide to do that again because it took far too much energy. She wasn't sure if he even meant to use it.

At least they knew that Keriam was distracted. It was a stroke of luck, and one that Shaleigh felt was too good to be true, but they had come too far to stop.

Tanwen stepped into the room, giving a menacing snarl—"Keriam."

There was an audible squeal of surprise and the rustling of feet as Keriam stepped out of the jail cell at the far end of the hall. He had blood on his fists and more blood on his shoes. He looked Tanwen up and down, his face a mixture of outrage and confusion. "Who—what are you exactly? How did you get down here?"

"The Dragon of Darkness sent me," Tanwen said. That made the color drain from his face. "I've come to collect payment."

There was a scream from the side, high-pitched and painful, and Tanwen swung her gaze to see that the other jail cells weren't empty like Shaleigh had assumed. There were others with their arms shackled and their legs chained to the cell walls. The one screaming was a young boy who couldn't have been older than eight. There was another boy with him, older and familiar somehow.

Then she heard Teagan's voice, filled with terror, whisper, "Lieutenant Varg's children."

The boys were huddled in the back of the cell, staring back at her with large eyes in frail bodies. They looked like they had been beaten up and were clearly living in filth. Beside them, leaning on the bars adjacent to them, was Madam Cloom. She was curled up in a ball, her fingers gripping a bar so hard her knuckles were white. She watched them through exhaustion and suspicion. She had...something that had to have been a mouth, but it was hard to see—or maybe Shaleigh didn't want to see.

A clatter from ahead drew her attention back to Keriam. He had picked up his staff, and the violet gem on top gleamed in warning.

"Stay away from me, I'm warning you!" he shouted, his staff shaking in his hands.

His threats were all empty and he was quaking in terror, but he still stood his ground. He still thought he had the upper hand. Tanwen didn't back down, and she brought up a ball of fire in one hand. "She gave you immortality, but you thought you could outrun your debt?"

"Yes," Keriam blurted out, his hands gripping his staff so hard that it was a wonder it didn't break. The violet gleam on the end of it wavered. He was panicking and it interfered with his concentration. They had the upper hand. Maybe her fears and worry were unfounded. Maybe they could actually win this. Tanwen gave a gleeful grin as she advanced, glancing briefly into the cell that Keriam had occupied.

The person was covered in dirt and was so bloody it was hard to even see them. Despite the blood all over them, there was none on the floor, and that sent a warning bell off in Shaleigh's mind. The man had a beard, but his face was pale and unrecognizable. At least, not for her.

A shuddering pain took hold of her, and Tanwen put a hand to her chest as a sob threatened to emerge.

"Owain!" Teagan cried with a sob, and it echoed on Tanwen's lips. "How is his body here?"

Keriam glanced to the prone body in the cage, licking at his lips. "I found him. The Pello Pines weren't the only thing the Scáil plants kept hidden in the Slumbering Forest. It was like he just died." He gave a wild smile. "Honestly I couldn't have asked for a better gift other than Cathal's bloody corpse coming back to life."

Teagan reeled and she felt it in Tanwen's very bones. The fire in her hand dimmed and then extinguished completely. Keriam's eyes narrowed; he was starting to suspect something was wrong. He was starting to see through their guise.

Shaleigh tried to summon it again, but it was too late, Teagan was sobbing and barely keeping the connection together. If she didn't get them out of there, their slim advantage was gone.

"Consider this your final warning," Tanwen snarled at him, coming so close that she could smell the sweat on his brow. "Next time there will be no warning."

Tanwen backed away, turned, and walked as quickly as she could back to the main room. She was almost there when the will of the others gave out completely, and Tanwen's body diminished. Her energy shot through the stairwell, past the Memorial Chamber, and back across the pile of stone and glass rubble. Shaleigh thought she caught a glimpse of a minotaur calling out something, but then it was gone, and her consciousness slammed back into her body.

Shaleigh was flung backward onto her butt with a grunt. She sat there a moment, trying to make sense of what had just happened. Her head throbbed and her body was covered in sweat. She took in big gulps of air, listening to her friends gasping around her. That was nothing like their training or even their off-course travels.

That was a brutal experience.

"I don't understand," Colin said, crawling back to his feet. "Why does he have Lieutenant Varg's kids? What does he want with them? They can't give him any information or anything, they're kids!"

"A threat to keep the Lieutenant in line, I presume," Talek said pushing himself up to his feet and going to Teagan. "Love, are you okay? You lost it back there. I was worried."

Teagan wasn't gasping like she thought, he was sobbing. "That was Owain, that was his body!" he wailed as Talek pulled him to his feet. "It was like he just died yesterday instead of centuries ago! How is he here? How did Keriam find him? What is he doing to him?" He pulled Talek close and cried into his arms.

Shaleigh watched him, a cold sadness spreading through her. She should have listened to her instincts. She knew something bad was going to happen, but she hadn't said anything. She should have. She should have said something so Teagan didn't have to witness his friend's body being defiled.

"Wait, that was Owain the Wise?" Mawr asked, looking around at the others. "The statue of the nice man in the library?"

Colin nodded. "Yeah, it must have been. I didn't recognize him either, but..." He shook his head. "I'm so sorry, that was terrible."

Shaleigh got to her feet and took a deep breath. At any other time, Teagan might have handled that shock better, but there was only so much stress he could handle. He had come back from being dead just the other day, and he had dealt with seeing the ruins of the High Castle and the Memorial Chamber better than she had. But they all had their limits. They all could only be pushed so far until they snapped. How could any of them have prepared themselves for that?

Seeing the children in cages, Madam Cloom's horrible wound across her face, and then to find Keriam beating up the corpse of a friend that had died centuries ago . . .

"That was too much," she whispered. She felt Mawr nuzzle her hand and looked over to see him hunched down, crawling to reach her. "Are you okay?"

He nodded. "I tried to help calm him down, but I couldn't. He was too upset, and now I'm upset. I can't imagine doing that to a body in front of children like that. He's more of a monster than I ever realized, Shaleigh."

She hugged him in the dark, cramped tunnel. She was tired. They were all tired. They might never again get another chance as perfect to take out Keriam, but there was no way they could handle that shock. She wasn't even sure if they could pull themselves together to try again: Teagan was still sobbing.

"What do we do?" Mawr asked.

Shaleigh shook her head. She had absolutely no clue. They had been so focused on strategy and training that they never considered another failure. They hadn't planned or prepared for any of that, and yet here they were, failing the only task they had: to kill Keriam.

She was about to recommend they regroup back to the woods and try to figure out how to last through the night, when Colin spun around. "Oh, shit!" he whispered, then turned to Talek, "Master Teagan, please be quiet, sir! We've got incoming."

TEAGAN BIT back his tears as Talek held him close. There were footsteps coming down the corridor—someone was running toward them. Mawr shuffled around to hide behind Shaleigh and Colin picked up a rock. Shaleigh stared at him for a moment, then realized that it might not be a bad idea and grabbed a rock too.

Down the tunnel, someone came out from a crossroad. They were big and Shaleigh felt a chill go through her as they turned and walked toward them. It was a minotaur; she knew that much. She thought of the warning that the Shadow Wolves had given them, how minotaurs were being controlled by Keriam. She clutched the rock tighter and drew back her arm.

"Master Teagan, is that you?" a familiar voice grumbled.

Teagan sniffled. "Graddic?"

He stepped forward into the light of the drain. "Oh wow, Colin, Shaleigh!" He rushed forward. Colin threw a rock at him, probably still thinking it was possible he was mind controlled, but it just bounced off his chest. Graddic was completely unphased and he pulled Colin into a big hug, sweeping him up off the ground.

"Oh wow, I'm so glad you're okay!" Graddic was so tall he had to crouch in the tunnel as well. He wore no harness around his chest like he used to when he pulled carriages, but she could see that he had some new battle scars on his arms and one across his nose.

"Me too, pal! Can you put me down now?"

Graddic put him back on his feet and smiled while Colin gasped out, "Glad to know you're still in top form." Colin patted his arm.

"Master Teagan, are you alright?" Graddic approached him, but still kept a respectful distance.

"Yes." Teagan smiled, wiping his cheeks. He stepped forward, still holding Talek's arm. "I think I'm getting better. I must ask, how did you find us? How did you even know we were here?"

"And are you under Keriam's control?" Shaleigh asked, still holding the rock in her hand.

There was a silence after her question as though the air around them shifted.

"Do you think I would be hugging you all if I was one of Keriam's puppets?" Graddic asked with chagrin. At the silence he received he gave a huff. "No, I'm not being controlled. But to answer your question, Master Teagan, I saw your magic in the rubble around High Castle! I would recognize one of your creations anywhere, sir!"

He gave a smile and pulled Teagan into a big hug. Teagan's eyes went wide but he hugged Graddic back.

Shaleigh wasn't sure she entirely believed he wasn't

being controlled by Keriam, but she doubted big hugs were part of Keriam's orders either and dropped the rock.

"We just failed big time," Shaleigh admitted. "We were going to have to leave the Garden and try again later."

He released Teagan and stared at her. "You're targeting Keriam?" There wasn't fear in his voice, but excitement, as though he was ready for anybody to be brave enough to stand up to him. Based on the violence she had glimpsed on the streets, she couldn't blame him.

Shaleigh nodded. "We tried once but failed. We need a place to regroup and gather our strength before we try again."

Graddic slammed a fist into his palm. "Finally! Someone's really going to take him on!" He looked around at them, adding, "You don't have an army, but I bet you all have some crazy magic going on, right?"

Colin burst into laughter. "Yeah, it's something like that."

"I knew it! That's where you've been, right? You all have been trying to find a way to fight back since Keriam destroyed the Garden!"

Shaleigh felt a pang of guilt rip through her at his words. Keriam hadn't destroyed the Garden, she had. The Garden would still be standing if she hadn't been so foolish, but then again, she reminded herself, if she hadn't been the pawn someone else would have. Keriam and Talek might have spent years waiting for the right person.

"If you all need a safe place for the night, I can help," Graddic said and put a hand on his chest. "I have a place out in the Pasture. We can use the tunnels to get pretty far without going top-side too."

"I don't know," Shaleigh said, remembering her last time in the Pasture. "I don't think the people there like me much."

"If you're aiming to take down Keriam, they'll support you no matter what."

~

THE TUNNELS CRISSCROSSED through the entire Garden, including the Marketplace, Graddic explained. They also led straight to the Pasture. Most of the soldiers didn't know about them because they were so old, but the minotaurs had been using them for a long time to get supplies around quickly and easily—that way they didn't have to wait so long in traffic.

"So, you could have cut through here with my carriage at any time and prevented me from waiting in that awful traffic," Teagan said. It was good to hear some of his wry humor come back.

Graddic gave a nervous laugh. "We never took customers down here, Master Teagan. We didn't want everyone to know about it."

Teagan hummed in response but there was a smile on his lips.

Shaleigh had to admit, it felt good to be walking around on her own two feet for once instead of controlling a world in her head. It felt like she had been living in her own mind for ages with all the practice they did back in Aife and the work they had done today.

As they passed beneath the streets of the Marketplace, she occasionally got whiffs of baking bread or of freshly cut flowers. Although she couldn't tell what the stores looked like from aboveground, she liked to think that some people were still carrying on with everyday life. She liked to think that the Garden hadn't been completely destroyed when she broke Teagan's magical pact, and it made her feel better to know there were signs of life. It gave her some power over the gnawing guilt that had only grown since she returned to the Garden.

They traveled beyond the Marketplace and then went uphill, and Shaleigh caught the scent of flowers. She knew exactly where they came from as soon as she smelled them because they seemed to fill the back of her throat and cling to her nose. It was the bridge of roses that they had passed through on their original journey to the Pasture. There was light at the end of the underground tunnel, and Graddic put hand up for them to stop as he went on ahead to check. The scent was incredibly strong and Shaleigh put a hand on Mawr's side, sad that her friend couldn't appreciate the smell like she could.

Graddic trotted back toward them, stopping to shake himself off like a dog before getting too close.

"It's going to be a wet walk," he said with chagrin. "The rain has come in."

"Maybe that's for the best," Talek muttered.

Shaleigh glanced to him, wanting to ask him why, but Graddic didn't let her get a chance to ask—"Alright, hurry up and keep quiet. It isn't really safe until we're deep in the Pasture."

Together they hurried behind Graddic, who was surprisingly fast for his size. They neared the entrance to the tunnel which curved upward and into daylight. Rainwater had already pooled at the base and Shaleigh winced as they stepped through the puddle and her feet got wet.

Graddic looked out of the tunnel one more time before gesturing for them to come. Colin was in the lead, sprinting on all fours toward the tunnel of roses. Teagan and Talek followed, and Shaleigh was one of the slowest. She wasn't a Faerie or a stoatling, so she didn't have their speed, but Mawr stayed close to her side as she hurried. Once they got into the safety of the bridge, the others paused to catch their breath.

"Did anyone see us?" Teagan asked.

Talek was looking out behind them. "I don't think so. Fortunately, it seems rather empty."

Graddic trotted over with them, water dripping off his nose ring. "It's been pretty empty out here since the High Castle fell. It's only really dangerous at night when the wolves come out."

The Shadow Wolves, Shaleigh thought. *That's why Talek was saying they should be glad for the rain.*

Graddic lead them through the bridge, then had them stop as he looked around on the other side. He took a while checking this time, and Shaleigh wondered if this side of the bridge was busier. She tried to think back to the plants that were being grown when they traveled through before, but she couldn't recall what they were. If the plants relied upon it to be eternally springtime, she imagined they were probably needing to be harvested quickly to ensure nothing went bad since fall was sweeping in quickly.

He turned around with a grunt and a shake of his

head. "It's no good. There are too many farmers out, and if I stare for too long, they'll get suspicious."

"We can travel quickly without being seen," Talek assured him. "We just need to know where to go."

Graddic laughed. "That must have been what I saw when I was looking through scraps at High Castle! You all must have been using magic to move so fast, right?"

"Something like that," Shaleigh said with a smile. "Do you know a place that's safe? I don't think many people will be really happy to see us back." She couldn't help but think of the three women that had mocked her when she came here before, and how Teagan had threated to remove the tongue from one of them.

"I've claimed a burned out barn not too far from here," he pointed in the general direction. "It's out that way."

Teagan sighed, saying, "That doesn't help us at all."

Talek crossed his arms and stepped closer to the exit, shutting his eyes tight. Shaleigh went over to stand with him to make sure that he wasn't seen while he was concentrating: Talek opened his eyes and they were clouded over again. "I see... several burned out barns." His voice was monotone.

"Mine's the one with the wood pile beside it."

Talek frowned.

Shaleigh said, "Just do your best. I know it's difficult."

Talek narrowed his eyes. "I think I found it. There's a barren fruit tree out front, correct?"

"Aye, that's it!" Graddic grinned. "That's some great magic you've got."

Colin was watching behind them, toward the entrance they came in, and his whole body went taut. Mawr was at his side, and they were whispering something to each other. Shaleigh wished she could be in two places at once, but she could guess that they didn't have long to wait here.

"That's it," Talek said, shaking his head and his eyes going back to brown again. "I think we can get there very quickly." He turned to Graddic, "You go on ahead and we'll meet you."

"You sure? I don't want to leave you out in the open like this."

Shaleigh went to his side. "It's a complex ritual and we don't want it to freak you out." She gave him a smile and Graddic matched it, giving a slow nod.

"If you say so, Shaleigh, I believe you. I'll go on ahead that way there's no suspicion." He looked around at all of them with a snort. "Good luck. I hope you make it." Without another word he bounded out of the covered bridge.

The rain was coming down harder now, and fat drops were dripping down between the roses and onto their heads. Shaleigh felt a roll of water go down behind her ear and shivered.

"We need to hurry," Colin muttered. "I can hear the Shadow Wolves in the tunnels talking to each other."

"Are they following us?" Mawr whimpered.

Colin glanced to him. "Seems like it."

Shaleigh reached out and put a hand on Mawr's flank. "We don't have much time. Come on." They all got into formation, shuffling through the dirt and mud to form a circle. "Okay, Talek, you know where we're going?"

"Yes," he said, with tension in his voice.

"Colin, give us speed. Teagan, see if you can keep us from destroying anything that might lead them to us."

Teagan blinked at her. "How am I supposed to do that?"

"You're resilient," she said, meeting his gaze. "Please, we can't let them follow us."

He pursed his lips and nodded.

"Mawr, be our strength. Don't let your fear overwhelm you."

He nodded.

"Okay, on the count of three: one, two—"

Shaleigh could hear the raspy voices echoing out from the tunnel. Even though she knew they were mind controlled and that they didn't even want to be there, she also knew how vicious and bloodthirsty they could be.

"Three!" she shouted and in a great dizzying spin, they flew out of the covered bridge. Shaleigh felt flowers smack her shoulder as they awkwardly took off. The panic made them unsteady. It didn't help that Shaleigh's adrenaline was coursing through her and she was having a hard time holding the steering wheel. Each of them were throwing all their energy into getting to where they needed to go, but that made them veer way off the path.

They passed by workers in the field wearing loose clothing and wide brimmed hats. None of them looked up as they passed, but Shaleigh hoped that they hadn't lead the Shadow Wolves to them. They skidded to the side and rolled through a patch of vegetables.

If the Shadow Wolves were following their scent, they needed to lead them on a wild hunt.

She felt Talek's path, straight and simple, and then

purposely avoided it. They pulled to the left, then to the right, and then circled back around to the bridge where she saw the shadowy forms of three wolves standing amid the roses. They looked angry and confused, good. She felt the fear, confusion, and panic of her friends, but Mawr supported her. She felt his warmth spread out to all of them, and their fear lessened. It didn't go away completely, but they at least trusted her judgment.

She took them on another half-loop, leading off in the completely wrong direction before shooting high into the air, and finally coming back down to the ground on Talek's path.

They started passing by burned out buildings everywhere, and Shaleigh wondered if this was from the initial assault with the Shadow Wolves. Had so much damage been done even this far out? It had been a week, and she had no idea the full story about what had happened in the Garden after it fell. Then she spotted a building straight ahead with a door held open wide. Graddic was standing outside, looking far too suspicious as he searched for them. Teagan did an excellent job of containing them as they traveled inside and landed with a sweep of wind in the center of the barn.

They stood on solid ground and Shaleigh took in deep breaths to calm her racing heartbeat. She smiled at her friends: Mawr gave a slow nod, his glasses glinting in the dim light. Colin was shaking and eased himself down to the ground against the wall.

"Are you okay?" she asked, going to his side.

"Yeah," he said, trying to catch his breath. "That was one heck of a joy ride!"

Teagan wasn't so thrilled. He had a hand to his chest. "While I understood the logic, I really wish you had warned us. For a moment I felt like I was going to pass out."

Talek let out a weak little laugh. "Was it when we were about to slam into the ground after being so high up that we could see the entire pasture? I didn't think we were going to stop in time."

Shaleigh felt a sandpaper tongue against her arm and turned to see Mawr at her side. "I wasn't scared. I believed in her."

"Psh," Colin hissed. "You were scared. Don't even act like that."

He hung his head. "Okay, maybe a little."

"Where did you all even come from?" Graddic was in the doorway staring at them with wide eyes. He looked like he was ready to bolt at a moment's notice. "That wasn't any kind of magic I've seen before!"

"I'm sure it wasn't," Teagan said, drawing himself up. "Now please quit your gawking and close the door behind you. We barely prevented a pack of Shadow Wolves from following us, and you seem determined to lead them straight here."

"Oh, sorry, Master Teagan." Graddic stepped inside and shut the door behind him with a snort.

The only light they had was through the cracks in the walls, and as her eyes adjusted, Shaleigh could see all the dust and debris floating in the air.

Talek came to her side. "Please don't do that again. After our debacle in the jail cells, that could have been dangerous for him," he motioned to Teagan who leaned against a wall with his eyes closed. "Any time we use that magic, it weighs on the mind, haven't you noticed?"

Shaleigh stared at him. She hadn't noticed, and in fact she felt invigorated after the high-speed flight. But Colin was still crouched down on the ground and Teagan was pretending to be in control, but he still had a hand on his chest—he was trembling. She might be strong enough to withstand using Tanwen's gifts again and again, but her friends weren't. In her desire to confuse the Shadow Wolves and to keep the workers in the Pasture safe, she had put them in danger.

"I didn't know," she whispered. "I feel fine."

Talek arched an eyebrow at her. "You lead this group when we use this magic. If you plan to lead well, you need to make sure you don't lose any of us." He glanced behind him at Teagan, then dropped his voice to a whisper, "Didn't you feel him cracking when we were with Keriam?"

Shaleigh thought back. She was so horrified by seeing Lieutenant Varg's children and seeing Madam Cloom's horrible injury, she couldn't remember. She should have been paying attention to her friends, but she hadn't. She had been too focused on herself. That was why Teagan had lost it. He probably showed signs that he was falling apart, and she probably could have felt it if she reached out, but she hadn't.

She wrung her hands. "I'm sorry, I'm still getting used to this, I guess. I always think that if I'm feeling well that everyone else must be too."

Talek put a hand on her shoulder. "But they're not. Teagan is struggling. He hasn't even come to terms with the fact that he *died*." Talek paused for a moment and took a deep breath, his eyes getting misty. "I haven't even come to terms with it."

"I know, and it was only a couple of days ago. So much has happened so quickly, I guess I'm just determined to take out Keriam before he kills anyone else I love."

Talek nodded, swallowing again as though trying to get himself under control. He was right, they had all been under so much pressure, and Shaleigh was the oddity in being able to handle it so well. The others were struggling, and she needed to take that into consideration before she did any more unexpected "joy rides," even if it was for a good reason. She couldn't risk her friends, not again.

"I'm sorry," she whispered. "I'll try to do better."

"Please. I know we're all learning how to handle this, but I worry about him. I worry about all of us. As powerful as our gifts are, this magic was never meant for us to wield. We don't know what kind of long-term damage it could cause... Just be mindful of us."

Talek wasn't talking about physical damage, but emotional and mental damage. That was just as important as the physical, and if they wanted to truly take down Keriam, she needed to take that into consideration too.

"Thank you for telling me," she said, rubbing on her arm. "No one else is as blunt and honest as you are."

He shrugged and gave a mischievous smile. "Once upon a time, Teagan hated my honesty."

"Well I appreciate it. Please, be honest with me. I can't help if I don't know, and I get caught up in everything else. I don't mean to; I care about all of you. I don't mean to hurt anyone."

He shook his head. "I never thought you did. You're too good a person for that. That's one of the reasons Keriam targeted you. He said you were naive." He gave an awkward laugh and Shaleigh smiled.

"I think he was right, but I'm trying to get better."

"Being a good person doesn't necessarily mean you're naive," he explained. "It just means you have a lot more to potentially lose."

The truth of his words was painful.

GRADDIC WAS AN INCREDIBLE HOST. He not only made sure they had places to sleep in his tiny little burned out building, but he also brought them freshly cooked vegetables.

The sun was slowly dipping toward the horizon and it sent long shafts of orange sunlight through the cracks of the barn. It was clear that the building they were in was meant to store food. She could see the remains of what she guessed were rat nests in some of the corners, though any vermin that had once made a home there had long fled.

It still smelled of charred wood. The corners of the walls were made of metal. She couldn't tell what kind because there was so much fire damage, but she could tell they were magically created and inserted into the ground. Normal metal pillars weren't made like that, and part of her appreciated that since it was still standing, it meant that Teagan had wanted it to be there in the first place. He probably put them in a long time ago. The wood that surrounded the barn was all blackened and charred, some of the pieces had fallen apart in the fire and were just propped up, leaning against the existing wood in an attempt to keep out the elements.

It should have been abandoned and demolished, not used as a makeshift house.

It turned out that the fall of the High Castle meant that the workers of the Pasture got to take the extra food they had grown. There wasn't really anyone to ask and nobody seemed to care, so the ones who survived the first onslaught took what they wanted because there was plenty to go around. It also meant Shaleigh and her friends were treated to a small feast.

Shaleigh had gotten so used to eating light, if she got to eat at all, that it seemed almost wasteful to have a giant plate of vegetables handed to her. There were even some slightly burned rolls that Graddic bragged about making himself.

"Some of the workers got controlled by Keriam," Graddic said, shaking his head as he ate. "It happened a few days after the Castle fell. They just came out and started setting the store houses on fire. Me and my buddies took out who we could and tried to put out some of the fires, but it spread so fast." He huffed. "They ended up destroying most of the living quarters, so the workers are now having to stay together. My buddies and I didn't want to cause any problems, so we offered to take the remains of these barns. The wood is still standing, though the rains tend to make them fall more than I'd like. And those pillars were built with metal, so they've held up pretty well. Like me, they're still standing strong." He grinned. "Sure, it gets cold some nights, but that's a small price to pay to have shelter."

Shaleigh could read between the lines. She saw the bigotry that many had against minotaurs in the Garden. She had seen how minotaurs out in the woods acted, how territorial they became, and how distrustful they were of anyone. It wasn't fair that Graddic should be forced to live in a burned out building just because the others saw him as more of a beast than an intelligent being. He was kind and hard-working, why couldn't that be enough to prove that he was decent?

"You deserve a real place to live," Shaleigh said to him, eating some sautéed zucchini.

He glanced to her with a small smile. "Thank you. Maybe one day, right? I'm not holding my breath though. I can make do. It's better than the shared barns we used to have to sleep in."

"You deserve better, you all do."

Graddic didn't say more on the topic and instead arranged sleeping locations around the room. Apparently the minotaurs of the Garden weren't comfortable even admitting the prejudices against them, and Shaleigh was too tired to convince him otherwise. There was so much about the Garden that still wasn't right, and it bothered her. She had originally thought that as soon as she broke Teagan's pact as High Faerie somehow the Garden would get better, that it would heal itself over time, but it was still upsetting to see that the bigotry was there even after the seat of power was toppled.

Fixing something that ingrained in the society would

take time, she realized. Sure, there were problems like that in her world, but there it felt impossible to fix anything—here there was a chance. She could see that there was a chance, she just wasn't sure how she would ever be able to help. Especially after she went back home.

As the sun set, Shaleigh began to understand just how dark it would be come night. Inside the small barn, she didn't have the luxury of starlight or moonlight really, and it was kind of frightening. The building they were in was barely livable and if someone did come out and set buildings on fire again, they wouldn't have any way to escape. But there was a place to sleep and a roof over her head, so she couldn't complain.

She laid down in her pile of hay and pulled up the blanket Graddic had given her. It smelled of hay. Everything smelled of hay. She had learned from Colin that half the blanket went down on top of the hay pile, and she folded the other part around her body to keep warm. It kept some of the hay from poking into her skin all night, but not all of it. Her whole body felt itchy as the others got comfortable for the evening.

"I'm going to keep a look out tonight," Graddic said, settling down on his only chair near the door. "I want you all to be able to get some sleep." He sipped on a cup of warmed water he got from one of his fellow minotaurs. "You all can stay here as long as you need to."

"We appreciate that," Talek whispered. "I know this is putting a strain on you. Do your friends suspect anything?"

Shaleigh couldn't help but smile. It would be Talek trying to pull information out of Graddic.

"I told them I have family visiting," Graddic said with a little laugh. "We don't ask questions here; we just support each other through thick and thin. We have to look out for each other, you know?"

Shaleigh was about to tell him how much she admired that, but the still night was cut with a high-pitched scream. The tiny barn fell silent as they all strained to listen.

"What was that?" Mawr asked in a terrified whisper.

"I don't know, I'm looking," Talek said.

As they waited, Shaleigh heard Graddic put his cup of water down on the ground and get to his feet.

"Shadow Wolves," Talek muttered to himself. "They're searching the Pasture..."

"Looking for us?" Teagan asked, but they all knew the answer to that.

There was another scream, a man's scream and Shaleigh flinched as Talek gasped.

"Don't watch, love," Teagan whispered. "It will only upset you."

Talek breathed hard, "I'll stop, sorry, it's just so... difficult to look away. They're going from building to building, searching for our tracks. I think they're confused because they can smell our presence, but they can't find our footsteps."

Another scream broke through the night along with shouts, followed by a child's wail.

"Oh dear," Mawr whimpered. "Should we just let them know we're here? Do you think that would make them stop hurting people?"

"He'll slaughter all of them eventually," Talek whispered. "We have to take out Keriam if we want to truly help them."

Shaleigh added, "These buildings are barely standing as it is. They have no defenses. I thought if we confused them on our way here, they wouldn't be able to do anything to track us, but—" She was cut off by a woman's scream. Dim orange light began to glint off one of the metal pillars. "Graddic? What's going on?"

He got to his feet and shuffled over between where Shaleigh and Teagan were laying down. He peered out through the cracks; his silhouette visible from the growing orange light.

"They caught one of the boarding houses on fire," he whispered. "It's a long way off, but this land is so flat and it's so dark..."

Shaleigh hunkered down in her blanket, watching the light pulse on the metal pillar and thinking of all the people who might be caught in the flames. There would be no way to get out. It probably only had one exit and the Shadow Wolves would monitor that doorway, killing anyone who tried to escape.

"Tomorrow, we finish Keriam," Teagan said. Shaleigh looked over at him, propped up on his elbow, watching where Graddic stood, a grim expression on his face.

She was surprised to hear such certainty from him after he had struggled so much before. "Are you sure you're up for it?" she asked, studying him.

"These are my people he's slaughtering. It's my duty to protect them."

Talek sighed behind him. "You're not the High Faerie any longer, love. You don't owe anything to them."

"I know," Teagan whispered, "but we're their only hope now."

Shaleigh hunkered down in her blanket, listening to the screams in the night as another metal pillar glowed with distant firelight.

They were the only hope these people had, like Teagan said. They had no option of failure tomorrow. She wouldn't hesitate next time. She had to kill Keriam or even more would die.

CONFRONTATION

Shaleigh woke sore and bleary-eyed. The smell of smoke was strong as she pushed herself up to a sitting position, wincing when her back and shoulder popped painfully. Gray, early morning light streamed in through the cracks in the walls and she could see Graddic sitting on his chair, arms crossed. He nodded at her as he gnawed on a piece of hay.

"Morning," he muttered. "I know it's not the High Castle, but it's more comfortable than a stone floor, right?"

Shaleigh gave him a sleepy smile. "It's great, Graddic. Thank you for helping us. I know you risked a lot."

He scratched under his chin, his nose ring shaking in the light. "Yeah well, it's a small price."

She understood what he meant. Others paid a much higher price last night.

Pushing herself up to her feet, Shaleigh's hip and knees ached from the uneven bed of hay. She had so much more respect for people who could sleep on this all the time.

"I'm sorry," she whispered, not really able to put into words all the reasons why she felt that way. She couldn't shake the feeling that she was responsible for those deaths.

Talek was right, she was the leader of their magical circle, she was Tanwen's Chosen, and she needed to be aware of who was struggling. She needed to know when to pull them back just like she needed to know when to strike. Next time she would be more cautious for her friends and more determined in what needed to be done.

Graddic shrugged. "We're all biding our time, to be frank. Every night the Shadow Wolves take a few, if not here, then in the Marketplace. Every night we bury more, and every night they come again. We're doing the best we can with what we have." He shifted the piece of hay to the other side of his mouth. "That's what I was doing when you found me on that rubbish pile, I was searching for more pieces of metal that I could use to strengthen this place. Most of it has already been salvaged, but I always try. You never know when you might find something useful."

Shaleigh squatted down, trying to look through the gaps out into the world to see what the damage was.

Graddic pushed himself up to his feet. "Careful with that, it's not a pretty sight out there." He said it like a father trying to protect his child from being scarred for life, but Shaleigh had already seen more horrors than she ever wanted to. She needed to see for herself what had happened. Perhaps it was the photographer in her, wanting to burn it into her own mind so she would never forget...

What did she want to remember? The guilt and the death that she felt partially responsible for? The weight of the failure on her shoulders and the knowledge that more had died due to her actions?

She took a deep breath as the cold morning air seeped in through the holes in the walls and looked out. A charred and blackened husk of a building stood only a short walk away and beside it blankets covered something lying in the dirt. She put a hand to her mouth. "Is that—?"

Graddic nodded but didn't meet her questioning gaze.

"I thought you said it was far away," she couldn't keep the panic from her voice.

He was silent for a moment, looking down at her; his brows furrowed. "I didn't want to worry you all. I was afraid you wouldn't be able to relax knowing how close they came." Shaleigh just stared at him, so he continued. "You needed rest! It was my duty to make sure you were guarded, so that's what I did. I made sure you were protected last night." He gestured to the bodies outside. "I feel bad for those people, you know I do. But you all have a chance to fix this. You have a chance to stop him and the Shadow Wolves for good."

He stared at her and Shaleigh saw just how exhausted Graddic was. He had deep circles under his eyes and there was a strain in his voice that hadn't been there before. He was acting like she was blaming him for those deaths, and that was when Shaleigh understood that Graddic felt just like she did. He held himself responsible just like she did, and that realization upset her.

She went to his side and put a hand on his shoulder, feeling his warm fur beneath her fingers. "Listen, you're not responsible for their deaths, do you understand?" Some part of her knew that she was speaking to herself just as much as she was talking to Graddic, and she accepted that. "You couldn't have stopped them even if you wanted to."

He blinked at her. "I've stopped Shadow Wolves before," he muttered.

Shaleigh grinned. "So have I. We had the power to stop all of this yesterday, but we didn't. We failed."

Graddic didn't respond and the silence filled the little barn.

"I know you don't want to think that we're capable of failing, but we are, and we failed horribly. I let down my team yesterday and we missed maybe our only chance at beating Keriam." She felt the tears building up in her eyes as she spoke, a mixture of exhaustion and weariness finally erupting in front of poor Graddic who didn't even understand what all they had been through. "We failed, and I don't know if we're going to get the chance again."

"You can win," he said. "He wouldn't have his Shadow Wolves out hunting for your scent if he wasn't scared of you. He knows you can beat him; he's always known."

Shaleigh shook her head. "No, he wants to see if I could be payment for a promise he made, but he's not frightened of us."

"Maybe that's for the best," Mawr whispered and Shaleigh turned to him with surprise. She had forgotten that he didn't really sleep and had been wide awake with Graddic all night. "If he's not frightened of us, then he won't think we're really a threat." Mawr started purring and Shaleigh could feel the vibrations in the ground. She went over and wrapped her arms around him.

"I'm just so tired of dealing with him," she admitted, embracing Mawr's warm fur and calming purrs. "He used me and now he wants to deliver me to a dragon."

"That's why Tanwen sent us to stop him," Mawr reminded her as he nuzzled her shoulder. "We're the only ones who can."

Shaleigh nodded and pulled away, wiping at her cheeks. "You're right," she muttered, her voice thick. "You're always right, Mawr."

He dropped his gaze. "No, I'm not. I just try to help is all."

"Well you're a great help to me," she said, rubbing under his chin. "I would be lost without you."

"And I would still be lost without you," he said with a weary smile.

ONCE EVERYONE WAS AWAKE, Graddic got them some more food. This time he gave them what tasted like raw pumpkin slices, but slightly sweeter. They almost tasted candied, and Shaleigh found herself eating not one but two helpings. Graddic left shortly after, claiming he had to help the others to prevent them from getting too curious about his visitors.

Talek didn't eat much but claimed that he couldn't eat much in the morning. Shaleigh wasn't sure if that was the truth or if he was still upset from watching the murders last night through his sight.

"I've been considering our approach today," Talek said while Teagan put an arm around his waist. "I've been monitoring his movements, and I don't think we'll be lucky enough to get him alone like we did before."

Shaleigh felt a pang of guilt in her stomach but then noticed that Teagan also lowered his eyes. She pursed her lips, feeling bad for him. As guilty as she felt, she knew Teagan had to feel worse about it. His breakdown had forced them to retreat.

"He spends much of his time in the Gully where the Games were held. That's been turned into a barracks for his soldiers, so clearly, it's one of the few places he feels safe. He has a tent setup there. It's large and well-guarded, but he does like to be alone. I think that's where we can strike."

"So, he's not going down into the dungeons any longer?" Colin asked through a mouth of food.

"No, in fact he's avoiding the place. I'm not entirely sure there is anyone else that knows that he's using the dungeon either. Each time I looked down there, all I see are the cell occupants."

"But those kids!" Mawr exclaimed. "They must be hungry."

"Keriam wouldn't want anyone seeing them," Shaleigh stated. "Who would he trust to handle that? Captain Briar said Shadow Wolves took Madam Cloom, so I imagine that's how he got the children too."

Mawr looked at her with horror.

"I'm sorry, Mawr. That's why Keriam needs to be stopped." She reached out and stroked his side.

He nodded and laid down with his nose between his paws.

"So, we can't take any detours with our visage of Tanwen this time. She needs to go precisely where she needs to be without any delay or distraction." Talek looked pointedly at Shaleigh as he spoke, and she gave an eager nod.

"Understood. No detours or anything, just exactly where she needs to be."

"Otherwise she could be traced back here, to these people, and I don't want that. I don't think any of us want that," Talek added with a sigh. They all nodded solemnly with understanding.

Shaleigh put aside her second plate, realizing that the person who had harvested the food might be one of the people dead outside. It put a grim perspective on her meal. "At least we can work from here without too much fear of being discovered," she said, exchanging glances with all of them. "Where is Keriam now?"

"I can look if we're ready to try to attack," Talek said, clasping his hands together.

"I'm ready," Teagan said, staring at the floor. "He's caused enough death."

"And enough pain," Mawr whispered.

"And heartache," Colin added.

Talek winced at his words. "Yes, he's certainly done that." He let out a shaky breath.

Shaleigh got to her feet. "If you are all ready, then I say we finish this."

Slowly the others joined her. The excitement and confidence they had felt the day before was gone, and in its place was a respect and duty for the task they had been given. This was the true purpose of their gifts; this was the final test of their abilities.

Shaleigh put a hand on Mawr's flank. "We can do this," she said, lifting her chin. "We've failed before, but we refuse to back down. We will not permit Keriam to control this land or the minds of his followers. We will not permit him to continue killing or to make his soldiers or his people do his disgusting deeds for him. We must stop him, even if it hurts."

Teagan closed his eyes and nodded, taking a deep breath. "We must stop him, even if we know others need us right now."

Mawr hung his head and gave a sad nod.

Talek added, "We must avenge our loved ones."

"We've got to kick his butt cause he doesn't deserve this place!" Colin cried. "He doesn't deserve the power he has. He's a jerk who uses people up and kicks them aside."

"Let's finish this," Shaleigh whispered.

Talek closed his eyes and opened them again. "I see him," he said with a serious expression. "He seems to be alone."

"Perfect," Shaleigh muttered.

SHALEIGH CLOSED HER EYES, feeling the energy of her friends mix together, and then opened her eyes from within Tanwen. The anger and determination of her friends flowed through Tanwen's body, but Shaleigh didn't allow herself to be swept away by the cacophony of emotions. She allowed them to exist separately from herself.

Tanwen turned to Talek, "Where?" Her voice was fire.

Talek smiled and glanced to his side where a clear path was lit up—Tanwen pursued it.

Flying with unprecedented speed and precision, Shaleigh felt her friends with her. Teagan didn't permit anything to stand in their way, either blasting through piles of rubble or skirting past buildings. Colin gave them speed, regardless of whether it was across dirt, grass, or piles of rubble, and Shaleigh could feel the heat rising in her legs from the energy he pushed in. Mawr's presence was the glue that kept them together, and Shaleigh appreciated his presence more than ever as the energy was difficult to contain.

Talek's path was perfect, moving out of the Pasture, through the rubble of the High Castle, and up the grassy hill toward the Gully. It was the same path Shaleigh had taken with Graddic and Teagan that fateful day so long ago when she thought she was going to be killed in combat. As they crest the hill, she expected to be blinded by the morning sun, but the day was overcast, and the Gully felt ominous.

No hot air balloons hung in the sky, and it was weird to see it so empty. Instead campfires were spread throughout the camp and gleamed bright against the gray world. All across the grassy land at the base of the Gully were small white tents and marching soldiers. There had to be dozens of them, moving along perimeters and more toward the center of camp. She could feel the press of Colin's words in her mind—"They're on high alert."

Of course, they were. It was clear that Keriam was shaken by Tanwen's visit the morning before, and he surrounded himself with soldiers to keep him safe. His tent was in the very center of the Gully, near the solid rock formation that used to lead to the stage and was the largest and most elaborate tent below. He must have thought that the location would be impenetrable and his enemies would find it impossible to pass through, but he didn't know what he was up against.

They hadn't lost their advantage yet, and Shaleigh felt a small flame of optimism build in her as they shot through the campsites, past the tents, past the caves that had been dug out for the Shadow Wolves to sleep during the day, past the soldiers who were on alert to spot and report anything.

Through the very walls of Keriam's tent, they finally paused, and Shaleigh understood why Keriam chose this place to hide. He had filled the tent with as many rugs, wine, decadence, and finery that he could find. He might not have a High Castle, but this was his equivalent.

She could feel the magic that made up his walls. It was strange to feel them through Tanwen's gifts. His magic was cold and warped compared to the magic that they wielded. His magic was a pale shadow compared to Tanwen's magic. Nothing was that powerful. Even their fake Tanwen couldn't hold a candle to her magic, but Keriam didn't need to know that.

Up ahead a pair of tent flaps were loosely pulled together, and Tanwen stepped forward to peer through the gap, her bare feet silent on the thick rugs. She thanked Colin for his attention to detail.

Keriam was in the next room pacing, back and forth from one side of the room to the other. His staff smacked the ground in time with his steps, dampened by the layers of rugs underfoot. Behind him was a chair covered in a thick fur blanket, and on the wall were maps. One she recognized easily as the Garden, with its Pasture, Marketplace, Gully, and the shadow of Pello Pines to the west. Another she recognized as the Land of the Fae and the Dark Lands. One map was very dark and hard to read, but it was the final map that made a shiver go down her spine. It was her hometown, complete with roads and bridges, homes and businesses. She even spotted the familiar shape of Ferris Factory that she and Kaeja had explored so long ago.

What was he doing with a map of her home? What was he planning? Shaleigh had too many questions and not enough information. For the first time she wondered if Keriam wasn't working alone, but if he had others willingly working with him. The Masked King planted the seed of immortality in his mind and also begged for Tanwen to help restore Teagan's life. Was there more to their arrangement than the Masked King let on?

She felt Mawr's concern, warm and comforting, sweep through her, urging her to be calm and to focus, but that was her home on the wall. That was where her father and Kaeja lived. The leader of the Shadow Wolves said that Keriam had allies, why hadn't she asked to know more? But Mawr was right, she had to keep her head, they had to finish this, even though she was seething.

So, with all the determination and fortitude she could

muster, she swallowed down the outrage and had Tanwen step through the flaps of the tent.

It took a moment for Keriam to realize she was there. Tanwen moved without a sound, so he had no indication he was no longer alone. Slowly he stopped, his back facing her, and sniffed the air. It was the scent that alerted him, the piece they had worked so hard to perfect.

The staff in his hand gleamed a vibrant pink and a ball of lightning formed above the crystal. He spun around and threw a great purple ball of electricity at her. Shaleigh felt Teagan shift and the electric ball slammed into Tanwen's chest but fizzled out. Shaleigh gave a confident smile, careful to not let it seep into Tanwen.

"How did you get through my guards?" he screamed. "How did you find me?"

"Did you think you could hide from me?" Tanwen asked. She advanced on him, making long strides over the worn rugs.

Keriam sliced his staff through the air, the crystal pulsed again, and a violet electricity shot out in front of him—it burst in front of his face and then seeped around his body. He smirked. "You won't take me off guard this time, dragon. I've sent plenty of people from the Human World to your sister's cave and she still won't accept my payment! So, it looks like I'm going to have to deal with you instead."

Keriam's confidence was incredible to think he could truly take on a dragon, but that confidence was his downfall. Shaleigh lifted Tanwen's hand and pushed through his barrier with ease. It should have resisted her or reacted with her presence. Shaleigh should have waited to let Teagan show it dissipate at her touch, but she was too caught up in Keriam, too determined to show him he was outmatched. Keriam gasped and backed away.

"That's impossible!" he snapped. "Even dragons aren't immune to magic."

Shaleigh realized her mistake and hurried to cover it. "You presume to know a lot about my kind, Keriam the Cruel."

"Do you think I would make an arrangement with a dragon of all creatures without doing my research? I know how they work. I know their limitations and I'm a master deceiver." The staff pulsed again and this time Shaleigh felt it rip through her body instead of Tanwen's. Her entire body trembled for a few moments and Keriam smiled. "Did you really think your parlor tricks would fool me? Clearly, you've stolen magic from someone, maybe Tanwen herself! I see all of you!"

Another blast of his staff and she felt it reverberate through them all. Shaleigh didn't know what to do. None of them had anticipated him finding out. None of them had known he could see through such powerful magic, but he could. She looked to the crystal in his staff and wondered for the first time where it came from. Did he have a dragon's gift too?

"Talek," he commanded with wild determination, "stop these fools. I order you! You are still bound to me, regardless of what that dragon did to you!"

Shaleigh felt Talek falter. "No," she whispered and wished she could see her friend, to hold his hand, to give him strength. They knew that Talek was still in a Pact with him, but they had no idea Keriam had control over it still.

"Don't do it," Teagan whispered.

Talek was struggling. She felt his energy started to fade, and she wondered if they would fail for a second time. Only she didn't think there would be a third attempt after this. Keriam knew their ruse, he knew their disguise, and he would hunt them down along with anyone who had helped them along the way.

They would all be killed if they didn't end this now.

She felt Mawr's comforting energy pour forward, enveloping her, overwhelming her fear. She felt Talek's affection too, and Teagan's and Colin's. They all knew the consequences if they failed, and none of them would let that happen.

Talek pushed forward and spoke through Tanwen's lips, "I refuse."

Shaleigh felt a surge of energy course through her and she rushed toward Keriam.

His eyes went wide. "I command you! You can't refuse me, no one can refuse me!"

Shaleigh reached out with Tanwen's arms and grabbed hold of his shoulders. His cloak caught fire instantly.

Keriam screamed. His staff caught aflame too, and he dropped it to the ground. Soldiers poured into the tent behind them, and she felt Teagan shift his energies again. Swords slashed at Tanwen's body but bounced off. Arrows were shot with crossbows into her back but bounced away as though she were made of stone. None of them could make a dent in her.

Tanwen dropped Keriam to the ground, his entire

body was engulfed in flame. He rolled around, trying to put it out, but it wasn't a normal fire. The fire Tanwen wielded came from the volcano on the Peak of Gwern, it was the fire from within Tanwen herself, a fire that Shaleigh knew hadn't been solely created by her and her friends.

The soldiers stopped attacking them. Instead they stood at the far side of the tent in awe. One soldier shot off a final arrow, but it bounced off like the others had. Finally, Keriam's cries subsided, and Shaleigh looked out at the horrified soldiers. "Keriam is vanquished after years of forcing others to do his bidding. Do any of you truly support him still?"

The soldiers began dropping their weapons, and metal clanged onto the ground. "You can choose a leader better than this..." Shaleigh wanted to say more, she wanted to give some kind of wonderful speech to give the soldiers something to empower them after the horrific sight, but she couldn't. Instead Tanwen was pulled back.

She shot through the soldier's camp, through the rubble of the High Castle, through the rose bridge, and through the burned out homes in the Pasture. Her form landed with a crash back to where she was formed, and the blast of Tanwen's landing flung all of them back. Teagan and Talek were flung against the walls of the barn, Mawr was pushed of his feet, and Colin landed in a pile of hay. Shaleigh smacked her head on the ground.

The room was filled with the smell of fire and ash, but it wasn't a smell they had created, it wasn't part of their illusion, none of them could make a scent that powerful. Exhaustion swept over Shaleigh as she looked up to the center of the room to see Tanwen standing there still. It was impossible though, none of them were conjuring her still. How was she still standing?

Tanwen turned to Shaleigh and their eyes locked; Shaleigh felt her stomach drop like it had on the Peak of Gwern as Tanwen gave a slow, respectful nod. Shaleigh heard three words reverberate through her skull, before she passed out: "You did well."

~

MOVING SHADOWS, shouts and cries, unintelligible words, crying... Shaleigh's dreams were filled with fear, despair, and fire. She thought she had woken up several times before being pulled back down into the blackness of unconsciousness again. She dreamed of smoke, of blood, of dragons, and magicians. She dreamed of the Dark Lands and Black Dogs, of sweet stone lions and beaten Captains, of scrappy kidnappers and two Faeries caught in an eternal embrace.

When she finally awoke, she heard birdsong, high and crisp and clear. It was the most beautiful sound she had ever heard, especially after her dark and disturbed dreams. She opened her eyes to see a window wide open, with white curtains moving in a breeze. A silver pitcher was sitting on a side table and she was in a real bed with pillows and even a mattress.

She pushed herself up onto her elbows and looked around in confusion. There was no one in the room, but the place reminded her of High Castle with great tapestries of unicorns and rabbits covering the stone walls and the wooden floor covered with rugs.

Where was she?

"Shaleigh!"

She looked to the doorway to see Lieutenant Varg wearing a big grin and rushing toward her. "You're awake!"

Shaleigh leaned away from him out of uncertainty. Wasn't he leading the soldiers who were trying to find them all for Keriam?

He composed himself and came to a stop a foot away from the bed. "I'm sorry, you must be confused."

"I am," she whispered, her voice hoarse.

He went over to pour her a glass of water. "You're in my house, and from what Graddic tells me, you've been asleep for two days."

Shaleigh stared at him. "What?"

He nodded, handing over a glass of lukewarm water. She drank it down quickly, eager to quench her parched throat.

"Graddic had you in his home for a couple of days, but none of you would wake. He began to worry that you never would. With Keriam dead, the Garden was without a leader, so I started trying to rebuild everything. The Shadow Wolves at first just stayed in their caves, not talking to anyone, it was strange. Then that evening they came out, asking who we were and where they were. Apparently Keriam was mind controlling them too. It was surreal." He laughed and sat down on the edge of the bed. He had a much thicker beard than before, but he also had dark circles around his eyes. He didn't look like he had been sleeping.

"What about my friends? How are Mawr and the others?"

"Still asleep," he said with a grim expression. "You're the first to wake."

She shook her head, suddenly realizing with terrifying clarity what she needed to tell him. She reached forward, grabbed at his shirt collar and spilled water all over the edge of the bed. "Your kids!" she cried.

He stared at her with wide eyes, putting a hand on hers. "Shaleigh, calm down."

"No, your *boys*! They're in the dungeons beneath High Castle, Keriam took them down there along with Madam Cloom. You have to help them!"

He put a hand over hers, warm and comforting. "I know, we found them the day that Keriam was killed."

Shaleigh slowly let go of his collar. "Oh."

He gave a patient nod. "They're getting better." He let out a sigh as tears came to his eyes. "I don't know if they'll ever fully recover after what they've seen, but they're better. I should never have let him find them."

"You didn't know Keriam was going to blackmail you."

He closed his eyes and winced at her words.

She shook her head. "I'm sorry. I'm not trying to upset you." The Lieutenant didn't respond so Shaleigh continued, "I'm glad they're doing well. I was worried about them. Wait, what about Madam Cloom? And... Owain? Did you find his body?"

The Lieutenant looked to the ceiling and sniffed, wiping at his nose as he tried to get himself under control.

"Yes, we found Owain, too. Madam Cloom is in the next room over actually." He gave another smile. "She's been a handful at times."

"I bet," Shaleigh whispered. She wished she could take back her words, but she knew she couldn't. Nothing could undo the damage that had been done to his children.

He reached over and patted her hand again. "I'm heading in to see how rebuilding is coming along. The Shadow Wolves help in the evenings, but some of the soldiers are still wary around them. I like to be present to make sure nothing goes wrong."

She nodded. "Thank you again."

"You all saved us from Keriam. You don't need to thank me for anything." He got to his feet and headed out the door. Shaleigh listened to his footsteps disappear and took a deep breath to calm down. Thank goodness those kids had already been found or they would have been in even worse shape.

She lowered herself down on the bed, bothered by how shaky she felt. How had she slept for two whole days? She dragged a hand over her face. She needed to find Graddic and her friends, she needed to make sure everyone was okay. Then there was Madam Cloom—

"Ow!" She hissed as the scales of her palm scratched her cheekbone. She brought her hand back and stared at the tiny scales along her palms. At least she knew it wasn't all a dream.

Shaleigh rolled out of bed and got to her feet, wincing as her body ached all over. She hurt, but at least she was alive. She poured herself another glass of water and did a double take at the clothes that had been left for her on the side table. A long-sleeved cotton blouse and a gathered skirt. She glanced down to her own outfit from centuries ago then changed. She kept the coat though; she had no intention of leaving that behind. Clothes were a rare and valuable commodity for her these days.

The clothes fit well enough, and when she pulled on the fur lined coat, she instantly felt more like she could handle whatever came next. She pulled on her shoes, grabbed her glass of water, and went off to find her friends.

They had better wake up.

She didn't want to deal with any of this without them.

THE MOST POWERFUL MAGIC

Shaleigh stepped out of her room and into the hall. She could see down the stairs to the first floor of the building, and the semicircle of rooms upstairs. Each door was closed, and she heard no noises coming from any of them. She turned to the left and went to the first door she came to; knocking caused a groan to come from the other side. Her eyes went wide as she turned the handle and pushed to go in, only the door caught on the doorframe at the top. She shoved it with her shoulder and the door gave, tumbling her into the room.

Madam Cloom sat up in a bed and arched her eyebrows at Shaleigh. Her mouth was covered with a white bandage that wrapped around her head.

"Madam Cloom," Shaleigh muttered, breathless and confused, "you're here."

She huffed an inaudible response then reached over for a chalkboard that was on her nightstand. She wiped at it with a cloth as Shaleigh approached.

"You're alive, I'm so glad. Captain Briar told me what happened to you. I was so worried he had—"

She held up the chalkboard and it took Shaleigh a moment to understand why. She couldn't talk. She couldn't use her mouth to speak. If she could, it was probably only basic words. When Talek had taken away her mouth, she had never truly gotten it back. Even after Keriam was dead, she was still unable to speak.

Shaleigh's gaze flitted down to her bandaged mouth again and she shook her head. "I'm so sorry that happened to you. I never intended that to happen. You know that, right? I mean, I know you wanted to kill me, but I never intended for you to be hurt."

Madam Cloom rolled her eyes and smacked a hand against the chalkboard, making Shaleigh jump. Then she tapped a fingernail against the board and Shaleigh had to step all the way up to the bed to read what she had written there. Her handwriting was sharp and jagged.

Glad you finally killed the bastard.

Shaleigh laughed and Madam Cloom's eyes crinkled with a smile. "I'm glad we did too," she finally got out through her laughter.

Madam Cloom wiped the board down again with practiced ease, then wrote quickly on the board again and flipped it around—*I shouldn't have tried to kill you. That was a foolish move.*

Shaleigh couldn't help but grin. Madam Cloom likely never apologized for anything, and even here she refused to admit any wrongdoing, only admitted that strategically it was a bad move.

Closing her eyes, Shaleigh sighed. She stared down at

the white bed sheets, and the words came out without her even meaning to—"Captain Briar asked me to make sure you were alive and well. She demanded that I help you even though she couldn't come herself. She loves you; did you know that?"

The shock was clear in Madam Cloom's eyes as she brought the chalkboard down to her lap. After a moment she shook her head.

"She told me after my friends rescued her in the woods. That's why she stood by your side after the Garden fell." Shaleigh felt her eyes threaten tears and wiped at her nose to fend them off as she tried to find the right words. "I know that you didn't care for your soldiers that night. I watched as you let your own city burn. You abandoned your troops. I don't know if Captain Briar knows that, but I do. The enemy was at the gate and you holed up in your throne room instead of helping them."

Madam Cloom wiped off the board and scraped chalk down it, holding it up with shaky hands: *She was a Captain of the Garden. That was her choice.*

Despite her words Shaleigh could see the tears in her eyes. She kept her voice low. She would not let Madam Cloom draw her into anger again. "I'm not sure if she'll make it back here alive, but if she does, please promise me you'll be kind to her. Promise me you won't just use her all over again."

Madam Cloom put a hand to where her mouth used to be. Her hand was bruised in places and it shook against the bandage as a tear fell down her cheek. She took a deep breath and leaned back against the headboard, staring up at the ceiling.

Shaleigh had never seen her look so vulnerable before, so shaken. Even when she spotted her in the jail cell, she was defiant and wary. She wondered if Madam Cloom had ever known love before. She wondered if anyone had ever cared for her that much. It had to be a lonely existence clawing to the top, only to find out she was surrounded by tainted loyalties and disgust. Even if she did choose that, it didn't mean she liked it.

Finally, Madam Cloom nodded and wrote on the chalkboard with shaky hands, *I promise.*

"Thank you," Shaleigh said with a smile. "I have to go check on my friends now."

Madam Cloom held out a hand and began writing again; Shaleigh waited.

Never forget yourself.

Shaleigh stared at the words for a long moment, letting the meaning sink in. Madam Cloom had forgotten herself, she realized. She had forgotten who she was and why she was doing things. Shaleigh met her gaze, feeling shaken from the inside.

"I'll try," she whispered. "Thank you."

Madam Cloom put down the board and then gestured for her to leave, her eyes crinkling again with a smile.

Shaleigh nodded. "I mean it. Thank you. You're a terrible teacher, but I did learn a lot from you." Madam Cloom gave a bitter laugh as Shaleigh left, closing the door behind her.

Stopping, she leaned against the wall, trying to wrap her head around what just happened. It felt surreal to know that Madam Cloom appreciated what she did, that she admitted to being wrong, that she lost herself along the way.

Had she lost herself too? Had she gotten so wrapped up in everything that was going on that she had forgotten who she was and what she was fighting for? She thought of her father again and of Kaeja. Soon she would see them, she promised herself. Soon.

ONCE SHALEIGH HAD COLLECTED HERSELF, she checked the other rooms. Teagan and Talek were in the next bedroom over, fast asleep, or rather, unconscious. They were a foot apart on the bed, their hands resting identically on their stomachs, and for a brief moment, Shaleigh thought they were dead. She went to Teagan's side first, shaking his arm, but he didn't budge. She went to Talek's side next.

"Talek?" she whispered, pushing some hair out of his eyes but he didn't move either.

Panic started to build in her. Why had killing Keriam caused them all to lose consciousness? She turned toward the door when a sudden thought occurred to her. Turning back to Talek, she pulled out his arm, inspecting his wrist —the black ribbon was no longer there.

So, their Pact was broken. It must have happened when Keriam died, maybe that was why they were all pulled back to their bodies. She tried to remember to the night that she cut Teagan's ribbon, but she didn't recall a magical explosion like this. All she remembered was that strange gong that reverberated everywhere. Was it because Keriam died? Or perhaps because the Madness that had infected the Pact originally?

At the door, she turned to look at them for several minutes, waiting for them to open their eyes, to look at her, or to call her name. Neither of them moved and as she pulled the door closed, she felt a weight fill her. Would they ever wake?

She tried the next door, the final door on this side of the semicircle. The bedroom was smaller than the others, reminding her of a child's room more than the large rooms everyone else had been in. Had this been one of Lieutenant Varg's son's rooms?

She found Colin curled up like a cat with his head on the pillows, sound asleep. His tail didn't even move. She went over and took his hand, waiting for him to crack a joke or make some annoying comment, but he didn't even squeeze her hand. She put his hand back down on the bed and took a deep breath.

None of them were awake. Why not? Why was she the first, a girl from the Human World? This was all their world's magic, so why did they have such a hard time dealing with it?

She checked the other rooms upstairs and found Lieutenant Varg's bedroom and another child's room that was empty. She couldn't find Mawr anywhere. She went downstairs, the wooden steps creaking under her weight. There she found the drawing room, the kitchen, a dining room, but still no Mawr.

Nobody else was home.

As she walked through the kitchen for the second time, she stopped and took a moment to think. Of course,

Mawr wouldn't be inside, he was too big to even fit through the front door. So where would he be? She went out the front door, wondering if she needed to check the Pasture or maybe the library to find him, but two guards stood on either side of the entrance.

"Oh!" She froze at the sight of them, thinking for some reason that they were going to capture her. But the woman smiled at her.

"You're Shaleigh, right? It's good to see you're awake!"

Shaleigh fought back the urge to run off and stepped forward. "I'm looking for my friend, Mawr."

"Who?" the other guard asked.

She almost just pushed past them to go look for him herself, but she was wary of the pikes they held. They weren't her enemy anymore, she reminded herself, but it was difficult to calm the flutter in her chest.

"Are you talking about the Living Statue?" the woman asked.

"Yes, I don't know where he is. I looked all through the building, but I couldn't find him."

She stepped closer and Shaleigh took a step back without meaning to. The woman had dark skin and a warm expression. She pursed her lips at Shaleigh's reaction and stopped before getting too close. "He's on the wagon still. We couldn't move him." She motioned to the side of the house. "Here, I'll take you to him."

Shaleigh stared at her for a moment, uncertain if it was a good idea to follow her or not.

"I promise, we're on your side," she said with a smile, clearly bothered by Shaleigh's mistrust.

Swallowing down her nerves, Shaleigh glanced over to

the other guard as she passed; he gave her a polite nod. Following the female guard, she kept her distance. "Why are you patrolling this house? I thought Keriam was dead."

"He is," she said, glancing back with a smile. "And we're very grateful. Lieutenant Varg asked us to prevent anyone from going inside as we're certain Keriam still has soldiers loyal to him. Many of the people reported attacks and abuse, and we expect to hear of more still."

Shaleigh thought back to the soldiers attacking people in their homes and in the shops in the Marketplace. The guards were meant to protect them, not keep them there... It was still difficult to quell her own distrust.

The guard led her to the side of the home to where a pair of wagons stood. A small barn was nearby where food was likely stored—she could smell herbs as she got closer. One of the wagons was weighed down far more than the other, only inches above the ground: Shaleigh didn't wait to be told this was where he was, she grabbed hold of the side of it even though her arms were shaking.

The guard put a hand out to stop her. "Is that a good idea? You just woke up!"

"I'm fine," she muttered as she pulled herself up, stumbling only once as her foot got caught. Her heart nearly burst at seeing Mawr: he was spread out on the hay in the wagon, his nose nestled between his front paws and his tail laid still at his side. He was breathing though, and that took away the fluttering in her chest. She crawled around to his face and scratched the bridge of his nose.

"Mawr," she whispered. "It's me. Please wake up."

Mawr grunted and twitched. She smiled as her eyes grew hot from tears. She moved to scratch his cheek.

"Mawr? Please wake up, I need you. I need my stars." She tried to keep control of her voice, but her throat tightened up.

Mawr opened his eyes slowly as if he were drugged. "Shaleigh?"

"Mawr," she cried, and wrapped her arms around his head. "I'm so glad you're alright! We did it! We stopped him!"

He started purring and the entire wagon vibrated beneath them.

The guard laughed from behind her and Shaleigh glanced to see her turn and head back to the house. "Don't worry, I'm sure the others will rouse soon!"

THE GUARD WAS RIGHT. Over the next few hours, the rest of her friends woke as well. Colin was the first, followed by Teagan, and finally Talek.

None of them liked the idea of being separated after all they had been through, especially alone in the empty house with Madam Cloom, so they all came outside to sit with Mawr. He wanted to stay in the wagon longer until he felt more awake, but decided it was too close to break-ing. So, he had to gingerly step out of it as the others trickled outside.

The smell of the herbs and vegetables wafted toward them from the barn, mixing with the scent of the river that wasn't too far away. They must be somewhere south of the Marketplace, maybe even near the ocean because she occasionally caught the scent of the sea. In the distance she could hear the bustling of people in the Marketplace, from the creaking of wagons, to hammers falling, to distant talking. The Garden, it seemed, was coming back to life again.

"I hope his kids will be okay," Colin muttered, stretching and cracking his neck.

"Lieutenant Varg said they were doing better, so I think they have a good chance," Shaleigh said. They might recover physically, but she knew that the mental scars would take far longer to heal.

"If only we had come sooner," Teagan sighed.

Talek gave him a squeeze. "Don't think like that, love. We did what we had to in order to kill Keriam."

Shaleigh stared up at the sky, the robin's egg blue color was turning purple and pink as the sun sank. She watched the clouds lazily float by overhead, oblivious to the danger that had passed.

Shaleigh thought back to the moment, the scene etched into her memory–Keriam had seen through their disguise. He had seen through to them. He knew who had killed him at the very end, and he knew it wasn't Tanwen. She remembered the smell of him catching on fire, she remembered his screams filling the air, and shuddered —"Do you think we did the right thing?"

Colin scoffed. "Of course we did! You see all the people he killed, all the lives he sacrificed for his own gain. What do you think would have happened to this place if we hadn't? More deaths, that's what. Tanwen knew that. She understood what he would do."

"All for immortality?" Talek asked. "Is that what it was all about, do you think? I don't even know how many he sent to the Dragon of Darkness trying to pay for his abuse."

Teagan shook his head. "No, he wanted power. That's why he did that to Owain. He hated Cathal and always wanted to show him up, to prove that he was more powerful. Owain was Cathal's best friend, so he took his anger out on his corpse instead of Cathal himself. Cathal died long before he could ever get close to him." He gave a heavy sigh. "I suppose in a way Keriam got what he wanted in the end. Only he could never hold onto that much power. He didn't know how to lead."

"Because he didn't care about the people he led," Shaleigh stated. "He didn't care about any of them, he just wanted them to look up to him and follow his orders."

IT WAS ALMOST dark when the Lieutenant came back, grinning ear to ear when he found them near his barn. "I'm so glad to see you all awake! How are you all feeling?"

"A little shell shocked," Colin replied with a lopsided smile. Talek nodded and put a hand on Colin's back in agreement.

"How are your boys?" Shaleigh asked.

"They're doing well, just recovering from dehydration." He turned away for a moment, swallowing down his emotion. "My youngest hasn't said anything yet, but he's eating and drinking. I just wish he would talk to me." He wiped at his mouth with the back of his hand and cleared his throat.

"If you think reading them a story would help, I don't

mind," Mawr said, his tail twitching behind him. "Reading a book always makes me feel better."

Lieutenant Varg laughed then sniffed. "I'll let them know that. I'm sure they would be thrilled." He smiled. "Here, let me get some food brought out and we'll celebrate. We have so much to be thankful for."

He went inside, and came back out with the two guards, all three of them carrying food. They ate, they shared stories, they laughed and cheered for the freedom of the Garden and an end to the violence. For a little while Shaleigh could escape with them, she could relish in their victory and forget the cost. She knew deep down that she still had one final decision to make, one that she had been dreading for days.

She needed to go home, to see her dad and her friend, but a part of her didn't want to. A part of her wanted to stay with her new friends, with the people she had fought beside and grown to love. She didn't know what to do.

The sun was nearly set, and the stars had spread out in the sky. The clouds were gone, and the waxing moon rose high into the sky before Lieutenant Varg finished off the last bottle of wine and excused himself for the night.

A stillness fell over all of them all, fragile and delicate. It was a moment that seemed to last forever but was also terribly brief. She glanced to each of them: Teagan and Talek were staring up at the sky, Mawr was curled around Shaleigh protectively, and Colin was staring right at her.

She didn't want the moment to end, but it had to.

"Are you still planning to go home?" Colin asked, breaking the spell that had held them together, the silence that cocooned them from dealing with reality.

It was such a simple question and her initial response was of course, that was what she had worked so hard for, what her friends had fought for. Yet, the words wouldn't come to her, and instead she pursed her lips. She looked at them all as if seeing them for the first time.

Colin, the stoatling who had kidnapped her but now was one of her best friends. She saw Teagan as practically a second father now. They had both seen each other fail and falter, but still they persisted. When she had first met Talek, she had thought he was a friend only to be ultimately betrayed. Then she slowly began to understand why he had betrayed her and found herself fighting alongside him too. Then there was Mawr, her stars. He was one of the most dedicated friends she had ever known. He stood beside her even when it was dangerous.

She cherished all of them.

Tears fell down her cheeks, but none of them said a word. They had all shed tears, hadn't they? She wasn't the only one who had lost, they all had. Could she really go back to being a high school student, feigning interest at her father's parties? Could she pretend that she hadn't experienced this extraordinary world and met these incredible individuals?

"I love all of you," she said, letting her heart find the right words to say. "You know that, right?"

They all nodded, and Mawr purred hard behind her.

"I don't want to leave any of you."

Colin nodded toward her. "But...?"

The words came again, like a mantra, memorized and repeated but barely understood anymore. "But my father... I don't even know if he's alive."

Teagan cleared his throat. "Let's be realistic. How can we send her home? There are no more Faerie pacts and I don't think the Magicians of the Sanctuary are keen on helping us right now."

"What about the bike?" Colin asked. "That might still be working, right?"

Teagan shook his head. "I never wanted to steal humans away from their world, regardless of what Madam Cloom said. When my Pact was severed, so was the magic of that flying bicycle."

"Maybe that's for the best?" Shaleigh asked, and they all looked to her. There was no judgment in their eyes, only pity. They found this as difficult as she did. They had brought her here against her will, and now she might truly be stuck here. After all this work, after all the battles and the words, she might find herself tethered here. She wouldn't mind it either if she knew her dad was well.

Talek let out a sigh and stared up at the sky. The waxing moon hung like a beacon, casting a blue glow over the world. The air was filled with crickets and the hooting of an owl in the distance. "You have a foot in two worlds now," Talek said. "You have lives in both, titles in both. You're both a high school student and Tanwen's Chosen."

Colin grinned. "Yeah but Tanwen's Chosen sounds way cooler, doesn't it?"

"I know how difficult that can be," Mawr whispered. "Living in two worlds at once. I used to find it just awful before I met you all."

Shaleigh rustled his stone fur. Her hands had callouses now from all the petting she gave him, and the thought of not being able to pet him anymore made her chest tighten.

Talek pressed on, "Straddling two worlds is a difficult weight to carry. You have every right to be confused, and you don't need to make a decision now. You can wait."

Shaleigh closed her eyes and listened to Mawr's purrs and the soft rhythm of the crickets. "Dad needs me. He doesn't have anyone else and he's so fragile on his own. You haven't seen him break down like I have. It hurts." She sniffled and leaned against Mawr. "But I still don't want to leave. I don't want to lose any of you. I need you all."

Colin got to his feet with a sigh. He kicked at a rock and it went scurrying toward the barn. "This is ridiculous. People go back and forth between the worlds all the time. Why can't we? If we can fight a fool Magician, surely we can help Shaleigh out."

Teagan lowered his gaze and Mawr shook his head.

Shaleigh couldn't help but smile at their frustration. She knew they didn't want her to leave either, but here they were trying to help her get home. Here they were, doing their best to fight for her even if it meant never seeing her again. She loved them so much.

Talek tapped a finger on his lips. "We might not have a convenient bicycle, but we are imbued with the magic of a great fire dragon. I would argue anything is possible if we put our minds to it." He glanced to Teagan and put a hand on his knee. "If I didn't believe that, I don't think Teagan or I would be standing here today."

"No," Teagan laughed. "No, you would have burned this whole city to the ground."

Talek nodded with a wide smile. "Probably, yes."

Shaleigh shifted her hand in Mawr's fur, feeling the scales of her palm catch on the tendrils of stone. She paused, pulling up her hand and staring down at the tiny little scales on her palms. "I willed my scales to be smaller when Tanwen gave them to me. She said I did that, not her."

"You are her Chosen," Talek reminded her. "I don't think she would have given that dedication lightly."

"Changing the look of some scales is different from traveling to another world."

Talek untangled himself from Teagan and crouched down before her. It was so good to see his calm, normal brown eyes instead of the swirling violet she thought would lead to their death. "You know, when I was younger, I never thought I would be a very good artist. I thought I was doomed to always be terrible at the craft. Living such a long life does not necessarily mean I have a natural talent, you know."

Colin laughed, hopping up into the wagon and letting his legs dangle over the edge. "Would you listen to this guy? He draws masterpieces in a matter of seconds and yet he doesn't think he's talented."

Talek rolled his eyes. "That is not talent. That skill came from years and years of practice. My earliest attempts looked like they were created by a child. I took my time and worked hard to improve my craft, and now I consider myself a fairly decent artist."

Shaleigh shook her head. "Making a drawing is way different than hopping to another world."

"Is it?" he asked with a gleam in his eye. "We practiced to make Tanwen. We practiced to give her life and to make her strong. She was more than just a figment, she was weight, heat, terror, even smell. That took practice. That was a skill we all had to craft together."

Shaleigh stared at her hands again. "So, you're saying we should all work together to create something?"

Talek reached forward and clasped her hands, drawing her attention to his face again. "No, I'm saying you have to create it. You are the one who needs to go to the Human World, but you also want to return. If you don't have the confidence to get there, how can you possibly get back?"

Shaleigh stared at him. She wanted to believe it could be possible. "What if it doesn't work in my world? What if the magic is like Tanwen's magic, and it only works here?"

"Because you are now connected to both worlds. You are both Human," he gently unfurled her fingers, "and dragon."

She stared at her hands. She had never considered that before. She had never thought that Tanwen had changed what she was, even though it was clear she had. She wasn't that different from Colin or Mawr in that sense—part dragon. The thought was both terrifying and invigorating.

Talek stepped back and smiled to the others. "What do you all think? I think she's capable of it."

Colin smirked. "I mean, she taught me what a kidnapper was, and I was a freaking kidnapper."

Mawr got to his feet so he could turn and look her in the eye. "She was a friend to me when nobody else was. I think she can do anything she wants."

"Do it for someone you love," Teagan whispered. She looked up at him, surprised. "The most powerful magic is born out of love."

She thought back to the Madness, and how Talek had gained it after feeling completely unloved by Teagan. She thought of the Masked King, and how he was prevented from being with the one he loved. Even Tanwen had spoken of her land as someone who truly loved it.

"Give it a try," Mawr said, stepping back to give her space. "And if it doesn't work, you can try again tomorrow."

Talek stared at her. "Use that spark, use that inspiration and that flame of creativity to create what you know you need."

Shaleigh closed her eyes, and her friends went quiet. She listened to the crickets and to the owl who was more distant than before. She wasn't holding her friends' hands, but she imagined she could feel their emotions like she could when they were casting magic together. They supported her, they loved her, they understood her, and they wanted her to be happy. They could tell she was struggling, and they wanted to help her.

Their love made her stronger.

She thought of Dad first, of his face when he sat beside her in the car that evening. She saw him first as her dad waiting for an explanation for his daughter's rude actions, then she saw him again bawling his eyes out in the garage; he had a hard time knowing how to talk to her sometimes, and they had more fights than she wanted to remember, but she knew he loved her. He had always loved her, and she loved him.

She remembered watching movies with him. She remembered laughing with him. She thought of his face, not sad but happy. Even when she lost her temper, he still loved her. Even when he embarrassed her, she still loved him.

She thought of Kaeja next, always at her side and ready to take on a new adventure. She took Shaleigh's quirks and weirdness with stride and was always ready for anything. She was perhaps the most supportive person she had ever known. Shaleigh missed her hugs. She missed sitting with her on park benches with their hearts pounding in terror. She missed her quirky fashion sense. Kaeja always cared for her, even when Shaleigh didn't know how to care for herself.

Mawr came swiftly into her mind. She felt his warmth and comfort. She imagined she could feel his low purrs and his sandpaper tongue over her hand. Then came Teagan, rolling his eyes and her. He was always supportive, annoyed, or both at the same time. She liked that about him. They understood each other, probably better than they understood themselves.

Then there was Talek and his intense, warm presence. She felt like she could always talk to him about anything, good or bad, and he would understand. He had been through so much and so had she. Both of them had made terrible mistakes, but they helped each other to stand and brave the world despite it.

Finally, there was Colin, always joking, always finding ways to deescalate a situation. And finding unique ways to put his foot in his mouth. She remembered his shock when she explained to him that he was a kidnapper, and how it had transformed his perspective completely.

She couldn't choose between them all even if she wanted to. She couldn't decide who she would keep and who she wouldn't. She wanted to be able to see all of them. She imagined a street where they each had a building in various styles and shapes. She wanted to visit any of them whenever she wanted, like she visited the Tree House back home.

An image of a door appeared in her mind, and Shaleigh recognized it. It was the same one in her house that led to her mother's room. The handle was polished, and the carpet vacuumed. It looked just as her Dad had always kept it. She reached out and tried to turn the handle, but it wouldn't budge in her grip—it was locked.

What she needed was a key.

She looked down to her hand and there it sat, small and silver, reminding her almost of the silver scissors she used to cut Teagan's Faerie Pact ages ago.

She opened her eyes, and looked down, staring at her hand. In her palm, the key still sat as though she had plucked it out of her own mind. Her mouth dropped open and she glanced to the others with wide eyes.

"Oh my gosh, did it really work?" Colin swung himself down off the edge of the wagon in an instant and peered down into her hand. "It's so tiny!"

Shaleigh covered her mouth, not sure whether to laugh or cry. How had she done that? How had she pulled it out of thin air?

She held it up to the moonlight and watched it gleam. It was freshly polished just like the doorknob had been.

Talek elbowed Teagan. "See? She just needed some guidance."

Teagan rolled his eyes. "I never said she couldn't do it. I just wasn't certain if it was possible."

She eyed them both. "You mean you both didn't know if it would even work?"

Talek shrugged. "It's magic, there's really no telling what will or won't work until you try it. That's why it's so damn dangerous."

"Personally, I enjoy experimenting with it, to learn its limitations and its dangers. It's what makes wielding magic so thrilling," Teagan said with a wicked smile. And that was why she and Teagan got along: they both enjoyed playing with fire.

Mawr shuffled closer and Colin had to move out of his way so he could see. "Shaleigh, it's beautiful!"

"Thanks," she said, her voice cracking. She moved the key to grip in her fingers like she was going to unlock a door. "I... honestly don't really know how I did it, but it worked."

Mawr looked up at her, his glasses glinting on his nose. "Does that mean you're going back then?"

A hush came over all of them and Shaleigh took a deep breath, turning to look at him. "If I do, I'll come back to you."

"Promise?" Mawr asked, his voice breaking.

"I promise. I can't possibly live without my stars, now can I?"

She wrapped her arms around him and gave him a big hug, feeling his tears fall. After a few moments, they pulled away and she wiped at her cheeks.

"So, do you plan to actually use it?" Teagan asked, folding his arms. "Or did you merely make it as an experiment?" Despite the question, there was a desperation in his voice. It was his own way of showing concern.

"Calm it, Teagan, I'm getting there." She looked around at all of them. "I love you guys, okay? Whatever happens. Don't forget that."

"Never," Mawr whispered.

"Ah, don't be like that. You'll be right back!" Colin gave a strained smile.

"If not, we'll see if we can send a Magician over to fetch you," Teagan said with a smile. "I hear they make terrible Seekers."

Talek added, "You don't need a Magician. You have plenty of magic in you already." He held up a finger. "But you had best not prove me wrong."

She smiled and held the key out in front of her. She waited for something to happen, but nothing did. She willed it to take her home, but it didn't. She scrunched up her face and turned the key to the side like she was unlocking a door.

The world seemed to slow down for a brief moment and Shaleigh watched a silvery outline of a door appear before her. There was the sound of a latch unlocking, and then the door swung upon. It was as if the door had been hidden there the entire time.

The door opened up to a room that was hard to see. It was very dark and strewn with leaves. She felt a cold breeze sweep out; it smelled familiar: old wood, moldy cloth, and the poignant scent of decaying leaves. The outline of a rocking chair was barely visible right where she had left it…

It was the Tree House, the very room she was stolen from so long ago. She stepped in, taking in the sights, the smells, the distant roar of traffic, and tears came to her eyes. The floor was warped under her feet, and she had to put her arms out to keep from tripping. It was the same, all of it.

"It worked!" she cried, turning around to tell the others, but the door she had stepped through was gone. A sinking feeling took over, and she wondered if she would be able to get back.

She had to try.

She had to make sure she could, and let the others know.

She fumbled with the key, her hands shaking as she turned it again and again. Only there was no lock this time or an outline of a door. "It doesn't work," she whispered, her voice filling the empty room for the first time in over a week.

TWO WORLDS

She tried again and again, turning the key and feeling the panic rise.

"No, this isn't right. I didn't mean to leave them. I was going to be right back! I promised!"

But the door back to her friends didn't appear. She turned around again to where the original door had appeared and tripped over the bulging floorboards and knocked her ankle into the rocking chair. "Ouch!"

Leaning on the arm of the chair to steady herself, Shaleigh rubbed at her ankle. She was too freaked out, too panicked—that had to be the problem. She had to remember Captain Briar's training. She had to focus... But how could she?

She was home. Her high school stood a few blocks away, and so did her house where she might find Dad. She would find a way back later. For now, she needed to focus on why she came. She needed to make sure her dad was okay, that's what her friends would recommend.

Shaleigh picked her way through the house carefully.

It was dangerous enough during the day, but it was even worse at night.

She clocked herself on something hanging low from the ceiling and winced, putting a hand to her forehead. "Oh wow, that hurt."

It wasn't bleeding, thankfully, just tender. She looked up at the hanging shadow and recognized it as a tree branch from the tree that grew up the center of the building. She snickered at first, then it grew into an outright laugh. She laughed so hard that tears came to her eyes and it took her a moment to calm down.

"Even here you guys are trying to kill me, huh?" she said to the tree. "Better luck next time."

She shook her head and ducked to avoid another shadowy limb. Finally, she found the front door, only someone had nailed it shut. Had there been an investigation? Had the place finally been condemned? She wasn't sure, but she wasn't about to be trapped in the Tree House of all places.

It took a solid five kicks to get the wood to loosen enough for her to crawl through, and even though her leg felt tingly afterwards, she was proud of herself. She was stronger than she had been before, and she wasn't afraid to get her hands dirty.

Outside a cold wind blew and she pulled her fur coat closer around her throat. She started down the path away from the Tree House and saw movement up ahead. She focused on it, straining her eyes to see what it was and going completely still. Was there something in the darkness watching her? Had Keriam sent something to the

Human World, was that why he had a map of her hometown on his wall?

Then she saw the movement again and realized it was from the headlights of a car bouncing through the undergrowth. She put a hand to her chest and chuckled. "What did you think it was, girl? A Shadow Wolf? A Pello Pine?" She shook her head. "Those don't exist here. There's nothing that wants to hunt and eat you anymore."

It sounded terrifying when she said it aloud, but to be honest, it made her kind of sad, too. The woods seemed kind of boring compared to the Slumbering Forest. As she climbed the hill; the sounds of traffic grew louder and she huffed. Why did she miss that? Who missed traffic anyway?

She got to the top of the hill and found a bus stop there. The plastic side of the bus stop reflected her appearance in the light as she approached, and it was only then that she realized how ridiculous she looked. She still had hay stuck in her hair. Her coat was literally centuries old, and her clothes looked like she was an actor in a historical fair.

Strangely, she felt like the clothes suited her more than her normal ones did, and even though she knew she would get looks, she sat down on the bench for the bus stop and waited. It was a cold night with a clear beautiful starry sky, and Shaleigh thought of her stars—she missed Mawr. She drew her arms around herself against the wind, and realized how empty she felt without Mawr's warm, purring presence everywhere she went. She missed him always being at her side. She felt so lonely without him. She closed her eyes and took a deep breath of the cold, exhaust-filled air.

She would see him again.

She promised.

It took a long time for the bus to come. Shaleigh had gotten to her feet and was trying to gauge how she would walk home by the time she saw the golden flickering headlights in the distance. When the doors slid open, the bus driver looked at her with suspicion. She was a plump woman with dark skin. Her salt and pepper hair was pulled back into a single plait on the back of her neck.

Shaleigh gave a tentative smile as she climbed the steps. "I'm sorry, I don't have any money on me."

The woman stared at her and clenched her jaw.

Shaleigh licked her lips. "I don't live far. I used to ride the bus all the time." She held her hands out, adding, "I just don't have anything."

The bus driver snorted and shook her head, whispering something under her breath. She looked Shaleigh up and down then gave a big sigh. "Did you leave the money in your other costume, honey?"

"Kind of?" Shaleigh said with a nervous laugh, feeling the sweat bead on the back of her neck. It was a gamble to joke about it, but she thought of Colin and channeled him to give the most convincing sheepish grin she could.

The woman nodded. "I remember you. Had your picture all over the news a while back. Take a seat and don't tell anyone I did this." She reached over and pulled the lever. "I've got kids to feed."

Shaleigh listened to the doors slide closed behind her,

not able to bring herself to move. There were pictures of her around? She thought of her dad and her heart sank.

"Don't make me change my mind, honey."

Shaleigh forced her feet to move and hurried over to grab a seat. "Thank you," she muttered.

The lights on the bus flickered dark as the bus began moving and it was then that Shaleigh realized that they were not alone on the bus. Farther down she saw two other people in the back, fast asleep under blankets with several rows between them. One of them was using an old newspaper as a pillow—they were homeless. And as they drove past several streetlamps, she thought she even recognized one of them: It was a cold night, a dangerous night to be out in the elements.

"We've all been through hell at some point," the bus driver said, watching her from the rearview mirror.

Shaleigh nodded and sat back in her chair, wrapping a hand around the cold metal of the handrail. She wondered how many times she had ridden this same bus and took for granted that everybody on it had a home to go back to.

THE BUS LURCHED down the dark roads, passing the occasional late-night driver. Shaleigh leaned her head against the cold metal of the handrail, seeing the houses she recognized still standing. It was as if the world hadn't changed at all, but she knew that wasn't true. If the bus driver knew her face, there had to have been news reports about it. She couldn't imagine how that must have been for Dad.

The bus slowed to a stop, the wheels squeaking in the empty stillness of the street. "This is your stop, honey," the woman said turning on the lights again. Shaleigh winced and got to her feet, starting toward her house just a few blocks down.

The cold wind swept in and she turned to the driver, "Thank you."

She gave a small smile. "Take care of yourself. Don't get lost again."

"I won't."

Shaleigh went down the steps and the biting wind forced her to pull her coat closer. She hurried down the sidewalk as the bus passed her by. She stopped at the driveway to her home. There was one light on in the living room where her father kept his fairy collection.

She hurried quickly down the cement, her feet moving her faster and faster until she was running. There was a light on. That meant he was home, didn't it? Surely that meant he was safe.

Would she tell him the truth? Could she lie to him about everything that had happened? How in the world would she even explain her clothes? She pushed the panicked thoughts out of her mind and hurried for the front door. She couldn't think of impossible questions right now, she had to see him. She needed his warmth, his smile, and his safety. She needed to know he was okay, that was all. She had to know.

She rapped her knuckles on the front door and waited, listening for any sound, any movement, anything that would indicate he was okay. What if he wasn't? What if he had killed himself days ago, weeks ago, and no one had noticed? What if no one still knew?

Her heart pounded in her chest, and she knocked again. "Dad?" She rang the doorbell, then rang it again. "Dad, it's me!"

There was movement on the other side of the door— someone was home.

She heard the deadbolt slide back and the doorknob unlock, her heart thundering in her ears. The door opened a crack.

"Who is it?" a nervous woman's voice asked.

Shaleigh froze. Her hands shook at her sides. "Where's Dad?" she asked, her voice breaking as her throat closed up on the words. "I know he has to be here. Tell me where he is!"

The door opened a little wider, and a familiar face came into view, but Shaleigh couldn't place it. Was it someone from work? One of Dad's co-workers? No, that wasn't right. She had very dark skin that was broken up in pale blotches across her cheeks, neck, and hands. She had her hair fixed in neat twists all around her head.

The woman gasped and put a hand to her lips. "Shaleigh?"

"Kristen, who is it?" Her dad called from a distance.

Shaleigh looked at the woman, at her familiar face, the blotches of her skin that looked so similar to the one she had on her lower back, her familiar eyes. "Kristen?" she whispered, taking a step back.

Her eyes were familiar, the same sad eyes she had seen in so many photos. Kristen put a hand to her mouth, frozen in shock and Shaleigh shook her head. What was she doing here? Why was she with Dad? What happened while she was away?

Kristen stepped aside, pushing the door open wider and Dad froze in the entryway, wearing a hastily thrown-on bathrobe and some worn slippers. "Shaleigh? Oh my God!" He rushed forward, his arms out to her, and Shaleigh ran forward to embrace him.

"Dad, you're okay!" Tears streamed down her cheeks. "I was so worried you would hurt yourself! I was so worried you would be dead!"

"Shaleigh," he said through a strained voice, "I knew you would come back to me. I never gave up on you."

They hugged and cried into each other's arms as the wind tore through the empty street.

SHALEIGH SAT in the living room with a mug of hot chocolate in her hands as her dad called everyone he could to let them know that she had been found—she watched him in a daze. It was just so good to see him moving around, talking, hearing him be happy. She had feared so long that he would be wrapped up in a depressed cocoon in his room, or in a hospital bed, or worse.

She felt a warm hand on her knee and turned to her mother, Kristen, sitting beside her with a worried face and a tentative smile. The woman who was more of a myth to Shaleigh than a person. She was the smell of perfume, a hung up dress, a perfectly poised room, not a flesh and blood human. After only seeing her through the eyes of the pictures that lined the walls of her house, it was surreal to see her in person. She had more lines on her face, and more worry in her eyes, but her smile was kind.

At one point in time Shaleigh wouldn't have wanted to meet her mother. She would have been angry to see the woman that had put Dad through so much pain and heartache for so many years. That anger was still there, but it was distant and disconnected. She just never expected to meet her in person. Shaleigh had always assumed her mother was happier living her life somewhere else without them, but here she was. There were so many questions Shaleigh wanted to ask but didn't know where to start or what to even say. So, she started as simply as she could. She couldn't live with the silence stretching out between them.

"I'm glad you came to help," Shaleigh said. "I don't want to think about what he would have done to himself if you hadn't."

Her mother sniffed and lowered her gaze then squeezed Shaleigh's knee and shook her head. "I should have been here," she said finally, her voice a hoarse whisper as though she had been crying for days. "I didn't know he was struggling. I saw him one day on a documentary, and he looked so in control of his life. I assumed he was doing well." She wiped at her eyes with the back of her hand, her fingers shaking. "I thought he was happy."

"It was a facade," Shaleigh muttered and shook her head. "He wanted everyone to think he was fine, but he and I both knew the truth. He's been a wreck without you."

"I should have been here for you, too. I just, I thought I could handle being a mother, I thought I could handle all the responsibility, but I couldn't." She took a deep breath and put her own mug of hot chocolate on the coffee table with shaky hands. The drink was untouched. "I turned to alcohol first, trying to force my way through it regardless of how I felt, but that only made it worse. I was such a coward; I couldn't even bring myself to divorce him."

Shaleigh closed her eyes. She never imagined that she would understand her mother so much. She had also run away from the responsibility of taking care of her father just like her mother had. She hadn't intended to leave him for good, but if she hadn't been kidnapped, maybe she would have one day.

It shook her to her core to know that they had that in common. Before she had been kidnapped, Shaleigh wouldn't have wanted anything in common with her mother, but now here she was talking to her and realizing how alike they were.

Shaleigh took a deep breath to steady herself, her eyes felt spent from crying earlier. She reached out and took her mother's hand and clasped it tight. "I couldn't care for him either," Shaleigh whispered. "I tried at first, but I got tired of it. I got tired of trying."

Kristen flattened down her tunic against her pajama pants. It didn't need to be flattened, but it seemed to help her. "He was in terrible shape when I got here, but I finally got him to seek help. He went to his therapist; he went on medication. I even got him to promise to stick to his schedule. It's helped him, but I worry."

She glanced over her shoulder at him before lowering

her voice, "I can't stay forever, Shaleigh. I have a job, a life, a home. I've told him as much, but he resists it. It's as if he thinks he can change the world just by willing it, but you and I both know that doesn't work."

Shaleigh nodded, registering what her mother was saying, but also noticing what she didn't say. Her mother hadn't asked once about where Shaleigh had been or where she had gotten her very old coat and clothes.

Already she was planning on leaving.

It wasn't really a surprise, that was how her mother was. She hadn't changed, she had just gotten older and maybe a little bit braver. She was still the same woman running away from her daughter and husband, running away from the mere mention of responsibility. Shaleigh should have expected it, but the realization still hurt. It was like an icy coldness that spread in her heart at the realization that her mother had never wanted to be in their lives. Instantly Shaleigh thought of her dad and how he would react if her mother just disappeared again, and she knew she had to say something.

She thought of Teagan leaving Talek in the middle of the night to run off with Master Cathal and how much that had destroyed Talek. It was bizarre to realize that Talek and Dad would have a lot to talk about if they ever met each other.

"Before you leave," Shaleigh said, looking her in the eye, "please make sure he understands you are leaving. Don't leave him in the middle of the night like before."

Kristen stared at her a moment, her bottom lip trembling and her cheeks flushing. She clearly wasn't comfortable committing to that, but Shaleigh needed her to be resolute about something. Part of Shaleigh wished her mother could stay, wished they could reunite and be a happy family together, but that wasn't reality. Kristen would never be happy in a marriage with a daughter, and it was guilt that had dragged her back when she heard of Shaleigh's disappearance, not concern for Dad.

Shaleigh mustered up all of the wisdom she had gained through her dealings with Madam Cloom, Queen Mab, and Tanwen the dragon. She took her mother's hand and gazed into her eyes, clearly making her uncomfortable, and said, "Promise me. It's the only thing I ask of you, and that's it. I could ask for far more, but I won't do that to you. I just don't want him to fall apart again, and I need you to promise me that you'll do your part... Mom."

Being called Mom broke her. Kristen's face scrunched up and there were tears in her eyes. Shaleigh knew she had hurt her, but she had to persuade her to act. Her mother had led Dad to having a breakdown before, and she could do it again if she wasn't careful.

After a tense moment Kirsten finally gave a nod and let out a shaky breath. "I'll talk to him," she said, pulling her hand away from Shaleigh's. "Maybe I'll even give him my number so he can check in. I'll see if he's interested in making our separation official too."

Separation. That word stung more than Shaleigh expected but having an official status would make it easier on Dad. It would help all three of them, even if it did hurt now. "Thank you," Shaleigh said, sitting back. "I'm glad I got to meet you."

Kristen shook her head and wiped her cheeks, only occasionally meeting Shaleigh's eyes as the silence grew between them.

Dad stepped back into the room. "Kaeja was the first person I called," he said with a pad of paper held up to his nose. "I've notified the police and they'll be notifying the joint authorities soon. We may have some reporters come by in the morning, but I can—"

"That's fine, Dad, I'll talk with them."

He looked at Shaleigh over the notepad. "Are you sure?"

Shaleigh nodded. She had dealt with queens and dragons; she could handle a few reporters. She had already put together an excuse in her mind: running away from home, trying to make it on her own, living homeless for a time.

He shook his head. "If you say so."

It was then that Kristen got to her feet. "Haki, can we talk for a moment? Alone?"

He clenched his jaw and swallowed. "Sure, that's fine."

They stepped into the hallway behind the stairs to talk and Shaleigh brought the mug of hot chocolate to her lips, reveling in the scent as she took another sip. The sweetness was so potent that it made her shiver as the warmth went down her throat. It felt amazing. She wondered if her friends had hot chocolate in the Garden. If not, maybe she could bring some to them. One day, at least.

She hoped Kristen did give Dad her phone number. She wanted to be able to get to know her better.

A knock came at the front door and Shaleigh jumped. She had barely put her mug of chocolate down when the door swung open and hit the wall—Shaleigh jumped to her feet. Surely reporters weren't barging into their house in the middle of the night. Her parents came out from the back room in shock.

"What—" Dad started to say but a cry cut him off.

"Shaleigh! Where are you?"

It was Kaeja.

Shaleigh ran to the front door and saw her friend standing there in her pajamas, her hair partway stuffed into a sleeping cap, and wearing slippers. She squealed in excitement.

"You came back!" Kaeja cried rushing forward, pulling Shaleigh into a big hug and swinging her around. Shaleigh felt tears in her eyes all over again and she couldn't get any words out past the lump in her throat, but Kaeja strung out a ton of words all at once.

"I turned around and you were gone! I was so scared! I looked everywhere but I couldn't find you. I told the police and they thought I was lying, and they looked for you all over the place. They searched throughout the school. They questioned so many people! And I never got to tell you how I felt about you!"

Then Kaeja leaned up and kissed her cheek.

Shaleigh felt heat rush to her cheeks that she hadn't expected and smiled. That felt so right.

"I'm sorry," Kaeja gushed, barely able to speak because she was crying so hard. "I meant to do that the day we went to the Tree House," she sobbed. "I meant to tell you how I felt about you! I meant to—"

Shaleigh smiled and pulled her into a warm embrace. "It's okay. I'm here now."

Kaeja sniffled and sobbed into Shaleigh's shoulder. She

had clearly been woken up by the phone call; Shaleigh grinned.

"You didn't take that shitty bike, here did you?"

Kaeja bit her lips, laughing a bit through her tears. "Maybe?"

Shaleigh laughed.

A WEEK LATER, after several interviews with news agencies, radio show hosts, and police reports, life was gaining some semblance of normalcy. Shaleigh was now known as a runaway at school, but she had been insulted by experts like Madam Cloom, so it didn't really bother her. She secretly thought it was cool.

Some of the students tried to make fun of her, but Shaleigh never let them have power over her. She never let them win. And after a few days, they moved on to easier targets.

Currently Shaleigh sat on the floor by her bed, hugging her body pillow. There was a whole pile of homework on her desk that needed to be done, but she didn't feel like it. Normally on a Friday night she would be looking for an abandoned building to explore, but that didn't seem as fun anymore. Besides she and Kaeja were meeting up tomorrow night, at an actual restaurant, not wandering around derelict buildings.

There was a knock at her bedroom door, and Shaleigh was pulled from her thoughts. "Yes?"

"It's me," Dad said through the door, "can I come in?"

"Sure, Dad."

He stepped in, carrying a big white dry cleaner bag with a hanger sticking out. He had a smile on his lips and Shaleigh couldn't help but smile back, it was such a wonderful look on him.

"I had this dry cleaned," he pulled back the plastic, and Shaleigh saw the leather and red fur of the coat Teagan had given her.

"Oh wow!" She shot up and rubbed her fingers over the soft leather. "I can't believe they were able to make it look so good!"

He chuckled as he pulled it out of the plastic and held it out to her. She grinned as she held it up to the afternoon sunlight streaming in through the windows.

"What happened to you out there?" he asked then, his brows furrowing. "And don't tell me what you told the police. They might believe that, but I don't. It's just the two of us now with Kristen gone back home. Will you share it with me?"

There was an intense curiosity in her dad's eyes, and she knew what he suspected. Shaleigh went over to the closet and hung up her coat in the doorway. She stared at it a moment, wondering if he would understand, wondering if he was ready to know the truth. "You know all about fairies, right, Dad?"

He was silent a moment. "Yes, of course I do. I've studied them for most of my adult life."

She drummed her fingers against her leg. "You know how they were said to come from a different land?"

He narrowed his eyes at her. "Shaleigh, you aren't suggesting that—"

She turned to him with a smile that Teagan would

truly be proud of. "I'm not saying anything, Dad. I just think the stories are interesting is all."

"Good." He gave a nervous laugh and rubbed his arm. "You had me going there for a minute." He laughed again, but his gaze lingered on the old coat, maybe truly seeing it for the first time.

"I think I'm going to turn in early tonight, Dad. I'm pretty worn out."

He nodded. "That's fine. You get some sleep." He turned to leave, but Shaleigh walked over and pulled him into a tight embrace.

"I love you; you know that? I'm glad you're okay."

He hesitated for a moment, his old hesitance and awkwardness coming back, before he hugged her back. "I'm sorry you were so scared for me. I hate being a burden on you, you do know that, right?"

"I know," she whispered, not letting go of him for a few moments longer.

He gave an awkward laugh, clearing his throat. "I love you, too." He pulled away and headed for the door. "Sleep well."

"Thanks," she whispered as he closed the door behind him.

Shaleigh walked over to her closet and pulled the freshly cleaned coat down. She slipped her arms into the sleeves, grinning as she rolled her shoulders against the fur. She reached for her cell phone and made sure it had a full battery, then she pulled the tiny silver key out of her nightstand.

She wasn't sure if Dad would ever believe where she had really gone, but maybe one day. Kaeja would love it though and Shaleigh loved the idea of bringing someone back through the doorway to meet her friends. Maybe tomorrow she would tell her about it over dinner. Maybe she would wait. She knew everyone was worried about her after having not seen her for so long. Next time she would be more careful.

She stuffed a pillow into the bed to make it look like her and made sure her curtains were drawn. Then she held the key out in front of her.

When she had tried to return that cold night in the Tree House, she was an emotional wreck. She had thought about that all week and worked hard to prepare herself to travel again. She had to practice, like Talek said.

She had to keep trying.

She concentrated on the silver key in her hand. She thought of her friends standing with her and supporting her. She imagined Mawr's warmth, Colin's laugh, Teagan's wit, and finally Talek's kindness. She was part of both worlds now, as Talek had explained. She envisioned the doorway outside of Lieutenant Varg's home, the steps that led up to the front door, and she turned the key.

The world slowed down, and the silvery outline of a door appeared in front of her. She felt giddy as she turned the key and heard the sound of a latch unlocking.

When the door swung open, she saw the afternoon light streaming across the steps of the Lieutenant's home and smiled.

Tears came to her eyes as she took a deep breath.

"She's back! I told you she would come back!" Colin cried as she stepped through the doorway and spotted a familiar stone lion bounding toward her.

EPILOGUE

$\mathcal{A}$ fog formed at the entrance of a dark cave deep in the land of Ciar, where the sky was forever black, and the land was filled with creatures from nightmares. The fog grew thick and spread out to cover the entrance, obscuring anyone who might be watching. Two black dogs stepped out, their eyes gleaming red, both clearly dead but standing despite it.

The Masked King emerged from the fog, holding his golden mask to his face as he entered the cavern and descended deep within. He walked the path with bare feet, through pitch black tunnels. The air grew cold and moist. He could hear the dripping of stalactites hidden in the darkness, but he continued onward, going deeper.

Finally, his feet met the cold water of the lowest cavern and he breathed in the stale air. It smelled delightfully of old, dried bones.

"I have what you requested, my dear." He held up a dusty jar that appeared to be empty.

Two yellow eyes opened in the darkness, bright and

gleaming like two bulbs. The Masked King had to blink until his eyes adjusted to the intense light.

"Is that all that's left of him?" Her voice was deep and echoed through the cavern.

The Masked King stepped closer to her, put the dusty jar on the ground, and then stepped away. "I'm afraid so."

A black claw reached forward, seeming to come from the walls of the cave itself, and smashed the jar: A smoke emerged, frail and fragile. The Dragon of Darkness snapped her jaws around it, flicking her black tongue in the air until she had eaten all that was left, then swallowed it down with a snarl of approval.

"My sister's magic. That's what destroyed him."

"It seems so, that's what the rumors say." He reached a hand down and a black dog appeared. The dog panted happily as he stroked its head. "Was his soul delicious?"

"Scorched," she said with a laugh that hurt his ears. His dog whimpered and turned to disappear behind him again. The Masked King winced but did not cower in her presence; it was unwise to cower before a dragon.

"I believe he may have slipped things into the Human World," he said. "I have no idea why."

"Yes, I see that. Dissipating magic into other lands and stealing it from our lands. I never should have trusted him." He heard her tail smack into one of the cavern walls, causing stone to fall and crash into the water.

The Masked King swallowed down his fear, "Unlike him, my dear, I fulfill my end of arrangements."

"Yes, you have, Fineen, which is why I will give you the gift you seek. You have been loyal to me and my sisters for a very long time, despite your cruel nature and chaotic magic."

He recoiled at the use of his old name, unable to keep his distaste from showing.

She gave a wicked laugh that made his ears ache again. "Yes, I know. You hate that name. You hate the word and wish to blight it out, but I cannot manipulate the minds of so many. Names are rarely forgotten, especially for your Faerie folk."

"Yes," he said with a shaky voice. "That is a very good point."

"I know you wish to pass through the veil and enter the Human World, but I need to know why? I have reason to believe you've traveled before through mirrors, which is where your dogs come from, am I right?"

He shuffled his feet in the water, "Yes, it's true. I do go there on occasion, but I am very limited in what I can do. A stolen child here, a push into Madness there, it isn't as powerful as I would like."

She stretched her neck, forward to look at him closer. "What do you plan to do there then? Other than fill your Dark Lands with more souls?"

"I would like to find and destroy the magic Keriam has slipped there. I would like to reclaim the energy he has so foolishly left behind. There is also a girl there, Tanwen's Chosen, she—"

"Ah yes, Shaleigh is her name, right?"

He nodded eagerly. "She too bears your sister's mark, and yet travels between the two worlds."

Bāhv huffed in frustration and he felt the air shift against his robes. "Who my sister chooses is her business."

She leaned in closer and he could see the gray teeth protruding out of her scaly mouth. "What is your true purpose there, Fineen?"

For a moment, the Masked King regretted coming. For a moment, he wondered if he had made a mistake, but no, if he truly wanted to claim the respect he deserved, he needed the power of dragons. Shaleigh and her friends had proven that to him. The only way to succeed in the land was not through grabbing soldiers and traders as they ventured too close to his fog, but to work with the dragons instead.

"Let me clean up Keriam's mess. Let me do more than work through mirrors, let me exist in their land. Let me pull whoever I wish to my realm and force them into servitude."

She stared at him for a long moment. "Greedy as ever, I see." She gave another laugh and he felt his ears throb. "Let us hope you do not share Keriam's fate in your greed."

He shook his head, "I merely wish to reclaim the magic that was lost there."

She snorted in amusement, "I'm no fool, Fineen."

He winced.

"I can give you the ability to pass through the veil, to enter the Human World fully, to take form there and retrieve whatever magic Keriam the Incompetent left there. If you betray me, I will slaughter you and destroy everything you have created."

He gave a deep bow. "You are gracious, and I am not worthy of your kindness."

As he stood up again, she reached a paw forward. He

could feel the chill of it before it touched him. She pulled his mask off and dropped it to the ground; Fineen shuddered. He hated having his face seen, especially by someone as great as her. But as she dragged the back of her claw against his mummified cheek, she felt soft and cool against his dried skin. Something like tears tried to form in his eyes, but he could not shed them.

"Easy, child," she whispered. "You have nothing to fear from me as long as you don't betray me."

He felt the prick of her claw against his cheek and gasped. Blood that he had forgotten he could even spill slipped down to his chin and she brought her paw back, lapping at the claw with her black tongue. For a moment, he wondered if he would be eaten, but then again, he had died once already, hadn't he? Why fear death when he already knew what it felt like?

"I grant you power to travel between our world and the Human World, Fineen. I grant you the ability to destroy as long as you do not leave your magic in that land."

The Masked King fell hard to his knees, and he felt his old bones rattle as the water seeped into his mummified skin. "Thank you," he whispered, no longer able to tell if blood or tears streamed down his cheek.

ALSO BY MARLENA FRANK

The Stolen Series
Young adult, portal fantasy, faeries
Stolen
Broken
Chosen

The Wolves of Kanta Series
Young adult, dark fantasy, steampunk, werewolves
The She-Wolf of Kanta
The Blood of Kanta
The Hunters of Kanta
The Fury of Kanta
The Howl of Kanta

Standalones
Young adult, horror, sci-fi, dystopian
The Seeking

Short stories, horror, dark fantasy
The Impostor and Other Dark Tales

Ocean horror, weird, short story
Undertow

Weird western, werewolves, vampires, short story

Night Feeders

Mystery, film noir, humor, short story

The Mysterious Disappearance of Charlene Kerringer

Join the Mailing List

The Blade Filled with Stars

A kingdom is under siege from a familiar enemy. Families and friends are pitted against each other without reason. Slaughter is imminent while the winged Queen Khafil soars overhead. Desperate and terrified, Anna works with her sister, Lilah, to summon aid from their mother's ancient spell book.

Determined to save their people, the sisters

summon Death to help them, but Death is not easily swayed. Neither of the sisters are prepared for the consequences.

Want a peek behind the scenes?
Want to preview my books before they get released?

Get exclusive access to book goodies, giveaways, and cover reveals by joining my mailing list. Not only will you get notified of all my new releases, you'll get an exclusive copy of The Blade Filled with Stars.

Subscribe to the Mailing List at:
http://marlenafrank.com/mailinglist/

Support Me On

Ko-fi

Follow me on Ko-Fi for regular updates on my writing progress.

Monthly subscribers get access to sneak peeks at stories way before anyone else. They also get access to cover reveals, monthly shout-outs on social media, and thanked by name in the acknowledgements in my books.

http://ko-fi.com/MarlenaFrank

ACKNOWLEDGMENTS

I have so many people to thank for making *Chosen* possible.

Kelley has been my constant supporter through everything that threatens to get in the way of my writing, and I wouldn't be productive at all without her guidance. My parents, John and Connie, have both been so supportive through the entire series, especially when the pandemic hit. Aunt Charmaine has always been one of my most vocal supporters through everything I encounter, and I wish I could give her a big hug. Candace, Carla, and Donna gave me a boost when I most needed it. Thank you so much for believing in me!

I will always be grateful to The Parliament House for taking a chance on me and my work. None of this would have been possible without them. As always, I have to praise my developmental editor Rae from A New Look on Books for her incredible skills. She knows this world and the characters who inhabit it almost as well as I do. Cindy and Erica did the final touches to make sure everything was perfect. Thank you all!

If you enjoyed this book, please leave a review and share this book with your friends. I would love an excuse to continue this world.

Readers make books thrive. Thank you for reading!

ABOUT THE AUTHOR

Marlena Frank is the author of young adult fantasy and horror novels, short stories, novellas, and book series. Many of her books have hit the bestseller charts, including her debut novel, Stolen. Her work has been praised by Readers' Favorite and featured in De Mode of Literature Magazine. Her stories have appeared in anthologies such as Emporium of Superstition, Catstruck!, Heroic Fantasy Quarterly, Georgia Gothic, and The Sirens Call ezine.

Although born in Tennessee, Marlena has spent most

of her life in Georgia. She lives with her sister and two spoiled adopted cats. She serves as the Vice President of the Atlanta Chapter of the Horror Writers Association, is an active member of the Science Fiction and Fantasy Writers Association, and is an avid member of the Atlanta cosplay community.

She is also an INFJ, a tea drinker, and a wildlife enthusiast.

Support her on Ko-Fi: ko-fi.com/MarlenaFrank